STEAMBOAT
ON THE
RIVER

STEAMBOAT
ON THE
RIVER

A Novel by

Darwin Teilhet

with drawings by John O'Hara Cosgrave II

William Sloane Associates

To Rowena Ferguson

"The early spring of 1832 brought to Springfield and New Salem a most joyful announcement. It was the news of the coming of a steamboat down the Sangamon River . . . I remember the occasion well, for two reasons. It was my first sight of a steamboat, and also the first time I ever saw Mr. Lincoln. . . . On its arrival at Springfield the crew of the boat was given a reception and dance in the court house . . . The Talisman lay for a week longer at Bogue's mill when receding waters admonished her officers that unless they purposed spending the remainder of the year there they must head her down stream. In this emergency recourse was had to my cousin Rowan Herndon . . . who recommended the employment of Lincoln as a skillful assistant. These two inland navigators undertook therefore the contract of piloting the vessel . . . through the uncertain channel of the Sangamon. . . . The average speed was four miles a day."

William H. Herndon, writing to Jesse
W. Weik, about 1888

"The splendid upper cabin steamer Talisman, J. M. Pollock, master, will leave for Portland, Springfield on the Sangamon River, and all intermediate points and landings, say, Beardstown, Naples, St. Louis, Louisville, on Thursday, February 2. For freight or passage apply to Captain Vincent A. Bogue at the Broadway Hotel or to Allison Owen."

Cincinnati Gazette, January 19, 1832

"On Saturday last the citizens of this place were gratified by the arrival of the steamboat Talisman, J. W. Pollock, master, of 150 tons burden, at the Portland landing opposite this town. The safe arrival of a boat of the size of the Talisman on a river never before navigated by steam had created much solicitude, and the shores for miles around were crowded by our citizens. Her arrival at the destined port was hailed with loud acclaim and full demonstrations of pleasure. When Captain Bogue located his mill on the Sangamon River twelve months ago, and asserted his determination to land a steamboat, there within a year, the idea was considered hysterical by some, and utterly impracticable by others."

The Sangamon Journal, March 29, 1832

NOTE

Remarkably little of this story is a product of my own imagination; most of it actually happened, and I should like to believe that here and there in the Illini country the legend of the *Talisman's* journey still exists. I know it did when I was a boy because I was born only a hundred miles north of the Sangamon River. I can still remember when the stars were out and the chores were done, I would listen to the soft drawling voice of a great-uncle who would mention the names of people who once lived not far from him: Rowan Herndon, "Slicky Bill" Green, Denton Offut, Simeon Francis and some of the young Rutledge boys who years before had moved to Iowa. All of them had a hand one way or another in the adventure of that steamboat on the river.

But when I was a boy it never occurred to me that I was listening to a piece of local history handed down from one generation to a much younger generation by word of mouth, with all the distortions and errors and elisions such a method has always entailed ever since elders spoke around a campfire. Finally I forgot all about the steamboat and the people who entered into its adventure. It was only much later, in 1932 or 1933, when I came upon a biography by William H. Herndon that I discovered a few paragraphs mentioning that same steamboat that I had heard about in my youth.

I have discovered no new Lincoln material. However, I have gone back to where others have gone before me and have collected every-

thing having anything at all to do with this steamboat from the far greater collections they have made. I have pilfered from old newspapers of the time, old letters, old books, new books—in short, I have ransacked everything I could lay my hands on which directly or indirectly concerns what happened to the steamboat *Talisman*.

I have gone and gone again to the two-volume biography *Abraham Lincoln* (1930 edition, D. Appleton and Company, New York) based on materials written by Lincoln's law partner, William H. Herndon, and rewritten and bowdlerized by his collaborator, Jesse W. Weik. Fortunately, Herndon's original papers became finally the object of assiduous study and research by the late Emanuel Hertz and in great part were brought together in his *The Hidden Lincoln* (The Viking Press, New York, 1938). In a second book, *Lincoln Talks: A Biography in Anecdote* (The Viking Press, New York, 1939), Dr. Hertz published the results of his years of collecting all the stories and anecdotes about Lincoln. I have lifted right and left from him—exactly, as he says in his introduction, as he "of course borrowed everywhere"—to obtain snatches of conversation as presumably the words were spoken at and around the time when the *Talisman* entered the Illini country.

While I have used very little direct material from Edgar Lee Masters' *The Sangamon* (Farrar and Rinehart, New York, 1942), the mood and feeling of what he has written has without doubt influenced my own mood and feeling when I was casting back in my mind to days long forgotten. I have borrowed from *The Illini* by Clark E. Carr (A. C. McClurg & Co., Chicago, 1904), a copy having been in my mother's family ever since it was purchased at the time of publication. I had assumed it had been forgotten by everyone until I saw that Carl Sandburg had also read it, remembered it, and used some of it for a few paragraphs in his *Prairie Years* (Harcourt, Brace & Company, New York, 1926). I cannot believe this great poet of my state will be too greatly displeased if by now I have almost memorized the first volume of his *Prairie Years* in ransacking its nooks and crannies for details which were not in the original material of the Herndon biography and letters.

The only people in this tale who are not historic personages are young Jim Owens, who has been my eyes and ears for what did happen, his immediate family, Thankful Blair, a young man who plagued Jim, the young man's mother, and two or three members of the steamer's crew. All the others once lived—even Captain Bogue, the steamer's pilot, and the scandalous woman who so badly

misbehaved and shocked all of Springfield. The poet did write and did speak his lines to welcome the steamer. The Haitian barber stood there at his barber shop. An appeal was made to Rowan Herndon. Ann Rutledge's father and his partner didn't much like steamer traffic on the river.

If it interests you at all, you might like knowing that when the young Lincoln of twenty-three speaks in this story approximately eight sentences out of every ten are lines from conversation he actually had with friends within that period of time. Often, to be sure, I have used his phrases or sentences out of their original context, as when he speaks to the fictional character of Jim Owens. Even so, it seems to me that this expedient is far better than the conversation a writer so remote from those days might invent for him. He was at a point in his career when he was almost speaking two languages or, rather, two dialects of the same language. One was the good limber prairie talk he had always heard. The other was the more thoughtful and tempered English he was beginning to discover in books and to hear spoken by men of greater education than he possessed.

I have assembled all that I have collected from greater collections and pieced it together as a labor of love to tell one more story: a story in which I have invented only a few trifling odds and ends. I have attempted to re-create something which seems important to me from our nation's past, the details of which in the course of time became scattered in a multitude of references. Brought together, even to be told as a story, they may also re-create the one incident in Lincoln's life which I do not believe has ever been told as a whole before.

Darwin Teilhet

Los Altos, California. May, 1952

9

The big sidewheeler *Star of Ohio*, of six hundred tons burden, docked at Cincinnati fours days before Christmas on a cold raw morning and as I sighted down from the hurricane deck the town was all bleak and miserable along the river. By using my elbows a trifle I was among the first to reach the wharf and I looked around through the crowd, expecting to be met.

Finally I saw Mother and Father off to one side, still sighting up at the boat. They hadn't appreciated I'd learned enough by now to get in ahead and be at the front of a procession instead of standing back and trailing along at the rear. I hesitated a couple of seconds. Their eyes passed over me, searching through the crowd, and again lifted toward the boat.

They hadn't even recognized me! Something began riffling up through my stomach. I never expected to have it take me like this. Why, only a few minutes ago I'd been such a young swell up there on the deck. Anyhow, I tried to make a joke of it, to show my mother and father how casual and languid I'd learned to be after three years of living in the biggest city of the nation.

So I walked up to them. I lifted my new beaver stovepipe hat, which all of us at the Philadelphia academy wore the same as men did, and I made a leg and I said, very polite, "Pray, sir," to my

11

father. "Were you looking for someone?" I was even laying it on a little, hoping in my heart, I guess, they'd see right away it was me and laugh.

My father didn't even turn his head. Very short, he said, "Yes, we are. My boy's supposed to be on that steamer."

But I didn't fool my mother for more than two long rotten seconds. She was staring at me, harder. Suddenly she exclaimed to Father, "Jim Owens, don't you know your own son even if he's grown half a foot?" and stretched out her arms. "Horace—" And I might as well admit here and not speak about it any more that that is my front name. It was given to me before I could argue against it. "Horace Owens! Bowing like that to your pa and me! Come here and give me a kiss. My stars, *what* have they done to you? Are those the kind of clothes my sister had you wear in Philadelphia?"

By the time they had got through greeting me and exclaiming over how I'd shot up from such a runty little thing in the last three years and my fingers ceased feeling so numb where Father had grabbed my hand, the two roustabouts had brought my hair trunk down the gangway.

From the fifty dollars my uncle had supplied me for spending money, I gave each a silver dollar like I'd promised if they got my trunk off first. The two roustabouts bowed and scraped and said I was a reg'lar gen'mum, real quality. It had been a pleasure to serve me. I wanted my mother and father to see I'd learned to command my way since I'd been gone. I must have impressed them, too, because my mother blinked.

My father swallowed a couple of times and said, "You gave those men a *dollar*, each? They won't earn that much in a whole day."

I explained if you wished to have your trunk off first without waiting your turn the thing to do was to pay for quick service. Next, I asked him where his manservant was to carry my trunk to his carriage.

Before he could answer, my mother said, "Jim, don't you dare let your own son tease us the minute he's landed. If you do, we'll never have any peace with him. I declare," she told me, "you'll do your pa good, now you're back with us. You'll give him something to think about besides his plaguey steamboat works. My, you've grown!"

She gave me a quick hug. Then she looked up at Father, grinning at him. Once more I had that feeling of not quite being here with them. Something warm and silent had passed between them. I

wished I hadn't asked where his manservant was. He'd kept one in Wheeling Town when he was superintendent of the big steamboat works there; but evidently he didn't have one here. Probably he didn't even own a horse and carriage. That was the stunner. How were we to get my trunk to their house? Father was already taking care of that; he'd hefted it up with one hand. I'd forgotten how strong he was.

Right then, though, somebody behind us said, "Mr. Owens, I'll tote it fer you. You and Mrs. Owens go 'long with your boy." I glanced around. A one-legged porter was waiting. He had one good leg and one peg leg and he was wrapped in even an older coat than my father's, and had a coonskin cap on his head, fiery red whiskers, and a black stub of pipe sticking out from his jaw.

"Thanks, Pete," my father said. "Horace, I'd like you to know Pete Wilmot."

I was surprised to have my father introduce me to a porter. A thing like that wasn't ever done in Philadelphia. But I remembered my manners and said, very kindly, "How do you do, my man."

The porter took out his black pipe and remarked, "Don't that beat the nation?" and gazed up at the sky. I looked up too, to see what was there, and couldn't see anything but dull-colored clouds. Right then my mother hastily grabbed my arm and said to come along. My father joined me on the other side.

When I looked back the porter, despite his wooden leg, had slung that heavy hair trunk on a shoulder as if it was filled with feathers. I still didn't understand what he'd seen in the sky to cause him to act so astonished of a sudden. I'd have asked Mother or Father but they didn't give me a chance. They were too busy asking how Aunt Iz and Uncle John were.

I scarcely noticed a couple of ragged boys maybe two or three years younger than me. They were standing on the corner of the street, watching us. One of them shouted, "Look! Oh, ain't that something?"

I sighted up into the air again, thinking possibly it might have been an eagle that was attracting so much attention. I'd seen wild eagles yesterday, swooping over the river; and seeing them had almost made up for not seeing any buffaloes so far.

But the other boy hollered, "That hat! Oh, that hat! And gaiters! Button gaiters!" And the first one slung a stone at me so I knew it was me they were shouting at. But the stone missed me by a foot. Well, I was too nearly grown up to let a couple of trifling boys

bother me. They couldn't even throw straight, either. I was willing to pass it off like it hadn't happened.

Father said, "Horace, they don't mean any harm. It's just that boys around this part of the country don't usually wear Sunday-go-to-meeting hats. Button gaiters aren't precisely the usual thing, either. Suppose I buy you a pair of good boots tomorrow?"

I said as politely as I could, "Well, thank you. But I've probably got used to wearing gaiters in winter weather."

I avoided saying it wasn't necessary for him to go to the expense of buying me new boots because if I could help it I wasn't planning to stay here long enough to have much time wearing them. I wasn't ready to come out with it and tell Father and Mother I was dead set against staying here for good and being shoved in some raw new academy, maybe with one room and only one master. Father didn't say anything more, either, about new boots. Maybe he was thinking of that letter he must by now have received from Uncle John as much as I was. But we were shying away at present, and so was my mother, from anything that might get us into having to discuss that letter. This was my home-coming. For a little while longer I didn't want to have to think about letting them see it was all for my best interests to leave them. I wanted to think of just being with them for a few days, once more being the third member of the Owens family.

We'd fallen into an awkward silence. We'd crossed two mud lanes cutting through the main street. We passed by frame houses and a new two-story brick house I'd hoped was where we would turn in; but we didn't. We passed by some vacant lots with dead snow covering the ground and a sod house and two or three log cabins and another frame house and somebody had put up a board fence to one side of the board walk and I could hear the porter stumping behind us, a good ways back, though, carrying my trunk.

Mother gave my arm a squeeze. "There are so many questions I've been waiting to ask you I don't know where to begin. You say your aunt Isabelle's well?"

"She's fine. She's on the go all the time."

"And your uncle John?"

"He's busy."

"Well, my heavens. I want to know all about them. What kind of a house do they have?"

Father was walking along silently. But I could see he was interested and listening.

14

"Big," I said.

"My stars, you're as hard to drag anything out of as your pa. You never wrote any news in your letters."

"Well, I didn't have much time for writing, Mother. That first year at the academy was perfectly ultra. I was—"

"What?"

"Ultra. I mean, I had to make up studies I hadn't had in Wheeling."

"Have you made many friends?"

"Oh, yes. Heaps, now. There's Whizzer Tucker, who's probably my best."

"Haven't you met any nice young girls your age? I'd have thought your aunt Isabelle—"

"Oh, she's always going on in that line."

"She has had you meet some, then?"

"Some? It's sickening."

"Well, my heavens, I'd think you'd be old enough to like meeting the daughters of your aunt's friends."

"Oh, they're all right. I was planning to take Whizzer Tucker's sister to the Christmas Ball this year until you and Father wrote to have me come here."

"I'm sure there are just as nice girls here, you'd like to meet. Did Thankful Blair ever write you? You and she were always such good friends."

Thankful was somebody I'd known back in Wheeling when we all used to live there. Mother and Father had been close friends of the Blairs until Thankful's mother had died and she and her father had moved, not long before my family had too.

"Thankful and I weren't *ever* good friends, Mother. I *never* liked her. When we were kids she tried to tag along."

"She never wrote you? I sent her your Philadelphia address the first Christmas we were here. She always sends us a Christmas letter."

"Well, she wrote me once. That was two or three years ago. I can't remember now."

Father stopped. Both Mother and I stopped. He opened the gate and said, "Here we are," and it seemed to me his voice sounded a little forced and too cheerful.

They both hesitated, waiting for me to go in first. I saw where they lived and I guess for five or six seconds I just stood there. In

15

all the three years I'd been living in one of the finest and richest homes in Philadelphia it never once had occurred to me that Father and Mother were trying to make a go of it in such a mean shackly little affair.

Their house was stuck out here on the edge of the little river town. Snow covered the fields beyond and the black rise of forest wasn't more than a quarter of a mile away with the road stringing out toward it and perishing off inside the trees. My eyes started stinging. While I'd been having everything anybody possibly could ask for in Philadelphia, it looked to me like my father and mother hadn't been having very much of anything at all.

Inside it was even more pathetic and crushing because Mother had tried to brighten up the front room for Christmas. She'd popped Indian corn, stringing the fluffy white flakes along the walls. Either she or my father had brought in pine branches and you could smell the piny smell; and I saw four or five packages wrapped in thick store paper on the plank floor off to one side of the fireplace.

Another package, long and skinny, about six feet long, all wrapped around in a piece of old cotton goods, was resting against the wall. It looked like it might be a regular hunting rifle, maybe with a percussion lock. I caught Father kind of grinning sheepishly at me after I'd sighted that long skinny package and my heart turned over and felt all dusty and sore. Had he bought me a regular hunting rifle as a surprise for this Christmas? He shouldn't have! What would I do with a hunting rifle in Philadelphia? My uncle never went hunting, didn't like even the idea of trifling his time that way.

Then Mother said awful soft, "Welcome, again. We *have* missed you loads," and unexpectedly pulled my head down and kissed my cheek. I should have helped her with her coat but Father'd already done it; I guess because he wasn't yet used to having another man in the house; and he was saying, "Here, I'll take your coat."

And for a second or so I felt his hand lie ever so lightly on my shoulder and drop away—and I was glad to have that porter knock on the door and walk in without waiting for somebody to open it for him. I was thankful for anything to distract me. The porter dumped my trunk on the floor and looked around and said cheerfully, "There you are." I fetched out a silver dollar, quick, and offered it to him; but he stepped back, asking, "What's that for?"

"For you, my man," I said. "Thank you for delivering—"

16

I never got to finish. My father said hastily, "Pete, my boy means well. I'm sorry."

"Why, that's all right, Mr. Owens. Will you be down to the works today?"

"No, I'm declaring a holiday for myself. You'll have to take charge."

"Why, sure. Glad to." Pete appeared to notice me again. "Sonny, I've been considered worse than a wharf hand in my time. Don't give it another thought. How old might you be?"

I thought asking that was pretty cool of him; but I told him.

"You don't say?" said the porter. "Even if you've growed up so sizable I'd still have figgered you a year or so younger . . . Mr. Owens," he told Father, "maybe younkers don't ripen so fast in Philadelphy as on the Ohio?"

I expected my father would put that Pete Wilmot in his place; but he didn't. He looked at Pete and then he looked at me, smiling a little, but not saying anything. You could almost think he was interested in learning how I was going to handle the thing.

Pete asked me, "I don't like to be cur'us. But was that a genuine silver dollar you was so free with?"

What kind of question was that? What did he think it was?

"Yes, certainly, it was a genuine dollar."

"I heard tell they growed silver dollars on bushes in Philadelphy only I never b'lieved it till now. No, sir. I thought it was a lie and I see it warn't. Sonny, did you bring one of them bushes with you?"

Then he gave a laugh, whacked me on the shoulder with a hand as big as the side of a ham, nodded to my folks, and stumped out. I could feel my shoulder tingling where that hand of his had whacked me. I was of a mind to lodge a complaint with my father.

I decided not to, though, after he finished laughing and explained Pete Wilmot was his chief engineer and not somebody it was safe to call "my man" and offer to pay for a friendly service. I saw I'd made a mistake. How could I have guessed a one-legged, slouchy, red-whiskered fellow like Pete Wilmot was chief engineer of my father's works?

Mother said she'd tidy herself up and get coffee started and lay doughnuts and cookies and corn bread and a cake she baked on the table. Now that I was home she expected the neighbors might be dropping in most any time to have a look at me after hearing so much about me. She told my father that he and I might as well get

17

my trunk up into the room they'd readied for me in the attic; and that was what Father and I did.

He said, "This isn't so much, I'm afraid. We considered bunking you in the front room."

"This is all right. I'm used to this sort of thing—"

That was the wrong thing to have said. It sounded like I was saying I was used to camping out.

"I mean," I said hastily, "I like a small place to sleep in. It's more comfortable."

"Well, we may have a better place for you not so long from now. I'll tell you our plans later . . ."

Then *he* broke off. Downstairs, again, Mother apologized because she didn't have any chocolate in the house for me. The stores in town had run out of chocolate three weeks ago. She didn't know when a new shipment would arrive.

I explained, "I never drink chocolate any more, anyway."

"I hope my coffee isn't too strong for you. Your pa always likes his so black."

Father said, "Here—" and came in from the kitchen with a tea-kettle of hot water, evidently thinking I'd want my coffee weakened.

So I said, "Well, no, thanks. Timmy always brings up my coffee black as anything."

Mother asked, "Timmy? I don't remember you writing about anyone named Timmy?"

"He's the new Negro boy Uncle John told off to look after my clothes and bring me . . ." And I heard my voice trailing away.

We sat around the table together. Mother tried to ask questions and I tried to answer and somehow it didn't go at all. More and more I was having the awful queer feeling of not belonging to them. Presently Mother said crossly to Father, "Well, my stars, Jim! Just don't sit there and look at him like you're studying a new machine. You can't take Horace apart and put him together again."

By and by some of their friends dropped in, with four or five boys. The boys were sharp-nosed and lean and stringy and too young to know much, two to four years younger than I was. While I was telling my folks' friends about the Friends Academy in Philadelphia I let go of a couple of Latin quotations, casually, you might say, only enough to indicate I was tolerably easy in Latin.

But those boys spoiled most of the effect by crowding into a corner to muffle their coughing. They must have caught colds. I was sorry for them, they looked so ignorant and unhappy. I even trans-

18

lated one Latin quotation for them, the one from Cicero. I
been willing to translate the other quotation I'd let off, too; I
said, no, thanks. They didn't want me to strain myself.

I wasn't straining myself. I'll grant I wanted to give a show of my
learning to impress my mother and father before their friends; and I
tried. However, I don't think it went down like I expected. I don't
know why. The minister was there. You'd assume a minister would
have a proper interest in the affairs of the world, wouldn't you? So I
spoke up, asking what he thought of the situation in the Malays.
Everyone in Philadelphia. couldn't talk of anything else. A tribe of
piratical Malayans had murdered the entire crew of the U.S. frigate
Friendship.

The minister smiled absently at me and kept on speaking to my
father. The difficulty of getting goods and supplies to the settlers
west of us in Indiana and Illinois had him badly worried. Roads
were impassable at present. That part of the frontier wasn't drained
by any big rivers, except the Ohio, which was at the south, and the
Mississippi, at the far west. The whole heart of that territory was
deprived of satisfactory means of communication during winter and
the mud season afterwards.

Furthermore, he said, no one was doing anything about it. For a
while there'd been talk here among the citizens of Cincinnati of
stringing a pontoon bridge across the Ohio at some point, such as
Rock Point. That would have assured transportation, at least as far
as the Indiana side, to the crowds of settlers arriving here in wagons.
But what had happened? The ferrymen had blocked the bridge.
Was that fair?

I tried to get a word in.

Father beat me to it. "Parson, if you'll forgive me, I'm a riverman,
and can't agree. According to our constitution and national laws you
can't obstruct a navigable body of water as that proposed pontoon
affair from Rock Point would have done. I've made it my concern to
know the law on that. More than bridges at present, I hold we need
improved steamers capable of navigating headwaters and small
tributaries to give communication to our frontiers." He paused.

He might have continued. This time I was there first, asking the
minister how he stood on Jackson's bank policy?

I never got an answer. Mother asked why didn't I go outdoors
with the other boys as if she'd forgotten I was old enough now to be
with grown-up company. But anything to please, I thought. Those
boys didn't say a word at first. To let them see how sociable I was I

said I'd tell them about the academy I went to in Philadelphia and they could ask me all the questions they wanted, afterwards.

But one of the boys stepped up to me and said, "I dast you to knock this off my shoulder," and I saw he had a chip of wood balanced there. So I knocked it off. Next a second boy said, "Wait! Take off his specs—" and before I could stop him he snatched them off. Everything blurred. None of the faces around me were very clear. Somebody knocked off my hat. If that was what was wanted, it suited me. I didn't plan to hit him hard enough to hurt him. But I'd teach him a lesson. So I started to shuck off my coat to square up to the nearest face I could see like we'd been taught at school by our grammar master, Mr. Taylor. He was born in England. He said all English boys were taught the manly art of fisticuffs—that was what he called it. And he'd taught us.

You stuck out your left fist, bent your right arm to protect your face, advanced, one foot forward, and when you'd finished your engagement, as he called it, and one of you'd had enough, you always shook hands. That was the way it was done. Only—it wasn't done that way in Cincinnati. I wasn't even given time to shuck off my coat. I don't know which one pushed me backwards over the boy kneeling behind me. They were like heathens. They were worse than Indians. They didn't know the first principles of fisticuffs.

I expect I lost my head. I don't remember very much afterwards except I ran all the way to the house while they chased after me, pelting me with snowballs. That evening I told my mother and father I didn't even want to stay in Cincinnati over Christmas. I wanted to leave by the first river-boat available, tomorrow morning if possible.

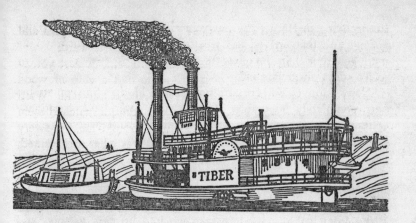

Father said, "Well, now, let's see. There's a steamer in tomorrow morning from Louisville that could take you north again, if it's what you want."

That cooled me down. Didn't he *want* me here for Christmas?

"*Jim Owens!*" cried my mother. "You'd *let* him go? He's going to stay here with us!"

"Well, now," he said, very calm, "possibly Horace has a few points on his side, Libby." He was sitting there as quiet as anything. Only you could see a hand move restlessly now and then like he was reaching for an invisible wrench to adjust maybe an invisible king bolt that no one but him had noticed was a trifle loose.

"Horace Owens," she told me shakily, "I'd hoped this would be the happiest Christmas we three had ever had . . ."

Father winked at me. I looked back at him, astonished. He was perfectly calm, no hurry, willing for Mother to go on if she liked. Mother said, "Well, my heavens!" and gave a halfway laugh. Then she thought of something. "The Whigs aren't planning to run your uncle with Henry Clay next year against Jackson, are they? I read last week in the *Gazette* that Henry Clay and Judge Springman were going on the Whigs' slate."

"Mr. Clay stayed a couple of nights with us last fall. He and Uncle sat up—"

"My sister had Henry Clay as a guest in her house?"

"Yes. I thought I wrote you."

"You *didn't* write me."

Father crossed one leg over the other. "As I was saying, Libby, we *did* pack him off to Philadelphia. Judge Springman's taken a

strong liking to Horace. So has your sister. In that letter of Judge Springman's that arrived last week, you couldn't ask for anything more generous than the offers he made—"

"To adopt our own son?"

"Now, Libby," Father said reasonably. "Judge Springman has been completely honorable. He and your sister haven't had any children. It means someday Horace would inherit everything they have if he returned to them. I don't have five thousand in cash. I expect the Springman estate must amount to at least half a million dollars. Horace would be a young nabob, Libby—"

"Oh, Jim! Who wants him to be a young nabob?"

I shivered. I couldn't help it but I wanted to be a young nabob. Uncle John had promised to take me into his firm as soon as I finished my education. I'd read law under him. In a very few years I could look forward to becoming a junior partner in the firm of Springman and Springman, established before the Revolution by my uncle's grandfather. I wasn't a riverman and steamboatman like my father. If I stayed here with my folks, what was there for me in Cincinnati? I *had* to return to Philadelphia!

Mother was saying, "We've lawyers in Cincinnati. They're good lawyers, Jim. You know Mr. Potts. Horace could read law under him in a year or so. Mr. Potts is a good lawyer, isn't he?"

"Not very," Father answered. "Lib, it's a problem. We have got to face it. We'd like Horace with us but it looks like your brother-in-law can do more for Horace than ever I can do, much as I hate saying so."

"*Jim!*" Mother said. She was so flushed and excited that her cheeks were all rosy. It seemed to me I'd never noticed before how pretty she was, maybe because she was my own mother. She was even prettier than that Mrs. Melrose whom I'd thought so gay and pleasant aboard the *Star of Ohio*. "You keep talking yourself down. I want Horace to be proud of you. I am. I wouldn't trade a dozen John Springmans for you!"

She leaned forward in the chair, taking my hand. She started telling me how, by now, my father's business had grown until he was employing ten hands. By repairing steam engines and building keelboats, he'd saved enough to build his first steamboat which he'd completed a month ago. The owner of one of the fur-trading companies in St. Louis, a Mr. Walker, had inspected it only last week, had decided he wanted it for upriver trading, and the deal had been closed.

My mother's eyes started shining when she said Mr. Walker was returning the first of the year to accept delivery and pay my father twenty thousand dollars in hard cash, not wildcat scrip or anything like that. With all that money in hand my father wouldn't have to scrimp so much. They both liked it here. They were planning to build a brick house. While the new academy here might not provide *quite* as good schooling as I'd received in Philadelphia, it had seemed to her that the advantages of all three of us again living together as a family might make up for any shortcomings a new academy had.

Now Father got up. "Libby, the new academy may or may not be what we think it is. But what Horace has to decide now is whether or not he wants to stay here and have Christmas with us."

Mother said to me, "You're joking. You haven't been away so long, have you, that you'd be willing to miss Christmas with us?"

I heard myself saying, yes, I was joking. I didn't want to leave tomorrow. The thing is, I didn't, either, as soon as I'd said it. Suddenly I *wanted* to be here for Christmas. Father said that all he asked of anyone was a fair trial. After Christmas, if it appeared, everything considered, that Philadelphia was best for me—much as they might miss me, they'd ship me back to my aunt and uncle.

That suited me. I wanted them to see I was as fair minded as anyone. So I repeated, "I'd enjoy staying here for Christmas," meaning it; and their faces seemed to lighten. Then Mother said she had to start dinner and I'd better wash up.

Although my clothes had been torn in the fight that afternoon, I had all the others I needed because my aunt had filled the trunk with an ample supply. I'd brought two other pairs of glasses with me, so it wasn't much of a calamity having the one pair broken. What graveled me the most was that the new beaver hat my uncle had bought me for the journey had been completely smashed.

But my father said he'd buy me a coonskin cap tomorrow, which was warmer and more comfortable than a stovepipe hat, when he bought me the pair of boots. He'd had a notion in mind, too, of taking me to his works. I could see the steam engine Pete Wilmot and he had repaired. After showing me his shop, he added, he'd take me aboard his new steamboat, the *Talisman*, if I cared to come with him.

Would I? I'd like nothing better. At dinner that night neither my mother nor my father said anything at all about the fight I'd had in the afternoon—if you'd call it a fight, after my running into the

house and probably making an awful spectacle of myself by wanting to have the law set on those boys. We had venison which my father'd shot across the river the week before. I'd forgotten what a wonderfully good cook my mother was, too.

When we'd finished Mother announced I didn't have to help with the dishes the first night home. Father got up and allowed that was one of the main reasons he'd been looking forward to having me return—he'd been expecting me to take over his chore of drying the dishes. But he was smiling. I could tell he was joking.

They pitched in washing and drying the dishes by the light of the tallow lamp and I couldn't help being reminded, in comparison, of how it had been in my uncle's house in Philadelphia when Negro servants would skim dishes on and off the white linen tablecloth. In Philadelphia you never once had cause to think of all the washing and drying and polishing of china and silverware going on behind doors in the huge kitchen. By and by it made me uncomfortable to see Mother and Father washing and wiping away at the dishes, with no one to help them.

So I stood and said, if it was all right with them, I thought I'd go up to my place under the roof and read for a little while before going to bed. It was what I usually did after dinner in Philadelphia. One reason my hair trunk was so heavy was I'd brought all six volumes of a set of books called *The Decline and Fall of the Roman Empire* along with me. My uncle had ordered them from England to give me as his Christmas present in advance. I told my mother I was on a chapter I'd like to finish because it was such instructive reading.

"Why, yes . . ." she said, and paused. "Yes, Horace. Go right ahead. I'm sorry we had to tuck you up in the attic. In our new house we'll have a nice corner room all for your own with a fireplace in it, if you decide to stay with us."

I didn't say anything to that because I knew now I wasn't going to have to stay. Father had said as much. In the attic I got into bed to keep warm and tried to read but somehow the Romans weren't as interesting tonight as they had been. I was restless. From downstairs I could hear my folks laughing, now and then. There they were, doing the dishes, no servants, having to skimp until my father was paid for his new steamboat. And they were laughing as if they were the two happiest people tonight in the whole land. I almost wished I'd stayed down there and had pitched in with them to clean up the dishes.

I sorted up another book from my trunk, a book of Mr. Robert Burns's poetry. My grammar master had given it to me for a prize. I hadn't much liked poetry, ever, until Mr. Taylor had put me on to Burns. There were lines in what Burns had written, like:

> If I should sell my fiddle,
> The warld would think I was mad;
> For monie a rantin' day
> My fiddle and I hae had . . .

They sort of sung in your head when you felt low and queer, even though Burns was a Scotchman and had never learned how to spell properly. I'd once asked Mr. Taylor why the printers hadn't corrected Burns's bad spelling, such as "warld" or "monie." Anyone knows they should be "world" and "many." But Mr. Taylor had snorted, walking off, never giving me an answer . . .

I shut that book too. It didn't "go" tonight, somehow.

For a minute, nearly, I was tempted to remain over an extra week and miss the opening of school in Philadelphia. However, I thought of those ragged boys who'd jumped on me this afternoon, smashing my new beaver hat, breaking my glasses, and I recalled how miserable and bleak the town of Cincinnati had been in daylight. I compared all that to the noble glorious times waiting for me again in Philadelphia.

No, thank you, I said to myself. Cincinnati wasn't for me. Philadelphia was where I belonged. I was sorry my mother and father might miss me but there was nothing I could do about it. When I grew a few years older and became rich and well thought of as my uncle was, with people bowing to me as I drove down Market Street in my own carriage, then my mother and father would be proud and glad they hadn't insisted I remain in Cincinnati with them. That was how my thoughts ran until I fell asleep.

Next morning I came out of sleep slowly and had to think for a minute where I was. I lay there in the warm bed. It must have been not much after sunup because there was only a gray dismal light against the oiled and split calf's hide serving as a substitute for glass in the little triangular attic window. I could hear the murmur of my mother and father's voices coming up to me from their bedroom below. I could remember to the days when I'd been knee high in Wheeling. Sometimes of a morning I'd wake up earlier than they

did. I'd feel so pleased with myself I'd find it impossible to stay in bed another lick. I'd jump up and go running in to them, shouting that they were the sleepyheads. And Mother would tumble me. Maybe Father would, too.

And once I thought of it, I was out of bed. I was going down the ladder to the front room before I began to wake up enough to notice how cold and drafty this house was compared to our big two-story house in Wheeling. We'd had real stairs in that big house, not a ladder running down from the attic. My foot missed on one of the ladder steps. I came down too hard. But I caught myself. Then I listened. Everything in the house was dismal still. I heard a cock crowing off somewhere and he quit. A dog barked faintly from miles away. He stopped. I didn't hear a sound from my father and mother's bedroom.

I could imagine them there, the two of them, whispering in bed to each other about me, worried. Maybe Father had been trying to assure Mother it was the best thing after all for my future for me to return to Philadelphia. All at once they'd heard me piling down the ladder. They had pretended they were fast asleep. They didn't want me to know they'd been whispering about me. They were so used to being alone and together, only the two of them, all these three years, they'd forgotten I might have been awakened by their whispering. They weren't any more accustomed to having me in the house than I was.

Even more strongly that shutout feeling swept over me. I slipped up the ladder as softly as I could and got into bed, shivering.

At breakfast Mother said, "I thought we heard you earlier?"

"No, I slept like a log," I said. "Can I have another helping of griddle cakes? They're good."

After I finished a second helping of everything and could hold no more, Father pushed his chair back. "Well, are you ready to have a look this morning at the Owens Works, young man?"

We walked the half mile into town. On the way I asked, "I don't suppose there are any buffalo left in this section of the country?"

"Last fall Injun Dave claimed he saw one."

"Who's Injun Dave?"

"He keeps a trap line in winter off west of town. You never did have a chance to see a buffalo, did you?"

"Not yet."

"Your grandfather Tate and you were always planning to go west

26

and hunt buffaloes as soon as you grew up. Remember? He was a fine old gentleman. You know, he saw something was wrong with your eyes before we did. Last evening I didn't—"

"Morning, Mr. Owens."

"Morning, squire. Let me present my son; Horace, Squire Denfield."

"I'd heard he arrived on the *Star* yesterday afternoon. Very pleased to see you, sir," he told me.

"Your servant, sir," I told him.

"Keep on," he told me, "and you'll be as big as your father in another year, young man . . ." He told my father, "I see the *Star of Ohio* laid over last night. Holden isn't taking her out until this morning. Engine repairs, I expect."

"No, it's probably boiler flake," Father said. "I didn't like the color of her smoke yesterday when she steamed in."

After Squire Denfield had gone his way I wanted to ask Father how he'd known one of the *Star's* boilers had started to flake but before I spoke he said, "As I was saying . . . Last night I didn't have much time to ask how your eyes were."

"They're better, I think."

"Good."

"Uncle John took me to a man in Philadelphia who doesn't do anything but grind lenses and fit spectacles to you—doesn't even pull teeth."

"Peddler Kebbee's was the best we could get you. His wasn't much, I expect. Let's stop in here and see what sort of boots they have."

I'd hoped he'd give up the notion of paying out good money to buy me a pair of boots; but he hadn't. He bought me a coonskin cap and a pair of boots the dovers and trappers wore, with soft oiled deerskin at the top to keep out the wet and oiled steer hide uppers and soles. While I hadn't believed I'd like them, I learned I was wrong. They fitted me from the beginning. They were easy and soft on my feet and the coonskin cap was warm.

So I slung along with my father, kicking away the snow where it had drifted over the board walk. The sun lifted higher. It looked like it was going to be a bright clear December day. We turned into Dock Street. There was the *Star of Ohio*, the gangplank hoisted, black smoke pouring from its twin stacks where the firemen must have thrown in a couple of barrels of pitch to make a show before steaming away this morning. Father and I moved through the noisy

throng of people on Number 4 wharf. We jumped out of the way of a big two-wheeled wagon drawn by a steaming horse. A man was shouting angrily from the cart, "Hey, wait! I got some barreled tallow for Louisville!" But he was too late.

I looked up toward the passenger deck. My heart gave the pleasantest sort of bound because I saw Mrs. Melrose was there among the passengers, trim and neat and handsome, wearing the same sort of India woolen scarf over her hair I'd bought in Philadelphia to surprise my mother with for Christmas. I reached to lift my stovepipe to her and bow. I'd forgotten I was wearing a coonskin.

Father remarked, "Well, if there isn't the Melrose woman—" He broke off.

Now she'd seen me and recognized me. So I bowed. And I followed Father, who hadn't waited. I heard the raucous whistle from the *Star of Ohio*. The steamer had started backing and plugging into the river.

I told him, "I didn't know you knew Mrs. Melrose."

"I haven't had that honor. But she's passed through here once or twice before. I've heard her name mentioned. There's not much for some people to do in a town this size but come down to see the steamers land." He pointed. "There's the *Memphis Queen*. She's one of the first steamers I had a hand in designing when I was with the George White Works in Wheeling."

He turned. He said, "Horace—" Another wagon pulled in in front of us. He drew me back. We had to push our way through another crowd of people boarding the two packets for the run north. Father and I recrossed the frozen mud street to the walk on Dock Street where we paused once again near a cattle stockade.

"Seeing you bow to a woman makes me realize how much you've grown while you've been away. In a year or so you and me are going to have a talk."

I was taking in all the sights. There was almost as much doing as you'd see along the Philadelphia wharves. I wouldn't have believed a little Ohio river town could have so much freight and traffic up and down the river. I looked at him, not certain what he meant.

"Maybe we'll have to have one sooner. I forget I was a full apprentice at the George White Works when I was your age. When I was eighteen I was earning six dollars a week, had men under me, and married your mother. She was just sixteen. Now here you are, nearly as tall as I am. I don't know where all the time has gone . . ."

Some cattle moved behind us in the plank stockade. To get away

28

from the cold wind we had stepped back from the walk, between the brick wall of one of the stores and the stockade. A couple of rivermen in steamer caps walked past us and didn't even see us.

He said slowly, "I can't say this very well but I'm going to try. Every year you grow older you'll find more things seeming to separate you from your mother and me. But distance doesn't count, if you'll think about it. Nothing counts unless you let it. Distance or time or doors can't shut you out unless your heart shuts you out, too. I fell in love with your mother the minute I saw her. I have loved her and she has loved me, ever since. After I saw your mother I have never cared to look at any other woman. She was all I needed. I wouldn't even have known that young woman's name, you bowed to, if Lawyer Potts had enough business to keep him from loafing around the wharves at steamer time.

"What I'm saying is," he went on, very steady, "your mother and I fell in love with each other from the start. We have stayed in love. You are what we have to show for our love. You *are* our love. Without you we wouldn't scarcely even be a family. Now . . . let's get to my works before you freeze. You're shivering. I forget you aren't used to Ohio Decembers."

We had walked about a quarter of a mile east on Dock Street, past the big hotel, the new buildings, by another hotel that looked second rate, a frame building that had been turned into a rivermen's boardinghouse, and I was wondering how much farther we had to go until I saw Father's works and his new steamboat. There was more business and go and push along this part of town, by the river, than I ever had imagined. Families had even set up camps in vacant lots, building leantos, with sod or old rubbish piled around the base to keep the snow and wet from leaking in.

I asked Father. He said it was like this all the year around. Cincinnati was booming and had been ever since the canal had been cut through to the river. It was why he'd located here. Half the people in Cincinnati were movers, arriving every day to get aboard a steamer here and continue west on the Ohio. Freight, he said, was twelve cents a pound to St. Louis, less than a third of what dovers would charge to carry it west by wagon and oxen across Indiana and Illinois; and cabin passage all the way was twenty-five dollars, with deck passage as low as twelve dollars. Even with those prices, each packet would earn her owners twenty-five to thirty-five thousand dollars in profits for each trip.

I stopped and stared back toward the big packets. I'd never known there was that much to be gained by river boats. Probably

30

I'd never before thought of it. My father explained most of the passengers struggling to get themselves and their goods on the two boats were going all the way to St. Louis, where they'd wait until after the spring thaw when the roads became hard enough for them to go east again into the forests and prairies of Illinois.

It seemed to me they were taking the long way around to go by boat to settle in Illinois. If they went directly west from Cincinnati, after crossing the Ohio, going by foot or horseback or wagon overland, it looked to me as if they didn't have more than three hundred miles to cover until they arrived in the new country. By taking passage on a boat, I knew enough from my geography lessons to know, they had to steam some four hundred miles down the Ohio to the Mississippi and nearly a hundred sixty miles up the Mississippi to the town of St. Louis. After passengers and freight were landed at St. Louis there was still a week or more of going overland, east and north across the river, by wagon and oxen, before locating in the Illinois country.

My father nodded to me from his height and agreed that was about it. The thing was, though, for at least six months of the year the only safe and sure means a family had of traveling westward was to go the long way around by river. During late spring, summer, and early fall, roads were hard enough for wagon trains. Even then a river boat could carry you and your goods three times the distance by river you'd have to go by land, almost as quick, and always more comfortably and safer than by oxen and wagon. If settlers had the price, if only enough for deck passage, they went by steamer as far as possible. The real trouble was, he said, there were only the two big rivers—the Ohio and the Mississippi. The other rivers weren't safe for steam navigation.

I remembered, yesterday, the minister had been complaining about the same thing. "What about the Missouri? I thought that was a big river?"

"It is at St. Louis, where it empties into the Mississippi. Above St. Louis it begins to flatten. It's filled with so many sand bars and obstructions a dozen packets've been wrecked the past few years trying to get up into the fur-trading country. When I built the *Talisman* I had the Missouri River in mind, all along. She's designed to shove high up the Missouri. If she runs into a sand bar, I've got some contrivances aboard to help her get off. You'll see, when I show her to you."

By now we were far enough east on Dock Street for the big pack-

ets to be behind us along with the crowd of settlers pushing across the gangplanks. The row of stores and shops and hotels, facing the river, had thinned into movers' camps and sod houses. I was more and more eager to catch sight of the *Talisman*. Still, all I could see were some keelboats tied along the wharves and a little stern-wheeler, not much bigger than a keelboat, when on the sudden at the last turn of the wharves I saw a proud handsome steamer of about two hundred fifty tons. She was smaller than the big packets but half again as long as that dumpy stern-wheeler. Just to see her, white and proud in the wintry sunlight, made your heart stand on end.

I was going to tell my father I didn't have to have him point out his steamboat to me. I'd recognized her at once. But from behind us came a call, "Oh, Mr. Owens!"

A tubby, cheerful-looking man dressed in a steamboat captain's blue cap and heavy blue overcoat with brass buttons down the front hurried, puffing, to us. He spoke in a hoarse whisper which put me in mind of how sometimes a plump, satisfied goose hisses at you, not in any sort of temper but merely asking to be noticed. "Mr. Owens, I saw you pass by, from the hotel. I'm wondering if you'd like to reconsider my offer to charter your steamboat? I'd raise my price to five thousand dollars and furnish the pilot . . ." He broke off, noticing me. "Well, well, I declare. This isn't your boy, Mr. Owens? I'd heard he was expected home."

My father looked down at the red-cheeked, smiling man as if he wasn't too pleased by what he saw. He answered in a reserved manner, although he was polite enough. He said for me to meet Captain Bogue. And Captain Bogue removed his mitten and shoved out his hand and said, "It's a pleasure, Horace. Honored, indeed." He had short thick fingers which felt more solid than they looked when they gripped around yours. And he kept pumping away, saying, "I declare, Mr. Owens, what a manly young fellow he is, too. I wouldn't say he's a boy at all. I'd say he's a young man—a young *gentleman*, by the looks of him. That's what I'd say, sir, if anyone asked me. Yes, I would. A young gentleman."

Well, even if Captain Bogue spoke to you in that curious goose-like whisper, he was so well set up and spruce looking, in that fine blue coat with brass buttons, and he had such a jolly way about him that I took to him almost at first sight. I was willing to bet he wasn't from Cincinnati. He was clean shaven, no whiskers at all, and he had little sparkling eyes. After hearing what he said about me I

stood a mite straighter and wished he could have seen me yesterday when I was wearing my beaver stovepipe.

Once more he said how pleased he was to make my acquaintance before turning to my father, asking, "I know you sold the *Talisman* but I understand you haven't been paid yet. Couldn't you delay delivery till you run my cargo for me into Illinois? It'd give you a clean haul of five thousand dollars in addition to the price you'll eventually get for the boat. What do you say?"

It surprised me to hear my father answer so curtly. He said he couldn't think of it. He'd given his word to deliver the *Talisman* in two weeks when the purchase price was paid over to him. It was out of the question. Then he bowed and said, "Horace, we'd better be getting along." All Captain Bogue did was smile and say he'd be at the Broadway Hotel over Christmas if my father changed his mind.

After we crossed another street of nothing but frozen mud my father explained that Captain Bogue had been an infernal nuisance. Captain Bogue came from one of the new towns springing up like mushrooms all over the middle of the Illinois country. He'd accepted orders from merchants and settlers of the town, promising to bring them in over a hundred tons of goods and supplies. To save himself the expense of paying freight charges to St. Louis, plus the cost of hauling his cargo overland by wagon and oxen from St. Louis, for the past couple of weeks Captain Bogue had been trying to charter the *Talisman* after learning my father had designed and built her to navigate small rivers. All of a sudden my father broke off and pointed and said, "There—there's a clear view of the *Talisman*. What do you think of her? Isn't she a little beauty?"

I looked. He wasn't pointing at that proud handsome steamer tied to the farthest wharf. He'd faced around. He was pointing directly at that snubby little stern-wheeler among all the keelboats. *That* was my father's new steamboat? She didn't look much wider or longer than an ordinary keelboat—not as big, even, as some of those floated down to the Mississippi and on to New Orleans. My heart dropped clear to rock bottom.

Why, at second glance you'd have decided all my father had done was to take one of his keelboat hulls, hang a paddle wheel at the stern with a wooden shack forward of the wheel to protect the engine from the weather and serve as engine room, build a second deck above to house paying cabin passengers, and on the third

level add a wheelhouse and a small narrow house next to the wheelhouse for pilots and officers. The lower deck or boiler deck was empty of cargo, of course, so you could see along the whole length from prow to stern through the spidery wooden pillars sticking up like stilts to support the two upper decks. The boiler was set out in the open, well forward as was the general custom so if it blew up it wouldn't blow up under the nobs paying cabin passage, with the furnace door opening forward to pick up the breeze when the steamboat was in motion and create a natural draft. This boiler was so small I couldn't believe my eyes. I judged it wasn't more than five feet long. It was as small as boilers on the new steam locomotives I used to see that pulled trains of cars over the line out of Philadelphia to Germantown.

I heard my father explaining that the *Talisman* was of a hundred fifty tons burden, which was even less than I'd estimated. He said she had an adjustable paddle wheel which would be raised and lowered when passing over sand bars, which was only one of the new wrinkles he'd thought of for his steamboat. Another was the boiler. It wasn't a steamboat boiler at all. It was a regular locomotive-sized boiler made and guaranteed by Beelan's Foundry of New York City to stand sixty pounds pressure.

"*Sixty*—pounds?" I said.

"That's right. In a pinch it might take up to a hundred. With a high-pressure boiler I'll get more work out of it for less space and less fuel, with weight saved for more cargo."

Hearing him say that, dead serious, too, made my legs go weak. The *Star of Ohio*, on which I'd traveled from Pittsburgh, was one of the finest steamers on the river and I knew she had two banks of twenty-six-foot boilers, the best to be had. They never ran on more than thirty pounds pressure. And calm as anything, here was my father saying he meant to run his steamboat on sixty pounds pressure. I wondered if he'd had to skimp so much that he'd been too short of money to buy a proper steamboat boiler. I could see the *Talisman* blowing sky high the minute her pilot hit a long hard stretch of alligator water and had to signal down to the engineer for a full head of steam. All I could do was silently hope Father'd get rid of her to that Mr. Walker, in St. Louis, and receive his money quick, before the *Talisman* was ever forced to extend herself.

"I tell you," he said, "I'll have Pete fire her up and as soon as I've shown you over my shop we'll go for an hour's cruise down the river and back. Would you like that?"

I swallowed. I could see he wanted me to experience how she handled. I wasn't going to admit the idea scared me of even having to go ten feet into the river after steam was fired up in that little boiler. So I said, "Yes, if there's time."

"We'll have time," he said. He glanced at me. I guess I didn't succeed very well in hiding my doubts, though. He laughed and in the most good-natured way possible he remarked, "Well, if the *Talisman* should sink while you're aboard, Horace, at least you can swim. Last summer your uncle wrote me he believed you could swim about as well as anyone in the river."

Yes, I knew how to swim . . .

Swimming was the one thing in the world you could do without having to wear spectacles. I don't know why it was, but the minute my eyes were in the water I was able to see as well as any of the fellows from the academy trying to race me. Two years ago, even, they'd started calling me "Turtle" Owens. At first I hadn't liked Turtle any more than my own name, Horace. By and by, though, I recognized it meant something to be called Turtle, same as Phil Tucker was called Whizzer because he was the fastest runner we had.

Perhaps that was one more reason why I kept missing Philadelphia so much even while my father was taking time to show me his works and his new steamboat. Here I was, hundreds of miles away from my friends who knew I matched up to anyone of them in the water even if I wore spectacles and was clumsy in games on dry land and always lost at fisticuffs. To them I was Turtle Owens, the best diver and underwater swimmer the academy had; and that counted. But how could I have explained that to those lean stringy varmints who'd pounded me into the snow, yesterday, and had chased me into the house?

My father's place wasn't a quarter of what I'd anticipated, either. Seeing it was another come-downer. We turned left from Dock Street. By a footbridge we passed above a slough or creek, which had ice crusting over it in this kind of weather. The slough ran to the Ohio, at the foot of the wharves, and Father explained he'd used the slough to float his new keelboats and the hull of the *Talisman* into the river.

On the other side of the slough was a long rambling frame building, of two stories, with a sign above the entrance which said: *Allison J. Owens Steamboat Works, Est. 1828.* I could remember

35

fairly clearly the big steamboat works at Wheeling, where we'd lived before my folks moved here and I'd been packed off to Philadelphia. Those works had covered nearly half an acre. Even on Sundays the furnaces were always blackening the sky with smoke.

It looked to me as if my father had merely taken over an abandoned livery stable and built on an upstairs to it. We entered a big noisy shed which reminded you of a blacksmith shop somehow all mixed together with a carpentry or joiners' works. Half a dozen men were shaping oak frames for what Father hoped was going to be his last keelboat. After that one was finished, he said, he was going to begin on his second steamboat.

Pete Wilmot stumped in from the engine shed, puffing at his black pipe. Yesterday morning his whiskers had been a fiery red. This morning they were a pinkish gray color, from all the ashes and machine oil and probably pitch which had collected on them. He wiped those big hands of his on his leather apron, spoke a greeting to Father, observed me, and said, "Sonny, did you bring along that Philadelphy bush what grows silver dollars on it? I'd like to show it to the men."

To be sure he was only joking. I'd ought to have answered back with something light and airy. But some of the men laughed. It graveled me to have him call me sonny. I couldn't help wishing my father had hired someone as polite and agreeable as that Captain Bogue I'd met on our way here. So I scowled and didn't speak; and Father scratched his ear a moment and asked if the engine was ready to run through its test.

Pete said, "I was busy on the *Talisman* this morning. But I had Clem Diggon give it ten minutes on half pressure."

"No trouble?"

"Smooth as silk, Mr. Owens."

"What about that thumping we'd had in the cylinder?"

"Nothing this morning, according to Clem."

"It couldn't be drawing water with the steam, could it, Pete?"

I knew enough about steam engines to understand why my father had asked that question. If the engineer allows the water level to stand too high in the boiler, or the gauge is defective, there's a chance of water rushing into the cylinder along with the steam. While steam both expands and compresses, water stays put. If you've ever done a belly-flop from a high dive you've discovered that water can be as hard as rock. So you can guess what happens if even a few drops are sucked into the cylinder along with the steam. Before the

36

heat converts the drops into more steam, back flashes the piston on the return stroke—and thump! thump! goes the piston. If there's too much water sucked in, why, watch out. That piston'll blow off the iron cylinder head like a cannon shooting out an iron ball.

"No, sir, I don't think so, Mr. Owens. Clem Diggon certified the level and gauge. If you've got any doubts, I can look at 'em myself."

Father said that wasn't necessary. He was satisfied by now that Clem was a capable hand, providing Pete was. It seemed to me that Pete took his time about replying.

"Why, now, I don't say he ain't a good hand, Mr. Owens. He 'pears capable, all right. But he don't yet fit in too easy with the rest of the hands. Mebbe he's still too fresh from New York State. I'd say to give him another month's try."

Father nodded. "Suppose Clem and I run the engine through this morning before shipping it? Meanwhile, I'd like you to take Sandy Jenks or Smoky Freeman with you and fire up the *Talisman*. Have her ready in half an hour. I've promised Horace to show him how she behaves on the river. He seems to have a few doubts about her."

"*Does* he, though?" Pete said, and looked at me again. "Mebbe you thought that boiler was a mite too small? Was that it, sonny? I guess you don't know all there's to know, yet, about high-pressure boilers. Don't you rile up. Most of the town's on your side. *They've* been claiming your paw's overreached himself this time, installing a locomotive boiler. But we might show you. We just might."

Then he winked at my father, like two men having a secret to themselves, and he called to one of the men and went stumping off, outside, toward the wharf where I'd seen the *Talisman* tied. I began to wonder more than before about that five-foot locomotive boiler I'd considered was too small to amount to anything. Pete seemed to have faith in it. While he continued somehow stepping off on the wrong foot with me, I was having a strong notion he probably knew more about boilers and steam engines than a person would have thought from looking at him.

I might have questioned Father about the *Talisman's* boiler, because my interest in it was growing; but he said, "Come along. We'll finish this job in a hurry and get on the river."

I followed him into the rear section of the works, going through a thick oak door. On one side sandbags had been piled up clear to the roof, but on the other side—away from the river—it was completely open. It was as warm as a summer day in here, though, because an old-fashioned vertical boiler already had steam up, and a fire was

blazing in the brick furnace. On oak stanchions was a big horizontal steam engine, with a cylinder about as long and thick as a man. On a boat it would be connected by a Pittman link-motion to one of the side paddle wheels. In here, while being repaired, the piston arm had been attached to a big six-foot iron wheel.

Near the engine a man with warts on his face and lank brown hair hanging over his collar was waiting. Father introduced me to him, saying, "Meet Clem Diggon, Horace. Mr. Diggon used to be an engineer with the Beelan's Foundry in New York State before coming to us last month."

"Howdee," said Diggon in a sour voice.

"Pete tells me you've got it running smooth as silk?" Father asked.

"It's ready any time you say, Mr. Owens."

"Let's try it first up to half power."

When Diggon turned on the steam, the machine began chugging, faster and faster. There's something about a steam engine—*any* steam engine—that rivets you to it once it gets going. Perhaps because I'd been brought up with steam engines, you might say, until I'd gone off to Philadelphia, they didn't have all the fearful attraction for me they had for some of the boys at the academy. Nevertheless, when I heard that big hard chugging and saw the piston beginning to go in and out, like a giant's arm and fist, the giant talking louder and louder to itself, I could feel a stirring in my blood.

Father listened. He got that same intent look to his face I'd noticed when last evening he'd been studying me. He signaled for more pressure. He stepped to the boiler and looked at the water gauge; and, presently, he nodded his head for Diggon to cut off steam. When the engine stopped, for a second everything seemed to go dead silent. You wanted to take a deep breath as if you'd been racing too.

Father said, "That gauge shows enough water. The engine *sounds* all right."

"Everything's fine, Mr. Owens."

I saw him lightly rest his hand on the engine as if he was trying to feel at something in it hidden from the rest of us. "I just don't know," he said thoughtfully. "It doesn't *feel* right, somehow. I can't say . . . I was afraid it might be sucking in water but I'll admit it sounded first rate."

"No, I checked them valves and the gauge. The wheel needed truing up a hair. That was the trouble."

"Well . . ." Father rubbed his jaw, still contemplating the steam engine. He put his hand to the metal again.

"Of course, if you don't think I'd know, Mr. Owens—"

"No, it's not that. No, when I hire a man I'm prepared to go 'long with him, Clem." He had made up his mind. "All right. We'll give her a try. I'll be down with you in about two shakes. Tell the men to stay on the other side of the wall. I don't want any of us in here, after we've turned full power. You've got wires arranged to shut off steam from the other side?"

"Yes, sir. It's just like we always done in New York State."

I'd have liked to stay on the other side of the partition along with Father and the men while they gave the machine a full head of steam. But he said he had some steamboat plans to show me and he led me up a flight of rickety stairs to the second-floor office. In here he opened his desk and unfolded the plans and drawings he'd made for building the *Talisman*.

I said, "I'd rather be down there with you."

"Your mother worries when I run tests. The men and I'll be behind oak planks and sandbags but if there should be any sort of trouble we might have to act fast."

"You don't *expect* any trouble?"

Father smiled. "Horace, we *always* expect trouble when we send a big engine through its final paces. That's why, so far, nobody's been hurt in this shop of mine. Up here, you'll be perfectly safe. It's the reason I placed my office on the second floor on the street side, to have all my drawings and accounts safe in here even if the worst happens and an engine does surprise us." He went to the door, and paused. "Remember—wait here until I come for you. Don't be alarmed, either, if you hear a roaring sound. It'll mean Clem's set the safety valve for steam to blow off."

After he shut the door I tried to get interested in his plans and drawings but I couldn't help having an edgy feeling as I waited. All at once I heard an eerie moaning seep all through the building. I started up. I sat back in the chair and told myself it was all right. My father had turned on the pressure.

There came that roaring. The whole building vibrated. I could imagine the piston link stroking back and forth so fast it was only a blur. I wasn't scared or alarmed, like my father had thought. I sat in the chair and crossed my legs and wished my father could walk in now and see how casual and slouchy I was, despite all the roaring. And next— It's hard to describe.

39

The whole building seemed to lift and come down again. The windows shattered. I was on the floor, deafened, and trying to get to my feet. I forgot my father had told me to stay where I was. All I could think was to get out of there. I ran to the door, opened it, a great cloud of steam gushed up from downstairs. The hot steam hit my face like thick gray wool, it fogged my glasses, it got into my lungs. I remembered that more people died from breathing in live steam after a boiler explosion on a steamboat than by drowning when the boat sank.

When my hearing returned all I could hear was a huge hissing, like snakes might make running loose somewhere, followed by a crackling noise. I lost my sense of direction. I heard someone yelling. "Father! Father!" At first I didn't even know it was my own voice. I had just enough wits left to sink down to my hands and knees, remembering the steam would be a trifle cooler along the floor than up higher.

In the first place, I never should have opened the door to the stairs, allowing all the steam to fill into the upstairs office and most nearly strangle and blind me. In the second place, I ought to have tried to find my way through that awful hot grayness to one of the shattered windows in front. I could have crawled out to the slanting roof built over the board walk below and have dropped to the ground, or slid, without risking much injury except being scared to death.

There's no explaining your actions once you let yourself go into a panic. Maybe when swimming you've come across a floating barrel and tipped it upside down to swim up under it and hear how strange and hollow your voice sounds in the couple of inches of air space between the water and the wood over your head. Now and then, though, a boy who isn't much of a swimmer'll try it to prove he can take a dare. He's liable to panic and start trying to fight through solid oak to get to daylight. Unless somebody comes to his help he'll drown. I watched it nearly happen, once, on the Schuylkill River, outside Philadelphia. My uncle had a summer house on the river and saw to it the first summer we stayed there that I was taught how to swim by his Negro coachman, who was as good as any fish in the water. The next summer I couldn't have too much of swimming and, one day, Whizzer Tucker took my dare. He almost drowned under the floating barrel before I knew he was in trouble. Later I asked him why he'd acted like a chicken with his head cut off, nearly drowning me as well before I could haul him ashore. He couldn't

give a reasonable explanation. No, he lost his temper. He claimed it was my fault for daring him in the first place and we didn't speak to each other the rest of that summer.

Well, when that hot steam blotted everything from my view, this time I was the one who acted with even less sense than a chicken with its head cut off.

On my hands and knees I began crawling down the stairs with some sort of idea, I suppose, of getting the shortest way possible through the steam to the street door. I was halfway down in a hot blinding grayness when that crackling sound got louder and louder from below me. Waves of heat flowed up through the swirling steam. I smelled smoke now, too.

Before I reached the bottom of the stairs, the opening below had changed from purely a gray murk to a glowing pink—next it went into a bright red. A tongue of fire shot up at me. I stopped. Something crashed. Next, the whole downstairs machine shed must have burst into flame. Probably the pitch barrels had caught on fire.

It was getting harder to breathe. I'd never experienced such heat before in all my living days. It hit me all at once that my way was blocked—I'd never get through. That steam seemed to be sapping at my strength, too. The fire through the steam was like something solid, trying to reach at me. I turned back—just as anything alive and still capable of moving will jerk away if you shove a hot poker at it. I was gasping and choking. Then there was another crashing sound. I felt the stairs shake under me.

There wasn't any reasoning to it at all. I simply knew that in another minute or so all the stairs were going to give way to drop down into the fire with me on them. I tried to crawl upwards and felt my arms and legs giving out. All that gray hotness went swirling and turning around and around inside my head and I hung there when of a sudden a voice seemed to go through me, telling me to hold steady.

I suppose my ears actually heard my father's voice from where he was shouting huge and strong, carrying over all that noise—but there wasn't any *sense* of hearing him. All I knew was that he was coming for me. I must have answered back, letting him know I was down here on the stairs. But I don't remember that part of it or any of the rest.

41

It was most nearly two weeks—not more than a few days before
my seventeenth birthday—before I placed where I was; and it
was a third week before I livened up enough to ask questions and
realized the academy in Philadelphia by now had opened the new
semester.

Even my birthday passed hazily. I knew, too, somehow, we'd
completely missed having any Christmas. I had to ask my mother to
open my trunk and fetch up her India woolen scarf and the real
Harts and Crabtree English hunting knife I'd bought in Philadel-

phia for my father; and there was a regular hunting rifle for me, there, as I'd thought. But none of it was very real. It wasn't until the third week came along that everything began collecting together in my mind.

The need to wear spectacles had always been a sore point with me but this time I could be thankful I'd had to wear them because they'd saved my eyes from being hurt. Dr. Hertz had showed my mother how to smear bear grease on my burnt legs and left arm and she attended me day and night for the first couple of weeks so by the middle of January most of the pain had ended, with nothing but a steady itching.

By degrees I'd learned all the sorry details. First, the steam engine had shot off its cylinder head because—yes, of water being sucked in with the steam. Somehow the new man whom Father'd hired had made a terrible mistake. At least that was what Father had thought. Pete had another idea. One day I heard him tell Father, "Mr. Owens, Clem Diggon did it deliberate. Even a new cub engineer couldn't have made such a mistake over such a simple thing as a water gauge. Diggon did it on purpose. He lied to you. Someday I'll learn why and if I ever get my hands on him I'll wring the truth from him. I hope I rot and perish if I don't."

The cylinder head had smashed into the furnace, exploding the boiler. Next, the barrel of pitch had caught fire, for a second explosion. If I'd kept my head, staying in the upstairs office, Father would have had me out in less than two minutes after the boiler exploded. What he'd done, directly, leaving everything else, was to run to the street, climb to the roof, and go through a shattered window. While it had seemed like an age to me, all told I couldn't have been huddled in the stairway more than three or four minutes before he located me and fetched me back through the office and onto the roof, where Smoky Freeman already had climbed, meaning to dive in after the two of us.

Instead of staying to rally his men against the fire, Father had slung me over his shoulder, running a full half mile, Smoky told me later, to Dr. Hertz's house at the other end of town. As a consequence of attending to me instead of directing the fight against the fire, no one was on hand at first to take charge. Pete had been on the *Talisman* with Sandy Jenks—and it was lucky Pete had been there. Otherwise the *Talisman* might have gone up with everything else. Pete threw off her lines and had just enough steam up to get her backed into the river where the current carried her safely free.

43

The rivermen and townspeople along with my father's men had stopped the fire from spreading west of the slough. But I learned there was nothing left of the Owens Works except a heap of smoldering rubble. The footbridge was gone. The two keelboats he'd expected to sell had burnt to the waterline, and sunk. Everything was gone.

Father'd had his legs blistered. In his excitement from seeing Father emerge from the smoke with me, Smoky Freeman had fallen off the roof, spraining his ankle. None of the other hands was injured although Clem Diggon was missing. People'd thought he might have been burnt in the fire. Finally, a keelboatman had reported he'd ferried Clem Diggon to the Indiana side of the river less than an hour after the fire. There couldn't be any mistake, either. Diggon had roomed in the same boardinghouse with the keelboatman, who said it was Clem Diggon, all right. Nobody could miss all those warts on Diggon's face.

Father believed Diggon had made a terrible mistake about the water gauge and had run off, not being able to face up to it. But Pete Wilmot growled and stamped around on his wooden leg and kept saying there was more to it than that. No one agreed with him, though. Diggon'd had no grievance against my father. He'd only worked at the Owens place for the last month. He'd been a good workman. Father had planned to keep him. Why should he want to blow up the works and lose his own job?

By this time—toward the end of January—I was being accustomed to where they'd located me. A bunk had been made for me in the small captain's parlor, high on the hurricane deck of the *Talisman*. Mother and Father had occupied the captain's berth, opposite the parlor; and I'd wondered about that too. I began to wake up and take notice.

That same evening evidently Mother and Father finally judged I was well enough for them to tell me how rotten complete the catastrophe had been. Hard after the fire, the very day after Christmas, Father had received a letter from a St. Louis lawyer with the information that Mr. Walker, the man who'd promised to buy the *Talisman*, had died unexpectedly. To be short about it, Father hadn't sold his steamboat. He wasn't going to receive twenty thousand dollars. To save paying rent money, Mother and Father had moved to the *Talisman*, having me carried along on a feather mattress. Hearing they'd given up their house left me with a scared feeling. I won-

dered if Father had enough money remaining to pay for food and living expenses. I didn't see how he was ever going to get started building boats again. I asked what he was going to do.

He said, "Do you remember Captain Bogue?"

Yes, I did. Captain Bogue was the short jolly man we'd met that morning before the fire. He'd been after Father, wanting to charter the *Talisman*. Well, it was what Father had done. He'd chartered the *Talisman* to Captain Bogue for a voyage into the Illinois country. Captain Bogue had paid half the charter price on signing, with the other half to be paid on arrival. Father said that meant he'd have enough after the voyage to set up in business in a small way, to pay expenses, and to wait until he received a good offer for the *Talisman* without having to sell her at a sacrifice price.

I asked, "How soon does she sail?"

"Bogue starts loading his cargo tomorrow. I ought to have the *Talisman* underway by next week, say the first of February."

I sat up, surprised. "You're not going?"

"Bogue wants the honor of being captain and he's welcome as long as he's paying. He's furnishing a pilot, but I'll supply the crew and be aboard as owner. I wouldn't miss the voyage for anything. We'll leave the Mississippi above St. Louis and start steaming up the Illinois and east into the Sangamon, where no steamboat's ever been. If the voyage's a success, once the *Talisman's* proved herself, I shouldn't have much trouble finding another buyer for her."

I started thinking. I hoped Mother would decide to return to Philadelphia with me, staying with Aunt Iz and Uncle John until Father got back from Illinois, sold the *Talisman*, and received enough money to start in business again. I said as much.

She shook her head. "You couldn't return for another month even if I went with you. If you could travel to Philadelphia by steamer, it might be different. You're not well enough yet to go by stage. Your father and I have decided the best thing is to have you go with us on the *Talisman* and wait with me in St. Louis until he returns."

"St. Louis? I can't. I'll miss school."

"I'm afraid you'll have to lose the winter and spring semesters. Mr. Blair's written Father. He's offered to help your father start a new boatworks in St. Louis. Father's accepted. It's where we'll live . . ."

I just looked at my mother. I remembered Mr. Blair. In Wheeling, he'd been in the mill business. He didn't own a mill. He went around and offered to build them and put up the wheel and construct the

dam for the millrace. The Blairs had lived next door to us until Mrs. Blair caught the milk fever, dying from it. They'd had Thankful, a sassy little snipe of a daughter, who was always getting in your way. But I'd felt sorry for her, afterwards. Her father had given up his business as millwright, taking a job with a trading company in St. Louis, and having to parcel his daughter on relatives in Memphis. That had been about a month before my father had decided to move to Cincinnati.

Now Mother was saying we were moving to St. Louis because Mr. Blair had done well enough to help Father. I wouldn't! I'd run off if I had to. I still had a few dollars of the Christmas money my uncle had given me. It was enough to pay steerage to Pittsburgh, where I'd write him to come for me. He would, too. My folks had promised I could return to Philadelphia. They had broken their word, it seemed to me.

Before I could start protesting and arguing and accusing them, Father was explaining that Mr. Blair had read of the fire in a copy of the Cincinnati *Gazette* carried by fast packet to St. Louis. Mr. Blair had written at once. He believed St. Louis offered better chances for starting a new boatworks than even Cincinnati. He was prepared to put money in a works, where Father could begin by building keelboats for the Missouri. As soon as possible they hoped to get orders for small upriver steamers. Father said he'd jumped at the chance. It was why Mother and he were moving to St. Louis. Inasmuch as I'd lose half the semester at the Friends Academy, anyway, before weather would be warm enough for me to go east, they had written Aunt Iz they were keeping me with them on through next summer's vacation.

Father said, "I know it's a disappointment to you. But we *can't* let you risk the journey by stage from Pittsburgh in dead of winter. As long as you'll miss so much school, we want you to stay with us through summer. By then, at least, you'll have been with us long enough for us not to be such strangers. Next fall, if it's what your heart's set on, you can return to Philadelphia. I wish it wasn't true— but if you've decided to be a lawyer, your uncle John can do more for you than I can. It might've been different if my place hadn't burnt . . ."

I saw his hands grip together. Then he added, "Anyway, it won't help to cry over spilt milk. We're trying to do what's best for you, and I hope you won't mind too much having to go to St. Louis with us."

I *did* mind. I didn't want to get shoved farther west to a river town probably even bleaker and more miserable than Cincinnati. But I saw Mother and Father waiting for what I had to say. I could guess it wasn't very cheering for them to have to pull up stakes and begin skimping all over again after their hopes and plans had been shattered here in Cincinnati.

I surprised myself by saying, "I wouldn't miss St. Louis. Think of all I'll have to tell Aunt and Uncle and everyone when I get back to Philadelphia next fall!"

"Yes," Father said. "You'll have quite a lot to tell them, won't you? Lib," he asked Mother, "did you give him his mail? There's a pile of letters stacking up for him from Philadelphia."

On Thursday morning, the second of February, the gangplank was raised aloft to the shear-legs, lines were cast off, and we churned into the Ohio River. Until finally we were on our way I still hadn't quite been able to believe it was happening. The last few days I'd been answering all the letters that had arrived on the Pittsburgh packets, after Christmas. I wrote a long one to my aunt and uncle, giving them the news about the fire, assuring them I was most nearly recovered so they wouldn't worry, thanking them for my Christmas gifts, and explaining that Mother and Father had finally agreed it was to my best interests to allow me to return for good next fall.

In my letter I hadn't said anything about being legally adopted by Uncle John. I'd let that part go. I pushed it away from my mind for the time being. I was thinking that, when next fall came and it was time for me to leave, I could explain to my folks I was certain I could persuade Uncle John to allow me to keep the name of Owens. Perhaps I could be legally called Horace Owens Springman or something like that. I answered Whizzer's letter, stretching all the details of what had happened to me so far so he'd be perfectly green with envy. Then I had answered his sister's letter, with not quite so much in it as in Whizzer's. She was a year younger than Whizzer and me although to see her I wouldn't have guessed it if I hadn't known her almost from the time I'd started living in Philadelphia. In that three years Matilda had suddenly shot up from being somebody who was nothing more than my best friend's sister to a younger young woman with all the style and graces you could want, providing you liked tow-colored hair on a girl. I'd been more partial to red, somehow. But tow-colored hair on a girl was all right. Matilda's looked pretty, I'll say that.

47

My aunt said Matilda had lovely hair. Whenever there was a party my aunt and Matilda's mother seemed to assume I was supposed to squire Matilda. Maybe I did too. But sometimes I had uneasily wondered if my aunt and Matilda's mother weren't possibly *too* much pleased with having Matilda and me seen together. While I knew it was wrong of me even to think it, now and then it had struck me that maybe Matilda and I ought to have more say about whether or not we always wanted to go together to the balls, and such, we younger young men and women were beginning to be invited to. I'd, once, even mentioned it casually to Matilda. But she'd surprised me by bursting into a most awful thundershower. I had let the thing go after that. Anyhow I answered all the letters; that was finished. Everyone in Philadelphia who meant anything at all to me would soon receive my letters and learn I was off to see the far West and the Mississippi for the next six or seven months.

While the *Talisman* churned into the Ohio River and slowly got herself straightened around, my mother had let me watch from the hurricane deck. In his bright blue coat with its brass buttons all polished, Captain Bogue was bowing and smiling and waving his cap to the usual crowd that had gathered on the wharf to see us get underway.

He turned to me, winking, jolly, pleased with himself, the boat, and everyone aboard her this morning. In that hoarse goosy whisper which carried such a surprising distance he urged me, "Go on. Wave your cap at 'em. They like it. I'm sorry your pa couldn't join us on deck."

Father had remained in the engine room with Pete Wilmot, who had signed on as engineer. Big Sandy Jenks was along as Pete's assistant. Smoky Freeman had also decided to stay with Father. And black smoke poured from the two stacks after Smoky, on the boiler deck, had had his firemen throw pitch in the furnace to give the crowd a last show.

At the wheel was Mr. Pollock, the St. Louis pilot whom Captain Bogue had furnished. I could turn my head and see him through the big square windows of the wheelhouse as he moved the wheel, one way and another, bringing the *Talisman* into the center of the river where the current flowed the fastest. He was a tall thin man with black hair under a sugar-loaf hat. He was as cool as ice water while handling the wheel and feeling for the flow and ebb of river currents through the wheel and the long lines carrying away aft to the twin rudders behind the stern wheel.

I watched the wharves and the town drift behind us. Pretty soon we came even with a big piece of woods, black and bare under the morning sun, with a rock showing like glistening silver. Captain Bogue waddled to me, sawing his elbows a little. "That's Rock Point over there. See? A while back a couple of rich, no-count fellows got a preacher in with them. Together they schemed to do in the ferrymen by laying a bridge across the Ohio from Rock Point. But the ferrymen beat 'em." He chuckled. "Yes, sir. The ferrymen hired Senator Durney for their lawyer. Old Durney brought in the Constitution and a whole galaxy of laws provin' nobody could obstruct a navigable river like the Ohio and that killed that proposition. Think of a preacher wanting to see the wives and children of them poor ferrymen starve to death! Shameful, ain't it?"

Well, that wasn't quite how I'd first heard it from the old worried white-haired minister I'd met, the afternoon of my arrival in Cincinnati. But I decided Captain Bogue was a real riverman, same as my father. His hackles lifted if anybody tried to obstruct his passage through a river. I listened to Captain Bogue praising our pilot.

"I tell you, Horace. You can find pilots who know the Ohio and Mississippi, easy enough. But I needed somebody who knowed them rivers and the Sang'maw. I thought of Jesse Pollock. He'd floated flatboats on the Sang'maw before gettin' his steam license. I said to myself, 'Pollock's the fellow!' And I got him, payin' out of my own pocket. I should have charged your pa. I didn't. He had hard luck. I was sorry for him. 'Be kind unto others,' is what often I say, 'and they'll be kind to you.' That's how I am, Horace."

I wished I could have listened to him longer. But the wind was cold and I saw Mother step on the hurricane deck from our cabin door. This was the first time she'd permitted me to stay on deck for more than ten minutes. She didn't want me to overdo in all the excitement of getting underway.

Captain Bogue bowed to her and said he hoped everything was all comfortable for us. If there was anything Mother wanted all she had to do was speak a word to him, and he'd see to it in a hurry. Then he bowed again and climbed up the steps to the wheelhouse. He'd been as friendly as could be.

So I was a little surprised when my mother scowled after we'd stepped inside the parlor and said, half as if to herself, "Why, that man seems to think he owns this steamboat."

He didn't own the *Talisman*. To all intents and purposes, though, the steamer was his for the duration of the voyage. Before sailing,

Mother had showed me one of the advertisements Captain Bogue had printed in the Cincinnati *Gazette*. He'd promised the splendid upper cabin steamer *Talisman*, with J. M. Pollock master—and as the single licensed river pilot aboard, Mr. Pollock *was* the master—would leave for Portland Landing, at Springfield, on the Sangamon River, and all way points; gave the date of sailing; and asked anyone seeking passage or shipping space to apply to him at the Broadway Hotel or to my father.

He'd done a land-office business, too, by cutting price by a third under the big river packets to St. Louis and towns and landings in between. In addition to the passengers, we carried more than a hundred fifty tons of cargo, barreled flour, sugar, and iron nails; both cased and baled cotton goods; cased hardware; bar iron, for smiths and forges; and sundries. That first day I was afraid we'd swamp in a bad storm. It worried Mother too. She told Father Captain Bogue must have loaded the *Talisman* by half again more than he was supposed to but Father said no harm had been done. He'd built his steamboat with the expectation that she'd have to carry sometimes twice her normal tonnage when going high up a river where no steamer had been before.

On the way toward Louisville, I soon changed my mind about that little five-foot boiler too. Although I'll grant we were aided by the current, still we were charging along during the daytime faster than my uncle's two best bays could have run a mile. The steam stayed right up at sixty pounds. If Mr. Pollock, or whoever happened to be spelling him at the time in the wheelhouse, signaled down to the engine room for more power you could hear a kind of change of rhythm all over the boat. The paddle wheel would flash faster. The fireman, forward, would throw in more cordwood.

Small as it was, that boiler Father had installed never dropped pressure more than an inch—and in a minute or so pressure was back up to where it belonged. That boiler was a regular little giant. I was sorry I'd ever had any doubts about it.

Friday and Saturday shot by without any trouble at all. Of course there were fist fights among the trappers and settlers on the boiler deck but you always looked for that. The nobs paying cabin passage took it for part of the entertainment when traveling by steamer.

Even in the engine room I noticed Pete wasn't grumbling as much as usual because he couldn't find anything against either the new horizontal forty-five-horsepower engine or the boiler, or Smoky's handling of the firing. So he took to complaining about his

pipe, or remarking in a loud voice to Sandy that the engine room was too small for a body to move around in—referring probably to me being here; or he'd have hard words against Mr. Pollock, our pilot.

He liked to have you believe he knew every pilot and captain and engineer of any worth at all on the Ohio and Mississippi Rivers. Because he hadn't been able to place Mr. Pollock, at first he claimed Jesse Pollock was only a branch-river fellow who was acting above his rightful station on the *Talisman*.

That didn't do, though, after Friday night when it started snowing again and you couldn't see your fingers before your eyes on deck. Father and Captain Bogue were ready to tie up at the first landing. Mr. Pollock said in his languid manner, "No, gentlemen. I'll take her through." He did, too. That night he stood fourteen hours without relief. At daylight he turned in. Instead of sleeping until we landed at Louisville, he was there on the minute for his regular shift, four hours later, a little pale, maybe, but steady and collected as ever.

So Pete began saying, yes, he'd met Mr. Pollock somewhere before but couldn't remember what steamer it was. He claimed the reason was because Mr. Pollock must have dyed his hair black or somehow changed his appearance. That was like Pete. He'd never admit he was wrong. I couldn't help laughing. Pete stepped forward and said above the noise of the engine, "Sonny, if you was mine, do you know what I'd . . ." Just then, Father entered. Pete clamped his teeth shut on that black pipe of his. Sterner than usual, Father told me Mother was looking for me. I wasn't supposed to be in here, bothering Pete and Sandy, particularly when Dr. Hertz had left orders I was to stay in my bunk most of the day for at least a while longer.

We arrived at Louisville, late Sunday afternoon. Here we unloaded a dozen passengers, took on that many more, and waited over Monday for a ton of bale leaf tobacco Captain Bogue had purchased. We departed Tuesday, with St. Louis six days to go. The river was too high for it even to be very exciting when we rode the falls below Louisville. Past Battery Rock the stern wheel walked over a big log the early flood had carried into the river. For a couple of seconds the *Talisman* quivered, and you could hear a grinding noise. But that was all. Pete reported no damage had been done.

We put Tower Rock behind us, piling along at a good rate through

the precipices and bluffs on each side of the river; and, once, I thought I saw a buffalo. When we steamed past Shawneetown, the ferry landing for the passing between Illinois and Kentucky, I could hear the roustabouts strike up a song for the passengers:

> *"Come bring your fam'lee west'ard,*
> *Bring all your gels an' boys,*
> *An' cross at Shawnee Ferree,*
> *Fer th' State of Illinois . . ."*

Not long after, we put both Cave-in Rock and Hurricane Island behind us; and Captain Bogue stopped along side of me to say Cave-in Rock was where the Wilson gang had hidden with Whitey Morgan, the wrecker, until they'd been cleaned out by Mike Fink and some of the tough rivermen a couple of years ago after the scuttling of the *Memphis Belle.*

He went on: "When I was captain on the Ohio I never had trouble from the Wilson gang. I stayed clear of 'em by hugging the far side of the river till we were five leagues down from Hurr'cane Island. But five or six years back all this river and on into the Mississippi through the Sugar Coast was resky. A friend of mine, Abe Linkern, was living at Pigeon Crick, then, on the Ohio. He was hired to take a 'broadhorn'—what was called a flatboat—to N'Orleens. I've often heard him telling of that trip—Abe lives at New Salem now. He runs a grocery store there for Offut. I got cargo aboard for Offut. You'd prob'ly meet Abe if you was to go on with your pa from St. Louis. Abe can tell stories funny enough to make a cat laugh . . ."

A big fish plopped up from the water not more than two feet out from the *Talisman's* passage. Captain Bogue paused and spit tobacco juice into the river. He didn't hit the fish, though. He was too slow.

"Well, sir," he went on some more but still eying the river for another fish. "Abe passed Cave-in Rock, all fine and square. He was sharp enough to get to the Mississippi. Abe hit the Sugar Coast, tied up, and one night was set on by scoundrels—and nearly got his eye knocked out in the fight. Scar over his eye's still there. Oh, no question—the Ohio and Mississippi used to be roaring rivers. Now they're safe as milk, though. So's the Illinois and Sang'maw. The old days've gone."

Probably to save expenses he was acting as his own clerk. Because I was feeling better every day, and growing restless, more and more often I'd join him in the clerk's office on the larboard aft side of the

officers' cabin, just above, almost, and forward the paddle wheel. I said maybe I could help him. We'd learned to draw up and close bills of lading and do accounts at the academy.

He answered, "Why, go ahead. Let's see."

It had ceased being a pleasure to visit the engine room. Pete's face got so black from engine grease you couldn't tell his whiskers ordinarily were red. He had less manners, too, than an Indian, puffed strong tobacco smoke in your face and the fact is, I took to him less and less. Ever since I'd happened to mention to him, nothing really more than a hint, that I didn't understand why our engine room was so oily and greasy and dirty, when engine rooms on the steam packets out of Pittsburgh were kept so smart and bright, I had the notion somehow he was prejudiced against me. I might have been wrong. But when someone calls you a spoiled insufferable pup and orders you to clear out in a hurry, trying to hasten your going with the toe of his boot, why, it was clear enough at least to me I was wasting time on him.

With Captain Bogue, it was altogether different. That first morning I found he didn't have a quarter of his lading bills even entered. He guessed he'd made a mistake by not engaging a bright young mud-clerk, which was what the assistant or night clerk was called aboard a steamer. He'd looked around for one, he explained. Young men these days didn't have any interest in that sort of thing. They liked learning to be a pilot or steam engineer.

I drew up a trial page for him. He said, "I declare. I'll bet there's not a mud-clerk on the Ohio who could do it that well. No, sir. Not on the Mississippi, either." He stopped, seeming to think. "You couldn't hit it off like that every time, could you? No, that'd be too much."

Well, I let him see I could; he couldn't praise me enough. Later he told Father, who said possibly life aboard a river steamer agreed with me because I seemed to be getting back my strength faster than anyone had thought. If I wasn't in the way, it was satisfactory with him for me to help in the clerk's room during the mornings.

"In the way, Mr. Owens?" Captain Bogue said. "With a little training from me, that young man of yours'll make the best mud-clerk I've ever had."

I'll admit, though, I hadn't counted on having a regular thing of it. But I stuck to it in the mornings. Time skimmed along. Because of having a chore to do, same as every one of the crew, I expect I enjoyed all the more the afternoons of loafing in the wheelhouse.

We hadn't had any trouble at all steaming down the Ohio excepting for that minute or so of walking over a log. And after we'd rounded Cairo, bucking the current of the Mississippi, the *Talisman* had swung right along, doing eight or nine miles an hour, nearly anyway. You'd have thought she was a regular New Orleans side-wheeler with double engines and a whole bank of boilers, not a little stern-wheeler particularly designed by my father for what Pete Wilmot once had said, disgustedly, were mud creeks.

I started thinking how dull and unpleasant it was bound to be in St. Louis, wishing my share of the voyage wasn't ending so soon. Mother'd probably want to shove me into some new strange school there, too. I thought to myself, Why couldn't I stay aboard and continue clear to Illinois and back with Father? I mentioned it to Father. He didn't say either yes or no. He said it was something that had never occurred to him. He'd expected me to stay with Mother at St. Louis. He spoke to her. Instead of being against the idea, she asked me, "Would you be strong enough? Suppose we decide when we reach St. Louis and have Mr. Blair's doctor look at you?"

Well, everything had been going along wonderfully and I was enjoying the voyage far more than ever I'd anticipated. The weather was sparkling clear ever since leaving Louisville. I could begin smelling a faint fresh tingle in the air, knowing spring wasn't too awful far away.

But Thursday, as I remember, when we were still two days below St. Louis we had a big storm in the afternoon, with shattering thunder and lightning, while rain poured down in a solid sheet. The sky got nearly as black as night. I'd been in the wheelhouse during Captain Bogue's shift. When he went off duty, I stayed there a little longer while Mr. Pollock came in for his four-hour shift. Ordinarily, I'd have left with Captain Bogue.

It wasn't that Mr. Pollock was disagreeable or showed like Pete did in the engine room he didn't like having company. No, Mr. Pollock would answer any questions you asked, polite and cool. But after a few tries with him, somehow you didn't feel encouraged to continue. It wasn't anything you could lay your hands on. Maybe it was because he gave you the impression you were of so little importance that he forgot you were there.

That afternoon I hung on in the wheelhouse because it was the only place on the boat where you could see much of anything and still stay out of the pouring rain. When lightning glared from the

darkened sky we could see the big river before us and the steep rocky bluffs on both sides. By and by I started up. "Mr. Pollock, look yonder!"

It was a steamboat that had hung herself on a rock, probably early this morning before daybreak. We were steaming directly for her and the lightning flashes set her off like one of those Fourth of July illumination spectacles of sinking ships. Only this was a real steamer, not one of canvas and fire-rockets; and it was sunk to the upper deck. I saw a chair there by a big bell with somebody's old hat on the back of that chair.

Mr. Pollock gave a turn to the wheel. We churned past, wide of the wreck and rock by at least a boat's length. He gave another turn, to put us back on course. He spoke up almost like he was speaking to himself, not me; and he said, "I wonder, now, how many were drowned?" And when I stared at him perhaps it was another flash of lightning which gave his long pale face such a queer shiny *pleased* expression. He didn't even glance around when I opened the larboard door and got out, shutting it quick against the rain—he was too intent on the river.

I grabbed for the slippery handrail and stepped down the short ladder to the hurricane deck, the wind taking hold of me and trying to carry me out into the river. Everyone was inside or under cover somewhere that afternoon. With the sheets of water flooding down from the dark sky the upper deck never looked so empty and lost and remote. For a minute or so I was afraid I wouldn't get aft to our door in the officers' house.

I tried to lie down as I was still supposed to in the afternoons. I couldn't rest, thinking of that steamboat that had killed herself back behind us on the rock. Up until now I'd been enjoying myself, wanting more and more to continue with Father on the voyage beyond St. Louis. But I'd never had any cause to dwell on the dangers you risked when you were on the river. I'd heard talk of steamboats blowing up or breaking themselves, to be sure. Somehow it had never touched close to me, not until we'd passed by that steamer on the rock and I'd heard Mr. Pollock murmur to himself he wondered how many had drowned.

Mother was below, probably in the passengers' cabin, helping a woman with a sick baby. I didn't know where Father was. No doubt he'd be in the engine room with Pete and Sandy, still making adjustments here and there on the new Beelan steam engine. I pulled

on my slickers again and ran aft along the hurricane deck to the clerk's office where Captain Bogue had lit a lantern, said I didn't have anything else to do, and I might as well help in here.

"Horace, that's right thoughtful of you. Now how'd you set down this consignment of printed cottons? It's for Denton Offut's store in New Salem, not for the Springfield merchants. I don't want my accounts mixed."

That was easy. We'd been taught the new entry system of book-keeping at the academy and he looked over my shoulder and said he wished as a boy he'd had the advantages of my education. But he'd gone into boats young, he said, rising to captain, before deciding to locate in Illinois. Last year he'd settled for good at Springfield, building a gristmill outside of town at Portland Landing on the Sangamon River. Soon enough, he continued, he'd seen what Springfield needed to start it booming was connections with the east by steamer. All last spring and summer he'd spent week after week measuring the flow of the Sangamon River which drained west from Springfield to the Illinois River. People had thought the Sangamon was too shallow for a steamer.

He'd proved they were wrong. Until early summer it flowed four feet deep all the way west. It had dried up a little during the summer months. Fall rains had it going again as good as ever. He was convinced it was navigable nine months of the year to a good-sized steamer. When he'd seen my father's *Talisman*, tied up at Cincinnati, he'd known right then, he said, that that was exactly the steamer made for the Sangamon. Drawing only two and a half feet even when loaded, she'd do for the Sangamon twelve months of every year.

If the first voyage was a success, he hoped my father might consider going in shares with him and repeating the voyage every two months as a steady thing. Then he started telling me about the buffalo and deer he'd shot in that part of the country and how corn and wheat sprung up without even having to plant it. Listening to him while I dug away at his accounts almost made me forget I'd seen that boat on the rock. I felt more cheered.

I was sorry when he looked at his watch and said, "Look here. It's nearly five o'clock. We've been working away on these plaguey ladings and accounts until I don't know where the day's gone. I'd *like* to stay with you but I promised Major Hill I'd have a segar with him before dinner."

Major Hill was one of our cabin passengers who was going on up

into the Missouri country after we landed at St. Louis. While I shouldn't say it, it gave me a proud pleased feeling to think Captain Bogue had enjoyed himself enough up here with me to apologize for having to leave to meet Major Hill. You can see now how much difference there was between Captain Bogue and Pete Wilmot, down in the engine room.

So I stayed on until I'd totaled the page I was doing, slipped into my slickers again, blew out the light, opened both doors to the deck, shutter door and the storm door, and if anything the storm had increased. I pushed my way forward on the slippery deck and it was so black and wet all you could see were a few red sparks, now and then, flying away from the stacks.

A flash of lightning lit up the river. In that instant I saw a raft out there, less than a quarter length from our larboard side. A boy was out there on it, holding up a dead lantern that the rain and wind must have blown out; and his face was staring up at me as we slid by and a big Negro man was behind him, on all fours, just crawling out of a kind of wigwam on the raft. It was all in a second. If the *Talisman* had veered two rods to larboard we'd have run them down and ground them up in our stern wheel. Both the boy and the Negro seemed frozen still in that bluish blaze of light.

Then everything went black again. The current had swept the raft on past our stern. I heard a kind of cry, or thought I did, anyway, of that ragged boy lifting his voice up at us for nearly running him down, or maybe it was only the howling of the wind and rain.

I know, after supper, I took to my bunk earlier than usual. For hours afterwards, though, I couldn't sleep. I heard my father step out quietly when it was his turn for the nine-to-twelve shift in the wheelhouse. I thought of that boy and that man on that raft and wondered what they were doing out here on the river. And at the speed the current was taking them, along about midnight I knew they'd come up to that big steamer which had killed herself on the rock, providing by then the steamer hadn't slid away and sunk clear under. For all I knew, the current might drive the raft with the boy and man on it directly into the sunken steamer and rock and smash them all. By the looks of her this afternoon, the steamer must have been one of the big New Orleans packets.

Last night she'd have been steaming toward St. Louis, carrying a hundred or more cabin passengers and possibly three times that many on the lower deck. All of them would have been eager, looking forward to landing and seeing their friends and families in

another two days. There would have been a shock when the steamer had hit the rock and hung there. I could imagine the cries, steam blowing, possibly the boilers exploding when water swept over the lower deck.

Even under the blankets I began shivering and couldn't stop. When at last I did fall asleep I dreamed somebody with a long pale face was looking down at me. He was beginning to smile, his face growing shiny and white as bleached bone. He asked, "I wonder how many'll be drowned the *next* time?" and you know how it is in a dream. I tried to get away and couldn't. His long fingers curved out and reached for me. I could hear them come scratching and scratching up the length of blankets toward my throat—

I woke up, feeling my lungs filling for a yell. It was black as pitch in the parlor. The door was closed to the captain's berth where my mother was sleeping in one of the bunks. I didn't yell. I hadn't been scared like that in my sleep for years. I was still scared.

The *Talisman* was pitching and yawing against the current. I could feel the movement tilt me back and forth on the bunk and I hoped I wasn't going to get sick. There was a great gust of wind and rain, with a rolling of thunder. Next there was a kind of lull, as you'll sometimes have during an early spring storm. And right then I heard a scratching on my door, like something with claws was outside on the deck, trying to get in. Next, something from outside spoke my name, saying, "Horace. Horace."

58

I shook myself awake. I knew *that* voice! I leaped from the bunk, flung open storm and shutter doors, and in the wet roaring blackness nearly stumbled over my father lying there on the deck.

He said, "Easy, Horace. I've hurt my leg," and somehow I managed to pull him into the cabin. I must have been shouting for help at the top of my lungs because Mother opened the door of her berth, holding a lighted ship's lantern in her hand.

She gave a cry, "Jim!"

I roused up Pete Wilmot in the engine room. It couldn't have taken him more than five minutes to strap on his peg leg, dress, send Sandy for Smoky Freeman, and join us in the cabin.

Pete knelt. "He's busted his leg. Don't move him till we git somethin' under him."

He ripped a shutter from the door—one of those long lattice steamboat window shutters—jerk, wrench, crack, and it was off.

He and Smoky slid the shutter under Father and got him to the bunk. Father explained what had happened. He'd left the wheelhouse at midnight when Mr. Pollock had taken over, shutting the wheelhouse door behind him. He remembered reaching for the handrail, slipping on the short ladder, and crashing to the deck. In all the storm, Mr. Pollock hadn't heard him calling. Father had crawled aft to my door.

He whispered, "Horace, I'm mighty thankful you've got sharp ears."

I felt weak, thinking of him lying all that time on deck, his hand scratching at my door, while he'd been calling to me I didn't know how long until I shook myself free of that nightmare. Captain Bogue wanted to put in at the first landing we came to after daybreak; but Father said weakly, no, he didn't know how badly he'd hurt his leg. Instead of trusting it to some village sawbones he preferred waiting until we reached St. Louis. He asked for the ship's medicine box and swallowed two brown pills. The pills were nothing but hard soap rolled up into pellets with something to stop pain —that was all there was available in those days.

Fortunately, the pills kept him asleep or drowsy most of the time but it was awful to see how white and haggard his face became. All Friday and Friday night we steamed under full pressure upriver.

Saturday morning, we tied up at St. Louis. Mr. Blair received news of our arrival before most of the passengers had time to clear off the boat. After that, Mr. Blair took charge of everything. He had rooms waiting for us at the Planet Hotel and his doctor arrived inside of fifteen minutes. Father had a compound fracture of the left leg from his fall and I waited by myself in our sitting room while Dr. Knox, Mr. Blair, Pete, and Mother were with Father in the bedroom.

I just sat there. I heard the doctor's voice, "Now, easy." Somebody made a sound. That was Father. I jumped up. They had locked the door. I didn't know what they were doing to him. I heard Pete's deep rumble. Then I didn't hear anything, much, just noises and somebody breathing hard. I walked around that room a hundred times. Then the door opened; Mother was there.

"Mother—" I said.

"It's all right," she said.

"Ain't this something?" Pete said. He held out two pieces of lead in the palm of his big red hand. It was a bullet bit clean in two. It

60

was the bullet Dr. Knox had given Father to bite between his teeth while the leg was set and bound in splints.

I walked in and looked at him and wanted to say something and couldn't. Dr. Knox said, "Well, we didn't have to shoot him, after all."

Father said, "You're supposed to laugh, Horace," and his voice sounded all hollow.

Then I guess it was Mr. Blair who said hastily, "Here, now," and shoved a chair under me.

That evening Father allowed he felt easier. He sent me to the steamer right after supper for Captain Bogue and Pete. I was to tell them he was calling a council of war. It was snowing and dismal in the street when the three of us returned to the hotel. Mr. Blair was with Father; and I shoved in along with Pete and Captain Bogue and sat off in one corner where the shadows were thickest and hoped nobody would notice me too much to send me out. Mother had propped Father up in bed, so he could halfway sit up.

Father said, "I'm sorry to have disturbed you gentlemen tonight but this confounded leg of mine is going to cause a slight change of plans, I'm afraid. We won't be able to sail as soon as I'd hoped."

At that Captain Bogue stepped forward. "Why, no, sir, I'd like to differ there. I reckon there's no reason why I can't take command of the *Talisman,* is there? I'll leave next week as soon as my shipment of English calico comes in from N'Orleens."

Father shook his head. "I'm planning to continue with the *Talisman.*"

"How can you with that leg, Jim?" asked Mr. Blair.

"I'm going to," Father said, "leg or no leg. I've got to see how the *Talisman* behaves in headwater country. I've got ten years of saving and planning and working to build that steamer. You don't think I'd miss being on her when she proves herself, do you? No, Captain Bogue, I mean to be aboard. I know my leg won't be ready by next week. I can't get away that soon."

"By heavens, you certainly can't, Jim Owens!"

That was my mother flaring up. In anything having to do with my father's safety or welfare she was like a little catamount, if you could call your own mother that. He meant more to her than a dozen *Talismans*—or a hundred—any number. I had the most mixed emotions. I was siding with Mother. I didn't want him to go aboard the steamship before his leg was healed. At the same time I was be-

ginning to see exactly how much the *Talisman* must mean to him. I'd never realized until now he had been thinking and dreaming and planning for ten years to build a steamboat for himself.

That was as long ago as when we were living in Wheeling. Father hadn't even been promoted to superintendent of the big George White Works. Mrs. Blair had been alive. She and Mr. Blair and that notionable daughter of theirs had lived directly across the street from our white house. I could remember long ago summer evenings when Mr. Blair and Father would be talking about steamboats or mill streams, depending on which one was doing the talking. And my mother would be on the other side of the porch gossiping with Mrs. Blair, now dead nearly four years. My grandfather Tate was still alive ten years ago. On a summer evening probably I'd be in the barn with him, while he was cleaning his old musket again. We'd both be yarning of how one day the two of us would go west to hunt buffaloes. The Blairs' daughter, Thankful, I expect, would be listening. Grandfather and I never did get to go west together to hunt buffaloes.

". . . care what that sawbones wants!" Father said more grimly. "As I was saying, I'm going aboard my steamer by the end of February if I have to be carried."

I had missed some of the conversation.

Captain Bogue protested. His voice lifted. It didn't sound as affable as it did ordinarily, either. "Now, see here, Mr. Owens. I'm as capable of commanding the *Talisman* as you are, I'd say. I commanded the *Joshua Melton* for three years, up and down the Ohio, until a no-good pilot of mine split her on a rock. I've got the *Talisman* under charter. I can't afford to wait till your leg heals. I'll go to law about this!"

Right then, Pete's deeper voice interrupted. He had to report one of the paddle buckets was badly split. It must have been when the *Talisman* had walked over that log south from Louisville. You had to dismount the paddle wheel, take it apart, find seasoned willow wood, have a new paddle bucket made, with iron bands forged, and everything put back together; and Pete said he didn't see how possibly all that could be done before the end of February. Captain Bogue argued.

Pete remained stubborn. He blamed himself. It was because he hadn't been accustomed to a stern wheel rigged to be lowered or lifted according to the depth needed. He must have let it hang too low in the water.

Finally, Captain Bogue said, "I must say, sir, that's a fine how-dee-do. Who's expected to pay expenses while the *Talisman*'s repaired? That's not in our agreement, Mr. Owens."

Father answered, fair enough; he'd pay all expenses during the wait.

"Mr. Pollock's too," Captain Bogue said. "If we let him go, I can't find another pilot who knows the Sang'maw."

So that was decided, too. After Captain Bogue had gone out, Father said, "Pete, you can't tell me it'll take you two weeks to repair a split paddle bucket?" But Pete, he just grinned and tugged at his red whiskers and mumbled he was sorry. Mr. Blair began to smile and so did Father, and Father said, "Pete, if you let Captain Bogue discover you're delaying on purpose until I sail, he'll have the hide off you. Bogue talks a lot, but fundamentally he's all right. He's even a fair pilot. However, I want to be aboard the *Talisman* when she tries the Sangamaw. That bucket wasn't too badly split, was it?"

"No, but it was sort of nicked," Pete answered. "I reckon inside of two or three weeks it'll be as good as ever, though."

After I'd undressed and had slipped under the covers of the hotel bed Mother softly opened the door, set the lamp on the stand, and came in to say good night.

I whispered, "Is it hurting him a lot? He made fun of me when I asked."

"He'll be all right. You've got to stop worrying. I almost wish I'd sent you out of the bedroom when that Captain Bogue was arguing and shouting. Your face got so white I was afraid you'd be—sick."

"I can't understand Captain Bogue. I thought he was our friend."

"Forget about him. I heard you tossing. I can't have both of my men under the weather, can I?"

"I wish there was something I can do."

"You can. Try to show your pa you're taking it with good heart. Be like he is—" she paused—"only, heavens to goodness, I hope you don't have *his* stubborn streak in you. Wanting to go on that steamboat! What's he thinking about?"

"I'd want to, if I'd spent ten years thinking of—"

"I declare! You'd want him to limp all his life? Suppose he got miles up in that wild Illini country and there was an accident. He doesn't know what kind of a river his steamer'll have to try to sashay through, does he? How could a man with only one good leg save himself?"

"We haven't got much money left, have we?"

"That doesn't concern you, young man . . ." Her voice softened. "Now try to go to sleep. Please."

"Mother—"

She'd picked up the lamp. The light shone through the rose-colored bowl, turning her face all soft and rosy.

"Horace, you'll be doing me a pleasure if you could forget the high and mighty way of speaking you picked up in Philadelphia during the time we're to have you. It may be old-fashioned of me, but I used to like having you call me plain 'ma.' Why can't you be more like all the other boys I see?"

"But I'm not a boy any more."

She sighed. "I suppose you think you're 'most a full-grown man? Maybe I shouldn't be in here, tucking a nearly full-grown man to bed?"

"I'm trying to tell you something important," I said. "I've been thinking. After I go back to Philadelphia to study law under Uncle John and enter his firm, someday I'm to have everything he has, anyway. It's what he wants. Well, why couldn't I write him and say we're hard up now and ask him—"

"Horace Owens! If you haven't any pride, your father and I have! Don't ever say such a thing again. You hear?"

"I wanted to help—"

"That wouldn't be helping. You'd be begging help from somebody else. I'm ashamed of you. Maybe it's the best thing after all that you are returning to Philadelphia next fall if that's what you've learned. Now go to sleep."

Those weeks slid by like drops in a river. I don't believe I'd have noticed their going if Mother hadn't kept worrying to herself about Father being determined to go aboard the *Talisman* long before Dr. Knox had said his leg would have safely mended.

Because there wasn't anything else to do, I fell into the habit of occupying myself aboard the *Talisman* while she was tied to the wharf, below Center Street, and two blocks from our hotel. The passengers were all unloaded, of course. The crew was staying aboard, Father paying their wages.

Because no steamer before ever had gone up the Illinois River and east on the Sangamon, Captain Bogue had scarcely any luck at all when he advertised for passengers. The whole town had learned of the voyage and so many people tried to come aboard to see the

new steamer that a sign had to be put up, saying no visitors allowed without permission. But people preferred to wait and see how successful the *Talisman* was with her first voyage before committing either themselves or much in the way of cargo.

Captain Bogue's English cloth arrived from New Orleans and the big wooden boxes were loaded. His ledgers were still in such a miserable state of confusion I was afraid they'd never be balanced and ready to show to his Illinois merchants before departing time. I spent one whole day and the next morning on one single example of a mixed lot of goods going to the John Williams store in Springfield, for instance.

I remember, still, how it opened my eyes to all the business and the variety of business and needs for one small prairie store, stuck away somewhere up north in the wilderness. In that list of goods we were carrying for that single store were cam knives, written down as ordinary pen, pocket & butcher; forks, steel & plated; razors; sockets & firmer chisels—in Philadelphia we'd have written it "chisles"; gouges; cast steel, both German and American; hand saws; braces and bits; knob-locks and latches; coffee mills; butts, both brass and table; screws; glass knobs; desk hinges; desk and cupboard locks; candlesticks, of brass, iron and tin; hammers and hatchets; iron and brass fire irons; shovels and tongs; both common and percussion gunlocks; percussion caps; bonnet wire; bridle bits; stirrups; steel-yards; teakettles; saucepans; both patent and common augers; marbles; shovels and spades; trowels; iron hoes; halter chains, and log chains; anvils and vises; sickles; fanning mill irons and screws; 4d, 6d, 10d, and 20d nails and brads; and Swedish and Juaniata iron, flat, round and square.

All of this, with the quantity or amount stated for each article, was only one consignment out of nearly a hundred which we not only had to have totaled on the books but located handily on the boiler deck and ready for delivery. Captain Bogue had a tremendous clerking chore on his hands. Captains of the six hundred-ton fast packets had even more of a responsibility; but they usually carried several clerks, as well as a mud-clerk for night duty, loading and unloading.

After about a week, he told me, "Horace, I declare—your pa's laid up in bed when he ought to be using the time here to boom up the *Talisman* to the big merchants in town. I can't help feeling sorry for him. He needs help. I'm giving him all I can. I'm making progress with Vairin and Reel, the two most important steamboat agents. If I get the time, I think—I don't promise—but I *think* I can persuade

65

'em to charter the *Talisman* for a good price this summer to Pekin and back, on the Illinois. Meanwhile, I just don't seem to have the time here for my ledgers . . ."

Well, it seemed only fair for me to continue helping him here. I told him so and he pumped my hand and said it gave him confidence in the human race to meet somebody as willing to even scores as I was.

Consequently, it rattled me badly when a few afternoons later Pete stumped into the office and said, "Captain, it's past five. You planning to work this boy all night?" That was unsettling enough. But he eyed me and went on to ask how much Captain Bogue was paying me to act as regular mud-clerk. I bristled all over. Before I could answer, Captain Bogue said, "Sir, I've made my arrangements with young Mr. Owens, thank you. Good day."

Pete waggled his red whiskers, said, "Sonny, tell your paw for me we're getting on handsome with that there bucket," and shut the door. I heard his peg leg go clump, clump, along the hurricane deck, the sound vanishing away. I looked at Captain Bogue and didn't know how to apologize for Pete. But Captain Bogue rubbed his hands together, explaining he'd been crediting me with twenty-five cents a day or a dollar and a half a week. He'd been planning to keep it as a surprise and pay me in a lump sum when it came time for the *Talisman's* departure.

More gray February days had slipped by. We never saw anything of Mr. Pollock, who was still living at the Commercial Hotel at Father's expense. Captain Bogue gave more and more of his time to booming the *Talisman* in town after he decided I'd got the hang of my job on his books. Mr. Blair still came down to the steamboat almost every day, sometimes bringing a friend with him.

Near the end of February I was able to do what at the time I figured was a favor to him. It was cold that afternoon in the clerk's office. I gave myself ten minutes off, to go down to the cooking fire on the boiler deck, warm myself, and jaw a little with Smoky Freeman and the roustabouts. Just as I arrived an elderly-looking man, with white muttonchop whiskers, came across the gangplank despite the "No Visitors Allowed" sign, and asked to speak to the engineer.

Smoky said both Pete and Sandy Jenks had gone to the forge, uptown. The old man said, "Hum, hum, dear me, I had a card from Mr. Blair to him," and gave Smoky the card. Because Smoky couldn't read he handed it on to me:

Peter Wilmot, Esq., Engineer, Steamboat Talisman—This will
present Mr. Bernard Pratte. Please offer him every courtesy.
                                        Timothy P. Blair

Mr. Pratte was so old and wobbly, and he looked so bewildered, that he reminded me of some of my uncle's older friends who sometimes had come to the house to ask for advice on legal matters. I said who I was and explained I might be able to show him my father's steamer, if he cared to see it.

"Hum, dear me, yes; very kind of you, if 't isn't too much trouble?"

He was so old it wouldn't have surprised me if he'd traveled by keelboat or stage to St. Louis. Maybe he'd never been on a steamer before. Well, he tottered along after me. First I showed him Father's adjustable stern wheel, explaining it could be raised or lowered depending on the depth of the river. He was interested in the steam winch and the new horizontal steam engine and began asking more and more questions until I wasn't as sure as I had been that he was so dead green to steamers.

He went tottering and trailing after me most nearly for an hour instead of the fifteen minutes or so I'd reckoned on. I could have continued longer but at last I had to explain to the old gentleman I was sorry; I was acting as temporary mud-clerk, and ought to get back to my job.

"I have detained you, haven't I? I didn't realize how the time had fled. Hum . . . forgive me. Here, thank you for your trouble, young Mr. Owens."

He gave me a penny. I took it and remembered to thank him, because that was one thing my uncle had managed to drill into me. Sometimes when leaving, elderly friends of his used to give me a penny, the same way, as if they were so old and nearsighted they couldn't see I'd grown up to three times the age of someone you'd hand a penny to when departing.

Mr. Blair's friend tottered over the gangplank. He waved at me. I waved back. There was an old shabby carriage waiting. An old colored servant helped him inside; and I felt guilty keeping him so long on the boat. I could imagine old Mr. Pratte having to take to his bed, with Mr. Blair blaming me for jawing so long with him.

Well, it passed out of my mind. I forgot to mention it that night to either Mother or Father because the doctor had been there, again, to inform Father he couldn't possibly leave in March on the *Talisman.* Father'd have to stay off his leg at least another month. Even

then Dr. Knox might have to reset the break. It was one of the glummest evenings I ever can remember.

I'd gone to bed but my door was partially open and I could hear their voices coming from their bedroom across the empty sitting room into my bedroom. Their voices sounded so worried and desperate I couldn't sleep. While I knew I shouldn't, by and by I got up and tiptoed across the dark cold living room and just stayed there, listening.

Father's voice repeated twice, "I've got to be on that boat, Libby. I've got to."

Mother's voice was too faint for me to hear her words through their door when she answered.

"Libby, you don't understand. I have got to. Bogue's a boomer. The country needs fellows like him. They talk up new territory and risk their money and other people's money in getting things going. But he's no steamer captain. I have got to get on that *Talisman* when she sails."

Mother's voice said something, again.

"Yes, Pete's the best there is. But all he knows is engines, Libby. I've got money invested in that steamer. Bogue still owes me half the charter fee. Everything I have is at stake in that steamer. Here I am nearly forty after working as hard as I know how since I was thirteen and began wanting someday to build steamboats of my own. Why, I'm nearly busted, Libby! I wanted by now to begin to do something for Horace. If he wants to be a lawyer, by God, Libby, *I* wanted to be the one helping him, not having your sister's husband . . ."

I couldn't listen any more.

I got back into bed after shutting my door; but it was powerful hard to sleep that night. Too late I wished at least I'd saved all that fifty dollars my uncle had given me, so I could have given the money to Father to apply on the expenses he was having during the delay. I could begin to appreciate, too, how much grief and trouble I must have caused them ever since I'd landed that first morning in Cincinnati. I'd been high and mighty from the start with Pete. I'd made a fool of myself with their friends. I'd showed off to those boys—and received my deserts from them, to go howling back into the house.

All next day it bothered me. Finally, I asked Captain Bogue if he'd like to keep me on as his mud-clerk all the way to Springfield.

His answer surprised me. He'd been complimenting and praising

68

me so much I expected nothing would please him more if I decided to go on with the voyage to earn at least my keep and twenty-five cents a day. It would have taken that much off what Father would have had to pay for me to remain in St. Louis, doing nothing at all, or maybe entering a new school.

That gooselike whisper of his didn't sound as kindly as usual. "I declare, Horace—no, I couldn't do that. Times are tight. I didn't succeed with Vairin and Reel. Everyone wants keelboats. Perhaps *I* made a mistake paying your pa such a big price for this voyage. Anyhow—no, I couldn't use you, Horace. While we're on the subject, I been meaning to tell you that I won't need you after this week. I'll take over the ledgers myself. You *are* inexperienced. You *have* been taking a powerful long time at the high rate I've been paying you."

I learned how it was to lose a job after I'd believed I was doing so well on it. Finally, Captain Bogue agreed to keep me on another week at fifteen cents a day but I could see he was doing it mostly out of charity. I'd never felt quite so low.

That evening when I started back to the hotel I didn't think I had the courage to admit to my folks, after all my bragging, that I'd failed at my first job. Snow was falling again. The wind whistled bleakly along the dark river and up over the wharves. I considered writing privately to my aunt Iz and explaining to her why I couldn't endure being here any longer and asking her to send for me.

As I headed through the cold darkness toward the hotel I wrestled with it back and forth in my mind. When I arrived at the hotel I still hadn't decided whether to write a letter tonight and dispatch it or try to hang on a little longer.

I'd reached a point in my life where I had to take a decision for myself, alone, with no one else being able to do it for me. It didn't give me an easy feeling. I climbed the stairs from the main or common room of the hotel. The lights were burning, with the fine pleasant smell of good whale oil from the lamps. It was warmer in the hotel—and possibly all the light and the blazing of a wood fire helped. Anyhow, I decide to hang on here for a little longer without weakening before writing Aunt Iz.

Father sung out, "You home? Hello, there. What kept you so long? We've news for you."

"Horace," Mother said excitedly, "you can't ever guess."

"Aunt Iz and Uncle John are coming—"

"*Horace!*"

"Tell him," said Father.

"Your father's received an offer at last for the *Talisman!*"

"Honest?"

"Honest."

It goes to show how quick the black side of anything can spin around and shine and sparkle. I asked if Captain Bogue finally had persuaded those ships' agents, Vairin and Reel, to contract for the *Talisman*.

By now, I was in the bedroom. Mr. Blair was in here. He was grinning away at me like a lean house-tamed wolf. Father wrinkled his forehead. He doubted if Captain Bogue had been doing much to

boom the *Talisman* while warming his feet next to the stove in the tavern with his pilot, Mr. Pollock. No, the man who'd done the booming was Mr. Blair, here. And it was Mr. Pratte who had decided to buy the *Talisman*.

"Mr. Pratte?" That name didn't signal my engine room.

"That's right."

Father, Mother and Mr. Blair were all looking at me so oddly that I saw there was something more to it. Mr. Pratte? *Old* Mr. Pratte? All my pull-cords suddenly started jangling at once. Why, I knew old Mr. Pratte. No—it couldn't be the tottery old man I'd led over our steamer. He hadn't had even enough money to buy a respectable carriage for himself.

I said as much.

Mr. Blair opened his mouth and gave a yelp of laughter. He couldn't help laughing, he told me. Did old Mr. Pratte have enough money to buy the *Talisman?* Mr. Pratte was the senior partner of Bernard Pratte and Company; and Bernard Pratte and Company was merely the largest fur-trading concern in St. Louis, one of the four or five largest in the nation.

"Oh," said I blankly, like you do when you see you've been dogged up a tree without knowing it.

Father took over. He said Mr. Blair was a junior partner. For weeks Mr. Blair had been urging his boss, old Mr. Pratte, to see the *Talisman*. Finally, Mr. Pratte had agreed to see our boat. But he'd wanted to see her by himself, with no one along to try to boom her to him. Instead of being so poor and so tottery, I learned Mr. Pratte owned about half the town. He worked from dawn to dark in his offices. Although he was close to seventy, regularly every spring the old gentleman still voyaged up the Missouri into the fur territories.

I felt my head spin, I'd have lathered myself all over with the finest honey in creation if I had known who Mr. Pratte was when I'd sprung my offer, coolly enough, to show him our boat. I'd thought he was green! Oh, my! It was a wonder I hadn't lost our chance to sell him the *Talisman* by the offhand way I'd finally dismissed him, too. I began to wither a little, all at once remembering that I finally had told off the old gentleman by explaining I was busy, had a job, and couldn't give him more time. No one needed to tell me what he'd said later to Mr. Blair. I only could hope Mr. Blair had been charitable enough to keep it from my father and mother.

Mr. Blair was explaining more of the details. After seeing the *Talisman* old Mr. Pratte had decided he wanted our steamer for his

71

firm. He was offering twenty-five thousand dollars. That was five thousand dollars more, I realized, than my father had hoped to receive! Furthermore, he wanted Father to begin constructing a second upriver trading steamer! Mr. Blair was resigning from Bernard Pratte and Company to go into the new works of Owens and Blair, as Father's partner.

He surprised me by shaking my hand. Now, what was up?

"I couldn't say anything sooner," he told me, the first man I ever saw who could grin like a wolf and have you like him. "Mr. Pratte cautioned me to hold everything in confidence, until he'd reached a decision. However, you might like knowing he took quite a fancy to you, Horace."

"Mr. Pratte?" I swallowed. "Did he?"

"Yes. He told me you tried to answer his questions, told the truth when you didn't know the answer, and were polite and well mannered. If you ever cared to learn the fur-trading business, I was also to inform you Mr. Pratte would see you any time you cared to call."

I heard Mother utter, "Polite? Well mannered?" as if speaking to herself. She saw I was looking at her, turned a rosy color, and exclaimed, "Horace Owens! I ought to shake you. Your father and I have been worried sick because Mr. Pratte didn't appear interested in the *Talisman*. Why didn't you tell us Mr. Pratte had been aboard?"

I didn't have any answer. The truth was—I'd clean forgotten ever showing that tottery old gentleman our steamer until Mr. Blair had brought it up this evening. Well, that shows you, too, I suppose.

I heard Mr. Blair ask Father, "Jim, what about Bogue? Pratte wants to take over the *Talisman* immediately."

"I'll manage Bogue. I've brought his cargo this far. Suppose I pay to have the cargo transferred and sent the rest of the way by wagon?"

"Fair enough. You can afford it now."

"Let Bogue pocket the remainder of the charter money due me. He'll come out with a handsomer profit than he anticipated. I'll turn over the *Talisman* Monday to Pratte and Company. We'll all be satisfied."

Not Captain Bogue, though.

Next day, Captain Bogue knocked all of Father's expectations in the head by refusing to relinquish the charter. He wouldn't con-

sider transferring the cargo to wagons. Or keelboats. He hissed like a fat angry goose. "Impossible! No, sir!" He wouldn't consider it at all. He had a charter. He had his legal rights. Father had signed the agreement to send the *Talisman* up the Sangamon River to Portland Landing, at Springfield. Captain Bogue held the charter. The *Talisman* couldn't be sold to anyone until she had filled her contract. He wouldn't budge. His whole interest was in proving to the merchants of Springfield and Sangamon County that their river was navigable. Using wagons or keelboats would defeat his purpose and all his promises . . .

Mr. Blair was the one who finally found a solution. He discussed the situation with old Mr. Pratte at the fur company. Mr. Pratte needed the *Talisman* for the spring gathering of furs. He'd planned to buy the *Souvenir,* from Vairin and Reel; but the *Souvenir* was three hundred tons and drew too much water to go high up the Missouri. If the *Talisman* completed her voyage and returned to St. Louis on or before April fifteenth, Mr. Pratte agreed to wait and buy her according to his original offer.

Father decided that was more than enough time, by at least half a month, for the *Talisman* to deliver her cargo at Springfield and complete the round trip. Captain Bogue said he was satisfied. He began to be jolly and affable again, like he'd been before. The *Talisman* would depart Tuesday, three days away.

Then I received another surprise. Saturday, Dr. Knox announced firmly that Father couldn't get out of bed and go on his steamer unless Father was prepared to be crippled the rest of his life. Pete Wilmot had arrived to discuss final preparations with Father. I never in my life expected a time would come when I'd hear Pete say anything in my behalf; but he did that evening.

"Mr. Owens," Pete said, "Sandy and me and Smoky Freeman can take care of the boat. Pollock's proved he knows piloting. What I'm saying is—haven't you got Horace available? Him and me haven't fitted together too well. That don't mean we can't if we try. I been watching him. He's dug in at them ledgers and worked like a hound dog at 'em. Let Horace come 'long with us. Sign him as mud-clerk, at reg'lar pay too, fifty cents a day and keep."

Mother said, "He's too young."

"I was three years younger'n him, m'am, when I signed on the *Henry Adams* as prentice striker."

"And you lost a leg when it blew up."

"Here, now," Father said. "My steamboat isn't going to blow up."

73

"Please," I said. "I'd like to go."

"You'd *like* to go?" Father asked from the bed.

There was a dead silence. I expect they were all watching me; but I was watching only Father. He had that same absorbed expression on his face I recalled he had had that first day or so after I'd landed in Cincinnati. It was when he had been studying me thoughtfully like I was a particularly delicate piece of machinery new to him.

"You'd like to go?" he repeated. His voice had changed. It was deeper.

"I wouldn't do all *you* could. I'd try, though."

Pete said, "Sure, Mr. Owens. Me and him can—"

"Just a minute, Pete," Father said. "As I was about to say, Horace, I'm a tolerably good steamboatman. At your age I could even captain a steamer in a pinch. Not very long from now you'll be returning to Philadelphia to make a lawyer of yourself. I wouldn't try to take hold of anything in your line. But steamers aren't in your line. Don't you figure you're spreading yourself to think you could try doing something in my line?"

I saw he didn't want me to go. He didn't believe I'd prove out on a steamer. Unexpectedly, though, I was stiffened by recalling that morning after landing in Cincinnati. Father and I had walked the half mile south from that shackly house of theirs to the center of town and east along Dock Street. It all came back to me. I'd thought I had forgotten. I hadn't. That morning I'd been thinking more than ever I was shut out and closed off from Mother and Father. I didn't belong to them. Their door had been shut when I'd come down earlier that morning from the attic to wake them up. I'd never had Father talk to me like he had that morning, offhand, almost casual, not quite, though, and at the same time saying things you never thought of fathers saying. He had been in love with Mother from the day he first had seen her. He had stayed in love with her and she with him; and I was tied in with their love, all a part of it, never really to be shut out by anything, doors, distance, or time. We three were the Owens family. We three were all there was to the Owens family. It all came back to me. I shifted from one foot to the other.

I said, "Didn't you tell me I was as important to the Owens family as Mother or you?"

"That's right. I did. You are," he said. "Well?"

"Jim—" Mother began.

"Libby, I'm sorry. This is important."

74

I said, "Then isn't your steamboat as important to me as it is to you even if it isn't exactly in my line? Maybe I would have to go some to be as good as you were at my age when you could captain a steamer in a pinch. Let me sign up with Captain Bogue. Nobody's asking me to captain the steamer in a pinch. That was your line when you were my age, maybe. But could you be a good mud-clerk at my age? You never had the schooling I've had. I can go on a steamer right now and go hard as a mud-clerk. If you were my age I could probably," I said, "beat you as a mud-clerk. It's the one thing I *could* do better than you." And after I'd finished speaking I held my breath. It was the first time in my life I'd ever matched myself up against my father.

"You think so?" he said in no way at all.

"Yes," I said. "Yes, sir."

"If you signed up for the *Talisman's* run, you'd be just a mud-clerk. You understand that? Mr. Wilmot, here, would be my representative aboard that steamer. He'd have full authority from me to make any necessary decisions. If you didn't prove out, you'd be yanked off your job. You'd be set ashore like any mud-clerk that failed. Of course, I'd have Pete give you money to take the stage line, south, back here. But while you were on the steamer you wouldn't be my son. Nobody'd know you were Judge Springman's nephew, either. If they did they wouldn't care. You understand?"

I felt my face grow red. "Yes, sir. But if you were my age, now, I could still beat you as a mud-clerk."

To my surprise Pete Wilmot said, "I don't like interferin' 'tween your son and you. But I've knowed you long enough to see you get your back up many a time. You got his back up and it ain't quite fair. I'll say this. Mr. Owens, if you was to match against him as a mud-clerk Horace jist might beat you."

"I've served my time as mud-clerk. I was younger than he was, too."

"I still say, he jist might beat you."

"You think so? All right, Pete. Sign him. If Horace is bragging, it's your responsibility to fire him."

"Jim—" Mother began.

"Libby, if Horace can even half match up to what I know I could do aboard a steamer at his age, wouldn't it be a great day for rejoicing in our lives? We'll know he can match up against anything that comes when he leaves us next fall to return to Philadelphia. Wherever he goes, wherever he is, we'll both know he is an Owens,

a part of us, and nothing, by God, will ever make him forget he is our son."

That was the second time in my life I'd heard him cuss. Generally, my father was a mild-speaking man even if he was a riverman. I didn't quite know how I'd gotten myself into trying to match up to how he was at my age, either. All at once it had become something tremendous and huge, I felt, to us three members of the Owens family. It was so important we never even mentioned it again. It stayed there under the surface, waiting. It was like that letter my uncle had written to my folks which I knew had arrived a week or so before I arrived, when I landed last December in Cincinnati. While my folks had been welcoming me, that letter had been in all our thoughts. But we'd been hesitant to begin discussing it for fear it would spoil our pleasure in being together.

When Father spoke to him Sunday morning even Captain Bogue didn't have any strong objections to my signing for the Illini voyage. Now the *Talisman* was sailing, with himself as captain, he had become as affable and anxious to please as he ever had been. When Father finished, he said, "If you say so, Mr. Owens. But Horace don't know much about steamers and voyagin' on rivers. I'd hate to have anything happen to such a promisin' young gentleman."

"To tell the truth, captain, I don't see very much that could happen to him unless he chanced to fall overboard. If he did, he knows how to swim."

"Does he, though?"

"Yes," I said.

"I declare," Captain Bogue said. "Who'd have thought? I ain't even learned how to swim. Never bothered with the thing, somehow."

"As we were saying . . ." Father said. I was beginning to see how Father always stuck to the main course in a conversation. Others might steer off to one shore or to the other for a landing but he always kept on going straight to wherever he had meant to go. "As we were saying, Captain Bogue, I believe my son can take care of himself satisfactorily while aboard the *Talisman*. I wouldn't put my word in for him if I didn't believe that."

"Why, I don't have no doubts," Captain Bogue said hastily. "Why, I wasn't implyin' nothing 'gainst him. 'Zactly the contrary."

"Besides, I've spoken to Mr. Wilmot. He's promised to keep an eye on Horace."

I said, "Then isn't your steamboat as important to me as it is to you even if it isn't exactly in my line? Maybe I would have to go some to be as good as you were at my age when you could captain a steamer in a pinch. Let me sign up with Captain Bogue. Nobody's asking me to captain the steamer in a pinch. That was your line when you were my age, maybe. But could you be a good mud-clerk at my age? You never had the schooling I've had. I can go on a steamer right now and go hard as a mud-clerk. If you were my age I could probably," I said, "beat you as a mud-clerk. It's the one thing I *could* do better than you." And after I'd finished speaking I held my breath. It was the first time in my life I'd ever matched myself up against my father.

"You think so?" he said in no way at all.

"Yes," I said. "Yes, sir."

"If you signed up for the *Talisman*'s run, you'd be just a mud-clerk. You understand that? Mr. Wilmot, here, would be my representative aboard that steamer. He'd have full authority from me to make any necessary decisions. If you didn't prove out, you'd be yanked off your job. You'd be set ashore like any mud-clerk that failed. Of course, I'd have Pete give you money to take the stage line, south, back here. But while you were on the steamer you wouldn't be my son. Nobody'd know you were Judge Springman's nephew, either. If they did they wouldn't care. You understand?"

I felt my face grow red. "Yes, sir. But if you were my age, now, I could still beat you as a mud-clerk."

To my surprise Pete Wilmot said, "I don't like interferin' 'tween your son and you. But I've knowed you long enough to see you get your back up many a time. You got his back up and it ain't quite fair. I'll say this. Mr. Owens, if you was to match against him as a mud-clerk Horace jist might beat you."

"I've served my time as mud-clerk. I was younger than he was, too."

"I still say, he jist might beat you."

"You think so? All right, Pete. Sign him. If Horace is bragging, it's your responsibility to fire him."

"Jim—" Mother began.

"Libby, if Horace can even half match up to what I know I could do aboard a steamer at his age, wouldn't it be a great day for rejoicing in our lives? We'll know he can match up against anything that comes when he leaves us next fall to return to Philadelphia. Wherever he goes, wherever he is, we'll both know he is an Owens,

a part of us, and nothing, by God, will ever make him forget he is our son."

That was the second time in my life I'd heard him cuss. Generally, my father was a mild-speaking man even if he was a riverman. I didn't quite know how I'd gotten myself into trying to match up to how he was at my age, either. All at once it had become something tremendous and huge, I felt, to us three members of the Owens family. It was so important we never even mentioned it again. It stayed there under the surface, waiting. It was like that letter my uncle had written to my folks which I knew had arrived a week or so before I arrived, when I landed last December in Cincinnati. While my folks had been welcoming me, that letter had been in all our thoughts. But we'd been hesitant to begin discussing it for fear it would spoil our pleasure in being together.

When Father spoke to him Sunday morning even Captain Bogue didn't have any strong objections to my signing for the Illini voyage. Now the *Talisman* was sailing, with himself as captain, he had become as affable and anxious to please as he ever had been. When Father finished, he said, "If you say so, Mr. Owens. But Horace don't know much about steamers and voyagin' on rivers. I'd hate to have anything happen to such a promisin' young gentleman."

"To tell the truth, captain, I don't see very much that could happen to him unless he chanced to fall overboard. If he did, he knows how to swim."

"Does he, though?"

"Yes," I said.

"I declare," Captain Bogue said. "Who'd have thought? I ain't even learned how to swim. Never bothered with the thing, somehow."

"As we were saying . . ." Father said. I was beginning to see how Father always stuck to the main course in a conversation. Others might steer off to one shore or to the other for a landing but he always kept on going straight to wherever he had meant to go. "As we were saying, Captain Bogue, I believe my son can take care of himself satisfactorily while aboard the *Talisman*. I wouldn't put my word in for him if I didn't believe that."

"Why, I don't have no doubts," Captain Bogue said hastily. "Why, I wasn't implyin' nothing 'gainst him. 'Zactly the contrary."

"Besides, I've spoken to Mr. Wilmot. He's promised to keep an eye on Horace."

At that Captain Bogue sawed his elbows faster. "That ain't required. *I'll* certify to look after him, myself, like he was my own son. Yes, sir. Be proud to, Mr. Owens . . ." He observed me a moment. "You know, Horace, I been wonderin' how I'd ever finish that there ledger 'ithout you. Now your pa's agreed to let you go 'long with us —" he gave his elbows another sawing motion—"I guess you won't want to loaf today even if 'tis Sunday. Will you?"

I went off with him. It was turning into an unseasonably warm day and when Captain Bogue opened the two doors to the clerk's office, he stopped and pointed to a green grasshopper sitting on the top of the iron safe, with its spindly joints sticking up. I hadn't seen a grasshopper since the end of last summer. It looked like a little old green man with spectacles on its nose.

"I declare," said Captain Bogue, surprised. "You know what that means, Horace? Sure as you're alive, it means an early spring. Shoo!" He swept his hand down to smash it. But the grasshopper gave a leap off the safe, a second to the door, and escaped. I'd waited to see if it would spit tobacco juice at Captain Bogue—but it didn't. I reckon it was too occupied clearing out.

By Sunday afternoon I was beginning to wish I'd never learned accounting at the academy. All the figures were starting to swim before my eyes and when somebody opened the door to look in, I turned my head, thinking it was Captain Bogue bringing more vouchers. It wasn't him.

It was a girl, wrapped in furs, almost as tall as I was, with one of those silly fur pillbox hats stuck up on top of her head which was covered with gingery hair cut short as a boy's. I said, "Visitors aren't allowed, miss."

She looked at me pleasantly and as if she was a little sorry for me being so slow—but not too much. "Hello, Horace. Aren't you glad to see me?"

I stared. I jumped up. "Snipe!"

She scowled. But right away she smiled again. "Well, I guess you can still call me that if you want to."

It was Thankful Blair, Mr. Blair's daughter. No wonder I hadn't recognized her at first. She had grown twice as tall and half again as thin as when she had been a pudgy nuisance, darting around like a little chipmunk and wanting to tag after me in Wheeling.

"What are you doing here?" I asked, standing. "Your father never told me you were arriving in St. Louis."

"Didn't he?"

That was how she had always been. If you asked her a question she would answer with another question. It all came back to me with a rush.

"No, he didn't," I said. "I thought you'd been parceled off on relatives in Memphis."

She gave her head a flick. A smile passed over her thin face, reminding me a little of the smile you sometimes think a young fox has when it's laughing over a private joke on you before picking up its legs and harking into the next county all in a single flash. She leaned against the door and said, "I got tired of Memphis and surprised Pa, I guess . . ." Then she said, as if it interested her, "I see you're still wearing spectacles, aren't you?"

That stung me. She always could sting me, I don't know why.

"No," I said. "I only wear them in the daytime. When I go to bed I take them off."

That wasn't very good but unexpectedly seeing her like this, after over three years, was bewildering.

"There you go," she said tranquilly. "You don't have to be so sensitive. I don't mind spectacles on you, much."

She didn't mind spectacles on me, much! That was cool!

I stepped forward. "You haven't changed, either."

"Oh, I've grown," she said. "Can't you see that?"

"Yes, I can see. Certainly, I can see. I wasn't talking about how much you've grown."

"You've grown considerably, too. That helps," she said, critically studying me. "Yes, you're going to be maybe taller than your father in another year or so."

As politely as possible I said, "Miss Blair, if it's all the same to you, how tall I am, my spectacles, what I'm doing, anything about me, doesn't happen to concern you. How would you like me to ask you, for example, why you've cut off all your hair?"

"Oh, I wouldn't mind. It'd show you'd noticed. It fell out when I had the fever. Now it's growing back in again and maybe it won't be so red this time. Stand up straight, will you? I'll bet you're nearly six feet less an inch or so. You're lots taller than me."

I was growing heated. She hadn't changed a particle. She had been the same in Wheeling, as long as I could remember knowing her and I guess we had grown up together. She never could discuss anything reasonably. If you started on one subject, before you knew

78

it she'd gone off in ten different directions. You'd end finding you were arguing with her that there was a man in the moon. You'd be on the losing side, too. She would tag after you. She'd never had any ladylike instincts at all. She wasn't like Matilda Tucker in Philadelphia, who had such fine sensibilities you had to watch yourself or it would start showering. When you tried to tell Thankful she wasn't wanted she'd convince herself of directly the opposite. It all came back to me. If she had a notion she wanted to tag after you stones wouldn't drive her away. She'd dodge yours, pick up hers, and heave them back at you, throwing boy-style, too, not girl-style.

She asked out of a clear sky, like she always asked something you didn't expect, "Horace, I wrote you when you were in Philadelphia, two or three letters. You never answered. I've always wondered. Didn't you get mine?"

"Well, yes, I did. I was too busy to write many letters that first year," I said. I should have answered hers. She'd been sent away to a new strange place, same as I had. I explained. "Going to a new academy was perfectly ultra for me that first year."

She nodded understandingly. "I know. All those new girls I had to meet in Memphis were too ultra for anything, too, at first."

"I guess I should have answered," I said.

"Oh, that's all right," she said. "I didn't mind, much. When I didn't hear from you I decided you were probably too young that first year to be much interested in writing to a girl. I suppose girls grow interested in young men before young men grow interested in them, don't they? You ought to be old enough by now, though, to be getting letters from some of those Philadelphia girls and answering. Aren't you?"

"Miss Blair—" I began coldly.

"Oh, we've known each other too long to be ultra with each other. It's perfectly proper for you to call me Thankful. You can say Snipe if you like. I don't mind too much. How old are you?"

"I'm eighteen and if it's all the same to you—"

"Oh, you can't be eighteen!"

"I'm going on eighteen—"

"I was seventeen two weeks ago. Horace, you're not more than a month or so older than I am!"

"I'll be eighteen in nearly half a year."

I heard a woman's voice from the lower deck call, "Thankful. Thankful, where are you?"

Thankful whirled around, listened, stepped back inside the door

79

and said hastily, "That's my aunt. I've got to run. But I'll see you again, soon. It's so nice to know you've grown tall. I did worry . . ." She laughed. But her green eyes gave me the coolest look. Then she legged it and was gone.

What did she mean, she would see me again soon? What was she doing here in town, on this steamer, with an aunt? It was the same as ever. We'd talked all around the tree and off she had gone with me no forwarder than ever, another afternoon smashed.

By the time I had picked myself up, so to speak, and stepped on the hurricane deck Thankful had skinned down to the passenger deck. I leaned over the railing, trying to see who was below me. I heard a woman's voice asking, "Where have you ever been, Thankful dear?"

"Oh, were you looking for me, Aunt Elvira?"

Ask her a question. She'd answer with another question.

I had to run aft to the crew ladder, leading down to the lower decks; and after I'd slid down, peering forward on the passenger deck I caught no more than a glimpse of a slender woman with a proud face and a back as stiff as a ramrod accompanying Thankful toward the main passenger gangway to the boiler deck. With them, to my astonishment, was our pilot, Mr. Pollock.

How had he become such friends with them? He was dressed more than ever to the hilt, new sugar-loaf hat, white linen stock, black coat, and tallow-colored pants pulled down over his boots instead of tucked in them and strapped underneath the heels. He was bowing and smiling and led them off the gangplank to a fine carriage. Well!

I couldn't wait until I got back to the hotel that evening to ask Mother if she knew Thankful Blair was in St. Louis. She nodded. Yes, she did. I heard the most disagreeable news. Thankful had been attending a girls' school in Memphis, run by her aunt, Mrs. Tanner. We'd been having a cholera scare all over the nation this winter. Last fall, in Memphis, Thankful had fallen sick from it. Evidently, she'd nearly died.

Mrs. Tanner's school had been closed and was going to remain closed. She'd received an offer of a teaching position from a Female Lyceum—as it was called—in Decatur, Illinois. So Mr. Blair had decided to send Thankful on to Decatur with Mrs. Tanner. Instead of having them go by the new twice-a-week mail coach line into Illinois, he'd arranged only this morning with Father for both Thankful

and Mrs. Tanner to take passage on the *Talisman* as far as Spring-field.

"That spoils everything," I said. "I can't stand Thankful. She pestered me to death when her father was a millwright in Wheeling. If she's going on the *Talisman*—I'm hanged if I will!"

"Horace Owens!" Mother's eyes sparked fire. "You know as well as I do how much your father's depending on the *Talisman*. If there was anything I could do to help Pete Wilmot bring her back before the fifteenth of April, *I'd* go on that voyage. I'd wash dishes. I'd clean the deck. I'd . . . Great stars above! I saw Thankful Blair this morning. She's grown into a very pretty young lady. *How* can you say you'll refuse to go?"

There—she'd completely forgotten that she was the one whom Father and Pete had had to persuade to let me go. I almost told her I'd bet my aunt Iz would have sided with me. I didn't though. Anyway, Mother changed around again as soon as I said, all right, I was going; but she needn't expect me to waste any time with Snipe Blair.

Monday evening, the night before we sailed, she helped me pack. She worried over me. She asked if I wanted to take along the volumes of the *Decline and Fall* my uncle had given me? I said, no; I guessed not. Somehow, my interest in them had petered out. She lifted a little green leather book with *Burns' Poems* stamped in gold and asked, "This?"

Well, one thing about Burns's poetry was it usually came in short pieces. Even if he never learned to spell and confused his printers so much they mixed up the spelling even worse, when reading what he wrote you got the impression he was somebody big and gay and pleased with things around him, liking people and liking to play the fiddle. You knew he never had to wear spectacles or worry about having rotten weak eyes.

So I answered, "Yes—" Because I was feeling peculiar about leaving I added, "Please."

She hugged me, quick, and let go quick—not lingering like my aunt used to do until I wriggled free. It gave me a warm feeling I can't explain.

And I can't explain, either, how I felt the next morning, March thirteenth, when the *Talisman* at last backed herself into deep river; and, from high up on the hurricane deck I watched the wharves, the people on the wharves, and the buildings rising behind, all grow smaller and smaller.

I should have remained on deck to keep waving to Mother, Mr.

Blair, and old Mr. Pratte, as long as I was able to sight them. But I stepped inside the clerk's office, shutting the door, ashamed because my eyes were smarting and my spectacles were blurring over.

It might have been half an hour afterwards when Pete startled me by sliding inside, quick, shutting and locking the door. I looked up, wondering what he wanted. He belonged in the engine room. We weren't more than five miles upstream from St. Louis. He didn't waste a second of time in explaining.

"I got to say this in a hurry, while Bogue's busy in the cabin house. He's helping to locate that Mrs. Tanner and the Blair girl, and acting like he was captain of a seven hundred-tonner. Now, listen to me. Sit tight. Don't be scared. Before very long we're likely to have trouble aboard this here steamboat. I don't suppose you brung a pistol with you, did you?"

What did Pete think I needed a pistol for? I hadn't even shot a pistol except once when my uncle had allowed me to pull the trigger of one of his French dueling pieces. I didn't have any pistol with me. I had even forgotten to bring the new hunting rifle along with me, the one my father had given me last Christmas. I was still feeling sore at myself for forgetting that in the last-minute rush.

I said, "Why should I—"

"Keep your voice down."

"No, I haven't got a pistol."

"That's more like it. Just stay calm. In a pinch I knew you'd be a reg'lar wildcat like your paw used to be in the old days. Now, listen. You recollect that handrail down the ladder from the wheelhouse? The one that busted off so unexpected-like when your paw broke his leg?"

"Yes. What—"

"When me and Sandy fixed it last week we found them screws had all pulled out like the wood was rotten. But that wood wasn't rotten —not on a brand-new boat. I tell you—somebody pulled out them screws and set 'em back in, again, loose. Why? For that rail to give at a touch and throw the pilot to the deck or overboard!"

I felt as if my head was slowly spinning around. "Somebody—tried to kill Father that night?"

"No. Don't you yet see? That handrail wasn't tampered with particularly to fetch down your paw. Think a minute. It was raining to beat the birds. Black as the inside of a chimbley. What's a pilot do on nights like that? Don't he sometimes leave the wheel a minute? He'll step outside on the ladder where he's got a better view of what there's to be seen than through glass windows swarmed over with rain. That there handrail was tampered with to fetch down whoever was at the wheel, that night. A pilot's up there all alone, some-

83

times hours at a time. If he'd gone sprawling on deck, in that rain he might've been washed overboard. At least, chances was good, he wouldn't get back to that wheel very quick. All right. In less'n five minutes, wouldn't the *Talisman* have swerved off? She'd have piled herself up on shore or against a rock before anybody woke up or thought to see what was wrong with the pilot. It was a try to get us wrecked."

"What did Father say?"

"What about?"

"*What* about? Why, just what you've told me!"

"I never told your paw."

"You—*never told* my paw—my father?"

"What for? He's stuck, ain't he? He couldn't stop Bogue from sailing the *Talisman* to Springfield. If we don't bring the boat back to St. Louis by middle April, your paw's even worse off. Your paw's laid up. If I'd atold him, it'd serve nothin' but to aggravate and worry him more."

"Who'd want to wreck the *Talisman?*"

"It's what I've been asking myself. Keelboatmen've always been against steamers, haven't they? They're being shoved off the Ohio and Mississippi by steamers. But they're still in full force on the Illinois and Sangamaw Rivers. What's to stop some of those Sangamaw keelboatmen from deciding to prevent the *Talisman* from proving steamers can take over their river? You remember that fire at the works? It was only luck it didn't catch to the *Talisman* and burn her down to the water. I told your paw, then, that Clem Diggon had lied and had jammed that steam boiler gauge on purpose. Keelboatmen could've hired Diggon to wreck the *Talisman*. He tried once, and failed. He could've slipped aboard at Cincinnati with all them steerage passengers, disguising hisself, growing whiskers, to've tried a second time. He tried twice, and failed. If I'm right, ain't he bound to try a third time?"

I took off my spectacles and blew on them and wiped at them but my hands had started shaking so much I didn't succeed very well. I said, "You think Diggon's got aboard?"

"It's what we got to find out. But we had a hundred steerage passengers before. With only ten aboard this trip, he ain't got so many to hide amongst. Even if he's wearing whiskers, cut his hair, and has got different clothes, them warts on his face'll give him away. I've already warned Sandy and Smoky. If Diggon's aboard, it's only a matter of a couple hours before we nab him. We—"

"Pete—" I had a sudden idea come to me.

"What?"

"No, it was too fanciful."

He said, "Say it."

"I just happened to think. Captain Bogue wanted to charter the *Talisman.* But Father'd refused. He thought he'd sold it to Mr. Walker. Well, Mr. Walker died just before Christmas. But Father didn't hear until *after* Christmas. Suppose Captain Bogue received news ahead of time—"

"Yes; certain—a man on a good horse could come across country in five days to Cincinnati, ahead of a packet." He tugged at his whiskers. "No," he said. "No, it don't make sense. What would Bogue gain to hire Diggon to blow up the Owens Works?"

"That's just it, Pete. If Father'd had the works still going and bringing in money, even if Mr. Walker died, Father never would have chartered the *Talisman* for a voyage up the Sangamon. He'd have waited, planning to sell it to some other fur company needing her on the Missouri!"

"You know, Horace . . ." Pete walked in a circle around the office. Finally, he shook his head. "For a minute, I was almost ready to agree. But, see here. *Bogue never would have trifled with that handrail.* By then, he had chartered the *Talisman.* All his cargo was aboard. He'd be the last man to want her wrecked."

That was true. I hadn't been very bright to miss that point.

Pete said, "I figure them keelboatmen've hired Diggon. But if he's slipped aboard again at St. Louis, he won't have any chance to do harm. Both Sandy and Smoky know him. Now they're on the watch for him, they can't help finding him. The thing is, we want to do it easy, so's not to alarm the other passengers and any of them women in the cabin. It might require a couple hours, yet. So, just sit tight. Here, take this—" He pulled a regular horse pistol from inside his coat and laid it on the desk. "Stick that into the drawer. Have you ever shot a pistol?"

"My uncle—"

"Good. Now, don't get scared. Another thing—" He hesitated. "Much as I dislike Bogue, in my head I know it's wrong to suspect him of wanting to wreck the *Talisman.* Anyhow, to be clear on the safe side, we don't have to mention to him we're on the lookout for trouble. And if you catch sight of Diggon—keep quiet. Get to me, quick. Understand?"

I nodded. My throat clamped tighter on me. I remembered Dig-

gon's warty face, the lank brown hair hanging over his coat collar, and his sour voice. He'd probably start shooting if he found he was cornered. Pete had reached the door—he stopped, turned back, and gave me a cheerful whack on the shoulder with that hand of his, big as a ham. Somehow, though, it didn't smart my flesh as much as it had that time in Cincinnati.

"That's how to take it," he said. "When you stick out your jaw I'd almost think I was seeing your paw if you wasn't wearing them spectacles. You want this steamboat back safe in St. Louis before the fifteenth of next month. Say, now, we ain't going to have nothing or nobody stop her, are we?"

Well, I hadn't known I was sticking out my jaw. I don't expect I was, come to think of it. To hear Pete say so, though, stiffened me in a way I didn't understand. I got my voice back and said, "No, sir; we aren't." Then I looked at him, and tried a smile even if probably it wasn't much of one. "No, Pete, we ain't."

"Horace," he said, "by the time we get back you'll even be talking like a steamboatman's well as acting like one," and he shut the door.

Before noontime we had thrashed beyond St. Louis and on by where the Missouri River discharges into the Mississippi. In the wheelhouse, Mr. Pollock had steered us along the far side, away from the big slick whirls of water that seemed to reach up and suck at your stomach just for a sight of them.

I had placed Pete's pistol in the drawer. But every time I heard a sound I jumped up, opening the drawer to grab for the pistol. Then the door behind me opened unexpectedly and I jumped so quick I knocked over my chair.

Thankful said, "My, you're nervy, aren't you? I guess when you take over a new job like you're doing it's a strain at first, isn't it?"

I said, "You're a passenger. You aren't supposed to be on this deck. Haven't you been on enough steamers to know that yet?"

"Well, how can I talk to you if I don't come up here to this deck?"

Ask her a question . . .

I hung on to myself, reminding myself after all she was a paying passenger. I said, "Miss Blair, passengers don't talk to mud-clerks."

"Oh, that's all right," she said, looking around my cubbyhole. "I don't mind talking to you. My, it's small in here, isn't it? Do you have to eat in here, too? I thought I'd see you at lunchtime but you weren't there. I guess maybe you were too busy to eat?"

I said, "I eat in the engine room, mostly." Then I saw it was be-

86

ginning all over again, same as it used to be when Thankful and I lived on the opposite sides of the street in Wheeling. I was going to have to put a stop to that sort of thing right now if I expected any peace on this voyage. I had too much else on my mind, worrying about Diggon probably hiding aboard, trying to ask myself what Father would have done if he'd found himself in a situation like this at my age. I didn't want having her thinking she could walk in here any time she liked.

"By Jerusalem, Thankful! I'm warning you. You stay out of here."

"See here, Mr. Owens. Even if I did grow up with you, you can't swear at me."

"I'm not swearing at you."

"If *that's* the manners you learned in Philadelphia! I don't even know why I came up to speak to you."

She slammed the door. I heard her shoes go tapping forward on the deck, the tapping fading away. Well, at least I had made myself clear. I sat down again at my desk and tried to get at the bills of lading but they didn't go so very well. That was like Thankful to put you in the wrong. Saying "By Jerusalem!" wasn't swearing. What was keeping Pete?

I stood, again. I walked around my office and opened the drawer and looked in at that big pistol and once more shut the drawer. It wasn't until early afternoon that Pete slipped in for another minute, looking worried. "Diggon ain't among the passengers. Sandy and Smoky've searched all over the boat. He ain't aboard."

"He couldn't be hiding in the hull?"

"Say, where've you been? This is a river steamer. She ain't one of them ocean tubs like in Philadelphy. Your paw's sealed the hull into watertight compartments."

"Could Diggon've gone ahead by horse, planning to sneak aboard later?"

"That's my notion, too. It means we got to watch all passengers trying to get aboard. Diggon might try to slip on when we tie up at night. But Bogue's concerned about thieves getting to his cargo. He's ordered Smoky to post watches all night long. I've talked to Smoky. But there's another thing. Diggon could be lying low somewhere, letting us think it's a safe, easy voyage and planning to slip on during the return voyage."

I thought a second or so. "Pete, we don't *know* anybody wants to wreck the *Talisman*. My father's a big man. When he slipped on the ladder he could have hit the rail hard enough to break it loose."

87

"Maybe," Pete said. "Maybe. Only let's don't rest down too satisfied. Them keelboatmen might've slipped somebody new aboard after failing with Diggon. Have you thought of that?"

I hadn't. It was a chilling possibility and it haunted me during all the following days and nights.

The rest of that afternoon Thankful Blair must have remained below in the cabin house with Mrs. Tanner and their colored servant woman. After having warned her out of my mud-clerk's office, I never caught another sight of her—not that I particularly tried. When I went to the hurricane deck railing a couple of times it was to look toward the shore not to sight down to the deck below to see if Thankful was there. When finally we did enter the Illinois River, though, I never knew it. I was in my office, deep into those plaguey ladings.

It was Captain Bogue who told me. He poked his head into the office, blinking rain from his eyes. "We're out of the Mississippi! That ain't making half bad time, is it?" He shut the door to keep the rain from blowing in.

"We're in the Illinois River!"

"Heading straight up the river." He hesitated. "Horace, I don't like mentioning this so early on the voyage. But I have got a sort of complaint against you."

"I'm sorry. If these ladings—"

"It ain't that. Mrs. Tanner mentioned it to me. You're a mud-clerk. You're being paid and you're a reg'lar member of the steamer's crew. Now, I'm captain aboard this steamer. I can't allow my mud-clerk to swear at one of my passengers."

"Swear at one—"

"Even if you used to know Miss Blair, you got to have better manners. I'm sorry I have to speak to you."

"I never swore at her."

"We ain't goin' to argue, mister," Captain Bogue said in a different tone of voice. "Mrs. Tanner mentioned that that young Miss Blair happened to pass by on this here deck. Because she'd known you she only thought it was polite to pay her respects. You answered by swearin' at her and orderin' her off this deck. That's not to happen again. Understand, mister?"

Oh, how I would have liked to get my hands on that Thankful Blair! What a sneaking, lying, deceitful creature she had changed into!

"Yes," I said. "Yes, sir."

"That's better. I'm sorry it was necessary to mention it . . . Now, what about our freight?"

"What?"

"The freight. In 'bout half an hour Mr. Pollock plans to run us to East Landing for the night. We got one passenger to let off. Well, what freight goes to East Landing?"

I didn't know; I should have. I'd been too distracted by the news Pete had given me to pay proper attention to my job.

I said, "I'm sorry, Captain Bogue. I forgot we were stopping at East Landing. I'll locate the freight right away."

"Well, now, Horace," he said, more easily. "That's all right. You got half an hour. I was only reminding you. I don't expect you to be perfect the first day *or* the next day, either. I ain't hard to get along with. Bring it down to me on the boiler deck soon as you can." Out he went.

I started thumbing over a pile of freight tickets in a rush. I didn't even have time to feel excited because at last we had left the Mississippi to begin the real journey up the Illinois River to Beardstown. From having previously studied our charts, I knew it was only a little beyond Beardstown that we swung east into the Sangamon for our final port of destination at Springfield. It still seemed a long ways off. If we'd planned to run night and day as we had done on the Ohio and Mississippi we could have counted on tying up at Beardstown, I'd heard Captain Bogue say, by the middle of the week. But we finally were entering new rivers for steamers. Even our pilot knew the Illinois and Sangamon only from having floated down them on keelboats. To be safe, Mr. Pollock and Captain Bogue had decided to tie up every night at the first convenient landing, going forward only by daylight. So it was estimated we wouldn't sight Beardstown until sometime late next Sunday.

Nothing much happened the next day. Pete was worried and anxious; but he said all we could do was keep our eyes peeled for any sign of trouble. It still graveled in me more and more to have had Thankful tell her aunt I had sworn at her and for Captain Bogue to have thought it necessary to call me down.

Consequently, I was cool as I knew how to be when she rapped lightly on my cabin door and slipped inside and even shut the door. She looked scared and kind of breathless. She said hastily, "I haven't got but a second—"

"You aren't supposed to be in here, Miss Blair."

"Horace, I know I'm not. But I couldn't sleep last night. I was so angry at you yesterday I wanted to—to kick you. I just boiled. So I told Mrs. Tanner you were dreadfully rude. I shouldn't have. Please forgive me."

I swallowed. "It's nothing to me what you tell her, Miss Blair."

"Oh, it isn't?" She stood straighter.

"No, it isn't."

She opened the door behind her. "Very well, Mr. Owens. I'm very sorry I ever troubled you."

"Not at all. Your servant."

She didn't even slam the door. She shut it, soft and easy. After that she stayed on her deck or in her cabin and I never saw anything of her. Wednesday, Thursday, and Friday marched by before I knew it. I was trying for a sight of buffalo on the shores; but I didn't see any. Captain Bogue had said the Indians had left a few, still. I saw my first crane of the year, though. It was standing on a sandbank, with its long thin legs stretching down like stilts. It gave out a shrill caw and went flopping heavily into the sky.

I considered I was working tolerably well by now into my job. I couldn't have said how I might have matched up with my father if he was my age and alongside of me; but I still thought probably I might have worked in quicker on Captain Bogue's ledgers than my father might have at seventeen or eighteen. I hoped so, anyway. When we got back, more than anything I wanted to hear Pete Wilmot tell my father that he, Pete, had been satisfied with me. I wanted so much to have it a glorious day of rejoicing for the Owens family before finally I shoved off toward Philadelphia!

So whenever we were in a rush to get off cargo I slung down to the boiler deck and heaved on the barrels along with the roustabouts. Captain Bogue was as affable and generous and filled with grand prospects for the future as I'd ever seen him. You wouldn't have known he had a mean streak in him. Perhaps he didn't have. Perhaps it was the way he was, a boomer at heart, as my father had said; and when Captain Bogue was thwarted, or his plans teetered and went downhill, he couldn't help puffing up and hissing at anyone in his way like an angry goose.

Nobody tried to slip aboard. I hadn't forgotten what Pete had said about Clem Diggon but the thought of him began to fade off, a little. We saw more cranes, with their long thin legs. When we tied up, one night, a cluster of violets were peeping up along the banks. Captain Bogue caught a grasshopper. "What did I tell you?"

he said. "We're plumb into an early spring this year." He let the grasshopper rest a minute on the back of his hand, the grasshopper's leg joints sticking up above its green body. Then he put his thumb on it and if the grasshopper spit tobacco juice I didn't see it. When Captain Bogue wiped his hands on the seat of his trousers, I turned away.

So far it had been a safe voyage, safer and easier than I'd expected. Because rains were washing the winter's snow from the land the Illinois was having an uncommon early rise; and it seemed to me that was a good thing. The high water gave us clearance over all the shoals and bars and even most of the snags. In the wheelhouse, Mr. Pollock kept us steady in the main channel, not even trying to gain time by cutting around little islands and side channels from the rise of spring water.

Now and then Captain Bogue might spell him for a quarter of an hour or so, or during meals if the sun was shining and the river looked reasonably clear of trouble. But most of the time, from dawn to sundown he'd be at the wheel, his face pale, the sugar-loaf hat tilted to one side of the black hair, his left eyelid drooping a little, a lighted segar at one corner of his mouth.

We dropped off half our original steerage passengers and picked up a couple of more, for Beardstown. None of them at all had any resemblance to Clem Diggon. One man came on with more warts covering his face than I remembered Diggon had. But this one was a journeyman printer, half as big as Diggon, and twice as big around. At nights, Smoky kept roustabouts posted, not only bow and stern, but midships too. Nobody tried to sneak aboard in the darkness except a raccoon and Smoky caught the coon and next day cooked him for supper. I was beginning to feel a little foolish, hiding a pistol in my drawer. By and by I stuck it in the iron safe and kept it there.

Although ordinarily officers and clerks on a steamboat eat in officers' quarters, on the hurricane deck, because the *Talisman* was so small and we had so few of us aboard this voyage, Pete, Sandy Jenks, and I took to eating together in the engine room. The only cabin passengers we had were Thankful and Mrs. Tanner—that's not precisely true, because their Negro woman occupied the berth aft of Thankful's. But only Thankful and Mrs. Tanner sat at the table in the cabin house's common room. Even steerage passengers weren't allowed up there. So, Captain Bogue took to eating with them—"to keep the ladies company," he said.

Even Mr. Pollock began having his evening meal there, after the boat was tied up and he was off duty. Once or twice I'd thought, myself, of scrubbing myself up and changing to my best Philadelphia clothes and loafing into the cabin house common room some night and sitting down at the table—to let Thankful see I wasn't being kept away because of her. But when I put on my best rags, something must have happened to them. They'd shrunk a little, since my aunt Iz had outfitted me back last November. Rain must have wet them. So I decided to continue eating with Pete and Sandy. It was more fun with them anyway, the engine clanking and shuffing and talking to itself, never letting up, the big Pittman link turning the paddle wheel twenty-three revolutions every minute, hour after hour, day after day.

By Saturday morning you could feel the excitement going all through everyone aboard, even among the roustabouts. We'd come close to seventy miles up a new river, smooth as you could want. Rain had ended, with no sign of it except a few thunderheads off to the north. The blackness of the forests was beginning to change into a color hard to describe—like a very pale green had misted a little over the stark blackness.

By midafternoon we'd finished at Naples, unloading cargo there and two steerage passengers; and we had started loafing toward the town of Meredosia which wasn't much more than two hours away. Captain Bogue had planned to tie up there for the night, with a run of only about six hours next day, Sunday, before we put in at Beardstown—with the Sangamon waiting for us, just on beyond.

After raising our gangplank I'd returned to the office on the top deck and, for once, I didn't have anything to do. I'd written letters to everyone I knew in Philadelphia and a long one to Mother and Father. Because Meredosia was on the mail coach line to St. Louis, and towns south, I had planned to mail all my letters there instead of waiting another day until we stopped at Beardstown. I added a postscript to my letter to Mother and Father. I finished it. I yawned and stretched.

You could feel a kind of tingling running through your blood. If I'd been in Philadelphia I suppose my aunt would have wanted to dose me with sulphur and molasses for spring fever. The storm shutter was flung open from the window, with bright hard sunshine filling the little narrow office with a sparkle of light. I stepped to the window, yawning again—and felt my teeth snap shut.

Thankful Blair was out there, resting her elbows on the railing

and gazing off toward the east shore of the river. She was still wearing that silly-looking fur pillbox perched on top of her short hair that looked more of a fiery color in the spring afternoon light than even Pete's whiskers after he'd washed the grease and pitch out of them. Well, hello, I thought to myself, what was she doing up here again on the hurricane deck? I decided I would inquire, but loftily and ever so polite about it. I pushed open the door; she didn't turn her head. I stepped out. I went to the railing. She still didn't turn her head. Here we were. We'd grown up together. We were nearly grown up and acting like kids.

I said, "Hello," not too loftily, either.

"Hello," she answered, cool enough. But she wasn't too cool about it. "I'm not interfering with your work, I trust, Mr. Owens?"

"No, I just stepped out for a minute to see where we were."

I didn't see anything along this shore that was any different than what we'd been having ever since entering the Illinois River—miles and miles of timber, with now and then a clearing where you'd see a sod house or perhaps a cabin. Sometimes a man would be there, no bigger than your thumb at that distance, to sight at you and suddenly jump up, realizing it was a steamboat; and wave his hands, with a faint sound of his holler coming to you. Or, it might be a woman, a whole pack of children suddenly tumbling from the cabin at her faint cry, all of them watching the steamboat plow up higher and higher on the swollen river. Well, I looked back at Thankful. I noticed the sunshine was bringing out the freckles on her skin.

I said, "Where's your aunt?"

"In the wheelhouse with your pilot."

"What's she doing there with Mr. Pollock?"

Thankful slid a look at me and said, after a pause, "Why don't you ask her, Mr. Curiosity?"

Here I was, stepping out to be sociable and to help pass the time of day with one of our passengers. If Thankful wanted to answer in that short style, that suited me. I didn't have to stay here. I had other things to do, anyway. But it shows how a girl'll be. Before I could bow, like I'd learned in Philadelphia, and walk off, cool and unconcerned, she gave me another quick look from those green eyes.

"Besides, Mrs. Tanner isn't my aunt."

That stopped me. "Now, see here. Haven't I heard you call her Aunt Elvira?"

"Not any more. Since she's become so int'rested in that dashing Mr. Pollock she's asked me to call her Cousin Elvira."

I turned that over in my mind. It hadn't ever struck me that Mr. Pollock was so dashing. I was beginning to think Pete had been right and that he did use hair dye to keep his hair looking so black and glossy.

"She can't be both your aunt and your cousin."

"She's just a 'kissing cousin,'" Thankful explained, something a little scornful in her voice. "In Memphis, she was cousin to my blood aunt's husband. Now Pa's sending me on with her to Lyceum at Decatur but next year I might go East to school, if I like. Pa's promised. I don't know I want to, though. I don't think so much of the East."

"I liked the East. I never had such gay times as in Philadelphia."

"Pa told me you were going back next fall."

"Did he?"

"Yes, he told me. Your pa told him . . ." Her green eyes had that critical look in them. "You didn't improve so much as I'd hoped."

"Didn't I?" Then I said, "I don't think you'd much care for the East. Course, if you went back next fall I guess your hair'd be long enough so people wouldn't notice you too much."

She tapped her foot on the deck a couple of times, but she collected herself and gave a little affected laugh. "Oh, I don't know. I may even keep it short if I feel like it. Do all the *men* in Philadelphia wear clothes so high above their ankles and wrists or is 't because boys just can't help getting gawky?"

I expect my pants and sleeves had shrunk, some. Privately, I'd been wondering about it, myself, thinking it wasn't possible for your legs and arms to have extended themselves, maybe an inch, in less than four months. I felt a kind of hot feeling on my face at her question. Instead of answering, I let it go. It wasn't of any account, anyway. With my eyes half closed, as if I was remembering back, I said, "Don't you miss those high times we used to have in Wheeling?"

"What high times?" she said suspiciously.

"Well, remember when you tagged after me and fell in the mud puddle in Mr. Denning's alley?" I let myself laugh at the memory. "You had such a tantrum, too. Poor old Mr. Denning had to send you home. I wonder whatever became of him?"

"Oh, I suppose he's still teaching the same old school. My!" She smiled. "Remember that fight you got into with that boy in the grade lower than ours? He chased you back into school, didn't he?

94

What high times we all did have, after all. Do you still jump and run if anything scares you or have you grown out of it?"

I sucked in my breath. It was too late to wish I hadn't touched her off by happening to mention her short hair. I expected she was more sensitive about it, being a girl, than I'd realized. She was watching me, waiting, with her smile seeming to run clear around her head; and I started to say hotly it was a lie. I don't know why I shut my teeth hard and didn't answer. Maybe the truth was— deep down inside me I'd learned by now I was a natural-born coward and couldn't do anything about it even if I wanted to be so much like my father. Maybe that was why I'd got my back up to him and had bragged I could have matched against him at his age as a mud-clerk.

The only place I'd never had to run very hard had been in Phila- delphia. That had been because Whizzer Tucker and Abel Buck- meister had taken me into their crowd after my uncle had taught me how to swim that first summer. But I hadn't grown out of the old fear of getting licked. When those Cincinnati varmints had jumped me, I'd run straight to the house. I was sorry I'd ever stepped on the deck to speak to her. I could feel a part of myself withering from her smile and the straight steady look of her green eyes.

So I said, "No, I'm same as ever, Thankful, except I can run faster now."

And I turned away, having a kind of blind feeling sweep over me. I didn't even see Mrs. Tanner. She must have been walking aft from the wheelhouse, Mr. Pollock escorting her, with Captain Bogue giving him a short respite from the wheel once more. I bumped into her, not very hard.

She gave a startled cluck or so, stepped back, straightening her big hat, and ruffling up at me like a prize white and red ginny hen. Before I could say anything, a hand fastened on my neck like a steel trap. Mr. Pollock stuck his face at me and said harshly, "Apolo- gize to Mrs. Tanner, d'you hear? I ought to break your neck." Well, it was like having something unexpected and impossible happen to you. It was out of all reason for Mr. Pollock to have grabbed me by the neck. I mumbled something. He flung me against the cabin wall, took Mrs. Tanner's arm, and they passed on as if I didn't exist.

"Elvira, my dear. You weren't hurt?"

"'Twas nothing, dear Jesse. Such a gawky young lout, though!"

95

They were already at first names with each other? Their backs were to me. Thankful had joined them. I was glad she didn't look around at me. But I don't think I'll ever forget how her voice rose up, thin and clear, to say, "He *isn't* gawky or a lout, Cousin Elvira!"

When I got back inside the office I wasn't sure Thankful had defended me. I might have imagined hearing her. I still had that feeling of something unexpected and impossible happening, like a door had opened where no door was with something stepping out at me and stepping back in again before I had collected my wits. You didn't grab hold of someone and threaten to break his neck for something like that. It had been an accident. I had enough manners, I hoped, to have apologized without Mr. Pollock grabbing me and slamming me against the cabin wall. It beat me. I thought of telling Pete about it; and didn't, deciding, finally, I was making too much of a small thing.

But my neck was turning stiff when we hauled into Meredosia, about four-thirty or five early that evening. It was still daylight. We didn't have any cargo for Meredosia. Only three passengers got off, leaving three more for Beardstown, tomorrow. It was a big enough town to have a hotel so Mr. Pollock got off with the passengers, to stay at the hotel for the night in a bed where the sheets and blankets weren't continually damp, if not moist, like ours were aboard the boat. River pilots led such free-and-easy lives when they weren't on duty, having no responsibility for the boat's business, that sometimes I'd wonder if maybe I shouldn't think of trying for a pilot's license instead of planning ahead to be a lawyer.

As mud-clerk one of my duties had been to collect all letters from passengers and crew and see that they were mailed at any of our stops having coach lines. Captain Bogue stuck his head into the office. "You haven't forgotten to get the mail off?" I said, no, I was just going. "You'd better hurry. Someone said the mail coach was in from Benham, early, and would be leaving from the Planter's Friend Hotel in a few minutes!"

I legged it into town, pleased at the chance of being on land again. Most of the stores and houses were weathered pine shackly affairs that maybe once had been white-washed and they'd been stuck a couple of feet above ground on posts in case the spring rise of river got too rambunctious. The town was strung along the one street and generally that street was mud except at two or three crossings where somebody once had laid planks but the planks had rotted and I guess you went on them at your own risk.

96

A pig was rooting after something on one side of the street and a couple of men were sitting under a ragged store awning, tilted back in their chairs, whittling and chawing tobacco and sunning themselves; and as I passed by I heard one man say, "Thet sure is the rootinest hog what I ever seed," and the other said, "If you don't watch out thet thar hog is goin' ter root cl'ar under yore store by this summer." I went on. They were still talking about that pig but neither of them had lifted an inch from his chair.

At the far end of the street I located the Planter's Friend Hotel, away from the river and the landing. It was a two-story frame concern and drawn up in front was a rackety-looking old mail coach. The two horses were ankle deep in mud, with heads and tails hanging so dejectedly and so covered with caked mud you had to look twice to be sure they were hitched right end to. Humped up on top of the coach, the driver was reaching down into his pocket for his horn to toot to the passengers and let them know he was tired waiting.

I crossed the sagging floor of the hotel porch, opening the door to the big common room—and stopped, frozen. Sitting with his back to me at one of the tables was Mr. Pollock. But it wasn't the sight of him that pulled me to such a quick stop I could feel myself lurch forward and steady back. On the other side of the table with a bottle between them was Clem Diggon, his warty sallow face just the same as I remembered it, his hair lanker and longer if anything. Probably by my spectacles, Diggon recognized me the same time I did him. He jumped up. His chair crashed. I didn't wait. I whirled and began legging it back to the boat. I heard the coachman blowing his tin trumpet. A man shouted, "Say, whur's the fire?" I never once risked looking back. I knew I had to get to the steamboat and warn Pete and Captain Bogue before Diggon caught up with me and stopped me.

Captain Bogue was on the landing, talking to a couple of men who looked like town merchants. And he saw me running and started coming toward me. I gasped, "Diggon," and pointed. But when I looked behind no one was following me. The old mail coach had rattled off behind its horses, disappearing on the other side of the low bluffs. I explained as fast as I could about Diggon. As soon as Captain Bogue understood why I was so excited he got red in the face and said, "I declare. *That* scoundrel? Fetch a constable!" and went hustling toward the hotel, followed by the two men.

Where did you find a constable? I lost more time, going aboard for Pete. He was with Smoky, who had some of the hands cleaning out the fire grate; and I said what had happened and Pete grabbed a stick and said, "Come on, Smoky," and they started for the landing but by that time Captain Bogue was returning with Mr. Pollock.

Well, Captain Bogue said there must be some mistake. By then, too many of the hands and deck passengers were interested. I noticed Thankful had stopped on the forward stairs to listen, her freckled face bright and lit up with excitement. Captain Bogue said the man I'd seen had registered at the hotel as Mr. Weik, a tallow buyer from Vandalia; and he'd taken the mail coach east.

We could send a constable on horse after the coach, to bring the man back—Captain Bogue looked worried and wiped at his face with a red bandanna handkerchief. But it'd be plague's own luck *if* the man was hauled back and I was wrong about him or failed to prove I was right. If the thing was hauled into courts, I might get stuck here a month or so. The *Talisman* might be sued for damages. All of us, Pete, Mr. Pollock, Captain Bogue, and myself, shut ourselves into the captain's parlors on the hurricane deck.

Mr. Pollock acted concerned—but not for the reason I'd have expected. He appeared concerned and worried about the steamboat and me getting into trouble. He stretched out his legs and, grave and serious, explained he'd never seen that man before this afternoon. The man had introduced himself as a Mr. Dereck Weik, tallow buyer from the state capital. Weik had wanted to know how soon the *Talisman* would return to St. Louis and what cargo rates per hundred pounds for barreled tallow were.

I said, "But he jumped up when he saw me. He *recognized* me."

Mr. Pollock studied his segar a second, taking thought. "I'm not arguin' 'gainst you," he said finally. "I never saw the feller before so I can't say who he was. All I know—he jumped up, bellowed that his coach was leaving, rushed through the door and got inside the coach. I had an idea he'd heard the coachman blow his trumpet."

You could take it two ways; one was as good as another. I wasn't as certain as I had been, myself, that it was Clem Diggon. I'd only met Diggon that once, briefly, in Father's works, months ago. Pete decided it was too late to do anything by now. If it was Diggon in that mail coach, by now he'd have been smart enough to jump off somewhere and make tracks in anticipation of a constable coming for him. If it wasn't—or if we couldn't prove it *was* Diggon, we'd merely get ourselves in hot water.

That evening, though, Pete and I returned to the hotel. The tavernkeeper let us see his hotel book. Sure enough the name, "Dereck Weik, Vandalia," was written there. He'd been here a couple of days, the tavernkeeper said, asking about tallow and prices. He'd even said he was planning to get back in a couple of weeks when farmers began rendering beef fat into tallow to barrel it.

We talked about it in low voices while we loafed back to the steamboat. Pete said, "Everything that tavernkeeper told us supports what Pollock claims. If I believed Pollock was in cahoots with Diggon, I'd have Pollock fired—or hold the boat here till we heard word from your paw. But it don't 'pear that way, Horace. If we fire Pollock, how we going to get the boat up the Sang'maw? He's the only licensed steamboat pilot I know of who's had experience on that river. We'd be in a bad hole. Captain Bogue could sue your paw, claiming failure to deliver the cargo. I asked 'bout Pollock in St. Louis. He came down from the lakes a year or so ago, got his license for the Mississippi and Ohio and was on one of the Vairin and Reel steamboats to Memphis before Bogue hired him. I figger I've seen him before. But I got to admit I've seen dozens of pilots in my time, so maybe my mem'ry ain't as good, quite, as I'd like to think. I've *asked* him where I might've seen him. It didn't put him off. He thought it was out of Detroit. Well, I never been to Detroit."

"I might have made a mistake."

"Yes, you might've made a fool mistake," he said. Even if we had begun knowing each other better and were getting back, you might say, to stepping with the right foot toward each other, Pete still was blunt as ever. I was learning, though, that was his style. It didn't rub my fur the wrong direction to hear him say I might have made a fool mistake, like it would have even a few weeks ago.

"I guess if it had been my father, he'd have done better."

"No, I don't say that. *Maybe* you didn't make such a fool mistake. It's hard yet to tell. Let's be fair on the thing. No, Diggon could've been laying round here, waiting for the *Talisman* and wanting information on her return trip. If that's so, you scared him off. I say we still keep our eyes peeled, keep on with the voyage like nothing had happened, and be ready to jump faster a next time. But you should've run direct to me, not stopping to trifle with Bogue."

That was true; I could see that now. I felt sheepish about it but Pete said not to harp on it. We had to feel our way. It might be all

100

had been for the best and I had scared off Diggon for good. Anyhow, he'd know—if it was him—that he was recognized.

That night, though, I got out the pistol from the safe, determining to sleep with it under my pillow henceforth. It nearly lifted the hair off my head, too, when the door opened unexpectedly and Thankful slipped in, looking as scared probably as I was to have somebody step in without knocking. She wasn't high and mighty at all. In a frightened whisper she said she'd risked a second to run up here after Mrs. Tanner thought she'd gone to bed. She wanted me to know she'd listened to Mrs. Tanner and Mr. Pollock talking this evening on the deck, in the darkness. Mr. Pollock had told Mrs. Tanner there wasn't anything to be alarmed about. That fool mud-clerk had taken a harmless tallow buyer for somebody else; that was all. Mr. Pollock hadn't understood what all the commotion was for and hadn't cared.

"I thought you should know," she whispered. "If it was the man who was responsible for your pa's fire, it'd be dreadful if the pilot was mixed in with him. That's why I listened. But Mr. Pollock *acted* honest, when he was speaking to Mrs. Tanner, even if he was laughing some at you."

Then she whispered angrily, "He shouldn't have laughed at you. I dislike him intensely, if you want to know. I don't see what Mrs. Tanner sees in him. He *isn't* dashing!"

She ran out before I could think to thank her . . .

It gave me the most peculiar feeling to realize Thankful had been interested and worried enough to risk stealing up here to tell me all of that. It was a comfort to have added proof that Mr. Pollock hadn't previously known that warty-faced man at the hotel—if the man was Diggon. More than that, it let me see maybe I'd misjudged her. I resolved to be friends with her next day; but next morning after we began chugging upstream, when I spoke to her, she gave me the coolest look. In that high affected voice she said she could see the deer on the shore as well as I could. She didn't have to have somebody point them out to her, thank you. And wasn't a mud-clerk supposed to remain on the upper deck and not trouble paying passengers on the passenger deck?

Well, that sort of talk kicked the legs, so to speak, out from under me. I saw she was same as ever, or worse. Last evening she'd been sweet as honey and pretending to be helpful and the minute I'd tried to show natural appreciation, here she was waiting to see me

turn blue in the face and look more gawky, I expect, than ever to her. I told myself it was a mistake ever to have anything to do with a girl, particularly Thankful; and, in my own mind, decided to see nothing more of her until she and that Tanner woman got off at Springfield.

It wasn't a long run to Beardstown, that spring Sunday. A whole crowd was there to meet us, with people giving speeches of welcome, Captain Bogue standing on the gangplank and answering for near half an hour. I was beginning to realize by now what a huge thing it must be to all these settlers in western Illinois at last to know they were having communication with the East by steamer.

Instead of continuing that day north to the Sangamon River, Captain Bogue said we'd tie up here until tonight. He'd arranged in advance, I learned, to send a man on horseback to Springfield to inform men that the *Talisman* was on her way. They were to ride north along the Sangamon to chop and clear any branches of trees which might have obstructed the channel during the winter.

It was the first I'd heard that the Sangamon was so narrow that you had to have tree limbs cut clear. It was the first Pete had heard of it, too. But Captain Bogue said it was nothing to be concerned by; the river was wide enough; it was simply that he was taking every precaution the first trip. That was all. He was paying for the men out of his own pocket. We didn't have to worry.

That afternoon there was a church service in honor of the arrival of the first steamboat at Beardstown and Captain Bogue was there, to be sure. And Mr. Pollock, rigged in a new fawn-colored clawhammer coat went along, bending his head down to Mrs. Tanner. And Thankful accompanied them, looking perky and proud in a hat so big you could scarcely notice her red hair wasn't any longer than a boy's.

Sandy Jenks and I attended. Pete said he'd like to go. But he said he didn't feel too comfortable in a church; he didn't know why. He thought maybe he got more aware of all his sins inside a church and he preferred not being distracted by such matters when he had the running of the *Talisman* on his mind. So he stayed with the boat.

A visiting preacher named Peter Cartwright did the sermon. Somebody told me he was the most famous preacher in the state. He was a fine big man with a voice like thunder and he preached on the text, "Let us draw near with a true heart . . ." twenty-second verse, tenth chapter of Paul's Epistle to the Hebrews.

After remarking how faith had at last brought steam navigation to the rivers of Illinois, gradually he branched off on the need of having faith and true hearts to stand against the perils now threatening Illinois by the treachery of the notorious Indian chief Black Hawk. Men were needed to volunteer to the call of Governor Reynolds and Generals Gaines and Whiteside.

He said, awful solemn, that always a few men were tempted to stand aside and let others take the burden. Invisible demons were always awhispering into your ears, urging you to do the wrong thing. You had a good angel trying to help you. But a demon perched on the other shoulder, whispering and whispering until the moment you let yourself listen. Well, the preacher's big thundering voice took hold of you. When he finished a dozen men stood up and answered they were ready to volunteer right now.

Off and on for months I'd heard talk and rumors of the threats that old Chief Black Hawk was making, from across the Mississippi. I hadn't realized until now how serious it was for these Illinois settlers. Suppose Black Hawk's tribe should attack and catch the *Talisman* still upstream on a trifling little river?

In the crowd waiting to shake hands with the preacher, and to speak to Captain Bogue, I noticed Thankful standing off by herself as if she was lost. Mr. Pollock had gone on ahead with Mrs. Tanner. So I walked to Thankful and she said, "You don't think the Indians will attack, do you?"

I answered, if they did, we'd be safe on the boat. They couldn't get to us, very handily. I sounded more assured than I felt.

Thankful and I started walking back together to the *Talisman,* more or less just going along in the same direction. By and by we came to where a lane branched off toward the river from the main road down to the town from church. Some spring flowers were growing. There was a smell of spring in the air.

I said, "Maybe this is quicker?"

"All right," she said.

It wasn't quicker because the lane wound along to the east past a deserted cabin and back again toward the river.

I said, "I guess we took the long way."

"It's pretty here. I don't mind."

By and by she stopped and sighed and said, "It won't be very long now before spring's really here, will it?"

The lane had gone through a kind of dell and on beyond, not so very far, I could see the houses of town through the trees. We

103

weren't lost. But it was so silent here you almost could think you were in the middle of the wilderness.

I looked at her and said, "Your hair's beginning to grow out curly, isn't it?"

She said, "Do you think so?"

I said, "Yes, it's getting curly. I always did like red hair."

She took off that big hat of hers and ruffled her hair with her hand. She said, "It feels funny when it's all short. I guess people still look at me and want to laugh."

"No, it looks nice."

"You're making fun of me."

"No, I'm not. It looks pretty."

She ruffled her hair again. "It just feels funny. I hate it."

Without much thinking I said, "Let me—" and I reached out and she didn't move. I ruffled her hair a little and her red hair was soft and curly and I pulled my hand away.

She said, "It feels funny to you, too, doesn't it? Oh, I *hate* having short hair. I wanted you to think I was as pretty as any of those Philadelphia girls."

I said, "Thankful—" and didn't know what suddenly came over me. All at once I crooked my arm around her neck and tried to kiss her. It was such a new thing to me perhaps I didn't get quite the right hold.

She jerked away and cried, "Oh, my hat! My lovely spring hat!"

I picked up her hat. I hadn't dropped it; she had. I hadn't even known I was stepping on it. I tried to straighten out the thing where the straw was a little torn and muddy. She snatched it from my hands, stared at it a second, and flung it away.

"Oh! Don't you know how to kiss a girl yet? I suppose when you kissed all those Philadelphia girls you pulled their hats from their hands to trample on?"

That was unfair of her. I hadn't even known she had let go of that hat of hers. So I said, "They don't let go of their hats when they're kissed."

"Oh, don't they? How do you know? No girl would let somebody as clumsy and big as you are try to kiss her!"

"Oh, I don't know."

"Name one," she cried in even more of a blazing temper. "You're lying. You can't name one."

"I could if I was of a mind to."

"Who? Who, then?"

"It was somebody aboard the *Star of Ohio,* if you want to know."

"You're lying! What was her name?"

It hadn't been lying. But it wasn't quite as much as it was blowing up with Thankful. I'd sat at the same table with a young widow probably ten years older than I was. She was on her way to New Orleans. Because it was near the end of the year not many passengers had been on that run and she'd put up with my company. She had been friendly and polite, very much like some of the older young women I had met at my aunt's in Philadelphia. The last evening before we'd docked she had said she hoped I had a merry Christmas with my family, good-by; and had turned her cheek, and I had given it a peck; and that was all there had been to it. But I wasn't going to give Thankful the satisfaction of knowing it hadn't been any more than that.

"All right," I said. "If you're so interested, her name was Laura Melrose. We had such a gay time together on the *Star of Ohio* she was sorry I wasn't going all the way with her to New Orleans—"

"Laura Melrose? You're lying! You're lying!" Then she took me by the ears, pulled down my head, kissed me hard, let go, and while I was still perfectly stupefied she slapped me as hard as she could in the face and marched away. It was convulsing.

I followed after her and she wouldn't speak to me. When we got back to the *Talisman* she was too proud to let anyone see we had quarreled; so she would speak to me, but it was in the most casual and airy way. Off and on during the next week I tried to ask her what was wrong, what had I done? But it didn't go. It wasn't of any use. I even admitted I'd lied about having such a gay time with anyone aboard that dismal *Star of Ohio.* But Thankful wouldn't believe me. It was still convulsing to me. When I hadn't wanted to talk to her she had been around bothering me every second. Now I began liking to talk to her she had changed her mind.

Late Monday morning we finally steered into the Sangamon River, going east. It was rushing and boiling where the river entered the Illinois, two hundred feet wide across, maybe more; but by noontime it was narrowing and closing in toward us. While the day remained bright enough, no rain at all, all the country had a bleak look to it. You could see big sloughs or ponds pushing off from the river into the gloomy sycamore tangles. Once we scared three buffaloes. They went charging back into the timber. I only had a glimpse of them, huge humped beasts with heads on them

three times the size of a bull's head. We steamed at quarter speed, stopping every fifteen minutes or so while Captain Bogue and Sandy, and I, and sometimes a couple of the hands rowed ahead in the yawl to sound for the main channel.

The main channel passed for miles along the north side. In mid-afternoon the boughs of a big sycamore reached out and whacked our starboard chimney a crack you could hear all over the boat. Again we had to stop while Sandy and Smoky set up a ladder, fetched off the top piece, and added new guys. I was beginning to have the queerest feeling take me by the stomach, as the river went rushing and boiling past us, shoals throwing long dark-yellowish streaks off to one side.

I expect everything had been too easy coming up the Illinois. Until now I'd never had much real cause to wonder just what would happen to all of us, as well as to Father's great hopes, if the *Talisman* did split herself on a sunken sycamore snag or rock.

I helped row the yawl. My muscles ached. Despite the coolness of late afternoon my shirt stuck to my back. When we'd return to the *Talisman* and Pete would open the engine again at a signal from Mr. Pollock, I wanted to throw myself on the deck and pant. But I'd see Thankful up above, on the passenger deck. She'd be looking down at me, probably wanting to see me fall on the deck. So I'd stick my hands in my pockets and say something to her, like, "Don't you wish you could row a boat?" It wasn't ever anything worth mentioning. But she was beginning to grin a little, every now and then. I still couldn't understand, though, why she had exploded in such a perfect white fury after I had happened to step on her hat.

We tied up early that evening. Captain Bogue told us the horsemen from the towns below would be here by morning to begin cutting the trees and branches. He didn't know why they had delayed.

I saw Pete staring through the hazy dusk toward the bank and he pointed and asked, "Ain't that a high-water line, there, captain? That don't look right. This river of yours can't be dropping, already, can it?"

Well, Captain Bogue stared at a sort of dull clayish line a little above the river's edge. He admitted it might be the river'd pushed down a mite. But it didn't count. Early rains must have slushed most of the snow off from the land, giving a higher rise than usual—that was all.

"Suppose we don't have more rains, captain?" Pete said, his voice

sounding strangely grim. "Why, sir—" Captain Bogue turned and seemed to swell a size larger. "That don't happen. I know this here river and this country. We'll have a pile more of rains. All this land drains into this river. It'll keep steady at this level till May, maybe longer. Haven't we got three full feet draw under our bottoms?"

That was true enough, except when shoals lifted. Tuesday, we stayed tied up to the bank until close to ten o'clock, when some horsemen came through the sycamores on the south shore. One of them hollered across to us, asking for Captain Bogue. At first I thought he had his stirrups pulled up uncommon short. Next, I saw he was riding on that horse with his knees lifting nearly to his elbows because he was so tall. His face was so dark and his hair so black and coarse I took him for an Indian, wondering what an Indian was doing here amongst white men after all the talk and worrying I'd heard at Beardstown.

Captain Bogue hollered, "Abe, where've you boys been?"

"Half of 'em are below Salt Fork, clearin' south," the tall man hollered across the river to us. "Our bunch'll clear east from Dodson's Slough t' the Fork."

"I'm obliged to all you boys, more'n I can say. You're staying with the job till it's done?"

"The boys hev agreed to stay on, capt'n; but I can't hang on longer after t'day. I hev t' get on back to New Salem t'night."

That news didn't appear to sit too well with Captain Bogue. He sawed his elbows back and forth, like a goose flapping its wings, scowled, and called in a half-jeer, "At Beardstown I heard you was going to join up 'gainst the Injuns. Aren't you feared old Black Hawk'll scalp you, Abe?"

High, almost squeaking, a laugh rippling through it, the holler from that tall man on horseback came over the water. "Well, I guess not. I'm no chicken t' run from a hawk!"

The other men on horse whooped at the quick reply, waved, and off they rode east along the river into the sycamores and pawpaws. Not long after they had vanished I heard the sound of an ax ring distantly, bright and clear. Captain Bogue was put out of countenance. He muttered to himself that Abe Linkern was good enough in his way, but never stayed serious very long. He spoke to our pilot, ordering the boat to proceed at three-quarter speed.

Mr. Pollock answered, "Captain, I'd dislike having a chimbley knocked clear loose. I'll proceed as fast as circumstances warrant."

It was hard going. I stayed in the yawl most of that afternoon,

helping Captain Bogue plant markers—nothing but board flats with a second edged down to plant itself in the current, the whole contraption strung to a rope knotted around a stone at the other end which you dropped into the river and hoped would hold. We scared up turkeys and wild cranes. They went squawking overhead in a sky filled with thunderheads, but no rain ever falling.

It was turning almost overnight into spring. I noticed how the high-level marks in the clay banks showed in places the river had fallen three or four inches. When we came into marsh country, with Dodson's Slough running greasy and black into the river, I saw all the branches overhanging the south shore for miles ahead had been lopped off. Mr. Pollock followed the turn of channel, now hugging the other bank; and we picked up time until early evening, when again we tied to a landing which wasn't any more than a half-sunken flatboat.

A stocky man in good clothes was waiting for us on a horse. He spoke to Captain Bogue and said the whole country south was swarming with the news that the *Talisman* was on her final stages. Captain Bogue introduced us to Squire Godby, who told us we only had a few days more. At Salt Fork the river ran south to New Salem, turning east again, there; and it wasn't more than an easy day from New Salem to Springfield, where the whole town was roused and planning a celebration to honor our arrival.

Well, just hearing Squire Godby gave you the sense of knowing it was almost over. I could feel prickles of excitement going through me. By Saturday, maybe Friday, we'd be there, unloading, and ready to start back on the return trip. It meant with any kind of luck at all we'd be in St. Louis by the end of March, with fifteen whole days to spare.

That evening we could see the campfire through the trees where the men clearing our way had bunked themselves in for the night. They must have been enjoying themselves, for now and then you could hear snatches of "All Chaw Hay on the Corner" or "Pig in the Parlor." By and by Captain Bogue said he guessed he'd see how the boys were coming along; and he was in such good temper, and so pleased with what Squire Godby had told him, I judge, that he surprised Pete by asking Pete to stretch his legs and come along with him. Pete said, "Why, sure. Thanks. Sandy, watch the engine room." He noticed me. "Come along. It won't harm you any to feel land under your feet."

About six of them were there, around a big fire, with a lean-to

they'd built of saplings behind them. You could hear their horses stamping and sometimes neighing out loud in the darkness. I saw how careful they'd laid out their sharp axes and their saws and their hatchets on top of dry rocks or pieces of wood covered with blankets. Squire Godby was with them, having evidently brought grub to them from his farm. They were all good-tempered and cheerful even if they'd been hacking away like roustabouts during daylight.

The leader of them was a thickset young man, with a broad flat smiling face like a piece of new hickory quarter sawed; and he didn't appear to be more than eighteen or nineteen, not very many years older than I was.

I envied him a little, he was so easy and sure of himself. He got to telling stories and he was one of the best I ever heard. He had us all laughing by the way he joshed Squire Godby—who chuckled and acted like he enjoyed it as much as anyone else. Last year, it seemed, three fellows had floated a raft down the Sangamon—although he called it the "San Gammaw," making two words of it. They'd stopped off at Squire Godby's for pigs. The pigs wouldn't go on the raft. Finally, one of them had said the thing was, you had to sew up the pigs' eyes. Well, Squire Godby had been taken in and had decided it was the thing to do. Evidently he'd tried to get at those pigs, and had been upset by one and thrown in the mud.

When everyone had finished laughing, Pete asked the young man his name.

"I'm plain Billy Green. But folks down thar on the San Gammaw whar I live call me 'Slicky Bill.' I don't partic'lar know what fer, either."

That broad flat face got such an innocent pained look to it, of a sudden, you'd almost have thought he didn't know, either. Somebody hooted. Even Pete smiled so much inside his whiskers you could see by the firelight how his whiskers spread out. Pete said, "Billy, you're the best storyteller I ever heard."

"I ain't a primin' to a curis feller who keeps a grocery down whar I live and hires me. I've seen the hull neighborhood turn out to hear *him* tell stories. He helped run a flatboat to New Orleans last fall. He was the feller who sold the squire on sewing them pigs. Laffingest thing you ever heard, hearing him tell. He's a great big feller with a big mouth an' he kinder acts it all out, smilin' an' laffin'. He come along with us ter start us off; but he had to git on back to New Salem, early. He's gittin' ready to go ter the Black Hawk war."

Pete said, "If he beats you he must be a clown."

109

"I never seed a real clown but he'd make one. But I've seed him, when he was the solemnest man in ten states. When he kem back from New Orleens last year if anybody said anthin' 'bout nigras he'd git so solemn an' tell of a nigra auction he seed in New Orleens —how they sold a fambly, the man to one planter, wife to another, an' passeled the children out among the highes' bidders. An' he thought it was awful. I've seed him when talking about this here auction turn pale and seem ter take sick ter his stomick. An' I've heered him say he'd ruther tend store all his life than ter sell slaves. I never once heared him swar 'cept when talkin' of that nigra auction."

Because my father was one, I couldn't help saying, "He sounds like an abolitionist. I didn't know many abolitionists were in this part—"

"Ab'litionist?" Slicky Bill jumped up. "Ab'litionist? You bet he ain't. He's a true loyal feller who loves his country. Hain't he going right inter the Black Hawk war soon's he can fix his affairs ter go?" He looked at Pete. "Like I said, he's the most curis feller you ever saw. But he's loyal. He's good as ever lived—kinder common—sorter jes' like ever'body. No better. No worse." He nodded his head. "But, mister, thar's another feller in the country who beats him—Dick Yates of Jacksonville. Talk 'bout the Amer'can Eagle an' the Star-Spangled Banner. I've seen Dick Yates make people hold their breaths and wipe their eyes and blow their noses, jes' by Dick's talk. Dick'll be pres'dent someday."

"But who's the other fellow?" Pete asked, amused.

"Him? Oh, Abe Linkern. You seed him this mornin'. Till noon he worked like a beaver 'long the river with us. He's the best feller with an ax thar is in the nation, I guess. But he hed ter ride fer home. He's goin' ter run for state leg'slature this fall. Leastwise, my paw an' Mr. Cameron an' some of the inflooenshul fellers've backed him. But he's leavin' for the Injun war next week an' he needs all the time he can git fer 'lectioneerin'. He's runnin' on the platform to make this here river nav'g'ble to Salt Fork and further, effen the state'll put up the cash. Ef you're plannin' ter bring more steamboats this here way, you ought ter hire Abe on one."

Well, Slicky Bill had such a humorous style of speaking I knew he was joking when he claimed that that young backwoodsman we'd seen this morning, and had heard call out he was no chicken afraid of a hawk, was running this fall for state legislature. But Captain Bogue took Slicky Bill seriously, and he said, hastily, he wasn't

planning to bring more steamboats here this year. Besides, he had the best pilot available, as it was. Next, he decided it was getting late. It was time we returned. I wished we could have stayed longer.

It was my first experience close at hand with Illinois frontiersmen —"Suckers," they called themselves, why I don't know. They weren't like any people I'd ever seen before, somehow. Even their talk sounded different. For one thing, I noticed, they said "hain't" instead of "ain't" half the time. Altogether it was a little graveling after listening to them. Because Pete had remarked, once, when I was beginning to know him better, that a reason I'd "throwed him off" was that I spoke like a foreigner, I'd been deliberately trying to cure myself of the careful, Philadelphia style of speaking which I'd picked up. Now, here we'd reached the pioneer country of Illinois— where all at once even the way Pete spoke, by comparison, sounded a trifle city-like. Even Pete would be looked upon as something of a foreigner by these rough-and-ready Illinois Suckers whom Captain Bogue had hired to clear the river for us.

On our way back through the trees, I heard the frogs croaking from the river. The torches glimmered redly and I wondered how anyone could find you if you stepped off the path and got lost somewhere in the middle of that great black tangle of forests and virgin ground lying for miles and miles along the banks of the river. Bear would be somewhere in these forests and so would catamounts and other animals and probably out along the rim of the forest, near the prairies, if you got that far, you'd still run into buffalo that the Indians hadn't killed off or driven west of the Mississippi.

I was relieved to catch a sight of the *Talisman* at last, with the fires for lighting our way back shining in the iron baskets. By now Thankful was probably asleep, up there in her cabin on the passenger deck. Against all the blackness our steamboat looked mighty small, all squatted down close to the river. I wished my father was along. I wished I hadn't made that brag to him. I wished with all my heart we were unloaded and on our way back to the Illinois River and steaming toward St. Louis.

I didn't like admitting even to myself how much the Sangamon was beginning to worry me.

Wednesday was slow enough. Thursday, the twenty-second, the river finally took us out of the timber country. The Clary Grove Boys rode south over the rolling hills. We grounded once on a mud reef, stuck fast. Pete lowered our paddle wheel down to its last notch. The boat still couldn't pull herself free. We had to use the steam winch.

Sandy and I rowed ahead two hawser lengths in the yawl. I sloshed ashore through ice-cold water, crawled up a bank and fastened our hawser to the biggest oak I could find. Sandy signaled we were ready by waving his hands to Mr. Pollock.

In the wheelhouse, Mr. Pollock signaled us back, tooting our big whistle, one short to get ready, and two short blasts to stand clear.

Father had said a steamboat needed a big whistle, particularly when the boat was designed to go into new country where people were scarce and distances were great. That whistle was probably as big around as Pete's arm and almost seven feet in length and it could release such a piercing blast your ears and even your skin hummed for seconds afterwards.

Our steam winch wound the hawser in and the oak held and we got the *Talisman* off the reef in less than an hour. We didn't have to unship our grasshopper poles and "walk" the *Talisman*. I almost wished we had. I wanted to see how the poles managed.

112

We tied up that night some fifteen miles above the nearest town, New Salem. Country people were always along the banks now, watching us, marveling. Many of them had never seen a steamboat before in their lives. To find out where you were, all you had to do was holler across the river. Someone would answer. Then you'd hear him bragging about it, later.

Sandy found somebody who would give him a lift on a horse to New Salem and he decided to see what sort of life a prairie town had for a steamboatman. A moon came up. After eating, I met Thankful on the passenger deck and for a while we rested our elbows on the rail, not saying much to each other, listening to a meadow lark somewhere in the soft darkness. It was real spring weather, except that the rains had ceased.

Finally, she said, "We'll be in Springfield by Sunday, won't we?"

"Looks like it."

"Perhaps Cousin Elvira'll want to stay over Sunday night before we take the stage for Decatur." She sighed a little.

I nerved myself up to ask her if she'd write back, if I wrote her.

"I wrote you three letters the first year you moved to Philadelphia," she said.

"Well, if I write you *four* letters, will you write one back?"

"*Did* you go around kissing somebody before waiting for me?" she said.

Ask her a question. Sometimes she'd come back with one that would lift you off your feet. She didn't get to answer mine and I didn't hers because Mrs. Tanner called. It was time for Thankful to turn in. She squeezed my hand a second—and was gone.

For a long time afterwards I stayed up there on the deck and watched the moon curving high in the sky. All the stars were shiny. It was a tremendous pretty night.

Later, I was awakened—and probably everyone else aboard was, too—by Sandy arriving and singing at the top of his lungs:

> *"When I was young I used to wait*
> *At Massa's table, 'n' hand de plate,*
> *An' pass de bottle when he was dry,*
> *An' brush away de blue-tailed fly . . ."*

Pete must have took hold of him and hushed him down. In the grizzly light of next morning I saw Sandy was sporting a black eye. Pete was still joshing him.

Sandy just grinned. "New Salem is sure a friendly town. It's got a tavern there owned by the nicest fellow I ever met, kind of moony and absent-minded, but goodhearted. He had a dozen daughters, too. I never saw so many pretty girls in one place in my life. Some fellows was in there, too, and one was playin' the fiddle. They learned me that 'Ballad of the Blue-Tailed Fly' I was singin' when you stopped me. Later, we got to rasslin' outside the tavern. I was matched with another fellow, even taller than me. He downed me. First time in my life. Name was Linkern. He was one of them fellows who helped us by cuttin' trees west of Salt Fork. Why, I guess that was one of the finest evenin's I ever had in my life . . ."

I wished I'd gone with him.

Except for mushing into a few more shoals, and having to steam-winch ourselves over, we muled along. We ate grub on the run. The river untangled itself and stretched almost due east, a big bluff rising on our starboard side. Sandy joined me on the hurricane deck.

"There, see? That's New Salem. Up on top of the bluff—the far end, where the river slings south behind the bluff."

The town wasn't much to see—only a few stores and cabins, nearly hidden by the thick grove of oaks. Snaking down to the river was a road. And thirty or forty people—men, women, children—had gathered on the west bank to cheer and wave. Mr. Pollock usually answered cheers from shore by a toot from our shattering whistle. He didn't this time.

We were approaching a long grayish ripple extending from the larboard bank clear across the river to a gristmill and sawmill, built near the opposite shore. Beyond the milky-looking bulge of water the river seemed to shallow down and rise up again. I knew enough of river water by now to know somewhere under that milky bulge was a dam.

I heard Mr. Pollock jangle on the pull-bells for full steam. I started running down the forward passengerway to the boiler deck. I never got there. We closed up over the dam. I heard a rumbling—next the *Talisman* seemed to stop dead. Captain Bogue was shouting, "Back away! Back away! We're struck!" The shock sent me sliding the rest of the distance to the boiler deck, plumb among the firemen.

The stern wheel dug in deeper. Mr. Pollock knew his job. He never paid any attention to Captain Bogue's yells. I felt the huge grating and shivering passing all the length of the hull. Enough of a "head" of water, all milky colored from air boiling in it, had piled

114

above the dam to carry us over. A gray-haired man stuck his head through the window of the gristmill, shaking his fist at us and bellowing that we'd broken his dam.

We never stopped. We might have scraped a few logs on that dam but that was all. We steamed around the curve, south, the big bluff shelving to the river's edge. We had to go powerful slow. Less than a mile further we passed another landing, where a crick came down to the river through oaks and sycamores. A man in buckskins hollered, answering Sandy's yell, that this was Green's Branch and to look out for Bales' Slough.

I guess Bales' Slough was where a second crick, half a mile more farther, poured into the river, throwing up mud shoals. Here, we had to yawl and hawser again. This was timber country, once more, dark and gloomy. We carried on. Next, we muled into the worst bend we'd had. The current had eaten into the banks, spilling over into a great stagnant slough filled with old drift and dead trees.

That bend scared me. I didn't see how Mr. Pollock ever located the channel. He ran us through little chutes between islands of old drift and matted rubbish and tied us up at dark at a place called Sangamontown. Tomorrow we would be at Springfield unless we hit more bends like the last one.

Pete told me it was time to start thinking ahead and begin planning for our return voyage. I knew we were low on fuel for our boiler. It looked to me as if we should think of getting wood. He answered, "Someone here might have a supply of cordwood, don't you reckon?"

"Where should I ask?"

"Try the tavern first. Want me to go with you?"

"Well, no. It's not necessary, thanks. I'll manage."

He lit his pipe and pulled on it. It was clogged again, as usual. In an absent-minded way he said a couple of hard words about his pipe and laid it on the steam cylinder and unexpectedly told me, "Horace, you know what? You've begun growing up on this voyage, in more ways than size. If you keep on with steamboating, in a couple years or sooner you'll be swaggering into river towns and sparking girls and collecting black eyes like Sandy, here, does every so often. Now —get on to your job. Don't offer more than two dollars and a quarter a cord. Hear?"

"Yes, sir."

Sandy looked at me with the eye that wasn't covered with a piece of raw steak and grinned. Probably he wished he was going instead

of being set to wiping every speck of grease off the engine, to have the brass all shining when we arrived in Springfield. I stepped off the gangplank to the landing, not using my elbows but easing through polite and careful, like I'd watched Pete do whenever he had cause to go ashore.

I looked up and back and saw Thankful on the second deck and I waved to her. She didn't wave back. I didn't expect her to; too many country people were at the landing, watching the steamboat people. I felt powerful good that evening. I wished my father could have seen me.

As I passed under a torchlight I heard a man say in a loud admiring whisper, "Thar! Hain't he one of the off'cers?" I stuck my hands in my pockets and hummed that tune about the blue-tailed fly. I didn't even much mind when a girl in a beaverskin winter coat answered scornfully, "Him? I bet he's only a mud-clerk. You kin tell. He'd hev a reg'lar brass-button uniform ef he was off'cer, wouldn't he?"

On the way to the tavern I started wondering why maybe I couldn't afford to buy a blue uniform in Springfield out of the pay I could draw when we arrived. The tavern was of logs, chinked with mud; but lights were shining through windows with proper squares of glass in them, not oiled paper or stretched pieces of split cowhide. From inside came the music of a fiddle.

When I got closer, I saw the common room was filled full, forty or fifty men and women, young and old. Near the fiddler, sawing away, was an old smiling foxy-looking man doing juggling tricks with four bottles of medicine; and he was shouting how good the medicine was while he kept the bottles flashing and tumbling in the air. He didn't drop one.

I stepped around to the side room. In here was a great barrel of a man who I judged was the tavernkeeper. He was sitting back, comfortable, hands clasped over his stomach, a boot stuck on his deck, ignoring the fiddling and noise from the common room behind him as if he had seen enough medicine men jugglers to last him all his life.

He was speaking to another man, youngish, dressed in good clothes, with a kind of bitter expression that made you look at him again. The youngish, bitter-looking man said, "Well, Toby, I'll be on my way," and he didn't have anything of the country style of speech I'd been hearing along the Sangamon.

116

The tavernkeeper stood. "What brung you here, McNeil? The steamer?"

"I wanted to have a look at her, I suppose. I'm no better than any of the other clodhoppers. I never expected Bogue to get a steamer down this far, to tell the truth. I don't yet see how he imagined a steamboat'll wriggle through the narrows above here, either."

"I heard he has a smart pilot . . ." The tavernkeeper nodded toward the door opening into the packed common room. The fiddling had ceased and I could hear the juggler beginning some sort of a funny speech. "Bogue's steamer an' ol' Doc Kickapoo hez brung me in some bus'ness ternight. Better stay on an' j'ine the fun."

The younger man shook his head, picking up his plug hat from the desk to depart. But his eye was caught by a big circular tacked to the wall and he paused to look at it. I was close enough to see the date and the beginning of a printed announcement: "MARCH 9, 1832. PEOPLE OF SANGAMON COUNTY . . ." before the tavernkeeper stepped in front of me. "Abe put that up thar a little while ago, McNeil. He won't hev much time 'lectioneering ef he goes ter war. That circ'lar reads good, don't it? Mentor Graham must hev helped Linkern with the grammar, him or young Green."

McNeil turned away. "No, the truth is, at his request I corrected some of the grammar in it, Toby. Not to amount to much, however. Lincoln's no fool."

I pricked up my ears at that, while waiting for the tavernkeeper to finish with the stranger. It was the third or fourth time I'd heard someone mention the name of Abe Linkern—although the stranger had pronounced the name "Lincoln"—and you know how it is when gradually you begin to hear of somebody who's being talked about. You can't help being interested.

"No, sir," I heard the tavernkeeper say. "Abe's least there is of a fool even ef he likes ter act one, often enough. He'll hev my vote." He turned to me. "Wal, young feller? What kin I do fer you? I hain't got no more beds to let."

I told him I was looking for wood.

"Wood fer the steamboat? There hain't much wood sold here, bub. I got a few cords stacked fer myself but not to sell. McNeil, you wouldn't know nobody, would you, with wood?"

"What about Jack Armstrong?"

"Has he got some?" the tavernkeeper said.

117

"He was trying to sell me a quantity only a few days ago. He told me he'd brought in a good supply of oak last fall."

I asked where Mr. Armstrong lived.

In that courteous educated voice with a kind of New England twang to it, the bitter-faced man said, "Four miles south of New Salem on the river road, sir. Armstrong'll be pleased to sell you all the wood you require and he'll saw it in any lengths. He offered me wood at a dollar and a half a cord. I'd advise you to see him by all means. Good night, sir. Night, Tobias." He shut the door behind him.

A dollar and a half a cord was cheap. We wouldn't have cargo to carry on our return voyage. There was no reason we couldn't load up with all the wood we needed to take us to St. Louis. I asked how I could send a message to Mr. Armstrong to tell him we'd stop at New Salem next week on our return to buy a hundred cords from him.

"You don't need no message, bub. Jack Armstrong kum here with Linkern tonight ter see the steamboat an' ter help Abe tack up a few circ'lars. Armstrong's somewhere in that crowd—" he thumbed toward the other room—"watching Doc Kickapoo do magic tricks before sellin' his Carthoticin Panacea. You can't miss Jack. He'll hev the widest shoulders. He's bound to be nex' ter a tall feller, the tallest here—that's Linkern. Jes' march in there—

"Here, I tell you what. Stay here. Don't budge. Jack needs the money bad. You wait here. I'll fetch Jack out ter you."

He walked across the plank floor to the door where three or four boys were standing on tiptoe, trying to sight over the heads of the crowd inside to watch the magic tricks. "Here, you, Wash," he said roughly, to the nearest. "Git. Go on, git home. Don't you know no better'n to be in a public tavern with no shoes on, like you was a Black Hawk Indian, here on steamboat night? The first steamboat night Sangamontown's ever had. Now, git! You hear!"

The boy sidled away; the tavernkeeper pushed forward between two yellow-haired men in coonskin caps. One of them said, "Toby, you're agittin' too beefy fer lardin' in with gents like us," and I lost sight of the tavernkeeper.

I moved in closer, lifting on my toes to peer over the shoulder of the nearest yellow-haired man. An elbow dug into me, nearly cramping out all my breath—and I never did see the magic tricks. The crowd was laughing again. I tried to see but I couldn't. That elbow kept knocking me off balance.

From the other end of the room the unseen magician was saying,

118

loud and big, "Come, gents. Who's goin' ter offer up a hat fer me to prove as how I c'n fry eggs in a hat, all 'thout enny fire to be perceeved by the naked eye? 'Twon't harm your hat. Ef the hat is touched by them fried eggs after I'm done, I'll buy the gent a new hat." Then somebody called, "Abe! Go on, Abe, give him yer hat ef you got one with you," and there was more laughing.

I looked around angrily, saying, "Hang it, don't shove me like that, understand?"

The boy looked at me out of eyes in a head as brown and shaggy as a bear's. He said, "*I'm* shovin'? By jings, ain't that cool?"

I had missed more of what was going on at the far end of the common room. There was a kind of hush. Next, very loud a voice asked, "Abe, why the delay? You hain't concerned what a few eggs'll do ter thet old shackly hat of yourn, are you?" Immediately a squeaky, amused voice answered, its sound carrying to where I stood with the same penetration of a rusty saw going through hickory:

"Why, Jack. It was out of respect f'r the eggs, not care f'r my hat that made me delay offerin' it."

That answer was like touching off a barrel of gunpowder. You couldn't hear yourself think from the shouts of laughter that followed.

I forgot I was supposed to wait here until the tavernkeeper returned with the man who had wood for sale. I wanted to plow and edge in there, among the others, and get forward to see what was going on between the medicine man and the other fellow who'd been making fun of the condition of his own hat. But I never did.

I suppose the boy digging his elbow in my ribs felt the same that night as I did. It didn't occur to me then, though. He was half a head shorter than I was, a year younger, I'd have judged; and he was dressed in nothing but an old jacket, foxed at the elbows, a ragged shirt, a raggier pair of pants, and wearing no shoes despite the coolness of the March evening.

Backed up behind him were three more like him, all a little younger than he possibly. Until now I hadn't particularly noticed any of them, thinking of myself probably as a full-fledged steamboatman and the four as being too far under my dignity to consider.

One said, "Wash, hain't he the furriner from the steamboat?"

By now I'd been long enough on the river to know a "foreigner" wasn't necessarily from another land but anyone who spoke, acted, and dressed differently than the people he happened to be with.

119

"Why, sure," said the second, grinning like a bobcat. "Wash, you hain't goin' ter let a furriner lord it over you, be you?"

I hadn't looked for this. "Now, see here—" I said. I admit I didn't say it in very strong style. The boy they called Wash—if you could say he was a boy—he appeared too near the age I was, where you didn't much like to be thought of as a boy—well, he pushed me harder.

Instead of pushing I reached out of habit—or instinct—to protect my spectacles. It was the same thing that happened at Cincinnati, all over again, except when I fell over the boy crouching behind me this time I managed to hang on to my spectacles. I landed with a jar. They rushed me; I expected to be held down and it surprised me when I had the force to shove to my feet, shaking them off. I was half through the door, shielding my face and spectacles with my arms.

Next, to admit the whole ignominy—I was running. Those four Illinois varmints went hooting and yelling after me. A dozen or so people were still on the landing, with light shining down from the smoking torches, lanterns, and iron baskets hung from the boat's masts.

A path was opened for me. Instead of streaking over the gangplank I came to a full stop, skidding a little on the wet planks of the landing. Thankful was up there on the second deck, with Mrs. Tanner and Mr. Pollock, staring down at us.

All at once it came over me that she must have witnessed the whole thing. I swung around, not knowing exactly what I was going to do. Those four caught up with me—couldn't stop in time—and perhaps they were as surprised as I was to have me wheel around at them like, sometimes, even a rabbit'll do when it's cornered. All five of us skinned off the planks into soft mud.

I don't *remember* stripping my spectacles from my nose and slinging them away. I must have had some sort of knowledge of doing it, though, because I stopped being afraid of getting glass splinters in my eyes.

I rolled around in that soft mud until I fell on one of my tormentors and started taking out the way I felt on him as hard as I could go. I dug into him—and it was the pleasantest thing in the world to hear *him* begin to howl. Probably, now I think of it, he was the smallest of the four. But *that* didn't sashay anything, at the time, to me; no, I went at him.

The other three piled in a swarm on me and probably fetched at each other in the blackness as much as they did to me. Roustabouts jumped into the mud, pulling us apart like they were breaking up a dog fight. Pete's voice said, "That's enough. All of you!"

He lifted me to the wharf. "Where's your specs?"

"In the river, I guess. Let go of me. I can walk."

"Can you see?"

It was the first time I knew he'd ever been that much aware of my rotten weak eyes. I hated hearing him ask that question, out loud, for everybody to hear. So I said, "Certainly. Let go."

And I stepped away from him toward where I thought the gangplank was—and down I plunked, again, into soft mud. By then everyone was laughing. I guess they couldn't help it. I must have been a whole circus for them when they saw me rise up a second time, covered with even more mud. I felt Pete's hand clench hold of my arm. "Here, step up," he said, sounding grim.

But somebody from one side asked, "Blind as a bat, hain't he?" and Pete released my arm for a couple of seconds.

I took hold of the edge of the wharf. The same voice said, "Here, now—" A sound followed like a log falling. Nobody spoke afterwards. There was a dead silence.

Then Pete got hold of me once more, hauled me up, and said, "Direct ahead, Horace," breathing hard through his teeth.

I let him steer me aft along the boiler deck. Thankful must have come down there but all I heard was Pete saying, sudden, "Miss, you clear out. Understand? Hike!" in a way to make anybody jump. I guess she did, too. I never asked her if she saw me like I was that night. I was steered aft and up the crew ladder past the second deck to my office on the hurricane deck. I didn't know Sandy had followed until he lit the lantern and I saw him, like seeing something big and wavery-looking through muddy water, his head all hunched down under the cabin ceiling. Sandy was the biggest man on the boat. He said, "Say, ain't this a lively town? When you plugged that fellow he just keeled over and curled up his legs. Pete, why didn't you call me to join the fun?"

But, short and gruff, Pete ordered, "Belay your jaw, Sandy," and asked me, "Maybe them specs fell to the mud and didn't shatter? I told Smoky to find 'em."

"I've another pair . . ." Next, I said, "Everybody saw me running, didn't they? Pete, don't tell my father. I'll never run like that again."

"Horace, I've run some too when I've had too many 'gainst me.

121

'Bout tellin' your paw. Why, I'll have forgot all this tomorrow. So'll you."

"But this time I didn't run *all* the way."

"No, you didn't. I saw that, too. Now, wash off with this water."

I wanted to ask if he thought Thankful might have noticed I hadn't run all the way back to the boat. I didn't, though. I was too much ashamed by what had happened. My father would never have backed an inch.

Smoky looked in. Pete said, "Find them spectacles?" Smoky said he'd looked through all that mud, himself, with a torch. He hadn't been able to find my spectacles. He sounded worried. Again I said it didn't matter. I still had a third pair I could wear. Then Pete spoke up in an ordinary voice, like nothing had happened; and he said we all were rousing at four tomorrow. It was time we called it a day.

I remembered about the cheap wood I'd located and told him but his voice got sort of thick and he said, "We ain't going to buy *nothing* at this here poky town, Horace. Nothing. The only thing I'd give anybody here is my fist." They all cleared out.

After I'd stripped and finished washing off the rest of the mud, it was hard to get to sleep. Inside, I still felt shaky. Something had happened to me I couldn't quite yet understand: *I hadn't run all the way.* I told myself if ever again I had to meet trouble I wouldn't run even part way. I'd stay and face to it, even if it killed me. I was through having people like Pete and—and, well, Thankful Blair— see me running like a scared pup with its tail between its legs.

When finally I fell asleep I dreamed of that shaggy-headed young fellow, whom his friends had called Wash. I seemed to be going to him, hating him, and he was laughing. Somehow his face altered. It became covered over with warts. He grew taller. Then it was Clem Diggon slyly laughing at me, knowing I was scared and going to turn and run harder than ever. And, you know how dreams twist and change—standing behind Diggon I seemed to see somebody else, with a long shiny pleased face, just waiting there, waiting for Diggon to deal with me. I woke up in a cold terror.

It was full morning, close to six o'clock. Pete must have left orders I wasn't to be disturbed. I don't know why he did that because when I jumped to the window I saw we were underway, the river-banks floating off behind us, people there, watching, some cheering, an old man even shooting off a musket. I was afraid we'd be in Springfield before I got dressed!

122

Early next morning, after steaming east from Sangamontown, we entered into the narrows which I'd heard that bitter-faced man mention last night. Here, Pete completely lost his temper. He said if my father ever had known the river was like this he'd have refused to charter the *Talisman*. But Captain Bogue wasn't disturbed. He told us, "Pollock knows his bus'ness. You watch. *He'll* get us through." And Pollock did, too; but it was painful slow going.

Altogether there were six miles of twists and turns. Most of the way there was a channel of sorts. The river was still boiling and rushing through water about as high as a man's shoulders. But shoals were being thrown up at the turns. Brushwood, old leaves, mud, sand, and accumulations of all the rubbish swept into the river by melting snow would lodge like dams at the turns, obstructing our way, with little islands growing while we watched, piling up, until the river again broke through, sweeping them away.

I didn't see why it was called the "narrows." The river bottom lifted here, if anything, with the water flowing sluggishly over the banks into a kind of marsh beneath the trees. It was dark and cold even in daylight. We had to stop while overhanging branches were sawed off to make way for our stacks. More than once Pollock was rowed off in our yawl, and he would tell us where to sound; and twice he cut around small islands through channels you wouldn't have known were there. We scraped our hull. Once I thought we'd have to unload our cargo to lighten the *Talisman* and unship our grasshopper poles. But Pollock said coolly, "Let's try it again, gentlemen," and our stern wheel bulled us over.

We halted at a place called Antrim's Landing while Pete and Sandy inspected our paddles. They decided no important damage had been done when passing through the narrows. Besides, Captain Bogue was in a fever to complete the voyage. He promised we didn't

123

have much further to go. Off we started again. From what he'd said we anticipated a clear run the rest of the way.

But, no, we mushed into Pigeon Creek Shoals, climbed a big log, had to crawfish the log off our bows, and got savaged up twice—once almost slewing into a shoal of hard sand, not mud at all.

For the first time since leaving Cincinnati our steam pressure fell so low from using both winch and stern wheel, at full power, that Smoky had to cut off the valves at the boiler until he could hastily repump and pile in more wood.

We were in such a tearing rush to reach the last landing that we had let lunch go by back at Antrim's Landing. By now, every ten minutes or so another horseman would ride, lathering, up to the south bank, all filled with his own importance, to yell did we know the welcoming delegation had been waiting for over a day? How much longer?

We wished we knew. We'd never expected to find anything like the narrows or Pigeon Creek Shoals. If the river had been three or four inches lower we never would have made it.

Well, the sun had dropped halfway down the cloudless March sky when we steamed around the last bend. Smoky threw in a whole barrel of pitch. Black rich smoke gushed from both stacks like a seven hundred tonner was coming in. I heard the band playing "Hail, Thou Dauntless Sp'rit," which, while perhaps not exactly the tune I'd have expected, was loud and jouncy enough for even a parade of the Philadelphia Blues on Market Street. We passed a gristmill.

Captain Bogue said, excited, "That's my mill!" and ran forward on the hurricane deck, bowing, lifting his hat, sawing his elbows back and forth as he called out greetings to everyone waiting. He was dressed in a new steamboat uniform, one he must have saved for this day, with bigger brass buttons than ever and gold stripes running down his pant legs.

Mr. Pollock sashayed the *Talisman* around against the current. He put her into Portland Landing, in the neatest piece of piloting I'd ever seen. I didn't know it then, but later I learned Portland Landing was only two miles northeast of Springfield by the river road. I guess that afternoon almost everyone in town including the entire population of dogs had come by carriage, horse, or shanks' mare to see our arrival.

It was like a big fair. Stands had been set up under awnings to serve grub. Peddlers were there. Big dray wagons, with their horses,

were lined up in the meadow waiting for cargo to be unloaded. Mud was almost dry under the afternoon sun. A warm haze filled the air, enough to let you think it was the middle of May, not the tag end of March. Here we were at last! I couldn't have described how I felt, listening to all that noise, the shouting, the whooping, watching men pound each other on the back, while women would look on, their faces shining with joy.

I stayed there by the hurricane deck rail with Thankful, neither of us speaking, while we snubbed to the landing and the gangplank was lowered. I reminded myself to write Father and get a letter off by the first mail coach, informing him we'd safely arrived at about four in the afternoon, March twenty-fourth. We'd left St. Louis on the thirteenth. When plugging up the Illinois it had seemed a powerful long time. Now I wondered where all the time had gone so fast. We'd done it in twelve days. It wasn't mail coach time; but it was good time, everything considered.

If we finished unloading Monday, I thought, by Tuesday morning we could cast off, head downstream, no longer against the current. Even if it would require another twelve days to return—which it shouldn't—that still would put us in St. Louis by the seventh or eighth of April—with a full week to spare. If we crowded on steam and had any luck at all, I ought to reckon on seeing Mother and Father possibly as early as the third of April.

The band had stopped. Next, a little fat man in a clawhammer coat stepped in front of the crowd, raised a plug hat off a head covered with cottony white hair. He shouted, "Now, everyone—my new song to welcome Captain Bogue and his steamboat!" But the words were new words.

I don't guess many in the crowd'd had time to learn them, for the singing was ragged. The little fat man sang out good and strong. So did a tall thin woman in a calico dress, going at it in a piercing soprano, until she fetched to the second verse, where she ran into mud shallows and got pink in the face. Still, she carried full steam at the end:

> "O, Captain Bogue he gave the load,
> And Captain Bogue he showed the road;
> And we came up with a right good will,
> And tied our boat up to his mill.
>
> "Now we are up the Sangamaw,
> And here we'll have a grand hurra.

So fill your glasses to the brim,
Of whiskey, brandy, wine, and gin.

"Illinois suckers, young and raw,
Were strung along the Sangamaw,
To see a boat come up by steam
They surely thought it was a dream."

Those were the words. I know, because I copied them down from the Springfield newspaper when the *Sangamon Journal* published them the following week. I thought my father would like to see what was sung.

Well, I listened; and I saw all those hundreds of faces looking up at Captain Bogue. I became aware I'd dropped my hand over Thankful's, on the railing. She didn't move her hand away. Neither of us still said anything. When I should have been pleased and cheered at last finally arriving, and looking forward to turning around and getting away inside of forty-eight hours, I wasn't too much.

I suddenly had the strangest pang. Now we had arrived, thankful would be leaving shortly for Decatur with Mrs. Tanner and their servant woman. I didn't know when I'd see Thankful again, maybe never, if I returned next fall to Philadelphia.

Captain Bogue was down there on the wharf by now, shaking hands with four or five important-looking men. Smoky and Denny and some of the roustabouts were holding the crowd back from the gangplank, having previously received orders from Captain Bogue that no one but his special guests was to be allowed to visit the boat until all the cargo was safely unloaded. The band was playing, again. A peddler was selling American flags. A woman fainted. A horse ran away—and a pack of boys and dogs took after it through the north meadow where the dray wagons were waiting.

I was trying to work out in my mind what to say to Thankful but all of a sudden it seemed to me there was so much I had to say to her I could never finish, such as, perhaps, did she know if there were any good boys' academies near Decatur? I didn't even start.

Unexpectedly she snatched her hand from mine, like lightning, wheeling around, giving a little gasp. It was only Pete. He said, "Horace, you got a minute?" Below, Mrs. Tanner began calling impatiently, "Thankful! Where can that girl be?" I had just the time to say, "Can we see each other before you leave the boat, maybe?"

126

She nodded, quick, and ran like a colt to the passenger stairs. I could feel my face growing hot as Pete squinted at me. But all he said was, "In here. Hurry." I expect he was so occupied he never noticed I'd happened to lay my hand over Thankful's, as if both of us had been feeling lonely even if there wasn't any cause for low feelings on a great day like this one.

Anyway, inside the office he made it clear, fast, why he wanted me. Captain Bogue was planning to begin unloading right away, this afternoon. According to the agreement he'd made with my father, the remainder of the charter price was to be paid over on arrival and by Pete's reckoning that meant before any of the cargo was unloaded.

He lit his pipe. "I figgered you might like to remind him." He banged the pipe a couple of times on the deck. "He could've forgot."

"Me?" I said. "Ask Captain Bogue for Father's money?"

"You're your paw's legal representative, ain't you?" he said, very fierce. "It's none of my concern if Bogue unloads the cargo and walks off and says he's sorry but he can't pay right away. I don't say he would, either. But seeing as how you've decided you're capable of tending to providing us with fuel and dickering on prices, I'd think you just might like to square up to Bogue and ask for the money. Course, if you're scared to . . ." He got his pipe drawing, again. He was puffing hard, when I walked out.

I found Captain Bogue had returned to the captain's parlor, accompanied by five men in top hats, gaiters, and clawhammer coats. He was so set up and pleased with his triumph he could hardly speak for all his emotion. He presented me as "young Mr. Owens, son of the builder of the *Talisman*" to a Mr. Matheny, who I learned was president of the town trustees, the same thing as a mayor in Philadelphia; Mr. Simeon Francis, town clerk, and publisher of the new newspaper, the *Sangamon Journal;* Dr. Merryman, the chubby white-haired man who'd done the main singing—and *he* asked, "How'd'doo. Did ye like my little effort, Mr. Owens?" referring to his new song, I supposed; and to two town merchants, a Mr. Cowgill and a Mr. Britton.

I had trouble getting Captain Bogue away. When he did leave he said, "Gentlemen, excuse me. Only a minute. You have no idea of all the cares a captain of a vessel this size has." After I got him to my office I was surprised to see Pete still waiting, smoking his pipe, despite the gruff answer he had given me on my being my father's representative. "Well, now what?" said Captain Bogue, in that goose-

127

like way he had when he was riled. "Disturbing me like that. Shocking. Well, what is it?" I told him. "What?" says he, drawing back as if he'd been hit by lightning. "Pay—now? Nonsense. I'll pay Tuesday or Wednesday at my convenience."

I didn't answer; but I showed him a copy of the agreement Father and he had signed. Captain Bogue had promised to pay five thousand dollars in specie or legal tender in addition to furnishing, at his expense, a competent pilot to bring the *Talisman* to Portland Landing; and half the five thousand was to be paid on signing the contract, and the remainder, twenty-five hundred dollars, was to be paid over to Father or his representative, which was me, at the safe arrival of the steamboat. Captain Bogue read the contract over once; and he read it a second time. Gradually his elbows ceased sawing so vigorously. That line: ". . . *at safe arrival*" had him. He knew it.

Pete spoke up innocently. "Course, if you can't pay now, cap'n, we could hold your cargo while you collect the money. If you don't read the contract like I do, bring in a justice of peace or sheriff and let him decide what the contract says."

In a hollow whisper Captain Bogue admitted, "I was expecting to get money from the merchants to pay the remainder. I'll pay Tuesday."

"Cap'n, me and Horace mean to be started for home by Monday. I don't like the looks of this river. We can take Mr. Pollock's advice, if you want."

"Now, now, we don't have to trouble him. He's already driven to town to make himself ready for the banquet tonight at the courthouse in my honor. *You're* expected, too, Mr. Wilmot. Everyone's looking forward to meeting the chief engineer—and, you, too," he said, nodding hastily at me, "my boy. Now, can't we adjust this sensibly? Can we do this? Allow Cowgill and Britton to unload today. I'll raise the twenty-five hundred from them, pay you on the barrelhead first thing tomorrow morning, Sunday, and we can unload the rest of the cargo then. You'll be ready to turn back Monday. How's that? Isn't that fair and square?"

"Horace?" Pete said, leaving it to me.

I nodded. We all shook hands.

Until nearly sundown I was kept busy checking off cargo items for Mr. Cowgill and Mr. Britton. When their carts were loaded and they were finished with, afterwards I lost more time by having to pay off the crew.

With the exception of Smoky, Denny, and Sandy, who'd volun-

teered to stand watch with me tonight, we were allowing all hands liberty ashore until sunrise tomorrow morning. That was short shrift, after our voyage; and I knew it and so did Pete. But Pete gave a short speech on the boiler deck. He explained how important it was to get turned around and on our way back by Monday morning to prevent getting permanently grounded in the narrows or shoals if the river continued falling. As my father's representative, I'd agreed to pay every man a full extra day's wages in return for cutting short their time ashore. That satisfied the hands.

Pete was getting ready to depart with Captain Bogue. He followed me up to my office, taking another minute or so to promise he meant to keep a weather eye on all the hands that rode into town. He'd herd them together and fetch them back to the ship in time for them to begin the final chore of unloading tomorrow morning. He hesitated. "You sure you don't want to join us? From what Bogue says, it'll be some banquet. Everyone of importance in town'll be there."

I was tempted. However, I knew I had to get a letter written to Father. I expected tomorrow, Sunday, would be a full day. Monday morning, we planned to cast off at daybreak. Tonight would be about the only free time I'd have to complete a letter and have it ready to send by the Monday morning mail coach south toward St. Louis. I shook my head.

"I'd better stay, Pete."

It was nearly six in the evening when he went down to join Captain Bogue and to arrange to hire carriages for the crew. I'd grown impatient, waiting for him to clear away before I sauntered along the passenger deck and offered to take Thankful's handbags to the wharf and find a carriage for her and Mrs. Tanner and their servant. I'd caught sight of her off and on while I'd been busy with the cargo, so I knew she was still aboard and hadn't gone off before we could say good-by to each other.

As soon as Pete got himself out of sight, I used up a few seconds trying to decide if I had time to strip, stand in the washbasin, pour cold water over me, and change into my best Philadelphia rags before seeing Thankful for possibly the last time. I had a good look at myself in the mirror. My hair had grown almost as shaggy as that bearheaded fellow's who had chased me with his friends from the Sangamontown tavern and rolled me in the mud, costing me my second pair of spectacles. I felt a sudden hot glow of anger again at the memory. I needed a haircut. I rubbed my hands over my cheeks. While there wasn't much to be seen in that mirror—the mirror was

old and wavery and needed resilvering, anyway—I did feel a kind of fuzzy feeling which wasn't entirely from my skin. I'd have liked to have rushed down to borrow Sandy's razor. But there didn't appear to be time to start learning from scratch how to shave, right this minute.

I'd settled for stripping and changing to my best duds when somebody knocked. Before I could say, "Stay out," thinking it was Sandy or Smoky, a big burly woman of about forty opened the door and asked, "Are you the young feller who sells tickets to St. Louis? I'm Mrs. Hicks—Mrs. Percy Washington Hicks—an' my little boy an' me are goin' ter my sister's in St. Louis ter live since my poor husband he passed away."

She stepped in, still talking. I couldn't shut her off long enough to ask her to see Captain Bogue. "My husband was a surveyor—doin' well, too—but he liked t' fish. Last fall he went fishin' fer catfish below the dam at New Salem—fell overboard—not two rods from shore. Couldn't swim a stroke. People on shore saw him—throwed him a line. Wasn't no use." She sighed. "*They* couldn't swim, neither. 'Here today,' they say, 'gone termorrer.' Best man a wife c'd hev. I tell my little boy, 'See what happened ter y'r paw? *You* learn ter swim.' But he's like the rest of 'em. They're all landspeople, here. I was born on the lakes. People thar learned ter swim early. Wal, kin you sell me passage fer my boy an' me an' six hundredweight of baggage? How much?"

I told Mrs. Hicks that was Captain Bogue's job. She'd have to see him. She surprised me by replying she'd already seen him. Captain Bogue had said this was as far as he went on the *Talisman*. He'd sent her up to speak to me.

In my mind I knew Captain Bogue wasn't returning with us. Nevertheless, it brought it square in front of me, so to speak, to hear Mrs. Hicks saying he'd sent her to me. I didn't know how much a ticket was worth. We'd charged seventeen dollars cabin passage from St. Louis to Beardstown. I was in a hurry, afraid Thankful might already have gone. I said was twenty dollars a fair price? Forty, for two people?

"Sounds fair, young feller. Includes baggage?"

We were returning empty. While six hundred pounds of baggage by mail coach line to St. Louis would have cost a small fortune, it was nothing for the *Talisman*. I told her to bring aboard all the baggage she wished. So she shelled out money from an old knit purse. I refused a couple of wildcat notes and she laughed and handed me

ten dollars more in government tender. Because we hadn't printed any tickets I scribbled on a piece of paper: "*Received $40.00 in payment cabin passage to St. Louis for Mrs. Percy Washington Hicks, child, and 600 weight baggage,*" signed my name, "*H. J. Owens, Purser S.B. Talisman,*" giving myself a quick promotion, decided I'd done a good piece of business by signing two passengers for a return trip, and answered, "Monday morning, m'am, about six o'clock," after she asked when we departed. "I'll hev ter jump ter make it," she told me. "Summow, my little boy an' me'll be thar, ready an' waitin'. You're sartin of leavin', aren't you? I can't afford to pay shippin' charges fer my furniture by coach an' I got a chance ter sell my cheers an' table an' dishes ter my neighbor. I druther pack 'em with me, if you're sartin, an' not sell."

I repeated, we were leaving Monday, by six or not much later. I waited until Mrs. Hicks had two minutes to get herself out of sight and cut for the crew ladder, not even losing more minutes by changing clothes. I was afraid Thankful might have gone. But there she was, leaning against the door of her stateroom. Inside, Aunty Phoebee was lighting the lantern and turning down the sheets as if Thankful was staying here instead of leaving for Springfield. I didn't see any of their bags or trunks piled on the deck. Mrs. Tanner wasn't anywhere in sight.

I swallowed and said in a stiff voice which caught me by surprise, "Can I help any way, maybe?" when I'd planned in advance how easy and casual I'd be.

She shook her head. "Aunty Phoebee and I are staying here tonight."

"Here?"

That was a change of plans. I didn't understand.

"Cousin Elvira was afraid we all couldn't get rooms for tonight at the Springfield Hotel, with the crowd here to see the steamer. So she drove in early with Mr. Pollock and she's supposed to send for Aunty Phoebee and me—" She scowled. "If you want to know what *I* think, Elvira's planning to go to that banquet tonight with that pilot of yours. And I suppose she expects to dance half the night and she doesn't want to be troubled with me. So, she won't send for me tonight. You'll see. I'll miss all the fun. And tomorrow morning she'll come for me and—and she'll say, 'Dear, I told you yesterday that you'd have to stay on the boat with Phoebee. Can't you *ever* remember what I tell you, dear? Such a helter-skelter little girl, aren't you, yet?' That's what she'll say. 'Little girl—' I wish Pa'd let

131

me stay in St. Louis and keep house for him like I wanted to. I *hate* going to Decatur with Cousin Elvira. She's different than she used to be in Memphis where she had to toe the line and be sweet and soft ev'ry day to my *real* blood relatives. Horace, I just don't like her."

Thankful was almost crying. She turned her head away from me. It was the most meltingest thing, I expect, ever to happen to me. Then she looked back at me and there were a couple of tears clinging to her lashes. While it stands to reason a girl's lashes shouldn't be any different or longer or silkier than a boy's—Thankful's were.

She blinked her eyes and said defiantly, "All right. Make fun of me. I—I know I'm being as much of a nuisance as I used to be in Wheeling."

I heard myself saying, "You weren't ever a nuisance, Thankful," and I guess that was about the biggest lie I'd drawed on yet. But I didn't think about it being a lie at the time.

Well, Thankful was right. Mrs. Tanner never did send for her. We had dinner together in the common room. Sandy joined us and mostly spoiled it by talking steadily to Thankful all the time we were there.

She giggled and laughed at some of the most played-out old jokes I ever heard. I was disappointed in both Sandy and her. Aunty Phoebee stayed in with us, all the time. She was big and strong, her apron tied around her. She took the hot plates Denny brought up and served us herself.

By and by she said, "Young lady, hits time you an' me was gettin' our rest, so's you say, 'Good evnun' to the gen'men." And she carried Thankful off, like she was a watchdog, making Denny step aside for them both.

That night Aunty Phoebee bunked in with Thankful, in the other berth. And I heard her voice saying, "We's gwine shut boff do's t'night, de' sto'hm do' *an* de' winder too." By that she meant the shutter door.

Denny and Smoky alternated as watch on the foredeck. Each one had a musket—a percussion-lock musket, not an old flintlock—loaded with rock salt in case some loafer from town decided to try to slip aboard to fetch at a barrel or so of sugar or flour.

Sandy surprised me by padding along with me to my office, after how he'd taken up all of Thankful's time during dinner with those played-out jokes of his. Very short, I said, "Well, what do you want, Mr. Jenks? I've letters to write."

132

He looked down on me. He was a good inch taller than my father and my father measured up to six feet. "Why—" he said and was embarrassed. "See here, Horace, you know I'm not the fellow to cut in on a friend's girl. I see you were freezin' up at the table. I just tried to liven things up a mite. I wasn't cuttin' in on your girl. She's a year or so too young for me, to tell the truth. Not that she ain't pretty as a picture. I'll say that for her to anybody. But she ain't somehow my style. That's all."

"She's not my girl," I said. "I don't care if you talk to her so much nobody can get a word in."

"Horace," he said, worried, "I *do* talk too much. Pete says so. Why didn't you stop me? I won't do it again. How's that?" He stuck out his hairy hand. "Thar, naow."

I don't know when it had started but since we'd listened to Slicky Bill Green telling his yarns back up there at Salt Fork all of us, that is, Pete, Sandy, and me, the three of us as a joke had begun trying to imitate how the Illinois Suckers talked. Sandy he could do it the best, even better than Pete.

So I said, "Thar," and stuck out my hand. I tried to squeeze as hard as Sandy did and failed although Sandy jumped back and pretended to wince and said, "I vum. You near cracked my fingers, Horace—" And stopped. "I wish you didn't have that name, to tell you the honest truth."

"Why don't you call me Turtle?"

"Turtle?"

"That's what I used to be called in Philadelphia."

"Why didn't you never say so? *Thar's* a name." He grinned. "Wal, g'night, Turtle. Ef Pete don't git back by midnight waken me an' I'll stan' watch till he does."

I wrote my letter to Father, another to Mother. Then I got started on a long breezy one to Whizzer Tucker in Philadelphia. After I finished I went on deck. A moon was up. You could hear a catfish, now and then, plop out of the river. I saw Denny's pipe down by the gangplank, where he was awake and on watch. I covered the whole boat, stem to stern, thinking of Thankful asleep with her Aunty Phoebee; but it was a waste of time. It was a quiet night.

Then I started to wondering if Thankful was my girl, without me ever having known it. I wondered if maybe, tomorrow morning, before she departed, I shouldn't say something about it or at least hint in that direction. But I didn't know how it might strike her. Then I

went into my office, meaning to lie down but not fall asleep until Pete and the crew returned.

After I shut my eyes, though, I never did open them until Pete stood over me, shaking me awake. A meadow lark was singing. Morning light was streaming through the shutters. I said what kind of a time did he have last night and he answered, gruffly, "Not much. After they finished with the speaking they brought in the band for dancing and I got away to herd up the crew."

"What time is it?"

"After seven. Get down for breakfast, quick, if any's left. We're starting to unload." He fired off a lucifer match to light his pipe. "Say, what's Thankful Blair and her woman servant still doing aboard? A fellow came riding up from town a few minutes ago with a message for her. I asked her what was wrong. She just looked at me as if all the breath had been knocked out of her."

Well, I slammed into my clothes fast.

I didn't bother about grub, either. When I saw Thankful it looked like she hadn't bothered about grub either, for her face was a dead white. Without speaking, she handed me a note. It was from Mrs. Tanner:

> *Dear Thankful—I'm sure my news won't displease you too much because I must say, during this voyage you have ceased being the sweet obedient little girl I used to know. I've realized it was a great mistake on my part to have so kindly offered your father to accompany you to Decatur. You have not thought of my feelings on this voyage at all!*
>
> *Mr. Pollock has done me the honor to ask for my hand and last night we were married privately by Justice Snodgrass. This note is to inform you that this morning Mr. Pollock and I are departing for the State Capital where he has important affairs to look after before we continue to New York.*
>
> *In view of the fact your father overlooked paying me any stipend for, first, conducting you to St. Louis, and secondly, for conducting you safely this far, I am certain you will agree 'tis only my right and due to take with me the small purse your father intrusted to my keeping. I suggest you ask the officers of the steamboat for an advance required for you and Phoebee to continue to Decatur as they will know your father will gladly reimburse them for any small amount loaned you. . . .*

134

I felt the blood rush to my head and drain away again, leaving me with a numb sensation. That mealy-mouthed, genteel-written note from Mrs. Tanner scorched my hand. My heart went out to Thankful. I was stunned. That woman had run off, stealing all of Thankful's money? She'd run off and married our pilot? Next, all at once I realized Mr. Pollock evidently had scamped, too. What were we going to do without a pilot to navigate us back through that wicked dangerous stretch to New Salem? I felt struck by a second thunderbolt.

Pete's voice said, "Here. What's wrong?"

I couldn't speak. Silently I gave him the letter to read.

Thankful wailed, "Horace, what will I do? It's awful! Pa gave her three hundred dollars to pay all expenses and my tuition for the term. Can't you go after her? Can't you find her?"

Pete finished reading that letter.

He had to try a second time before he could speak and it came from deep down in his throat. "Both of 'em have run off! Ain't that a nice pickle?" He regarded Thankful. "It ain't the half having your woman take out. No. What 'bout our pilot? I'm none. Neither's Sandy—"

"Trouble, gents?"

I felt myself jump. There was Captain Bogue come toward us, sawing away at his elbows.

"Trouble?" asked Pete, getting his voice back. He shook the letter under Captain Bogue's nose. "Pollock's married that Tanner woman and run off. Read this."

Captain Bogue didn't bother reading it. He gave his elbows another jerk. He began smiling, a little, a soft smile that wreathed his head. "Why, now you mention it, after I paid Pollock off last night I do b'lieve he remarked he had business to tend to in Vandalia after he got married."

"You—let him go without telling us?" I cried.

"'Twasn't my concern to get a pilot for the return trip, young Mr. Know-it-all. Get the contract what you stuck under my nose yesterday. What does it say? I was beholden to furnish and pay a pilot only till we landed here."

"Ain't you proud of yourself?" growled Pete. "Why, I ought to—"

"No violence, sir, or I'll fetch the town constable." Captain Bogue stepped back. "Read the contract. It wasn't my job to produce a pilot for the return trip. If you want Pollock bad enough you'll find him

136

and his new wife at Vandalia, providing you hurry. He might—I *think* he might be willing to pilot your steamboat back for five hundred dollars."

"Five hundred dollars! Is this a swindle you and Pollock figgered out together? I'll see myself hung before paying him or you, either, five cents."

"If we don't soon have rain and you don't find a pilot, sir, you may see your boat hung up here in shoal water to perish and rot before the river rises again ten months from now. But suit yourself. 'Do unto others,' I say, 'as others do unto you.' Now, here's your twenty-five hundred dollars you wanted this morning—"

He handed me a leather bag. "Part in silver and the rest in government tender. Count it. I'll thank you for a receipt, if you please. Now, that quits me, don't it? My responsibilities are ended. I've played square and fair. Meanwhile, if you want to stay tied to my landing I'll have to charge you fifteen dollars a day wharf fees. If you don't like that price you're free to move to Sangamontown Landing, always providing you can pass Pigeon Shoals and the narrows 'ithout the val'ble services of Mr. Pollock . . ."

After Captain Bogue went hopping and waddling to the wharf, holding the receipt for the money in one hand, using the other to hold where Pete had helped him leave, shouting back to us that nobody could kick him like that and not have cause soon to regret the liberty—afterwards, we had a council in the cabin parlor. First, we had to decide what to do with Thankful. I promised her we'd lend her any sum she might need from the twenty-five hundred paid to us by Captain Bogue.

But she shook her head. She'd had enough of Mrs. Tanner and of the Young Ladies' Lyceum in Decatur whose praises Mrs. Tanner had sung. She wanted to stay with us and return to her father in St. Louis.

Pete agreed with her. He believed her father would prefer having her get back to him rather than going on to a strange new place which might not come up by a quarter to Mrs. Tanner's fine talk. Aunty Phoebee could continue bunking with Thankful every night. Thankful would be safer with us, friends she could trust. So we agreed to restore her to her father—always providing we found a pilot who could run us back through the Sangamon to the Illinois River. That brought up the most pressing and urgent problem we had. We hashed that over nearly an hour.

Finally, it was Pete who decided.

"This boat might get stuck here and rot," he said, "if we don't find us a pilot. I'm an engineman. So's Sandy . . ." He squinted at me. "Now, listen. I want Sandy to stay on this boat and be in charge, day and night. I meant to hunt up the newspaper fellow—that Mr. Francis. He looked honest. Maybe he can help me find a reliable pilot in the neighborhood. Meanwhile, I want you to get away quick to Vandalia. Tell Mr. Pollock he can have five hundred to pilot us back. It's a swindle, yes. But it's better to save the boat. *If* I locate another pilot, we'll keep our promise, pay Pollock his money, and kick him off. I'll have him blacklisted by the Pilots' Association . . ."

Pete struck a deal with one of the draymen to take us to town. We arrived about noon. At the Springfield Hotel the owner, a Mr. Ransdoll, answered, yes, he did recall seeing our pilot and a tall proud-looking woman get on this morning's mud-wagon for Vandalia. He explained "mud-wagon" was the name everyone had given to the mail coach. Well, that certified Captain Bogue had told us the truth, so far. But we were six hours too late to stop Mr. Pollock.

The hotelkeeper scratched his neck and said he jes' might save me from heving to hire a hoss. He had a party here, Mr. Josiah Pugh by name, eating lunch, who planned to drive to Vandalia. It was eighty miles to the state capital and a lonesome ride. Mr. Pugh might like having someone along as company. When I was introduced, Mr. Pugh said, "Shore. Pleased t' hev you . . ."

His two sorrels stepped off mile after mile through a rolling prairie country already beginning to turn green. I learned Mr. Pugh was going to the state capital on a lawsuit. He was about fifty and wonderful good company at first, interested in the difficulties we were having with our steamboat. But he happened to mention troubles of his own he was having with somebody he named "thet wildcatty scoundril, Abner Jefferson." He told me, "Fer the fust time, last week, I seed a handbill declarin' thar was swindlin' done by the road commission. It was signed by thet scoundril. My name was referred to in terms too strong t' mention. Ef thet scoundril is any man of standin', I'm goin' t' dare him to disavow hisself or take the consequences from me. I'll hosswhip him. I'll . . ."

It caused my blood to run cold to hear Mr. Pugh, after that. I never did fetch to the bottom of the feud he was having with the Jefferson fellow. When Mr. Pugh'd try to tell me he'd choke up, turn

purple, gasp, and say despairingly, "I'm goin' t' hev another spell. Jes' grab the reins, will you?"

I got so interested the day passed before I knew it. I almost forgot my own anxieties. He shared his grub with me. We hunkered along at that slow steady pace his sorrels set. There wasn't much of a moon.

By and by we were going through a piece of timber and the horses snorted and shied. Mr. Pugh said, not excited, "Wolves. Mebbe we'd better stop fer the night t' the nex' taown?" That suited me. He might have been accustomed to wolves; I wasn't.

It was the first time I'd ever stayed in a tavern so small and mean that I had to sleep three in a bed with all of us wearing everything we had but our coats and boots. Mr. Pugh shook me awake in that green washy-looking light of early morning. I reached for my spectacles underneath the bed, by my boots, hooked them on, and got up. In the bed next to us I saw four men sleeping, each on his side, laid together like logs. As I got up the stranger who'd been asleep at the far side of our bed, last night, when the landlord had lit our way in with a candle, he roused up, rubbing his eyes. "Wal, what time is it?" he asked and stared at Mr. Pugh, who was putting on his coat. Mr. Pugh stared back.

"Josh Pugh!" said the stranger.

"Abner Jefferson. I hain't seen you in a coon's age."

I waited, petrified, for Mr. Pugh to leap on the man in the bed and kill him, maybe, tearing his legs and arms from his body as he'd sworn he was going to do. But Mr. Pugh eyed me, looked back at the swarthy unshaven man sitting up in bed, swallowed, and said meekly, "Wal, Abner, nice t' hev seen you. I hev a right smart distance yet. Give my reegards t' Mrs. Jefferson."

"I shore will, Josh. Drap in someday for dinner, will you?"

All the rest of that morning, Mr. Pugh never said a word. He was like a clam. He acted as if he had something on his mind. We arrived in Vandalia toward eleven, Monday, and he set me down at the Commercial House. He was insulted when I offered him pay for the ride. He refused to accept a cent.

But he leaned down to me from the buggy and said, "Thar is suthin', though. Thet Abner Jefferson . . . He's a desp'rate feller. I'd ajumped him this mornin' ef you wasn't thar. 'Twasn't I was scairt. No, sir. Not me. I jes' didn't want t' hev you resked gettin' shot. You understand, don't you?"

139

I nodded and allowed that I did.

He looked more relieved. He tipped his hand to me, wished me luck finding my pilot, clucked to his sorrels, and shot off down the corduroy street.

My joints still ached from the long pounding in the buggy and probably, too, from that crowded cornhusk bed last night. Because Vandalia was state capital it had more hotels and rooming houses for a town of its size than either Pete or I had anticipated. After inquiring at the Commercial House and learning nobody resembling Mr. Pollock or his wife had arrived, I used up most of the remaining day tramping down one street and up another.

I covered every hotel, tavern, and rooming house to be found, stopping only for a bite to eat toward the middle of the afternoon. At the very last place the landlady asked tartly, " 'Stead of botherin' me, why don't you ask the livery stable whar the stage comes in?"

I was sore at myself because I hadn't thought sooner of doing that. Well, the mail coach had arrived late last night. Nobody at the stables could say what passengers were on it because the driver had gone off to his farm until he took the stage out again, Wednesday morning. They told me his name was Nebbles; he lived at Hog Creek, a mile south of town.

By the time I got there it was dead dark. I kicked off a dozen dogs and Mr. Nebbles opened the door. After listening to me, he said a couple of that description had come with him from Springfield. He couldn't say where they went after arriving. Had I asked at the Commercial House?

I'd tried there the first thing. Now I'd learned definitely Mr. and Mrs. Pollock were somewhere in Vandalia I couldn't quit to return to Pete and admit I'd failed. That night I took a room at the Commercial House. For a dollar I had a bed to myself and breakfast Tuesday morning. Tuesday was even more discouraging. I even backtracked over the places I'd called on yesterday. I couldn't see how it was possible for two people as smart looking and as well dressed as the Pollocks to be here in town with nobody having noticed them.

Finally, someone asked if I'd tried Perkens' Livery, by the bridge east of town. No, I hadn't. I hadn't known a livery was that far away. I walked there to have Mr. Perkens' men bring me up short by a hammering sensation, first of hope, next of despair. Yes, he'd seen a man and woman of that description. Monday morning they'd paid hard cash for a secondhand buggy and his best pacer. They'd

told him they were driving east to Indiana. However, their names weren't Pollock. As he recalled, it was a Mr. and Mrs. Wilmot Owens.

Wilmot Owens! That was Pete's name joined to mine. I felt staggered. It seemed to me I could see Mr. Pollock laughing at me for the joke he had played on us. He'd left just enough of a trail of himself here in Vandalia to have me waste two days hunting him. Now he'd driven off somewhere. Indiana? I didn't know. I knew he was beyond finding.

Somehow I dragged myself to town. Nobody would rent a horse for an eighty mile jaunt to Springfield, starting out at night, to a stranger like myself. I learned the stage departed at six next morning. I'd have to take a room for a second night.

Returning to the hotel I passed by a notions store showing ladies' spring hats in the window and remembered that hat of Thankful's I'd ruined. The store was closed. I rapped on the door. I stepped back and hollered. Presently a man stuck his head out of the upstairs window. I called, "Open up. I want to buy a lady's hat!" He shouted, "That ain't my idee of being comical this time of ev'ning. You let another peep out you and I'll call the constable. Now, git!"

I was too tired to argue; I got. That night I couldn't sleep. I'd failed. If Father had been sent down here to find a pilot, at my age, he probably would have succeeded. At least if he had been courting my mother, he'd have had the gumption to get her a hat he had ruined.

I asked myself if we'd been given a red herring in the shape of Clem Diggon while something had been hatching under our noses. Captain Bogue had sent me on a wild-goose chase. He'd wanted me to lose more time while the Sangamon dropped lower each day. No, that was giving myself excuses for failing. I wish I knew the truth. Suppose Captain Bogue *had* sent me on a wild-goose chase? It was no use thinking about it; I'd ask Pete what he thought when I saw Pete.

I was up at four, on the stage an hour and a half before it departed. The weather was so warm, after the first stop I climbed up to the boot seat. Sitting next to me was a farmer or storekeeper of thirty or so, short in the leg, long in the body, with a pleasant tanned face; and he nodded to me. He never said a word, though.

We went cracking along at a fair rate of speed. There was something so kindly and good humored about that farmer sitting with

me, even if he was chary of speech, that somehow I began speaking to him. I told him how we'd brought the *Talisman* up the Sangamon and before I quite knew it I was pouring out all my troubles and grief and worry to him. I had to tell someone that day—or split. He was the best listener I'd ever had, too.

He'd nod his head. He was attentive. He started scowling and clenching his fists when I came to Pollock scamping off. But he scarcely spoke. When finally he did, I understood why he didn't often commit himself. He took too long. He'd say a word, halt, say another, halt—and it took us nearly a mile through prairie and timberland for him to get out with a dozen sentences. It was a relief, though, to have someone to unload my grief on. I felt better, some. I tried to make myself believe Pete would have located a river pilot while I was away, with the help of that newspaperman.

The farmer beside me left the stage at one of our stops in late afternoon. I shook his hand saying I hoped I hadn't ruined his journey by jawing so much. He began a slow smile. "No—" he said. "As—a—matter—of—fact—"

You couldn't help it. You leaned forward, wanting to get hold of those words to pull them out faster. I learned for half a year or so, once, he'd been pilot on a steam ferry at Shawnee, across the Ohio. After listening to me, he'd considered offering his services to pilot the *Talisman*. He'd decided not to, though, because he didn't know the Sangamon well enough. He'd never even floated a broadhorner down to the Illinois.

Well, for a minute I was beginning to get excited. By chance, I thought, I had got hold of a pilot! But a pilot who didn't know Pigeon Shoals or the channel through the narrows was of no use to us. He said, "I—wish—I—could—have—done—business—with you." I wished he could have, too; but we couldn't, worse luck.

It was growing chilly again, as the sun began sinking, and I climbed inside the coach, the only passenger remaining. They say misfortunes never come singly. Nobody ever warned me misfortunes came by the bushel. We broke an axle ten miles south of Springfield. By the time it was patched to hold and we'd crawled into town we were three hours late.

I had to walk that lonesome road to the river and I was dog tired and it was past midnight when Smoky's voice hailed, "Who that?" and let me by. Pete hadn't gone to bed. He'd been waiting. Later, I learned he'd been planning to send Sandy to Vandalia after me if I hadn't showed up before morning.

I told Pete what had happened. He said it beat him. He didn't understand. Anyway, he'd had some luck; how good he couldn't yet say. That newspaperman, Mr. Simeon Francis, had known two or three river pilots who'd settled around Springfield. All of them had enlisted for the Indian war. However, he'd gotten on the track of a fourth man, promising to bring him to the boat tomorrow to see if he suited us.

Pete said the way he felt now any pilot would suit him. We'd have to get away by Friday if we ever expected to pass the narrows. It was a risk. What else was there for us to do? He'd written my father; but the stage south to St. Louis didn't leave until Saturday. We couldn't get a reply until it would be too late. If we didn't get a pilot, Pete was ready to try to steer the boat himself, with Sandy in the engine room, and Smoky and me going ahead in the yawl to sound. It was our only chance. We'd have to place Thankful and her Aunty Phoebee on the stage—it was too much of a risk for them to remain with us if we tried to run the Sangamon without a proper pilot. He paused, thinking.

"Oh, yes . . ." He asked, "Did you sell passage to a Mrs. Washington Hicks—" I remembered and said, yes, why? I'd sold passage to her and her little boy. "Little boy?" Pete growled. "He's a young catamount. They both came aboard Monday. She's pleasant enough 'bout it, but she says she won't budge. If we put her off she'll go to law 'less we pay for her and the imp's fare by stage and also the baggage. Never mind . . . *That* don't help now. Get to sleep. Tomorrow . . ."

I sat up; I'd forgotten something. I told Pete I had come across a ferry pilot on the stage but he hadn't known the Sangamon. "See here—we don't care any more. If he can pilot, that's all that counts. What's his name?" I hadn't asked. "Well, what town did he get off at? We might find him, still." I couldn't remember the town. We'd stopped at dozens. I was so chagrined I wanted to crawl through the floor. Instead of laying into me with his tongue Pete said it didn't matter, much, anyhow. Probably Sim Francis, the newspaper fellow, would bring the right sort of pilot for us tomorrow. We'd have all our troubles ended.

"Get to sleep. We ain't licked yet."

I was still asleep when Denny came in to awaken me the next morning, Thursday. I was late for breakfast and Thankful had waited for me. Mrs. Hicks was there, too. She was as talkative as I remembered. She told me she'd lost her chance to sell her furni-

143

ture. If she and her boy had to go by stage, she'd have to ask us not only to pay the fare but the price of sending six hundred pounds of baggage by coach, too. It would come, maybe, to an extra forty or fifty dollars. She was pleasant enough but she knew her rights and was firm.

I was too drained by all our misfortunes to bother much with one more straw on our backs. I answered we'd do whatever was judged fair, considering the circumstances, and turned to Thankful. In a low voice I began telling her what I'd told Pete last night. I was much too intent with Thankful to hear anyone enter our cabin's common room until somebody at my left said, good and loud, "Wal, hain't this a joy? I see yore back at las'. Got yore specs too. Are you thievin' critters goin' to git this tub started or are you goin' to square things with Maw?"

"Wash!" exclaimed Mrs. Hicks from the other end of the table. "Washin'ton Hicks. You sit down afore I thump yore head!"

I started up, looking at him. It was the same one who'd shoved me at the Sangamontown tavern and had helped chase me to the wharf and roll me in the mud. The whole shameful mortifying scene flashed in my head again. He was aboard? *Here?* From the way his mother had spoken, I'd assumed she was bringing a child of three or four.

At the sound of his jeering voice, calling us thieves, I felt a furnace being stoked inside me, with pitch thrown on my fires. Having Wash Hicks aboard was the last straw. I'd told myself I'd settle with him if ever I saw him again. Here he was, asking for it; and I reached for my spectacles, to place them somewhere in safety before going at him. I felt a kind of wild delight.

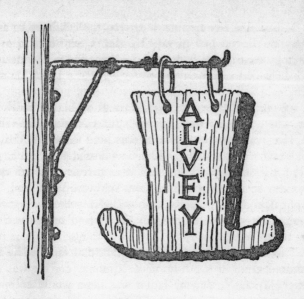

It was a shock to have Thankful grab my arm and hear her cry indignantly, "Shame on you, Horace Owens. You're bigger than he is. He's a passenger, too!"

I'd have thought she would have been on my side.

I had to stick my spectacles back on to see her face. She was blazing angry and that was perfectly bewildering. Next, Wash jeered, "Yay, that's right. Shore, I'm a passenger of this tub. Yay. Horace. I'm 'shamed of you."

He'd lost two of his front teeth and sort of spluttered and I suppose it was comical, hearing him. It stung me to the quick, though, seeing Thankful beginning to grin. All at once I recollected I'd signed his mother's name, *Mrs. Percy Washington Hicks* on the receipt I'd given her. There's only one name worse than mine and that's Percy. If I do say so, it was pure inspiration on my part.

As cool as could be, I said, "Why, Percy, if you don't like this tub I'll give your mother her money back and two dollars, extra, to get you off before we use you for kindling in the furnace."

It did my liver good to see how that name, Percy, jounced him. He yelled back it was a lie; his name wasn't Percy. But he gave himself clean away. I don't know what next would have happened if Pete hadn't shoved head, whiskers, and pipe in to say, worried, "Horace, Bogue's here again with something to tell us."

For the time being I put aside the fact of Wash Hicks being

145

aboard and spoiling for trouble. I entered the cabin parlor to hear what Captain Bogue had to say. He didn't take long. He began by claiming it wasn't his fault rains had stopped early. He told us he'd driven west to New Salem, yesterday. He said not more than fourteen inches of water was above the dam, not enough by six inches, for our hull to scrape over. Pete growled, "A bar'l of gunpowder will open that dam for us." But Captain Bogue he just smiled. That was something else he was here to explain. Mr. Cameron, half owner of the dam, had been against steamer traffic on the river from the start. We'd find armed men ready to stop us if we tried to blow up any part of that dam. We were stuck here.

Captain Bogue was prepared to buy the steamboat. We might as well realize we were stuck fast and prepare to settle for the best we could get. He was ready to pay us five thousand dollars in legal tender. That and the twenty-five hundred he'd already paid, seventy-five hundred in all, was a tidy piece of money and he was certain my father, Mr. Owens, if my father was here, would accept. Pete gave a kind of jump. "That's a lie. Bogue, you rigged this! You got Pollock to scamp off."

"Prove it, sir. My offer remains good till Monday. Good day . . ."

Pete let him walk out, slammed the door, flung down his hat and stomped on it with his peg leg. By and by he quieted down enough to listen to me. I asked—couldn't this be what Bogue had schemed all along? Suppose he knew the Sangamon wasn't navigable south of Salt Fork except for a few weeks of the spring rise? He'd seen his opportunity to get the *Talisman* cheap. He'd taken it. Last Christmas, from a man riding overland to Cincinnati, couldn't he have heard of Mr. Walker's death in St. Louis before Father had by packet? Yes, and couldn't he have paid Diggon to lie about that steam gauge. By losing his works, Father had been desperate enough for cash to charter the *Talisman*. Next, Captain Bogue had to get rid of Father—so Father wouldn't be on the voyage to order the *Talisman* to turn back when he saw the condition of the river east of New Salem.

"Horace, yes, he might have. I just don't know."

"Who else could it be?"

"Pollock perhaps."

"*Pollock?*"

"It's been coming slow but steady in my mind. I've seen him before. I know he dyed his hair black. What if his hair was *white*— naturally white at an early age? There used to be a Mississippi River

146

pilot I met once, years back. His name was Whitey Morgan. *He* turned into a wrecker, joining the Wilson gang at Cave-in Rock, on the Ohio. When the Wilson gang was cleaned out, Whitey Morgan vanished. Nobody ever's seen him since. I should have thought of it sooner, but I didn't. I kept thinking Clem Diggon was the danger to us. Suppose Pollock is Whitey Morgan, older, thinner, his face changed by that droopy eye he might've cut in some fight? *He* was in St. Louis, wasn't he? He'd known of the death of that man who'd promised your paw to buy the *Talisman*. *He* could've dickered with Clem. *He* could've talked Bogue to hiring him as pilot. Maybe Bogue ain't even all the way in it. If it's Pollock who's pulling the strings, arranging through Bogue to grab hold of this steamer, I say this. If that newspaperman can't locate even a second-rate pilot for us today, let's put Thankful, her woman, and the Hickses on a stage—pay whatever it costs—don't get held up by an argument—and we'll take the *Talisman* as far as we can get her by ourselves. The way the river's lowering, tomorrow's the last day we got any chance."

"What about the New Salem dam?"

"Can't you see Bogue's bluffing? If we have to blow up part of that dam, we'll pay costs to have it rebuilt. It's not the dam—it's Pigeon Shoals and the narrows that worry me. In another forty hours the river'll be so low even an experienced pilot couldn't walk us through. If I have to tackle the job, I say—start this afternoon. I won't promise nothing. I may land us on the shoals so hard nothing'll get us loose 'cepting gunpowder. You're here, acting for your paw. You say."

I caught sight of my face in the gilt mirror on the wall. It was so strained and clenched together that for a second I didn't know it. What Pete had said about Pollock was just beginning to filter through to me.

I remembered when Captain Bogue had pointed out Cave-in Rock and Hurricane Island to me, on our way down the Ohio. If Pete was right and Pollock was Whitey Morgan, I could see everything having happened to us gradually forming into an awful and terrifying scheme. I'd rather we wrecked the *Talisman* ourselves, trying to get away, than to cringe and have it fall into the hands of someone like a Whitey Morgan, or his agent, for even five thousand dollars. Five thousand dollars!

You could almost see Pollock's hand in that price, too. It was just high enough for people in Springfield to decide Captain Bogue was

offering us a close price, but fair, for a boat hung up here all the rest of the year. I knew how my father would decide. He never in his life had given in to people trying to pressure him. So, that was what I told Pete.

"Turtle," he said, "I hoped you'd say that." He grinned and stuck out his big hand. "Thar."

I felt my eyes open wide. "Sandy told you?"

He nodded. "Now, Turtle's a first-rate handle for a steamboat fellow like you're beginning to be. I tell you what. If we get safe to St. Louis you can teach me how to swim. I never learned."

"I'd like to."

"That's a promise . . ." He looked at his watch. It was nearly noon. "Now—if only that newspaper fellow keeps his promise and finds us a pilot. We'll give him two more hours. And"—he warned—"keep it between me and you what I said on Pollock, will you? If Pollock's the wrecker, we might be laughed at trying to prove it. It would just warn Pollock we had more on him than he knows. Lie low. Don't show our hand till we get the best chance."

We waited. The publisher of the *Sangamon Journal* didn't arrive. Pete gave him two more hours. He and Sandy kept themselves busy in the engine room. For nothing else to do, I brought out the green leather book of Burns's poetry, hoping I'd find something with a rousing enough lilt to take my mind off my worries.

Maybe my eyes weren't very good but I'd always had a sharp ear for words and sounds. Perhaps that was why the swing and singing of good rousing poetry had an appeal for me. I *liked* sounds. I liked all the different ways people spoke. Burns was a Scotchman and by now I'd gotten it through my head he hadn't spelled wrong —he'd been trying to spell the way country people spoke in Scotland. To tell the truth it wouldn't surprise me if I'd known it all along and had tried to plague my English master in Philadelphia by asking him why Burns couldn't spell.

I took the book with me to dinner. Thankful wasn't there yet. She hadn't been feeling well and was keeping to her berth. If somebody had run off from me with my money, as that woman had with her, I wouldn't have felt so very gay either. At the other end of the table, sitting with his mother, was Wash Hicks. He got up and looked over my shoulder. I thought to myself, here it comes. It did.

"Whut's thet?"

"Can't you read?"

"Shore I c'n read. It's a po'm, hain't it? Why, thet's the jolliest thing yet! You read po'ms. Only girls reads po'ms."

"Wash!" his mother called sharply.

Well, nothing happened. His mother marched him away. We didn't settle anything right then and there but I lost my interest in that poetry. I began thinking of what I'd like to do with Wash Hicks. I remembered that preacher, Parson Cartwright, who'd spoken of demons sitting invisibly on your shoulder, back at Beardstown; and if there was such a thing, I guess a demon began whispering to me right then.

"You can't fight him square," it seemed to whisper. "He'd bust your specs. Think of something else. What? Pick up a chair. Lay it across his head. That might do. No? What *is* there?" It was like that. I went on deck and saw Aunty Phoebee bringing a tray of empty plates from Thankful's stateroom and asked how Thankful was.

"Bettah, Mist' Owens. She'll be perkin' up soon."

So I joined Pete on the wharf and saw he was sighting toward a buggy, drawn by a bay and a pure white, approaching us. He said excitedly, "I believe it's that newspaperman. But he's brought two fellows with him."

After we tied the horses I recognized one of the men and stared. It was the same short-legged man who'd ridden with me on the mail coach. Mr. Francis introduced him as Rowan Herndon and looked at me, amused. "Herndon and you've already met, I hear. I had trouble persuading him to come and talk to you fellows. You didn't seem to want a ferry pilot."

But Pete spoke up, quick, shaking Mr. Herndon's hand. "When young Owens talked to you he didn't know quite how hard up we were for a pilot. If you've been in charge of the Shawnee steam ferry, that suits me. If you'll accept the job, young Owens can do the sounding for you in our yawl. He's the best we can offer but he was with Bogue and Pollock when they sounded."

"Well—" Mr. Herndon answered in his slow fashion, "I—don't—yet—know. I'm—rusty—in—a—wheel—house. Can—I—see—your—boat?"

"See everything we've got. Welcome to. I'll show you now."

I'd noticed Pete had been shifting to his one good leg and back to his peg leg while waiting for Mr. Herndon to finish. Hearing Mr. Herndon was like waiting on a cold morning and watching

your hot cakes cool while someone tries to pour molasses from a bottle with a small spout. I'd almost forgotten the third man who'd arrived in the buggy. Mr. Francis introduced him as Denton Offut, saying he'd come along for the ride to see our steamer.

Mr. Offut appeared considerably older than the other two. But he had a kind of guileless, candid, hopeful face which put you in mind of a boy half your own age, even if his hair was shading into iron gray. And while his speech was much more countrified than the newspaper publisher's, and a cut broader than Mr. Herndon's, he was one of those men with the sort of drawling, honey voices that causes stray dogs to come following behind and stray horses and, probably, sometimes horses not too long strayed. I might as well add that Mr. Offut had a strong smell about him that afternoon. It wasn't entirely a horsy smell, though it was a fair guess that he no doubt enjoyed a good horse race as well as any of the taverns he might have been visiting recently. He looked all around the lower deck, wagging his gray-haired, oddly young-looking head.

"Say, it's some steamboat, hain't she, gents? I never expected seein' one this year, though. We been waitin' for the state leg'slature t' vote funds for improvin' the San Gammaw for steamer traffic."

"Mr. Offut—" Pete removed his pipe. "If we'd known your river couldn't hold its rise past March, you'd never seen us this year or any other. Bogue stole a march on us."

Mr. Francis gave a birdlike hop of protest. "Now, now. Vince Bogue means well enough. He's a good advertiser in my paper, too." There followed a short uncomfortable silence you could feel. He looked at Mr. Herndon, who was contemplating our boiler. "Well, Row?"

"Small—boiler—I'd—say—" Mr. Herndon smiled that slowpoky smile and added, "But—maybe—I'm—sorter—behind—times?"

You couldn't help liking a man like that. Pete stepped in. He explained why we used a small, high-pressure boiler. He went on to show Mr. Herndon Father's grasshopper poles, telling of their purpose. We all trooped aft, Mr. Herndon listening and watching while Pete described how the winch was used, praised our engine, and called Sandy to help him raise and lower the stern wheel in a demonstration. Mr. Herndon looked impressed but he never said a word. I began to feel prickles all over my skin. It was like having a sudden case of hives.

Finally, Pete said hoarsely, "Any man who's had the wheel of the Shawnee steam ferry could spin this little steamer round like

a top. If you'll help take the *Talisman* out of this river, young Owens and me'll offer you a hundred dollars. How's that?"

"Too—much. It's—jes'—that—I—don't know—this—river. I'd like—t' accept—but I'd—pile—your—boat—on the—banks—'less—I—had—someone—'long—with—more experience—of—the—San Gammaw. I'd —recommend—Abe—Linkern—as—a—skillful—assistant—Mr. Wilmot. He's—flatboated—this—river. But—he—hain't—avail'ble. He's—gone—with—the Clary—Grove—boys—to fight—the Injuns—"

"Hold on, Herndon." Denton Offut stepped forward. "Linkern hain't gone ter war yet. You been away, buyin' flax seed. You hain't heard the news. Gen'ral Whiteside won't be ready fer Linkern's volunteer company fer two weeks. I come ter town with Abe this mornin'. He was goin' ter canvass fer votes fer the 'lection next fall w'ile I seed Bogue ter ask if I could git my goods an' pay next month. Bogue—" He laughed, unembarrassed, and didn't say whatever Captain Bogue had told him. Now I remembered we'd carried a small shipment of goods for a Denton Offut in New Salem.

"But, looky here. Abe'll help. Don't I know him? Who hired him ter take a flatboat ter New Orleans when I fust seed him a year an' a half ago at John Hanks's, in Coles County? Me. Who got him ter move ter New Salem an' run my store? Me. Since, hain't I told people time an' agin we'd soon hev a reg'lar steamboat runnin' up an' down the San Gammaw with Abe as her cappen? The boat would run the y'ar round, too, in all weather, hevin' rollers fer shoals an' dams, runners fer the ice. By thunder, with Linkern in charge she'd hev to go! Go git Linkern now. Bring him here before he gits away an' rides back to New Salem!"

Mr. Herndon began, "If—Abe—is—avail'ble—"

But this time no one waited for him to finish. Hastily, Mr. Francis asked, "Offut, where'd we find Lincoln now?"

"Why, he said he'd stop in at Alvey's hat store last thing before leavin' town."

Mr. Francis picked up his plug hat. "Herndon, you stay here. Let Mr. Wilmot continue acquainting you with the boat. I'll whip my buggy in and fetch Abe if he's still there."

"If you'll unhitch one of your horses," Pete said, "young Owens, here, can ride your horse in quicker than by any buggy."

"He doesn't know Abe, does he?"

My heart began pounding so hard I was afraid it would get lodged in my throat when I spoke. "Yes, I know Mr. Lincoln. I've seen him."

We ran across the gangplank.

Helped by Pete, Mr. Francis had his big bay unhitched from the buggy inside of three minutes. I looked around. Wash Hicks was watching us with Thankful, Mrs. Hicks, and Aunty Phoebee looking down at us in wonderment from the second deck. Wash asked, "Whar you goin' on that hoss, Hoe-race?"

Mr. Francis didn't even appear to notice him. He told me, "You'll find Alvey's hat store directly across from the post office. You can't miss Abe. He'll be the tallest man you'll see." He tossed me the reins and gave the horse a whack with the flat of his hand.

That big bay sprung like a thunderbolt toward town, with me on it, riding bareback, gripping my knees for dear life. If Mr. Lincoln had left Springfield, I told myself, I'd ride west in the direction of New Salem, by the river road. I was dead certain I'd recognize him at sight. Besides, hadn't the newspaper publisher assured me that Lincoln would be the tallest man I'd see?

Alvey's store was across from the post office where Mr. Francis had assured me I'd find it. I tied the bay to the nearest hitching post, one in front of a barbershop with a brown-colored man visible through the window shaving somebody sitting on a stool; and I hurried as fast as I could walk, trying to keep myself from running to the hat store. I needn't have rushed. Only two people were inside. One couldn't be anyone else but Lincoln. The other was a spade-jawed man behind the counter who I learned quick enough was Mr. Alvey, the store's owner. I cleared my throat. I said, "Excuse me—"

Both were too busy, Lincoln talking politics, Mr. Alvey listening, to pay attention to me. So I had to wait a minute or so. How well I recall my first sight of Lincoln at close hand! He was so tall and thin and awkward and ungainly he reminded me of one of those sand cranes I'd seen along the Illinois River. I know, now, I saw him about at his worst in the store. I'd previously heard he was planning to run for the state legislature if he got back from the Indian war.

At the time, though, I hadn't learned how much it always cost him to ask a favor from anyone, even a vote. All I knew, after I rushed in and had to wait, was that he seemed to be laboring hard to express himself. I noticed he was carefully saying, for example, "have" instead of "hev," and trying to pronounce every word correctly as if someone with more education than you usually found in this part of the West had taken hold of him and attempted to give

153

him some proper instruction. But he was nervous. His voice sounded as shrill as any of the cranes' who'd cawed at the *Talisman* on the Illinois.

From that one previous glimpse I'd had of him, I had thought his hair was Indian black. When I saw him close enough to touch him, the blackness had the faintest glints of red in it, as if a fox's tail had lightly brushed the coarse black hair to leave a trace of another color in it. He was inclining forward, toward the counter, as he spoke, but not touching the counter. His legs extended so far to the floor from his body I saw his old tow-linen pantaloons lacked by an inch of meeting the tops of his darning-wool socks, exposing sharp shinbones. He was so thin through the chest he looked stoop shouldered.

As he bent down from his height to speak to the storekeeper, he placed his hands behind him, the back of his left hand in the palm of his right, thumb and fingers of his right hand clasped around the left arm at the bony wrist.

I didn't have to wait more than a couple of minutes. I'd expected him to go on longer; but he ended abruptly by saying, "That is that, Mr. Alvey. My politics are short and sweet—like the old woman's dance. I am in favor of a national bank. I am in favor of an internal improvement system, and a high protective tar'f—" instantly he corrected himself—"tar-*iff*. These are my sentiments and political principles. Ef you care to vote for me I shall be thankful." He paused. "If not, it will be all the same." He stopped.

How was that for asking a man to give you his vote? In Philadelphia I'd heard politicians appealing to my uncle and they could bring tears to your eyes. For all his talk of sentiments and political principles, I saw Lincoln didn't know the first thing about running for office. You had to act like you cared. You didn't tell a man it was all the same to you whether or not he gave you his vote. It was no surprise to me when the storekeeper turned Lincoln down. Mr. Alvey shook his head.

"Abe, yore a goodhearted feller. I admire yore heart. But you hain't got the head ter be 'lected dog catcher."

Well, it was blunt and cruel. I was watching Lincoln. For a second, maybe, he had a dull look to him as if all the light inside him had been extinguished. You could have heard a pin drop. He began moving, but awfully slow. He was so loose and leathery, all of him seemed to work slowly as if he needed oiling. But he was lifting up his head. The shriveled, woebegone look had vanished.

154

His mouth was stretching in a smile so wide you'd have thought a cartwheel could have slipped in it.

He picked up his old straw hat from the counter. He gave a laugh which reminded me exactly of one of those shrill piping cries I'd heard the sand cranes give. He dropped his careful, elevated style. As easy as slipping into an old shoe he slipped into the broadest possible sort of country talk:

"Alvey, I hev ter admire yore nat'ral candor. But you hain't got the manners, by jings! ter vote fur dog catcher!"

Mr. Alvey chuckled. Before I knew it, Lincoln's long legs had carried him past me out of the store. In my ear Mr. Alvey was asking me if I wanted to see some fine new hats. I shook my head, and cut for it to the street. "Mr. Lincoln, can I see you for a minute?"

He seemed to go on momentum a few steps before coming to a stop. He turned, wiry, sinewy, rawboned, wearing a linsey-wool shirt under a clawhammer coat that looked new but was short in the sleeves and tail. Despite the changeable March weather he had that old straw hat on his head, as if it was summertime. His gray eyes studied me. I expect they must have seen I was dead serious and in trouble.

"I've been dabblin' again in politics an' neglectin' my business as usual. I'm a trifle short of time. But I never yet seed when I couldn't spare a minute, though."

He spoke to me betwixt and between his high elevated political style and the broad countrified style he'd used later on the store-keeper after failing to obtain a vote. Afterwards, too, with me, he was always shifting up and down, sometimes broad, sometimes not. Most people get set in one fashion of speaking and stay put. He didn't. I began to wonder—and I wondered more. Later I learned why he didn't stay put. It was deliberate, not accidental. He was trying to improve his way of talking, mainly by reading books . . .

Well, I tried to tell him everything in a minute—couldn't, of course, and ran out of wind. He suggested we cross the street and warm a bench in the courtyard while I chalked a fresh start. As he walked beside me his long arms and enormous hands swung down by his thighs. I saw he walked with an even tread, inner sides of his feet parallel, not outwards or duck fashion, as so many people do who walk hard city streets most of their lives. But where most people have a kind of springiness or jounciness, some more than others, like Captain Bogue, Lincoln put the whole foot flat down on the road, all at once, not landing on the heel, and he lifted his foot

all at once, not rising from the toe, so he had no spring to his stride. I noticed another thing: When he sat down on the bench beside me his head didn't come much more than an inch taller than mine. It was his legs that were so uncommon long. They had carried his head at least half a foot above mine when we'd crossed the road together.

I began explaining to him in a hurry because I was in a hurry. I knew Pete and Mr. Herndon would be waiting for me to bring him to the boat. But he wasn't a good listener. He wasn't anything like Mr. Herndon had been. He'd ask questions. When you tried to rush through something, he'd stop you.

How much water did the boat draw? Two feet? Was I certain? Well, I hadn't looked. I *thought* it was two feet. It might be two feet and a couple of inches. How did I know Bogue had lied? Had Bogue made any written promises? No. Why hadn't we approached our pilot before he'd married and gone off? Well, we thought Bogue had. But we hadn't asked Bogue? Well, no, we hadn't. We had *thought* . . .

It went on like that for perhaps twenty or thirty minutes. It seemed to me his questions weren't important. I was beginning to sizzle. I finished in one long stretch, to keep him from interrupting. I filled my lungs and said, "If we don't get the *Talisman* to St. Louis by the fifteenth, my father'll be ruined."

"What's his name?"

"Allison J. Owens."

"What's the J for?"

"Jim. James."

"I don't know him. Yours?"

"Horace," I said, by now not caring. "Horace Owens."

"Warmish day, hain't it?"

It wasn't a warmish day and I knew it and he knew it. He was smiling at me, a little. I said, "Mr. Herndon won't pilot us unless you join with us. He doesn't know the river. He told us you did."

"I been on it. Last year I took Dr. Nelson's flatboat all the way through the San Gammaw River. I guess I run that flatboat three miles off and more onto the prairies . . ." He started the process of rising from the bench. He went towering up and up and his voice drawled down, with a thread of laughter in it, "But I always got that flatboat back on the main channel, somehow. Let's go see your steamer an' Herndon. I'm on foot. Hev you a hoss we can ride double?"

156

I nodded and was so rigged by impatience I ran ahead of him, across the street, to unhitch the bay. When I looked back to see what was delaying him, he'd stopped to speak to a man driving two oxen. The driver said, "Abe, I heared yore organizin' a comp'ny of volunteers?"

"We leave New Salem two weeks from now. You mou't look me up, Bap, ef you decide to j'ine. Say, how's that red rooster of yours doin'?"

It was infuriating, having to wait for him. Red rooster? Who cared? What would Father do if the *Talisman* got hung up here the rest of the year? I heard the driver answering, "That rooster? The little cuss is great on dress p'rade in the barnyard an' hain't wo'th a tinker's nail agin hawks. Tawl!" he spoke to his two big oxen. "Taw. Taw on!"

Lincoln crossed the street with that same steady, careful, even stride. "You must put up with me, Owens," he said, speaking as one man to another, not as most would to somebody like me with still considerable distance to travel before I could reckon myself full grown. "I'm not neglectin' your business but I must hev time to think it out in my mind. Here. Hop!" He took my arm in one hand, bridle in the other—the next second I had the sensation of flying. I must have weighed a hundred fifty pounds that March afternoon. Lincoln hoisted with one hand, setting me square on the broad back of that bay. It was as if a hickory tree had reached down one of its branches to send me flying upwards to the back of the horse. One hundred fifty pounds lifted by a single sweep of arm and hand! No man was ever that strong. There had to be a trick to it, somewhere.

I looked at him. But he wasn't looking at me. "Well, Flory," he said, sounding pleased.

The door of the barbershop had opened and a thin little brown-faced man stepped out, acting as if he wasn't entirely certain Lincoln would bother with him until Lincoln let go of the horse and turned to him. I saw the barber was a Negro and that was a surprise. You wouldn't in those days have expected Lincoln or any white man to lose time to greet a Negro even if, as I suspected, the barber was a freed man. The brown-faced barber didn't speak like any of our roustabouts, either; he had a high, almost singsong voice, as he said, "Mr. Linkern, I wanted you to have a look at a po-em I jes' writ. I'm goin' inter the clothes-cleanin' bus'ness, too, an' writ

this to run as a bus'ness announcement in the *Journal*. Kin you look at it?"

"Why not?" Lincoln said. And he glanced at the sheet of paper the brown little barber had anxiously given him. Next he said seriously, "Flory, now that ought t' do the job good," handing me the sheet of paper to read as if as a matter of course I ought to be interested, too. You could read the doggerel in a single snatch of the eye:

> *I renovates old clothes,*
> *And gives 'em sich a glossy hue,*
> *That you'd believe, almost,*
> *I make 'em all quite fresh and new;*
> *The chin I scrapes, as well you know,*
> *And cuts the hair as I us'd to do.*

Without a word I passed the paper back to Lincoln, who said, "Some po'm, hain't it, Owens?"

I answered, "Some poem, yes." What else could I have answered. Somehow it sounded wrong, though, even to me.

Lincoln still paused. I was so snarled by my anxiety for us to get back to the *Talisman* that if Lincoln paused to give me a small lesson on something, say on being too curt in front of someone I considered below me, at least the lesson didn't take until long afterwards.

With increasing impatience I heard him say, "Owens, Mr. Fleurville comes from Haiti. He had to l'arn our language and grammar which is more'n sometimes I figger I've yet done. I even hed to ask him whur Haiti was. Never knowed till he told me, did I, Flory?" He gave the poem back to the barber and flung his legs over the bay.

Fleurville grasped at the horse's bridle. "Now, Mr. Linkern, don't say sich things before gen'mum you're with. You was jes' jokin'. You knowed whar Haiti was. Sure, you did." Then he asked hastily, "You liked my po'm?"

"Hev Francis run it like it is in his newspaper with no changes."

"I'll do jes' that. Thank you. Say, that's a new coat you got?"

" 'Pears so. Flory, we're kinder in a hurry."

Kinder in a hurry? I liked that. Oh, my, how I liked that! You'd have thought the barber was more important than what became of the *Talisman*. But the barber had released the bridle. He stepped back.

"Mr. Linkern," he called. "Hain't thet coat jes' a mite too short fur you?"

"Yes, perhaps so. But it will be long enough, Flory, before I get another." He clapped his legs against the bay's ribs. Off we jogged on Adams Street and I heard that brown little barber laughing behind us.

I didn't even smile. I remembered Slicky Bill Green telling us that he'd never "seed" a real clown but "Abe Linkern" would make one. I'd been present at the store when Lincoln had tried to get Mr. Alvey to vote for him. Failing, he'd joked it off. He'd had some sort of joke with that driver of the oxen about a red rooster, but I hadn't understood it. He'd joked with the barber. All of it didn't lay very easy with me. He knew his friends were waiting for him at the boat. He knew how urgent and important it was for us to get something settled. He'd delayed and loafed and slouched, holding up my explanation by all sorts of questions.

My doubts about him increased as we jogged those two miles north on the mill road toward Bogue's mill and Portland Landing. I didn't say anything. Neither did he until we were almost there. He turned his leathery jaw against his shoulder to sight back at me. In the slant of hard March sunlight I could see the mole on his right cheek and a scar above one eye. I remembered it was Captain Bogue who'd told me that that scar was there. Four or five years ago Lincoln had taken a broadhorn down the Ohio and Mississippi, had got in a fight with thieves on the sugar coast, had been struck over one eye, leaving a small scar for life.

"Owens—" he began.

I waited. He'd had time to think over all I had told him about our predicament. After all, Herndon had claimed that Lincoln knew the Sangamon River. Perhaps by now Lincoln *had* found a solution of how we could get back through it to the Illinois despite the low water!

"I hev been thinkin', some. I b'lieve it's bound to rain in the next few days. What do you think?"

What did *I* think? I felt myself slump.

"Rain?" I said dully.

"I smell rain off some'eres, Owens. It takes a big nose to smell rain fur off. I hev got a bigger nose an' c'n smell fu'ther off than most."

I had been expecting him to say something important in connection with the *Talisman,* not to joke about the weather! *Rain?*

159

The sky was clear of clouds. It had a bright gauzy blueness with a suggestion of coldness high above the chilly light falling on us as if, if anything, the weather might backtrack a few notches and snow later on. I felt chilled to the bone after hearing Lincoln make that carefree, reckless, joking remark about his big nose. I saw he hadn't even been *thinking* about our steamboat.

They were all still waiting for us at the boat.

I expect, all told, for nearly two hours, until dusk anyway, Lincoln went over that steamboat of ours like you'd go over a horse with a currycomb. The minute he settled down to business, he changed. It wasn't the same man. He was silent, abstracted, his expression looked dull if you could say there was an expression on his face; and the only time he spoke was when he had a question to ask. Then he wasn't polite about it. He'd scarcely wait for Pete or Sandy—or me—to give him the full answer. The only time he came back into something like that other easy slouchy self was, at first, the first time around the deck, when he saw Mrs. Hicks and Thankful on the passenger deck.

"Howdy, Mrs. Hicks," he said, stopping, but never remembering to lift that old shackly straw hat of his to her. "Hannah Armstrong

told me you'd decided t' go by river but I didn't somehow hev a chance to drop your way in time t' say good-by."

"Abe—" she asked, and I saw all the worry and anxiety come out in her broad strong face as it lifted up to Lincoln's. She'd successfully hidden her anxiety from us, squatting here like a big hen, you might say, on an egg, defying us to remove her. "Abe," she asked, "are you agoin' ter show these steamboat fellers how ter git their boat down the San Gammaw?"

I waited, wanting to know probably even more urgently than Mrs. Hicks did what he was privately deciding about our chances.

"Why, that reminds me, Mrs. Hicks," he drawled, his face lighting up all of a sudden as if just struck by the thought, "when somebody at Mentor Graham's school up thar on New Salem hill asked ef he wasn't goin' t' show how Christopher Columbus had done with thet egg, Graham replied, 'Ef each child amongst you'll bring an egg ter school temorrer I will be pleased ter show how Christopher Columbus made the egg stand on end—' An' then Graham added, 'Those who cannot bring an egg will kindly bring a piece of ham.' Wal, ef these steamboat fellows hain't got an egg, Mrs. Hicks, mebbe they kin give me a small slice of ham t' show 'em how et's done."

I expected her to answer something sharp, because he'd given her no kind of reply to her question at all—but she didn't.

"You'll try ter help?" she asked.

"Now, Mrs. Hicks, suppose you jes' let me worry."

"All right, Abe . . ." She turned to where Thankful was watching him and introduced her.

"Howdeedo, miss," he said, rather curt.

I'd guess he wasn't as easy with strange young women as he was with men of all sorts, new or old. He was going on, but Mrs. Hicks blocked his way. "Abe, don't this Blair child put you in mind strong of somebody? She hain't so old, yet, as Ann Rutledge, but she's got Ann's same hair, only Ann's is longer, an' the same colorin'."

I didn't know who Ann Rutledge was, didn't care, and saw Thankful was being badly embarrassed. Lincoln muttered something I didn't hear, shied off the subject, and for once appeared to be in a hurry to get on to his job. But right then Wash Hicks came up from the forward stairs, saw him, and hollered, "Mr. Linkern!" and ran aft to us, carrying a fishing pole. Wash had been east of wharf, fishing. I'd seen him. But how he had expected to catch any catfish while sitting back at least four feet from the edge of the wharf, his

feet plowed up before him like he expected the wharf to crumple under him, I hadn't known.

He asked Lincoln to come with him and help him catch some fish. He spoke to Lincoln like he'd known him for some considerable time. He was demanding and almost impudent, hanging at his sleeve, not letting go, so it was a surprise to hear him keep saying, "Mr. Linkern, won't you—won't you?" and not just plain "Abe," or, even, "Linkern."

Lincoln was patient but he was in a hurry. Wash still pestered at him, the rest of us acting like we all had fiddles out of tune because of the delay.

Mrs. Hicks said, "Wash! Wash Hicks! Abe, I don't know what ter do with thet boy since his paw passed on!"

Then Lincoln said, "*I* know what t'do with him—*drown* him," and quick as a cat picked up Wash by the arm, same as he'd done to me. Wash weighed ten pounds less, I'd say, than me. This time I watched how it was done. If there was a trick, I missed it.

Lincoln's big hand just lifted Wash up over the railing and hung him above the water—and while it had started out as a joke, you knew he wouldn't drop Wash, it didn't end that way. Wash started clawing and screeching and he acted like he was having convulsions.

Lincoln looked startled. He set him down gently, on the deck; and Wash streaked aft to his stateroom and slammed the door. Lincoln was disturbed.

Mrs. Hicks said, "I should hev told you, Abe. Wash is scared witless of the water since his paw drowned. But don't bother 'bout him. It served him good. Next time, mebbe he'll larn not to plague a body."

But that didn't satisfy Lincoln. He stepped inside Wash's stateroom and must have spoken to him. What he said to Wash, none of us heard. He opened the door again, came out, shut it, and like nothing had happened, said, "Now, let's see how much water she's drawin' empty . . ."

Even after measuring how much the *Talisman* drew, head and stern, he still wasn't satisfied he'd "larned the boat," as he said. All of us gathered in the parlor. It was a close fit for Lincoln; his head kept rubbing the ceiling. Pete was trying to make a good impression, and to show the boat's hospitality, asked Lincoln what he'd have.

Offut spoke for him. "Abe'll hev water. He won't tech nothin' harder 'cept mebbe Hannah Armstrong's buttermilk."

163

"Nothin' at present," said Lincoln.

I could tell that stumped Pete. In those rough-and-ready days most men weren't too particular about what was offered in the line of hospitality, providing it was offered. It made me wonder if Lincoln could have signed the Washington Society pledge, like my father had. Well, Pete didn't give up easy. He tried again.

"Segar?" he asked.

Everyone else helped themselves from the box Pete offered around—but not Lincoln. He just waited, with nothing at all showing on his yellowish face. I could see Pete thinking as he closed the box of segars. He was going to do his best to be hospitable if it killed him. Finally, he had an inspiration.

"Chaw?"

Again it was Offut who spoke, grinning. "Abe don't take *nothin'* in thet line. He's a curis feller. Hain't you, Abe?"

"Suppose we git down t' bus'ness?" Lincoln asked as if it was us, not him, who'd used up so much time.

He told us this was how he saw things. With Herndon at the wheel, he, Lincoln, believed the two of them might get us safe through Pigeon Creek Shoals although he wouldn't say how fast. It might require a day—might take more. The narrows were where the *Talisman* would get stopped. Only this morning, on his way in to Springfield, he'd walked the whole stretch of narrows on the left bank. The winding, twisting channel through it, he'd guess, still had a "draw" of about seventeen or eighteen inches of water. Tonight it would drop more. No steamboat with a twenty-four inch draw could make it . . .

Well, I saw how pinched Pete's face had got. Sandy Jenks turned away. He hit his fist against the woodwork. It's a wonder his fist didn't punch a hole through the wood. Next to Lincoln, I still think Sandy was the strongest man I ever knew. But Sandy was two inches under Lincoln even if he was broader at the shoulder and beam.

"Now, wait . . ." Lincoln said. "I *think* it's bound to rain soon."

He explained. We'd had an unseasonable dry spell for longer than a week. Rain had to fall. When it did, it ought to come in buckets. I saw now why he'd been so interested in the subject of rain when we had come riding together from Springfield and felt a little ashamed of myself.

If we got buckets of rain, he believed, the river would rise enough to give us the necessary inches of "draw" through the narrows to pass.

164

Pete asked, "What about that dam below the narrows?"

Lincoln said if we had water to carry us through the narrows we'd have enough of a head to push us over the dam, provided we didn't lose time. Pete took a big relieved breath. But Lincoln went on to say he *thought* we'd have rain. He believed he could smell it in the air. But he might be wrong. If he was wrong, we all could see where we'd be. We'd get hung up somewhere between Pigeon Creek Shoals and the narrows, stuck fast for months. It would be worse than being tied to the landing. He didn't want to take on such a job unless we saw the risks and made up our minds ourselves. He looked at Herndon.

"I—agree—with—you—Abe," Herndon said in that slow ponderous way.

I noticed all these men who were obviously close friends of Lincoln called him Abe, although he called them by their last names, even Offut, who was to all intents and purposes his employer. I couldn't quite understand that. It made you think Lincoln was the oldest of them all. At least Offut and the newspaperman were older. Herndon was close to thirty. Lincoln's age was hard to tell. I thought he was under thirty. How far I couldn't decide. While he had a young man's supple body, his face was as sallow and wrinkled as—well, as a monkey's.

Pete told me, "I'm for it. We can't do better than to try."

"All right," I said. I felt that way, too.

It was that simple and commonplace. Yet, somehow, it was one of the most exciting moments of my life. We were going to chance it! Then I remembered we hadn't settled on a price.

Pete didn't try to bargain. He said he'd sent me to find Pollock and we'd been prepared to pay five hundred dollars. It was the first time I saw Lincoln lose his temper. "By jings, Herndon! We hain't here t' rob these fellers!"

We could have obtained Lincoln for ten dollars, which seemed to me the robbing was on the other side. It struck me he didn't have any more sense about money than asking for votes.

But Herndon pointed out he'd have to pay somebody a dollar a day to help his brother tend their store, while he was piloting the *Talisman*. Offut said, "Abe, don't worry about my store. I'll take over. Bill Green and me c'n tend to it. Besides, bus'ness is sorter peterin' out, anyhow."

It was finally decided each would receive forty dollars to take us to the Illinois, conditions permitting. If we got stuck and laid up for

good, Lincoln was all for saying in that case Herndon and he should get nothing. But Pete said, "That ain't my idea of a deal," and it wasn't mine either. "Forty dollars, each, gents, is what we pay—come high water or come nothin'." So that was it. I remember how Lincoln said it would be the biggest sum he'd earned. He told us he had never had forty dollars at one time in his whole life.

They both had to return tonight to pick up their "truck," as Lincoln called it; and Herndon had to arrange for his brother to take over the store. They planned to be here by five tomorrow morning. We were to have steam up and be waiting for them.

To show how sharp Lincoln's eye was for details, he mentioned it didn't look like we had much wood left, even if our boiler was so small. I must have turned crimson. That was my chore. I'd been so occupied going after Pollock I'd forgotten. We had enough for two days, perhaps three, but no more. I'd said I had heard at Sangamontown that a man by the name of Jack Armstrong had wood to sell.

Lincoln nodded. "I know Armstrong. He'll give you good wood, cut to length. S'pose I speak to him t'night. He can meet you with a pile of wood day after t'morrow at Antrim's Landing. It's jes' below Pigeon Shoals."

We agreed.

After the four had gone, crowding into the newspaperman's gig, I asked Pete, "What do you make of Lincoln and Herndon?"

"Why, they're both honest. They'll get us through Pigeon Creek . . ." He sighted up at the darkening sky. A few stars were shining. "I don't smell rain."

By now I wanted to believe in Lincoln, so I said, "Rain *has* to fall soon."

"If Lincoln's smeller is wrong, say good-by to the *Talisman*."

"You won't give up?"

"Me?" he said fiercely. "No, sir. We ain't licked. We'll get through the narrows somehow. You'll see."

I hoped he was right as much as he did. I drew a long breath. "You didn't say anything about your suspicions of Pollock being—that Whitey Morgan?"

He looked uncomfortable. He started banging his pipe on the edge of the rail. One of these days he'd break that pipe at the stem. "I tell you," he admitted. "Mebbe I'm wrong. *We* don't know. We got to have Lincoln and Herndon, haven't we? We got enough troubles, I figger, 'thout giving 'em more. Suppose I'd scared 'em off by saying Whitey Morgan was trying to grab our steamer through

Bogue? No, let's hold back and lie low. If Pollock shows up and I'm certain he's Whitey Morgan or even half certain—why, I'll say it. I'll say it loud," he added, looking so stubborn and fierce it was a little frightening. "Jes' leave Pollock to me. You stay out of it. Hear?"

I nodded. If Pollock was Whitey Morgan, I much preferred to let Pete handle that part of it in his own way and in his own time. All I wanted was to get the *Talisman* safely to St. Louis before the fifteenth . . .

When we informed the crew, gathered on the foredeck, that we had a pilot and an assistant and were leaving early tomorrow morning, you should have been there to hear the cheering. Our roustabouts were as eager as we were to get off. They were ready to jump in and do all they could to help. Things began to move.

Next, Pete and I talked to Mrs. Hicks and Thankful in the parlor. When he finished and I'd backed him up, Thankful said, "Please. I don't want to return by mail coach. I'd rather stay. There can't be any real danger for the boat's passengers. If you get stuck—well, you're stuck, aren't you? But the river's too shallow for us to drown."

"Nobody's going to drown in this river," Pete said, "unless he steps in a sinkhole. Our trouble is there's not enough water for half floating the *Talisman* very far below Bogue's mill, much less than drowning a passenger."

She smiled. "I want to stay. Don't you, Mrs. Hicks?"

"Child, ef Abe Linkern an' Row Herndon is in this thing, me and Wash is in it, too. *I'll* look after you, Thankful. I'll see you git back safe."

Thankful said to me, "Well?" in her sassiest style yet.

"I guess I won't have to write you those four letters now, will I?"

A few minutes before supper I had a chance to speak to Mrs. Hicks on the passenger deck. I asked her how well she knew Lincoln.

"How well do I know him?" she asked me. "Ever since Linkern cum here, two years, nearly, I've knowed him. Before my man drowned we lived at Clary Grove, a piece of timber a mile or so south of New Salem. Jack an' Hannah Armstrong live thar, too. We all heared of Abe soon's he got here 'cause Jack Armstrong is—was the best rassler in the hull country. Soon's Abe cum, why, thet boomer, Mr. Offut, bragged up his new man. So he bet ten dollars Abe could throw Jack an' the two of 'em went at each other an' Abe, he did throw Jack, fair an' square. Then Jack an' Abe got good

friends. Jack an' Abe an' another Jack—Jack Kelso—you seed one, you saw all three.

"Why, often I've seed Abe at the Armstrongs'. Many's the time. Abe would go thar, drink milk, eat mush, corn bread an' butter, bring Duff, their little boy, candy, an' rock the cradle while Hannah got him somethin' ter eat. She'd make his shirts, an' he'd tell stories, joke people at the Armstrong parties, nurse babies—do anything ter accommodate you. After my man's funeral, my boy, Wash, tuk on so terrible, Abe was the one thet ca'med him down. They went huntin' together. No, you can't find a better man than Abe Linkern to work with Row Herndon. Abe's kinder lazy but he'll dig in when he hez to an' he'll git others ter work their bones off an' w'ile Row Herndon hain't so sociable as Abe, he's steady as a rock. I say we can't do better'n stay by the boat. You hev got two good men workin' for you."

For our supper, Denny and the cook did themselves royal proud. You could say it was nearly a celebration. Most all of us ate in the common room this time, including Pete and Sandy. Wash Hicks was there, at the far end of the table. He scowled at me over his plate. For once, though, he remained silent. Perhaps he was still thinking of the shameful spectacle *he'd* made of himself this afternoon, screeching and clawing when he'd thought he was going to be dropped into the river. He left the table as soon as he'd finished eating.

I had time to start pondering again on how I'd settle with him. I could almost *feel* something hunching itself on my shoulder and whispering mighty soft in my ear, "Don't you see? That's what to do. You haven't a chance with him on land. Get him edged toward the water, though. *Thar's* the thing. Give him a scare ter last . . ."

Our supper broke up in a hurry when Smoky entered, wiping his black hands on his pantaloons, apologizing for coming to the passenger deck, and saying Captain Bogue and somebody else was waiting to see Mr. Wilmot. I jumped up, following after Pete. I let all thoughts of settling with Wash Hicks submerge somewhere deep in the back of my head. I asked myself, alarmed, why was Bogue here tonight? Had he found a means to prevent us from sailing at the last minute?

He was waiting on the wharf with a huge man wearing good linen clothes, the light from our iron baskets illuminating them both, redly. "What brings you here tonight, Bogue?" Pete asked. Hastily,

Bogue explained that the man with him was Mr. Bowling Green, justice of peace of New Salem. Justice Green had a big shiny face like a newly split board and he straddled out his legs and he took over from Bogue without seeming to be aware he was doing it. He told us he'd traveled to Springfield to see about an estray horse. He called it "estray," old style, not "stray." He went on to tell us the horse was fifteen hands high, claybank in color, about four years of age, and he'd found it and was hunting for the owner, as if he considered all that important and necessary for us to know. Seeing as how he'd had to come to Springfield, he added, before leaving New Salem Mr. Cameron had asked him to collect a bill for him.

In no way at all, Pete said, "I don't believe we know Mr. Cameron, do we?"

"He's half owner of the dam at New Salem," answered Justice Green, serene yet watchful. Bogue started to say something. But I saw Justice Green reach out and push Bogue back—not hard, almost gentle. Bogue kept silent after that. "Let's see the bill, sir," Pete said.

It amounted to ninety-five dollars for money spent in repairing damages the *Talisman* had done when scraping over the dam last week. Well, Pete was smart enough to see Justice Green was neither for nor against us; and, he said, mild enough, we'd pay.

He sent me to the iron safe in my office, where I'd stored the money Bogue had given us. So we paid the money to Justice Green. He thanked us. That was all there was to it. I suppose Bogue had come along, hoping we'd refuse or that Pete would lose his temper and we'd be in more trouble. Bogue looked so discomfited he climbed into the justice's buggy, never saying a word. Justice Green paused another moment.

"I b'lieve you met my son, didn't you?" We must have appeared puzzled because he laughed. "Up at Salt Fork. He was helpin' with the Clary Grove boys to chop the tree branches away from the river. He likes to call himself 'Slicky Bill.' Watch out for him. My son'll take you in, sure as shootin' . . ."

He drove off with Bogue in the darkness and Pete just stood there a minute or so longer. He said it was hard to believe that that wild young Illinois Sucker at Salt Fork was the son of the justice of peace of New Salem. I agreed. Next, he said, still slow and thoughtful, "Bogue's licked, if you ask me. He never expected us to pay. If Pollock and he did try rigging a scheme to grab this boat, thanks to Herndon and Lincoln we're going to slip away from them."

"I hope," I said.

He looked at me. Then he said, "I hope," too.

Well, the *Talisman* raised her gangplank and backed into the river the next morning a few minutes after six. It was Saturday, the last day of March. We had arrived one week ago. By scamping off, Mr. Pollock had cost us seven days' delay. We now had exactly fifteen days to get to St. Louis. I didn't see the *Talisman* leave because Lincoln and I had been in the yawl for over an hour, laying markers and sounding; and we were around the bend when we heard the *Talisman's* shattering toots—four, all told. It was Herndon in the wheelhouse signaling he had cast off.

I'd forgotten how loud that whistle sounded to someone who hadn't previously heard it. Lincoln was aft, handling the oars. His knees stuck up halfway to his waist. In that greenish morning light he looked like one of those grasshoppers you'd see with their joints sticking up. He jumped at the shattering who-o-o-iee! who-o-o-iee! from our whistle. When you could hear yourself again, he picked up the oars and said, "Some whistle. It's always that loud?"

"Usually."

"With a seven-foot whistle an' a five-foot boiler, I'd think the steamer'd stop every time Herndon pulls the whistle cord."

His face was solemn enough but his eyes had sort of little dancing lights in them. I was beginning to learn when he was teasing you. So I said something in reply. As a joke it was no good; but Lincoln laughed like it was funny. I began to feel better and better about being with him. Later, I even asked him how old he was.

He announced, "Twenty-three years of age. Six feet, four inches high. Two hundred an' twelve pounds on the hoof. No prospects I know of. I am like a piece of driftwood, Owens. Any further partic'lars wanted?"

His face had that dull look again, too, as if he had no sense or spark in him. His reply took me under the ribs. It was as if I'd been brash by inquiring into something of no concern of mine. He had deliberately cut me down. It cast a shade over me.

We worked along for a time, not speaking except when he gave me directions. He had to keep sculling against the current. The *Talisman* crept up two hawser lengths behind us. After that Pete had to reverse our stern wheel to hold the boat off from running us down while we sounded our way down, planting markers. It was hard going for me. My muscles began aching. It must have been even harder for Lincoln, with the task of controlling that heavy yawl

170

against the current but he was like a machine. You could see more and more how powerful he was. He moved slowly—but strongly.

He never once indicated he had noticed he'd set me down hard by his gloomy reply to my question about how old he was. By and by, though, when we had a moment or so of waiting, he started questioning me about all our troubles with Bogue. It was tedious difficult, plunging a sixteen-foot sounding pole to the bottom, going on, repeating the same thing over and over again at Lincoln's directions; and it helped pass the time by talking to him after I lost the prickly sensation he'd given me. Probably I grew too heated when recollecting how Bogue had tried to trim us. I said what I most had against Bogue was his greediness. He'd seen the *Talisman*, liked her, wanted her, and was too greedy to have offered my father a fair price for her back in Cincinnati.

"Greedy?" Again Lincoln rested a moment with the oars. Later, I would see him pause the same way, many times, telling a story and holding your attention while he refreshed himself. "I wouldn't say Bogue's greedy. He reminds me of Squire Kirkpatrick who I hev been havin' some trouble with lately to c'lect pay from. I've heard the squire say, 'I hain't greedy. People are wrong to say I'm greedy 'bout land. I jes' want whut j'ines mine, that's all' . . ." Lincoln took hold of the oars. "Bogue got his mill. He got the wharf joinin' the mill. When your boat tied up at his wharf it was nat'ral for him to want the boat. He can't help it. He jes' wants whatever 'j'ines' his; that's all. He— No, *thet* direction, Owens. Let's try over *thar* a leetle."

Well, we tried. We tried hard. But the river was so low, despite our trying, the *Talisman* shoaled six times before reaching Pigeon Creek Shoals. We didn't enter Pigeon Creek Shoals until four in the afternoon. We had sounded a channel we hoped the *Talisman* might pull through. How wrong we were! She got stuck proper, piled up on sand—not mud, mind you, but sand; hard sand. The roustabouts were still working on her at ten o'clock that night when Pete told them to knock off; she hadn't budged an inch. Altogether that first day she must have made the grand total of four and a half miles progress. Four and a half miles!

We were still twenty-five miles to New Salem where the river ran north for another fifty or so, to Salt Fork, before going west again toward the Illinois. How long it seemed!

It was a cold dry night. The stars shone like diamonds. No sign of rain. I didn't see how we ever were going to get through Pigeon Creek Shoals, much less the narrows waiting for us on beyond. I

171

almost wished we'd eaten crow and had accepted Bogue's offer of five thousand dollars. At least, with five thousand, plus whatever we could save from the twenty-five hundred locked in the iron safe, my father still could get some sort of fresh start. That money was better than having nothing at all but a steamboat laid up somewhere on the upper Sangamon, rotting, starting at the seams, rusting away through a summer and fall and on into next winter.

I asked myself if we had made a mistake. I lay in the bunk, too tired to sleep. I wished Lincoln hadn't ever told us he smelled rain coming. How could anyone smell rain when there was still nothing in the sky at day but a sun and all the stars came out at night? It must have been another one of his jokes. Pete and I should have known—but we hadn't.

Pretty soon that old wish began hitting at me again, when I was too low in spirits to resist. I wished I was back in Philadelphia. There everything would still be noble and rich for me. I'd still be treated like a boy, with neither Aunt Iz nor Uncle John expecting me to take on a man's job and have a man's responsibilities and worries. In Philadelphia, too, no invisible little demon ever would perch on my shoulder to whisper and whisper about how I could give somebody such a scare it would last him all his life. I was scared, myself, that night about the future. I didn't much want to scare anyone, even Wash Hicks. It didn't appear to me that my father and mother would ever have that great day of rejoicing he had once mentioned.

All I wanted was to stop aching, to get to sleep, and to wake up to the rich easy life I had once known. I slept; but when I woke up we were still stuck on that sandbank.

It was still dark Sunday morning when the screeching of that whistle of ours exploded me off the bunk. I shook myself, and had to remember all over again where I was.

From dawn until a late breakfast the whole boat's crew, twelve of us, the roustabouts, Smoky, even the stewards, every man we had, along with Lincoln and Herndon, all pitched in to dig a channel twenty-five feet wide, one foot *below* shoal bottoms, and two musket lengths long, until the steamboat could walk herself over that hump and flop down into a deeper channel. Here, her grasshopper poles, the winch, and the stern wheel, all combined, once more began mushing her forward again.

Helping to dig that channel was the most killing work I'd ever

173

tackled. At first we were knee deep in water but toward the end the water was rushing waist high around most of us, boiling past, sucking at us. You had to dig down with the shovel to loosen the sand for the current to carry it away and I wasn't much good, because sand and water splattered my glasses. Every ten minutes or so I'd have to lay off and grab hold of the hull and shuck myself up and sit there, tucking my wet legs above the water, and just pant while the heat from the boiler dried me off enough to drop down again.

Because the river was tricky, the roustabouts had roped themselves together even if the water was low. Did I? No, that was too much trouble. When we grazed the next shoal and stuck there, Pete had me investigate, telling me to hang on to a rope he was holding with one hand.

I told Pete not to bother, dropped off, expected to touch mud—and went down into a sinkhole.

Instead of trying to fight the current, at least I had the presence of mind to claw at my spectacles while the water rolled me over and over along the mud and sand bottom. I came up spouting. Smoky hauled me aboard. Pete looked white. He said he was sure I was drowning. He'd kicked off his one boot and had started to strip off coat and shirt to go in after me.

Well, I said brash enough, I'd managed, hadn't I? I had saved my spectacles, which was what counted. I dried off once more in front of the boiler. You always went straight to that boiler as soon as you could. It was the warmest spot on the boat.

By this morning Mrs. Hicks was taking over. You began appreciating that woman the more you saw of her. Later in the morning she collected all our muddy rags—all we could spare—and had them sent off to people she knew at New Salem for a quick scouring. I didn't know where Wash was—didn't care. Probably he'd gone ashore to be with some of his friends there.

After church services people began coming by horse, buggy, and foot, for miles around, gathering on both banks, watching the *Talisman* lumber along, painful slow and awkward—but still moving inch by inch, once we had her grasshopper poles rigged. That single big shoal of hard sand was the only one where we had to dig like beavers for so long; the poles and winch and wheel crawfished most of the rest of the way along the line Lincoln had sounded and we, Lincoln and I, marked. But he said we needed more men if ever again we got stuck.

Pete told him we still had almost all of the twenty-five hundred

dollars from Captain Bogue. If necessary we'd use every cent we had to get out of this infernal river. Well, Lincoln answered he didn't reckon it would cost that much. He could get fellows for us at a dollar a head a day—but not Sunday. He'd have to wait until to-morrow.

It was the most tedious thing in the world. To lurch forward over shoals Pete and Herndon, and all concerned, every time had to go through a whole complicated series of orders and actions with the roustabouts. The grasshopper poles, standing on each side of the boat, acted, you might say, like one of Lincoln's long legs would have done to push him over an obstruction. Each boot-pole was slung forward, dropped, held there, the winch towed in, the whole hundred-some tons of empty boat crept forward inch by inch until the forward end was *lifted* a few inches above mud or sand level—hanging there, actually, in a kind of sling from the two hickory boot-poles on each side.

Meanwhile, at the stern the paddle wheel was crowding with everything it had. We still had enough draw of water in the river to help, the current sloshing under the hull and eating away the shoals. Then there'd be a bigger lurch—the *Talisman* would smash forward from ten inches to sometimes a rod or more, depending on circumstances. Then—it started over again until we struck a stretch of deeper channel.

After Pete saw I could take care of myself in the water, more and more he pulled me off the yawl. He kept me around handy, whenever we were grasshoppering—to go in after loose hawsers, shovels, anything the men dropped, or to dive down if one of the poles got stuck in a sink. That river wasn't exactly ice water. While you were in it and active you could endure it possibly ten or fifteen minutes before turning blue and feeling a numbness. So I was up and down, dripping, shivering, standing before the blazing furnace, and down again—but it was no rougher on me than anyone else.

We stuck to it until dark. That day, I reckoned up, we had gone less than two miles! Lincoln rowed back with a piece of encouraging news. He said he'd sounded the way by himself to Antrim's Landing and beyond. He believed we'd be clear of Pigeon Creek Shoals sometime tomorrow and ready to consider the narrows which were waiting for us. We didn't ask him if he still smelled rain. He didn't say. Right then, to get free of Pigeon Shoals looked good enough for us. Furthermore, we learned after we'd taken on wood at Antrim's Landing he had arranged to have Jack Armstrong join us as an extra

hand. I'd almost forgotten our need for wood and Lincoln's promise, last Friday night, to have wood ready and waiting for us. I was glad he hadn't.

"Armstrong's a reg'lar bull for work," I remember him saying, standing up there before us so long and thin while warming himself by our fire. "Jack'll do what any three other fellers can do, ef we get bogged. You'll see. Jack's a good feller."

I was beginning to learn, too, it was high praise when Lincoln said someone was a good fellow. For all of him seeming so good-natured and—and *easy* with people, he was chary of praising them. He'd laugh. He'd tell his stories. But when he told you somebody was a good "feller," if you didn't know he meant it, all the way, you soon learned.

Before eating grub that night I changed into the last of my dry clothes. Everything else I had was hanging on lines to dry, all along the boiler deck which Mrs. Hicks and Thankful had rigged—or had been packed off in baskets to be washed in New Salem to be brought back sometime late tomorrow. Gradually I had had the impression the whole countryside was aroused with unknown people wanting and hoping to have the *Talisman* get free, and being ready to lend a hand and help in any direction Lincoln or Herndon suggested.

It came over me that the best piece of business Pete and I had done had been to hire those two. I didn't yet know how we'd pass the narrows—but I had more confidence tonight than last night. We'd arrived this far, hadn't we? It might rain tomorrow. Who could say? I'd finished dressing when Wash Hicks opened the door and looked in at me.

"Yay, Horace. You shore 'pear sorter dragged ternight."

I don't know why he got so deep under my skin. I knew he was a passenger. His mother had paid his fare. He didn't have to help us. He wasn't supposed to, for that matter. I *knew* that. But his mother had been pitching in, all day. Thankful was doing anything she could. When Mrs. Hicks didn't need her she'd go forward to the prow, standing, bracing herself on the hurricane deck, to sight forward and holler back to Herndon in the wheelhouse if she sighted any snags. For a girl, she had sharp eyes—no, that's not fair. For anyone, she had about the sharpest eyes, probably, you could find. Five or six times she'd saved us from crawfishing against a snag, singing out, sharp and clear, before any of the hands below, stationed on the boiler deck. But here was Wash Hicks—and he hadn't done a thing to help. All day long except when it was time to have

grub he remained on shore. You hardly ever even saw him except at mealtime.

Well, I turned. It boiled up of a sudden in me, seeing him there, the lanternlight shining on him, with a space of black water separating us from the shadowy trees on the riverbank. I never said a word. Just seeing him laughing at me heated me inside as if a furnace was being stoked faster and faster. I snatched off my spectacles and remembered to shove them on the desk where they wouldn't get smashed.

Then I started toward him, now seeing him in a kind of blur. I wanted to settle it between us. But he laughed. He must have flung the door open just far enough for me to walk square into it, without seeing it. I slammed into the edge of the door. Next—I sat down with the most excruciating pain possible. He ran off. My nose began to swell. I didn't go down for grub. Later, when Pete looked in on me I'd stopped the nosebleed and had had time to wash off my face. I was there, humped over the desk, reading. He said, "What's wrong?"

A month ago, perhaps less, I might have told him. Now it appeared to me that he had all the troubles he needed. In addition, he was trying to save me from being worried about who Pollock really was by taking that problem on his shoulder. During the day I'd seen Pete sighting to the shore, looking at the people gathered there. I knew he was waiting for a glimpse of Pollock. But Pollock—or Bogue—never showed up. So, tonight, I answered it wasn't anything at all. I was too played out, I guessed, and tired to eat.

"That won't do. I'll send Denny up with grub."

So Denny came. I ate and felt better. By and by I heard him return for the empty plates. But it wasn't Denny. It was Thankful. When I opened the door, in the deep shadows I could scarcely see Aunty Phoebee also there, waiting. Wherever Thankful went, you were certain Aunty Phoebee was close behind. Well, I explained my nose to Thankful by telling her I'd bumped it while diving. And she believed me. By now almost all the hands had bruises and welts on them from where they'd been slammed against the hull. A swollen nose wasn't of any account.

However, instead of taking the empty plates away she handed the tray to Aunty Phoebee and looked at me again, while I waited. She hesitated. All at once she said, "I hate having them call you Turtle, Horace."

I hadn't even known until now she heard—or if she had, had much noticed.

She went on, all in a breath. "If you don't like Horace, what's wrong with your middle name? James is nice, isn't it? But you aren't a turtle. Ugh. You wouldn't go crawling underwater to snap at people's legs."

I don't know what made me say what I did, unless it was my nose hurting, and knowing privately in my mind I'd never stand any chance of settling anything with Wash Hicks on dry land. Maybe invisible demons do whisper in your ears, like I'd heard that preacher claiming, back at Beardstown. Anyhow, I said somebody'd soon find I was a turtle. And I mentioned Wash Hicks, by name. Thankful got almost white in that lanternlight.

"You—*wouldn't?*" she whispered.

She marched out, slamming the door, before I could explain all I meant to do if I found the chance to give Wash a scare. I was tired of jigging at his bidding. I didn't see why what I'd said had upset her so much. I thought about it, finally deciding to saunter down to the passengers' common room to see if Thankful was still there with Mrs. Hicks and Aunty Phoebee instead of having turned in for the night. It was still fairly early, around eight in the evening.

I delayed making up my mind too long, though. When I did go on the hurricane deck, Lincoln and Pete came aft with a stranger in tow whom, evidently, they had been showing over our boat. They saw me in the lanternlight from my office, and stopped. Lincoln introduced me to a wiry, sharp-faced man, Jack Kelso. He explained that Kelso had walked down from New Salem this evening to have a look at our famous steamer as if a twenty-five mile walk in the evening was an ordinary stroll.

He nodded toward me, telling his friend, "Jack, young Owens, here, has got a prime eddication. He went t' school in Philadelphy."

I wondered who'd told Lincoln that much about me. Probably it had been Pete, who was looking on, remaining silent, and smoking his old pipe. I looked closer at Lincoln's friend because his name of a sudden fit into a notch in my mind. Mrs. Hicks had said that Jack Kelso and Jack Armstrong were two of Lincoln's closest friends. Kelso wasn't anything like Lincoln or, for that matter, like any of the men in the crowds of Suckers who'd walked along the banks all day, watching our steamer wallow forward from one shoal to the other. He had long hair hanging over his collar, real Injun black hair, I saw, not the black with a fox-red glint that Lincoln had. And I saw he had an old fishing creel slung over a shoulder. And—I

opened my eyes wider. Instead of a pole he was carrying what looked like a fiddle, wrapped in old rags.

Kelso's voice, too, was different. When he spoke it was like hearing wild music from far away. And he was so dark and so slim and so proud in his bearing, somehow he reminded me a little of gypsies who used to camp every spring in Tenny Square, in Philadelphia. "So you hail from Philadelphia, do you, Owens?" he asked. While he spoke "slouchy" enough, you could tell he'd had schooling somewhere.

I said, "I was there only three years, Mr. Kelso." And I asked, you know, to keep conversation moving, the way you do when you've been rushed too fast at someone else—I asked what did he do and where was he from? Those were common enough questions in a new territory. They were the first people asked you.

But Kelso didn't give a common answer. He never even said where he was from. "What do I do?" he replied, like the uneasy stirring of hidden branches in the darkness on the shore. "Why, I fish, some," he said. "I read when there's a chance. I fiddle, too," he said after a pause. "And I let my good wife keep me, I dare say, although my neighbors would like for me to sell my fiddle for bread. However," he told me, smiling, all dark and sharp, "perhaps you've heard what someone a little like me, perhaps, once wrote?" He quoted:

> *"If I should sell my fiddle,*
> *The warld would think I was mad . . ."*

And stopped. I stood stock still. Those were two lines I knew from a poem by Burns, in the green leather book I'd packed with me. You could hear a horse whinny from the bank. I finished with the final two lines:

> *"For monie a rantin' day,*
> *My fiddle and I hae had."*

Then I became silent, wondering if I'd been too brash.

"Bless my soul," said Kelso. "Abe, he 'pears to have had some eddication at that. More than most, I'd say."

And Lincoln laughed, short and shrill. Pete looked puzzled. And that was all there was to it. Jack Kelso shook my hand; and he had a small thin hand, not enormous like Lincoln's or even big like

179

Pete's. His fingers touched yours with a feel of worn smooth leather, light and quick, and were withdrawn. He was courteous, like a great gentleman, even if he was in rags and his Indian-black hair hung down most to his thin shoulders. He murmured it was time he was off—and off he went, in the darkness, Pete and Lincoln seeing him down to the wharf. Somehow, I never expected to see Jack Kelso again.

I finished writing the *Talisman*'s log for the day, blew out the lantern, and turned in. Possibly an hour later, Lincoln rapped on the door and asked ever so softly, "Owens, are you asleep?" I roused up, said, "No, come in," and used one of Pete's lucifers to light the lantern, wondering what was wanted. I never did know, exactly.

Perhaps all he wanted was company before turning in; but I'm not quite sure. He set the light down low. He hunched himself at the foot of my bunk, his knees under his chin, not speaking, and finally hauled out an old mouth organ and played on it soft and low for a time. I'd been around him long enough by now to know, a little at least, when to hold my jaw with him.

The cat that had taken over our steamboat, like a cat will if you let it, padded in, all a gray shadow, and rubbed itself against his legs and purred. And I never knew that cat to put itself out for any-body before. By and by Lincoln asked where I'd learned Burns's poetry. He was "sorter" fond of poetry, himself, he said, sounding shy off there in the dim light. So I had an inspiration come to me and explained I'd brought a book of Burns's poems with me; would he like to borrow it, perhaps? He stood, answering it would please him more than I knew.

He added, "The things I want t' know are in books. My best friend is the feller who'll git me a book I hain't read . . ." And then his voice seemed to change and become droll and comical, as if afraid he'd sounded too serious. "Because, Owens, books hain't quite as plenty yet as wildcats in these parts."

I hunted for my book of Burns, didn't find it, didn't know where I'd put it; and he rose up, ducked his head under the doorframe, paused, and asked diffidently maybe I'd find it tomorrow? It lodged a funny lump in my throat, hearing him ask that way as if a book was so important to him. I promised I'd find it tomorrow. I knew it was in here somewhere.

Monday we wallowed forward a little faster than the day before. Early that morning I didn't have much time to search for my book. When I got into the yawl with Lincoln for another day of it, I ex-

plained I hadn't forgotten. Tonight I'd give my whole office a going over to see where I'd misplaced the thing. Again he promised to take good care of it, almost anxiously, as if he thought I might think somehow he'd soil it and that was the reason I seemed to be having so much trouble locating it for him. It wasn't the reason; I didn't want him to think it was.

We tied up at Antrim's Landing half an hour before noon, eating grub early. Mrs. Hicks had promised to cook us fresh cornpone, Kentucky style, and my mouth had started watering. We didn't have any that meal. Denny said the cook-galley had clean run out of eggs. I was reminded that part of my chore, as boat's clerk, was to see what the cook wanted in the way of provisions and have them provided.

When we finished grub we found a square-built, muscular man of thirty or so, his face shaved so close it reflected light like polished hickory, who was patiently waiting for us at the heads of a team of oxen yoked to a big country two-wheeled cart piled high with cordwood. "Why, Jack," said Lincoln. "Why didn't you say you was waitin'?" He turned to us. "This here's Jack Armstrong. One of the best fellers ever lived."

It gave me a thrill of excitement to see him. He looked as strong as one of his oxen, and about as patient and mild, too. You wouldn't know you were seeing the man who'd been the best fighter and wrestler in the whole county until he'd lost his match with Lincoln last year. Armstrong answered mildly, "Why, Abe, I was jes' restin' here. I was up near the hull —— —— night, acuttin' them —— —— logs to the four-foot size you asked. Most cuss'd —— size I ever seed —— ef they hain't."

Well, he couldn't say three words without saying one, extra, that knocked you on your heels. He wasn't like Lincoln, whom I'd never heard say anything more powerful than "By jings!" By and by, though, as you listened to Armstrong you saw he didn't know any more than a baby that he was lighting bombs every time he opened his mouth. Pretty soon you got accustomed to hearing him. Those words didn't even kick up dust any more.

I sighted at his big cart. At least ten cords of wood were piled there waiting to be unloaded. Later, I discovered every length of wood had been cut to exactly four feet to fit our furnace—not four feet one inch or three feet eleven inches, but the precise length. Lincoln had told Armstrong we wanted four-foot lengths. Evidently Armstrong had taken that literally. Lincoln stayed on the wharf until

he was satisfied Jack Armstrong and Pete understood each other. Pete seemed to take a liking for the square-built, powerful, mild-mannered friend of Lincoln's right off. Armstrong was one of the few men—grown men, I mean, not boy, or part boy—whom I ever heard Lincoln call by his first name.

He agreed to stay on with us at a dollar a day as long as we needed him. We began loading the wood—and Lincoln shoved off in the yawl, while the rest of us pitched in on the wood. With so many of us, it didn't take long and Lincoln had returned by the time we were getting back our wind—all except Armstrong. He wasn't even breathing hard, but he'd been a regular whirlwind, shaming the rest of us into extending ourselves out of pure pride, I guess.

Lincoln told us he considered the next stretch of river was well enough marked as far as Hamacher's farm, where we could tie to-night before undertaking to enter the narrows. Herndon, he thought, could manage all right this afternoon. Armstrong could go ahead in the yawl.

Lincoln's gray eyes glanced at me and he asked if I'd like to ride west with him as far as the narrows which we'd have to enter to-morrow, rain or not, or quit. Would I? I jumped at the chance. A gig and horse were waiting for us behind Antrim's barn. Next I asked myself how Lincoln had managed to conjure up gig and horse for us so quick, until I saw who was waiting, standing at the horse's head. It was that eighteen- or nineteen-year-old Sucker, with the broad shiny face, whom I'd last seen above Salt Fork. He recognized me, too, probably because I was the only one wearing spectacles. How I hated those spectacles. My nose was still swollen and sore from walking into that door and the spectacles on it rubbed it even more annoyingly.

Slicky Bill Green walked to me. "Wal, I'd hev knowed you ef yore nose was busted clean off. Mr. Linkern tol' me you was still aboard when he asked me ter fetch him a hoss . . ."

"Billy, don't play the fool on people I'm workin' for . . ." Lincoln turned to me, explaining brusquely, "Billy Green's s'posed to keep from mischief by helpin' me at Offut's store. Trade's been so whiney, lately, mostly he's been l'arnin' me grammar—"

" 'Teachin' me grammar,' Mr. Lincoln."

"What?" asked Lincoln.

"It's *'teachin','* " said Bill Green quietly. He had ceased playing any sort of fool at all.

Now, that made me wonder. He was dead serious. You could see

him leaning forward a little, his pale eyes watching Lincoln. He was wanting to help.

"Oh," Lincoln said. "Owens, Billy's *teachin'* me grammar. Now shake hands with him, for Billy's a good feller when he don't play the fool."

Bill Green looked sheepish, laughed, and we shook hands.

After that, to me at least he spoke with no more of a Sucker accent than I did, perhaps less, although now I noticed he did have something of the same bluffness I'd seen in his father, that huge Justice Bowling Green who'd collected a bill of damage from us last Friday night, before sailing. You know, seeing Bill Green grow serious and trying to help Lincoln set me to wondering. It made me wonder more about Lincoln, wanting to learn grammar, wanting to borrow my book, wanting an education which obviously he lacked so greatly —and unexpectedly I found myself wanting very much to know why he wanted to learn grammar at his age of twenty-three, a full-grown man, when it wasn't any of my concern. The *Talisman* had been my single concern. She still was my greatest concern. But slowly it was beginning to come over me that whatever happened to our steamboat more and more was going to depend on Lincoln and what he decided, now that we were approaching the narrows, had had no rain, and no rain or sign of it was indicated.

We followed the road west. It twined away from the river and back, in and out, and ran through a dark piece of timberland. But Bill Green didn't go along with us that afternoon. Thankful did—Thankful, and Aunty Phoebee, bundled up, behind us, and enjoying the ride.

Bill had said, no, he guessed he'd stay at Antrim's Landing now he was here and have a good look at the steamboat. He'd wait until we returned. Thankful must have been watching and listening to us from the passenger deck because she called down to us, "Let *me* go. Please! I'm perishing for a ride in the country!" I don't know why, but lately every time I'd seen her she looked prettier than ever and I'd get the strangest feeling, as if I was nothing but legs and arms and ready to stumble over myself if I moved.

She delayed us a few minutes, Lincoln appearing disconcerted at first. Mrs. Hicks bustled over the gangplank, a shawl around her head. She asked why we men always thought of only ourselves? It

would do Thankful good to have a ride in the country. Thankful followed, wrapping her warm fur coat around her, Aunty Phoebee trundling in the rear. So Lincoln gave that laugh of his which made you sit up and look around to see if some cranes had flown into the neighborhood. I assisted Thankful to the front seat, sitting beside her. Lincoln had stayed behind until he'd helped Aunty Phoebee into the rear. He even shook the straw from an old blanket and wrapped it around her skirt and feet, saying, "Thar, aunty. It mou't get chilly."

To hear him you'd have thought he never noticed any difference between her color and Thankful's. Aunty Phoebee regarded him, unsmiling. Next, she tucked down her head for a second like she was breathing a prayer to herself about something. Now, why would she do that? She didn't have to be scared of a buggy ride. The horse was old, as steady as a rock. But she never said a word to Lincoln for having wrapped her feet, not even a thank you. That shows you. She'd always had good manners, Memphis manners, better than most whites', come to think of it. I judge she considered Lincoln as too ordinary to bother about thanking.

We had nearly an hour's drive before coming to the narrows. Thankful chattered away and by and by Lincoln lost his constraint and began joshing with her as if maybe she was three or four years younger than I knew she was. She asked him the same two questions everyone asks at the start, where was he from, and what did he do when he wasn't helping a steamboat? He unlimbered that afternoon and gave full answers. We learned he'd been born in Kentucky, had moved young to Indiana, where his mother died and his father re-married. He even told us his father had been against "eddication," only wanting him to "larn readin', writin', an' cipherin'." It had been his new stepmother who'd urged him to study, standing between him and his father. Four years ago he'd seen New Orleans for the first time, after broadhorning down the Mississippi. A year later, when he was twenty, he said, his family had moved west to Macon County, Illinois. Here he'd met Denton Offut, floated a raft for Offut to New Orleans, and had accepted the job at Offut's new store at New Salem.

Although her father's people had settled in Virginia and stayed there, Thankful said, most of her mother's people had settled in Kentucky. Perhaps they'd known some of Lincoln's people? He shook his head. He said most his people, he guessed, were from second-rate families. Then he looked at her, beginning to grin. "But

185

the first ancestor that I know anything about was one Tim Linkern who came over in sixteen-thirty-four and settled at a place, Hingham—or perhaps it was Hang-him. Which was it, miss, if you say some of your people came from Virginny?"

Quick as a flash, Thankful answered, "Catch'em County, perhaps, Mr. Lincoln?" casting the most demure look ever you saw at him through her lashes.

He said he wished he'd thought of that and he looked across at me and told me I'd better watch sharp at this young lady because one of these days she was going to give somebody a run for his money; and I wasn't quite certain why he'd said that to me, and I don't think Thankful was, either. But she began to color up. And next she said, rather tart, "You seem to keep on the move, Mr. Lincoln. Where next, after New Salem?"

"It's hard ter say . . ."

I had the oddest notion he was using his broadest possible style, partly to amuse us and make the ride go faster, but also partly to make fun of himself.

"In a few weeks I'm goin' ter chase old Black Hawk, ef he don't chase me fust. I mou't end as gen'ral. Who knows? Why, nobody can say what's acomin' next, can they? Thar was a settler and his fambly passing through New Salem a few days back. He was headin' west. He sold me a bar'l full of rubbish. I didn't want it but ter oblige him I bought it jes' the same an' paid half a dollar for it. Now, who kin tell? When I finish this job with the steamboat, ef I hev time before goin' ter war, I'll sort the rubbish in that thar bar'l. I mou't find a peck of gold hiddin in it an' live like a king the rest of my nat'ral life."

Even Aunty Phoebee, behind us, had to laugh at that. I don't know how Lincoln did it. If he was in the right mood, though, he could liven you up, and cheer you, and give you a feeling of delight just to be with him.

We came to the river and Lincoln stepped down and hitched the horse to a hickory branch and told Thankful and Aunty Phoebee to wait. He nodded at me, his eyes still having that sparkle deep in them.

"Watch out for yoreself, Owens. Yore growin' fast. But you hain't yet growed legs long as mine 'pear t' hev growed. This grass is powerful clingin'."

We slung through heavy timber and into sour grass which had lifted nearly to my knees in the past few days of warm sun. I didn't

much like what I saw. Neither did he. Since the *Talisman* had steamed this way, the river had continued to fall. All the little chutes between islands of drift, through which Pollock once had steered us were now almost filled by more drift and accumulated mud. I had to wipe at my spectacles more than once, because the dampness under the trees kept steaming them over. Lincoln stopped and waited for me each time. Finally, I got embarrassed and tried to apologize.

"Now, here," he said almost roughly. "My mother—my stepmother, I should say—she wears them things. An' she's the smartest person I ever knowed, man or woman. Here—" He offered me a red bandanna from his ragged pocket. I hesitated.

"It's clean," he said.

So I used it. We got back to the buggy, drove on, stopped again, and continued going and stopping for a couple of hours. We covered the entire length, all six miles of the narrows, driving in and out through stands of mixed hickory, walnut, maple, elm, and some pawpaw.

Off and on we had views of the prairie country to the south and west. Once we saw a man with a bull-tongue plow of wood and iron, drawn by an ox, breaking sod. He waved to us. I was on the watch for buffalo but never sighted any. A couple of wild swans boomed low over us, streaking toward the north. The sky was going gray, ribbed through with blue.

Lincoln told us Sangamontown was a mile over yonder rise. Instead of continuing, he turned the horse around. A little later, for a second time, we tied up near the tightest bend of the river and Thankful and Aunty Phoebee waited while we plunged off through the timber toward the riverbank.

He said this was called Snee Bend. I remembered it from the time Pollock had taken us through, steaming east. That time we had almost banked ourselves here for good. We got as close as we could and my heart sank heavier at what we saw. I didn't understand why this stretch of river was named the narrows. It wasn't narrow at all. The water had melted the banks almost away and had filled sluggishly into old river bottom to form a dull-brown-colored slough. If any sort of channel remained, you couldn't see it. I tried to keep hopeful. I saw some driftwood floating past and pointed to it, thinking that meant the river hadn't quite lost all the water from the last rise.

Lincoln said, "Driftwood keeps floatin' after the river's done risin', Owens. See whar thet bank shelves, with all the sediment? That was

land yesterday or day before, when the water was higher. Now, the driftwood's beginnin' to strand, too."

"What are we going to do?"

He hunched his head forward, pulling his coat around him. You could hear the wind sighing through the trees but the river was quiet, too quiet here. All the current had lost itself in the slough. "Owens," he said, "it sorter 'pears like I hev traded Wilmot an' you a sawhorse, don't it?"

I didn't understand. He went on, not waiting to explain.

"I b'lieved 'twould rain. Mebbe 'twill, yet; but perhaps not. Ef it does rain, though, thet steamboat won't get by Snee Bend, yonder. I see thet now. The current has shoved agin the far bank an' eaten it away. Ef it rains, 'twill be only more so, not better. The current'll spread t' the slough an' fill up thar 'stead of curving *with* the bend for a channel. I am sorry, Owens. Herndon an' me won't take the pay. We'll get you back to Bogue's mill. You'll do better to tie thar for the year than at Antrim's Landin'."

"You're pulling out on us?" I said, wretched.

"I can't lead you astray longer, Owens. Why, don't you see? Thet bend is ruined for steam navigation. Mebbe next year, all the snow meltin', an' fresh rains will clear a new channel. I'd *like* t' help. But we're jes' plumb agin a river thet has beat me as much as you. Here—" He took my spectacles. "Hain't you got no sense, rubbin' 'em thet hard? You want 'em broke? Whar's yore case?"

I answered dully that I'd lost my case, somewhere, weeks ago. He blew on the spectacles, wiped them, careful, slow, sticking out his underlip, peering through them, wiping them again, until he was satisfied; and he said, "Thar, now," and returned them to me; and we walked back in silence. Thankful must have seen all the despair revealed in my face when we came out of the timber and climbed into the buggy.

"Mr. Lincoln," she protested angrily, "are you going to let a little old river stop our steamboat and ruin Jim's pa and mine, too?"

It took me a second or so to realize she was calling me by my middle name. I suppose that was her way. If she didn't like something, she'd go ahead and find something else that suited her better without asking you in advance.

I was too far down to bottom, though, to care what she called me. She was worrying away at Lincoln. He was waiting, listening, instead of starting up the horse. He explained to her exactly as he had to me why the *Talisman* couldn't pass the last bend. Even if it

rained, he told her, the added current and rise of water would merely eat away the soft outer banks faster to flow further into the slough.

"It doesn't have to," she said, growing excited. "I know because my pa started out as a millwright. He constructed mills and improved millstreams. I remember, once, he had trouble with a bendy stream below Wheeling. That stream had soft banks at a bend. Well, *my* pa just laid a weir there and fixed it for good. Can't you?"

"What's a weir?"

If Lincoln didn't know what something was he was never too proud to ask.

On our way back to Hamacher's farm, where the steamboat was to tie up after ending her run for today, Thankful tried to explain. As she remembered, her father had pounded stakes all along the outer bend. Afterwards, he had filled the soft places behind the stakes with stone, to hold against the current. I'd seen weirs along millstreams, back in Pennsylvania; and I tried to help Thankful explain.

Lincoln listened about as well as he ever listened. He let us finish a sentence or so before asking another question. But he kept at us until you could begin to see the steamer's smokestack above the roof of the barn. Hamacher's place wasn't much, only a clearing, stumps still there, with a log cabin, and a barn which was more lean-to than barn, with chickens scratching around where hogs weren't rooting, the usual dogs barking, and the usual five or six kids of assorted sizes running out to see who was coming.

Lincoln turned the horse into the rutty lane leading through a grove of apple and pawpaw toward a rickety landing. He said, "Stones?"

Then he said, "It'd take us two months to hew and cut and cart enough stones for that quarter mile at Snee Bend, wouldn't it?"

Thankful hung her head. "Yes," she said, so low you couldn't scarcely hear. I was afraid in another minute she'd begin leaking rain from her eyes. She felt as badly as I did.

I didn't know what Pete was going to say. Lincoln called to Herndon, and the four of us gathered in the captain's parlor on the hurricane deck. Probably tomorrow Pete would want to have a look at the narrows himself. When he saw them, he'd have the same answer we had. If it rained, possibly we could mull forward from Hamacher's farm three or four miles into the narrows—until we came to that last bend. Then—we'd be finished. I could see the *Talisman* wallowing there in that mud and drift until she rotted and fell apart.

189

Lincoln told Pete and Herndon what he'd told us. Herndon knotted his fingers together. Pete banged his pipe hard a couple of times to empty it. Well, his pipe snapped off at the stem. He just looked down at it. I reached down and handed him the two pieces; wanting to say we could fix it somehow; but I didn't, not then. My throat was hurting so fierce I didn't trust myself to speak.

Lincoln was watching all of us. His face got more sallow and more shriveled. You'd have thought he was closer to thirty or forty, an old man, instead of being only twenty-three, younger than any of us in the parlor except me. He said, slow, "There jes' might be one way . . ." Pete stood. "Say it."

Lincoln began explaining, sticking out his underlip, sometimes stopping to chew on it while he thought. As he bent down to explain to us, when he turned his back to me to speak to Pete, I saw he'd placed his hands behind him again, like that time when arguing politics with the storekeeper, the back of his left hand fitted to the palm of his right, thumb and fingers of his right working with a steady sort of squeezing around the left arm at the wrist.

If it rained, he figured, the rise would carry us as far west as Snee Bend. We'd be stuck there, in about a quarter of a mile of curving where the river had flowed over the far bank into a slough. That smart girl we had aboard, he said—meaning Thankful—had asked why we couldn't build a weir. He'd turned her question over in his mind. Hewing, cutting, and hauling enough stones was plainly impossible.

Did we need a stone fill? Suppose five hundred to six hundred split rails were driven three to four feet apart, all along the outer curve of Snee Bend, where the current would tear at the banks? Instead of filling with stone, couldn't men weave old drift and saplings through the split rails, Indian style, and fill it behind with mud or sand or anything a shovel could lift? Only a temporary weir was needed, wasn't it? If it stopped the rush of water, long enough for the current to slide around the natural bend, wouldn't the force of the current when constricted have enough pull to clear away the rubbish and eat down to the old bottom?

Pete said, "By thunder—"

Lincoln held up his hand. It looked twice as big as a ham, attached to that narrow bony wrist. There was something else. Herndon and he could find men, yes, to chop down logs and split them into rails. Suppose it didn't rain? We'd still be no better off—worse, if anything. While the going price for a day's work was a dollar,

you'd have to pay more than a dollar a day to keep those Clary Grove boys piling away, into the night with lanterns if necessary, and weaving brush and saplings in the river. It might cost us two hundred dollars. Lincoln could see our expenses growing huger and huger. He was afraid, he said, we were like fellows stepping into quicksand, only going in deeper the more we struggled to get free.

I asked, "Mr. Lincoln, do you think you still smell rain?" Looking back, I believe that was about the time I began calling him Mr. Lincoln, same as I'd heard Bill Green and Wash Hicks call him.

"I smell it, Owens," he said. "But it hain't yet here. That's one thing for sartin."

Pete said, "Get that weir built and we'll whistle for rain! What do you say?" and squinted at me. I tried to think of the answer my father would give. And I gave it.

Herndon nodded his head. "Abe—I'm—all—f'r—startin'—right—now—t'—git—our—men."

"Wait." Pete stuffed his broken pipe in his pocket. "That ain't quite all. You two've played square with us. Before you get in too deep in this thing you better know I been holding out something."

He told them why he suspected our pilot, Pollock, of being the notorious Whitey Morgan, the wrecker. Even if the telling should cause Lincoln and Herndon to think twice, and perhaps shy off from helping us, I couldn't help being proud of Pete. He was honest, all the way through. Holding out on them about Pollock had lain on his conscience. When he finished there was a short silence. Both Lincoln and Herndon were almost strangers to us. They were storekeepers. What happened to the *Talisman* would be no very great affair to them. I felt a withering sensation, waiting for one of them to answer Pete.

"Wilmot, that hain't—" Lincoln paused again, sticking out his underlip. He was trying to think of the exact word he wanted. "That hain't *relevant*. What yore pilot is or was hain't our concern. Our concern is this steamboat. Bogue, now—I don't b'lieve knowingly thet Bogue would j'ine with any wrecker. He don't worry me. Pollock don't, neither. Herndon?"

"Same—here. Let's—git—started—clearin'—Snee—Bend."

On our way down the forward passenger stairs, Lincoln caught sight of Aunty Phoebee, aft on the passenger deck. He stopped still a moment; and next his long gangling legs carried him to her.

I heard him ask, dead serious, "Aunty, will it rain soon? What do you think?"

He was speaking carefully, too, not in any way slouchy at all.

She thought for a couple of seconds before answering, "Hit's in my bones, Mr. Linkern. I kain't say no more en thet."

After Slicky Bill drove Lincoln and Herndon west in his buggy, I sighted up at the sky, even wiping my spectacles clean and looking again. The sky was all a dull inflamed red from the last light of the sun. I could hear the wind sighing in the trees along the lane toward that shackly cabin and barn. There was no sign of rain I could see. I didn't smell it. I didn't feel it in my bones, either. I ached, that was all. I hurt all over.

It was one of those glum suppers when even the grub is hard to swallow. Thankful had heard of our decision and she looked pale and scared, as if she was blaming herself for having thought of a weir. I didn't feel very brash that evening. I was down so low I didn't even mind, particularly, having her call me by my second name, Jim. I tried to have her see if her idea worked she'd be the one who could say she'd saved the *Talisman*.

"But if it doesn't work, Jim?"

I shook my head. Actually, we had only three choices—the same three we'd always had. We could push ahead, and take our chances of getting stuck fast for good. We could turn back, tie up to Bogue's wharf, pay him his wharfage fee, and wait until next year, letting the steamer rust away. Or we could sell the steamer to him. What we were doing was still pushing ahead. We weren't being licked.

I saw her up to her stateroom. I never quite knew how comforting it could be when you were in desperate trouble to have a girl like Thankful as a friend. She was smiling. Her eyes looked wet and big and soft and—but Aunty Phoebee was right there behind us.

"Good night, Jim."

"Good night," I answered, and climbed up to my office. Pete wasn't there to keep me company. Probably he was in the engine room, glowering at nothing, with Sandy keeping *him* company.

For nothing else, I searched my office high and low for that book of poems. It wasn't there. I couldn't understand what I'd done with it. Next, I remembered we were running out of provisions and I'd neglected that part of my job. Denny had mentioned it to me, again, after grub tonight.

So I opened the safe, took out five dollars from our pile, shoved the tin box of money back in, hard against that pistol Pete had given me, locked the safe tight, being thankful the iron was so thick, and

cut down to the boiler deck where Denny gave me his list. He wanted eggs, ham, corn meal, and anything in the eatable line I could buy at the farm.

It wasn't very late, not much after seven-thirty. I wished Aunty Phoebee wasn't so strict with Thankful, bossing her around like Thankful was five or six years old, and having her inside her stateroom so soon after supper. I'd have liked to have asked Thankful to walk with me to the farm. Every time I'd begin thinking of her, I'd start feeling a kind of warmness coursing away through me, all up and down from head to toes. Now, why was that? Not so long ago I'd thought she would be only a nuisance and had never given a tinker's nail for girls. I hadn't even written to Whizzer Tucker, my closest friend in Philadelphia, about Thankful being aboard.

Well, I got off on that rickety wharf. Smoky, as usual, had lit fires in the iron baskets so you could see your way some distance off the wharf. Four or five boys of assorted ages, probably from the farm, were there sitting around a useless little fire that Wash Hicks had built. They were cooking something they'd caught today—a raccoon they might have trapped, for all I knew.

Wash looked up as I passed by and said this was the cheapest tub he'd ever been on. We didn't even serve good grub. Well, he'd never been on any steamboat before. He was showing off to those farm kids, swaggering, stirring that mess in an old tin pot he'd found—or lifted from somewhere.

But I reckon those farm kids thought he was a great traveler; and they laughed with him; and I heard one say, swaggering like Wash was, that he wouldn't resk himself on an old tub like ours. No, sir.

I let them go. I got to the farm and the woman was ready to sell me two dozen eggs, all she had, at five cents a dozen. She'd been saving them to take tomorrow to New Salem. They only paid her four cents a dozen, there, she said, being straight out and honest. I also bought a salt-cured ham for fifty cents, and that was all.

She couldn't spare me any corn meal. She said her husband had reckoned on trying to kill a deer tomorrow, hoping to sell it to us for meat; but Row Herndon and Abe Linkern had stopped off a minute with that Slicky Bill Green. Her husband had grabbed his ax and driven on with them.

So I thanked her. She gave me a big basket she'd woven herself out of green split willow in which to carry the eggs. Wouldn't charge me for the basket, either. Those people living along the Sangamon were all poor as dirt, most of them anyhow; but they'd rather die

before taking advantage of you. She asked me to tell "them" boys of hers, if I saw them, it was time for them to skin home to bed. I promised I would.

Going back toward the boat, the lane seemed darker than before. We'd had a moon of sorts. It had slipped behind some clouds. You could hear the wind rustling and moving more strongly through the thick heavy pawpaws. Looking ahead it was like looking through a long dark tunnel to where, away off, were the dim lights shining from our steamboat.

I got to thinking if a man wanted to hide anywhere to pounce on someone, this was the best place. I remembered how white and strange looking Pollock's long face always had been, with his hair such a dead black; and I started walking faster; and pretty soon I thought I heard a rustling which was more than from the wind. It was as if a horse had started to whinny, deep in the pawpaws, and a man had grabbed the horse by the nose, if you know how to do it, choking off the whinny. I had a most powerful feeling of wanting to cut for it and run.

Then I remembered Wash and those kids were on ahead of me, near the wharf. They'd see me skinning for the boat, basket of eggs jouncing from one arm, the ham dangling over my shoulder.

No, I didn't run. I got by those dark shadows. I did hear something. When I looked back, startled, a big black shape all at once flicked out and away up the lane, vanishing against the black mass of the timber. For a second I was certain it was a man on a horse. But right away I told myself, nervously, I was wrong. All I'd done was to scare up a deer. So I walked on, seeing the boat lights grow brighter and, next, Wash Hicks standing, back to me, lit up by that little fire. He was holding something in one hand and gesturing with another and speaking at the top of his voice, stopping for those farm kids to laugh and to appreciate the noble play he was giving them, and going on again. He was reciting, if you'd call it that, from my book of Burns's poems!

I went cold all over.

Then I did several things, careful, not in too much of a hurry. I laid the ham and basket of eggs on the road, took off my coat, removed my spectacles, stuck them in a coat pocket, wrapped my coat around the spectacles, and placed the coat on the basket.

I could still see Wash's blurry shape, outlined against his fire; and I could see where the boat was, vaguely, by its lights; and I knew in my mind the river wasn't more than two or three rods on down from

where Wash was standing. Then I got all that set in my mind. I ran at him. I slammed into him as I'd counted and got hold of him so he couldn't slip loose. We went tumbling over. Sparks flew up into the night where we must have kicked at the fire.

I'd thought those farm kids might pitch in to help him—but they didn't. Maybe they were too surprised. Maybe they'd heard Wash blowing so much they figured he could take care of himself.

He was like a regular wildcat. He got on top of me and began punching at me. For once I didn't care too much. I kept hanging on, working to get the crook of my arm clamped around his neck. And I had the strangest sort of delight when I learned I was stronger than he was and I began tugging and pulling him down the slope of bank toward the river. And I expect if anyone had been watching we might have been like one fairish sized dog pulling and hauling inch by inch a smaller dog, more lively than the other, making more of a scrap of it at first.

There were more noises now. I could hear people beginning to yell but I hung on. I guess suddenly Wash saw what I was doing—or, maybe, when his leg splashed into the mud after we slipped down the bank he saw what I was up to. He changed around. He ceased hitting and clawing at me. He began screaming in a queer high way and trying to get free. At last it was beginning to be what I'd wanted, with him doing the jigging; and I pulled harder.

Of a sudden something fetched me up, straight up by the collar; and it was Pete. And his voice rang out in the hardest possible style. "Leave that kid be," he said.

And he gave me a cuff. And that did it. I'd believed Pete was my friend. I had that rage still on me and I tried to get at Pete and his peg leg got stuck in the mud. For a couple of seconds or more everyone seemed to be milling and flying around, like a cat and dog fight. And it was Sandy who hauled me up, next. And *he* gave me a cuff.

Pete and Sandy fetched me, like lightning, dragging me, past Smoky, past the roustabouts, along aft to the engine room. Here, one of them slammed the door shut. Pete looked down at me, fiercer than ever I'd seen him.

"You been spoilin' to go after that kid, ain't you?"

"He's no kid. Wash is nearly my age. He—"

"Shet up!" he said. "By thunder, you listen to me, Horace James Owens. Hitting me. Hitting Sandy. I like that. I sure like that. I seen you was growin' too big for your boots, lately. But I didn't say nothing. No, I figgered it was a change for the better from that high

and mighty Philadelphy snob, yes, snob, who I first seen in Cincinnati. I don't say you ain't worked neither. You have plowed in as good as anybody. But that don't satisfy you, does it? No, you have to get in that river and show nobody is half as good as you. I thought you was drowning. Did you care?

"That 'peared comical to you, didn't it," he asked, fiercer and fiercer, "when I got ready to go in after you even if I never did larn to swim. And that Wash Hicks. What about him? You knowed he's been scairt of water ever since his paw drowned. Why, that boy's nearly sick to death for missing his paw. It's why he acts like he does, hiding off day after day on shore like a young pup beginning to miserable away and not knowing the reason. Jumping him like that! Maybe he did steal your book. Why didn't you ask him for it, first? You're half a head taller. Someday you'll be as big as your paw, with bigger bones. By thunder, don't you know better'n jumping somebody younger and—and—"

He broke off. He pointed to the door. "Now, clear. Thank Smoky for fetching your coat and specs and that book. If I was Smoky, I'd have burnt that book. Sure thing. Now, clear; you hear: It ain't no use you starin' at me, like you can jump me. You ain't the size, *yet*, for that!"

I walked past Pete and Sandy but the rage was in me, as strong as ever; and I walked by mighty slow. If Pete wanted to deliver a kick, to help me clear, like once he'd helped Captain Bogue, it was all right with me. This time Pete wouldn't see me shy off from him.

So I walked out. I climbed the aft ladder to the passenger deck. In the shadows was Aunty Phoebee, all wavery and rippling like water without my spectacles; and she'd been watching and listening. That meant Thankful would know of my disgrace tomorrow. I climbed higher, feeling my way.

Inside Smoky had heaped my coat on the bunk. He'd laid my spectacles on the desk, just at one side of the lighted lantern for me to see them there. And my green leather book, burnt at one corner, was next to the glasses.

That demon, if there was such a thing—perhaps it was part of me, a new part I hadn't yet learned to know very well—began whispering in my ear, "The next time . . ." I didn't care if I was in disgrace. Wash Hicks was to blame. He'd cost me Pete's and Sandy's friendship. It was unfair of all of them. I knew what I was going to do the next time to Wash Hicks, when I found the right opportunity. It wasn't even a thought. I didn't let it get as far in my head as being a

thought. It was just there, back in a darkness in my mind, turning and twisting and beginning to take shape.

And I'd learned one thing, too, from that fight. It hadn't scared me to get hit. Afterwards, I'd even faced it out with Pete. All of that newness I'd discovered about myself rose up strong inside me, like fresh sap in a tree; and nobody was there to tell me you can go as far wrong on the side of laying over somebody hard as on the other side, of running away.

I was awakened in the middle of the night by what I thought
must be the firing of cannons. It was thunder, followed by fifteen or twenty minutes of rain. It emptied itself out and stopped.
Afterwards I lay awake, thinking over our chances and feeling miserable. Pete and Sandy were the only two officers the boat had.
Suppose they became so disgusted with me, after yesterday evening,
they decided to quit? That thought lifted my hair. Right then I resolved to eat crow and do everything possible to win back their
esteem and let Wash Hicks slide until later. I'd eat humblepie from
him, too, if necessary. The steamboat took precedence. How I
wanted to have her get free!

Tuesday dawned into one of those gray affairs, just generally
dreary, no rain whatsoever. Even if we were laid up here, I came
down for early breakfast. Thankful and Aunty Phoebee were there,
earlier. Thankful's eyes were green as grass this morning. Very cool,
she said, "Good morning, Horace." That meant she'd heard about
yesterday evening. It was back again to Horace. Well, all right. Why
should I care? Everyone knows how fickle and unreliable girls are
anyway. Thankful simply proved the rule; that was all.

I heard Wash and his mother on deck; and I shoved through the
larboard door. I didn't want to see either of them yet. There was
nothing for me to do that morning. We all had to fiddle our thumbs,
wait on Lincoln, the building of the weir, and whistle for rain. For
an hour I used up time rereading the *Talisman*'s log I tried to keep.

I started up when Pete entered. He acted constrained; so, I guess,
did I. But I remembered my resolve and told him I'd played the
fool, was sorry, had learned my lesson, and hoped I'd be forgiven.

I felt more mealy-mouthed after that speech than I ever had in my life because I wasn't sorry. I meant to tackle Wash Hicks again to settle a score, it seemed to me, piling higher in his favor—as soon as the *Talisman* was out of danger. The steamboat came first. Nothing else counted any more except the steamboat.

Pete peered at me from under his shaggy red and salt-colored eyebrows. He cleared his throat a couple of times and unlimbered a notch, but only a notch. He told me Lincoln had sent for me from Snee Bend. A boy had arrived and was waiting to take me where I was wanted. So terribly and urgently did I want our steamboat to get free that I'd have offered to cut off my right arm if doing that would have helped.

I said, "Yes, Pete. Thanks," and ran for it.

Waiting for me was a boy half my size. His name was Duff Armstrong—at least I think that was what he said.

He might have been Jack Armstrong's other boy, Will. One of the Armstrong kids, somebody told me that April, was still in the cradle. Which brother was the oldest I can't recall for certain. Because, later, when he grew to a man, Duff was put on trial for his life in a case that was famous, his name stays the strongest in my mind. But I believe he was the oldest of the two kids and the one who came for me Tuesday morning.

Instead of immediately climbing up behind him on the old plug he was riding, I walked as far south on the lane as the thick grove of pawpaw trees. I hadn't forgotten by any means the surprise I'd had yesterday evening, just before charging at Wash Hicks, when something or somebody on a horse had streaked off like black lightning from those pawpaw trees.

There were too many tracks of horses and oxen and even deer in the soft clayey lane, though, to tell if a man had led a horse with him last night into the pawpaws, while spying on our steamer.

I didn't know what to think. As far as those of us on the boat were concerned, Pollock and his new wife had vanished forever. Who would have wanted to spy on us last night? Pollock and Bogue already knew all there was to be seen on our steamer. It didn't make sense. I decided I'd sparked up a deer by accident last night. That had to be it.

I mounted behind Duff on his old plug. We trotted off at a sedate rate, seven miles on the river road toward Snee Bend. I looked back once, seeing the *Talisman* through the trees. She swung there like a ship already dead. I had such a desire to run to her and push and

199

shove that I felt my stomach cramp. The whole north quarter of the horizon was black. It made you sick, knowing people somewhere miles to the north were probably receiving all the rain today we needed so desperately.

My spirits kicked up a little when the horse brought us close enough for me to hear a steady ringing of axes, sharp and clear. That sound sent a rill of hopefulness through me. Even if the *Talisman* was tied up back there like a dead ship, here a whole crowd of men had gathered in the timber behind the slough and bend to drive away with everything they had to help get our steamer to good water.

In the clearing a big fire was burning. Ringed around the edge of the clearing four or five men were hard at it, splitting fallen trees. Another man was stacking hickory and elm rails. You could hear others, deeper in the timber. Somebody yelled. A tree crashed. "Thar's my pappy," said Duff proudly. He pointed. I saw Jack Armstrong at one end of the clearing, stripped to his red woolen shirt, his ax flashing up and down. It was like watching the Pittman link of a steam engine going up and down.

"Howdy."

Lincoln stepped into the deer run we'd followed, and wasted no time that morning. He thanked Duff for bringing me and told me to follow him. Was I ready for some hard work? I answered, without thinking, that I still shied from hard work but the steamboat seemed to be breaking me in to it, anyhow. "I'll tell you somethin', Owens. I hain't yet got broken good ter it, neither. But jes' let's you an' me keep thet for ourselves. Come on."

I followed him across the clearing and into rank grass at the south end of the slough. He was explaining on the way. From the top of the old buckskins he was wearing this morning he removed a "shake" of hickory, showing me the figures he'd scrawled with a piece of charcoal. He'd even "ciphered" the number of yards along the outer curve of bend to obtain a rough total of the quantity of split hickory and elm rails needed for a weir. He wanted five hundred rails, cut to twelve-foot lengths, for our weir posts. To fell the trees, trim, split each tree into "sides," split the sides, chop to lengths, and sharpen one end of each rail, he told me, took some doing when we were so pressed for time. Ordinarily, forty split rails was a good day's chore for any man.

He had ten men, counting himself. It was all Herndon and he could scrape up at such short notice. Because getting out the proper

number of rails was only half the job, he'd enlisted four or five older boys from New Salem and Sangamontown to cut brush and saplings to be used in weaving a temporary weir after men had pounded the rails all along the outer rim of the bend. Having noticed I could take care of myself in the water, he'd thought of me when he needed someone to pack saplings and rails over the slough to the river. Could I do it? I didn't see why not. I began hauling off my boots.

He called, "Dave," to a boy cutting saplings. "Here a minute, will you?" It was still sprinkling, only a trifle; still, it was enough to let you hope for more. I said it looked to me as if he'd been right about smelling rain. He shook his head, worried.

"Yesterday, I heared they had flood rains up Havana way, north. Soon, Pigeon Crick'll be drainin' inter the river again. Ef the river has a flash rise too soon, before we git all them rails split, jes' how are we goin' to finish our weir? Mostly, these fellers can't swim a stroke. . . ."

That was something I hadn't thought of, until now. I felt a tightening go through all my nerves. If it started pouring too soon, we'd still lose out. The boy came to us; he was about Wash Hicks's age, I'd say, slimmer, with ginger-colored hair not much less red than Thankful's shade. Lincoln said this was Dave Rutledge from New Salem. Dave would look after me and show what was wanted.

Dave did.

All day I packed back and forth across the slough to the river where Herndon and a man I didn't know were pounding rails down into the river bottom. The water was cold. The mud and slime and stagnant water south of the bend was even colder. The day wore on and got raw, rain sprinkling at us every so often, just enough to tantalize us and let us think it was worth continuing.

Herndon and the man with him could stand the coldness longer than I could. By middle afternoon I was stumbling from fatigue, covered over with mud and green slime, and stopping maybe every ten minutes or so to dry off by the fire. That young Dave Rutledge must have been made out of strap leather and steel wire. He kept along with me, began besting me and was cheerful about his job, pleased at earning two whole dollars a day. I had to grit my teeth to get myself up again for each new load. At first I'd thought Lincoln was offering big pay, three dollars a man, two for the boys; but I'd changed my mind by now. If it hadn't been my father's steamboat, you couldn't have paid me a hundred dollars to continue.

The whole air jarred with the sounds of axes, trees smashing,

shouts, the fire crackling, somebody calling to somebody else, with a woman or girl who'd brought us more grub or more black coffee sometimes laughing out, high and merry. But the air was gray. It was dark under the trees. The slough was like thick tar. The cold grew on you, it touched your bones and you never did get warm.

I stumbled, again, floundering. This time my spectacles slipped off my swollen nose. I was struck by panic. They were my last pair. Everything broke off and shifted into queer angles and flat vistas before my eyes. The sky was terrifying, slipping away at the edges of my vision like running water.

I got down into the cold mud, feeling with my hands, finding nothing; and, then Dave said, "Here, now. I'll help." And mud was in my eyes, on my face, over all of me. And he led me to the bank. I was trying to wipe off my face. I succeeded only in blinding myself by smearing more slime over my eyes. And somebody's light soft gentle hands took me from Dave. A girl's light soft sweet voice said, "It's all right. Sit down next ter the fire. Thar. Dave found yore spectacles."

"Shore," Dave said. "I found 'em and *told you so*. But you didn't listen. I got 'em here, safe. Jes' catch yore breath."

I could feel myself quivering. I hadn't known what I'd do without my spectacles. I felt that girl, whoever she was, kneeling next to me despite all that stinking cold mud and slime covering me. "Here," she said. "Take my bandanner. It don't hurt ef you git it dirty. I got plenty more."

I cleared the slime from my eyes with her bandanna and tried to see who she was. Without my spectacles all I saw was her great blueness of eyes, everything else about her melting and bending into shadows and light. I must have been staring harder at her than I knew. I heard her breath catch, like my staring was troubling her. I felt her rise up from me. Dave spoke again, promising he'd have my spectacles clean as ever in another minute.

Unexpectedly, Lincoln's shrill voice came from behind me, "Why, Ann, what's up with young Owens?"

It was Dave who hastily explained. Afterwards, that girl, who-ever she was, and Lincoln must have started slowly walking away from us. They were whispering sort of, as if they didn't want Dave or me to hear. But I'd always had good ears. I heard her whisper, "Abe, *can't he see?*" and part of Lincoln's answer, "Some with spectacles. A little, I guess. One of the fellers on the boat told me . . ." I didn't hear more of it because they had moved too far away. I

202

didn't know what anyone on our steamer had told Lincoln. I could see with my spectacles as well as anyone aboard, almost anyway.

Dave finished with them. After I hooked them on and thanked him I looked around to see what the girl looked like. I was too late. She'd vanished up the deer run. Lincoln was returning, taking those long steady strides. So I asked Dave Rutledge if he knew who the girl was.

"Ann? I oughter. Why, she's one of my sisters. I got 'leven, all told. But Pap runs the tavern at New Salem. He's got space fur all of us."

"Is she pretty?"

"Who?"

"Your sister."

"Ann? How'd I know? You seed her."

Lincoln returned and I didn't have to explain I hadn't been able to see her very distinctly without my spectacles to see through. Lincoln informed us we could rest for another two bits' worth. Because the weir was using up rails faster than they could be split, to get a pile done in a hurry Lincoln had promised a rail-splitting bee with a five-dollar prize for the winner. Was that satisfactory to me, as the only steamboater here? I nodded. I knew Pete'd pay any amount required to speed up the job. Then Lincoln said, "See here. When you go back inter that slough agin, can't you sorter foller behind Dave? Jes' stick yore specs in a case so you won't lose—

"By jings!" He put down his ax. "You don't hev a case, do you? I forgot. But I found one for you. You remember thet bar'l I told you of yesterday? The one I bought from the settler at half a dollar? I stopped inter my store last night while waitin' for Herndon to stop inter his. I hed jes' time to start sortin' through the top of thet rubbish. First crack, I found an' old pewter case for holdin' flints. How's thet for luck? I told you I mou't find something valu'ble yet in thet old bar'l of rubbish. A flint case is jes' the thing t' slip yore spectacles in an' keep 'em dry." His face got long. "But you know what? Herndon come by. We was in too much of a hurry. I plumb forgot t' bring the case with me."

I wished he hadn't. I needed something to keep my spectacles in. It was no use wishing. Jack Armstrong called that the "fellers was waitin'." Lincoln left us. I saw he'd already put that flint case out of his mind for something more important.

Dave nudged me. "Say, a rail-splittin' bee is fun. Linkern kin sink a' ax deeper inter the wood than any man I ever seed. But Johnny

Brewer over thar—" He nodded. "Thet little shorty feller, like a banty rooster. At anything fur a short spell, he's the fastest. Some rail-splittin' bees don't last more'n fifteen minutes. Brewer's been layin' for Linkern an' Armstrong. Brewer'd like ter be the big buck of these licks. Even ef he's sich a shorty, he's got arms like mule laigs. He jes' mou't win 'cause Linkern don't show up good in nothin' quick. It takes him time ter git started."

The rules were simple. Herndon was selected as timekeeper, probably because he was the only man with a watch. But they settled for twenty minutes, five more than Dave Rutledge had anticipated.

Each man had to fell a hickory tree, of a girth equal or larger than the circle of the man's arms, which I saw equaled the thing a little, for a big man like Lincoln would be set against a tree larger around than one Brewer, for example, would tackle; and after felling the tree, the man who finished with the most rails won. That was all. Seven all told entered. Lincoln had hung back, saying he was working for the steamboat people. He didn't rightly belong. But Brewer crowed up at him, "You skeered this time I'll run you out?" So Lincoln was among them when Herndon called, "Get set—go!" That whole place began ringing from the sound of axes. Dave and I watched Lincoln and tried to keep an eye on the others among the trees.

Lincoln went to work in his usual careful style, trying several trees before selecting one on a rise, a little off from the clearing. That seemed a mistake. He'd lost a couple of minutes, too. His hickory ax handle measured from the steel to the top of his hipbone and I guess it was the longest handled ax there. Chips flew. He stood to one side driving in deep and hard. Everyone was shouting.

A buggyload of women arrived from the deer run. One tree crashed. Somebody yelled. "Armstrong's!" Somebody else shouted, "No, it's Johnny Brewer's!" I forgot I was cold and covered with caking mud and began jumping up and down as excitedly as Dave or anyone else.

Presently Lincoln's tree crashed. Now I saw he'd cut it so it would sling down toward the clearing. He began trimming. Dave had run off, came back, said, "Brewer an' Armstrong are splittin', already."

I never heard so much noise. Lincoln set his steel wedges. Down came that ax in streaks of light. Hickory splits straight, yes; but those whiplash arms of Lincoln's had the power in them to split down the center with *only three* wedges. I saw it. Three wedges. He opened up that tree like a piece of old ashwood.

He got a single middle "side"—he didn't bother with the rest. Next, he split that side with the *ax blade* itself, not wasting more time to set the steel wedges.

I got so excited my spectacles steamed over. By the time they were wiped clear again, I saw Lincoln already had fetched out a long twenty-foot four-inch square piece from the side. He cut to length with single hard blows, like cutting off lucifer match splints. He took two strokes to sharpen the end, one stroke each side. Chips scattered.

Herndon called, "Eighteen—minutes—"

I didn't know where the time had gone. Off to my left, Armstrong like a bull, all red, somehow suddenly violent, had knocked out five rails. He was sharpening a sixth, taking three strokes. Lincoln looked just once over his shoulder.

"Nineteen minutes, boys!"

Lincoln used four strokes for his last and seventh rail. Armstrong had finished *his* seventh rail. He was starting to sharpen the eighth when Herndon shouted, "Time!"

Lincoln laughed, gave a final stroke, the fourth, and threw down his rail. "Jack," he called to Armstrong, "I guess you beat me."

"Fust time. What did Johnny Brewer do?"

"Five," said Brewer angrily from the left. "Linkern, you're losin' yore strength ter hev Armstrong beat you."

"Yes, I guess I am," Lincoln said. He picked up his ax by the handle and held it out, slow, steady, strong, at arm's length, sighted along the handle to the steel, his arm never wavering, said, "Wal, boys," and put down his ax.

I stepped forward and reached for his ax, so amazed I wasn't even very conscious of what I was doing. You had to tug up that ax in both hands. It was that heavy. Lincoln said, "Here, now. That ax is as sharp as any razor, sharper. You could shave with it." He took the ax from me, peering down, getting his wind, looking dark and sweaty, like good harness leather lathered a little from having strained against a running horse. "Mebbe, you mou't soon use a' ax fer shavin', too, Owens?"

Well, Armstrong was paid the five dollars. We got back to work, all of us.

By nightfall we had three-fourths of the rails needed and perhaps a quarter of the weir built. For the first time in my life I hunkered up for a night in the loft of a log cabin. Dave said it was too far for

him to go back to New Salem for the night. He hunkered with me along with two of the men. I don't know whose cabin we used. I was too dead played out to ask or care. The owners stayed downstairs. It started raining that night.

I woke up in the darkness and it was pouring. Next morning it was still pouring. We had grub in the cabin, corn mush, ham splits, acorn coffee, nothing else. The woman had dried our clothes by the fire. I learned now her husband was one of the men with us. Our clothes got wet through the minute we stepped outdoors.

Lincoln was already in the clearing as wet as the rest of us, wetter, if anything. He looked like the oldest and gawkiest and most drenched crane in the nation. He caught sight of me, reached into his pocket and said good-naturedly, "Here's what you need for them spectacles of yours, Owens." He gave me an old pewter flint case. It was the kind that used to be manufactured to keep musket flints dry. Lincoln had even thought to line it inside with a strip of linsey wool.

I felt something slowly swelling in my throat. To get that flint case for me last night he must have walked or ridden the dozen miles through pouring rain to his store in New Salem and all the way back.

You know it fastened on me all of a sudden. He waited a second or so, said, "Thet does it, don't it?" and walked back into the wet timber to finish splitting another side. I hadn't thanked him. I couldn't. I just couldn't. In my mind I'd blamed Aunty Phoebee a few days ago for not thanking him after he'd wrapped her feet in that blanket. I found myself wondering if perhaps she'd wanted to thank him, had tried, and like me now, had found something would start breaking in her if she said a word.

Even if most of the time I kept my spectacles off my nose and safe in that pewter flint case, I don't believe I was completely useless that Wednesday. There wasn't anyone better as a friend either than Dave Rutledge. I wished he was aboard instead of Wash Hicks. Dave stuck close to me. People passed saplings to me and I tied them to the stakes as fast as anyone. Maybe faster. By noon you could feel the water tugging your legs as it began rising. We never completed the weir. We had to leave a short stretch at the upper end because the river got too dangerous by early afternoon.

It was boiling by four o'clock, scouring out the natural channel as the current raced along nearly a quarter mile of weir we had finished. I nearly perished from surprise when I first heard the shat-

tering blasts of our big whistle. Nobody had thought to inform me that two hours previously Herndon had started worrying about the flash rise, had whipped a horse back to Hamacher's Landing, and was now bringing the *Talisman* all the way through the narrows. Under that pouring rain we lined up on the bank and watched her crawfish and mule and sashay her way around the bend. She made it. We danced and jigged and cheered and slammed each other on the backs until Pete hollered to us, from the steamer, that Herndon had said there wasn't any safe place to tie to here. They had to run the *Talisman* east to Sangamontown wharf and couldn't stop to pick Lincoln and me up . . .

After that everyone began scattering for home. I worried how we were going to collect the men to pay them. Lincoln promised he'd give Herndon a statement. Said he knew we steamboaters were honest, told Dave to look out for me, and hopped into a wagon Mrs. Armstrong had had waiting for him and her husband. Dave found me a ride in another wagon. We hunkered down in the straw. It looked like our worst was over. Dave assured me we wouldn't have any trouble at New Salem. He knew that dam, he said, because his father and Mr. Cameron had built it.

"Will this rise give us enough of a head?" I asked.

He was certain it would, more than enough. By tomorrow, Thursday, he was willing to bet his whole pay that we'd have at least thirty inches of a "head" to carry us over. It would have been bad luck to bet he was wrong. It would mean I was betting against our boat. But I knew we only had a two-foot draw, empty, so it did look like a sure thing. I was so cheered when we arrived I wanted to show him over our steamer and have him have supper with us. He explained he was "kinder" played out this evening. He'd go on in the buggy to New Salem, as long as he had a ride. When the *Talisman* came by his town he'd see me again. I said to tell his sister I'd get her bandanna cleaned somehow and return it after we went over the dam; but Dave said not to trouble. "A thing like a bandanner don't count, not to Ann. Jes' throw it away."

It was almost like I'd been away for a month when I got back on the boat again. When Pete and Sandy saw me they were grinning so much their grins ran nearly around their heads. It was back to old times with them. They didn't say anything more about the trouble I'd had with Wash Hicks; and neither did I. They were so pleased and tickled and set up with themselves and with Herndon for stealing a march on us and rushing the *Talisman* on the first tide

207

of the flash rise they didn't have any time to hear about the experiences I'd had at the clearing. Well that was natural. I was so crowded to the hilt with everything I wanted to say, I didn't have time to hear them. So we talked at cross-purposes; but it was all right.

I saw Sandy was all rigged up in what he called his "St. Louis duds." He stayed until Pete began pouring hot water over me. Then he said he guessed he'd stretch his legs. I said, "Where?" But he grinned, got out, and shut the door again to the engine room. Smoky brought me freshly cleaned clothes. Getting our clothes washed and dried despite the rain had been Mrs. Hicks's doings. While I dressed Pete said thoughtfully, "That Hicks woman is a nat'ral-born steamboater. I'd give her a job if she was a man, Jim."

I raised up my head. "What?"

He repeated himself, saying "Jim" again, too. I decided that must have been Thankful's doings. First it was "Horace." She didn't approve of "Turtle." Back again it had gone to "Horace" when I'd fallen into disgrace. Now, she must have privately decided my middle name "Jim" was what suited her and had gone to Pete about it. That was always her way. She never asked you. No, she made up her own mind and clipped in quick. But somehow after so much trouble with my names, being called plain "Jim Owens" suited me. That was how it always stayed, too, afterwards. Once you get a name you like, I say why not stick to it?

I finished dressing. Pete told me we were having a late supper. I didn't need to rush too fast. That suited me because I was having a reaction after the past two days. Excitement can carry you for a time even if you're three-quarters to a frazzle; but you start feeling even worse afterwards. I learned from Pete that our timbermen were having a shindig, with fiddle music, at the tavern to celebrate. It was where Sandy had gone.

"We've got to pay those men."

"I forgot to tell you. I did. Lincoln give Herndon a bill and he give it to me before you got here."

I asked how much, getting ready to brace myself. I didn't care though how much it had cost us even if it was two or three hundred dollars. To get the *Talisman* around Snee Bend safely had been worth almost any price.

"Ninety-two dollars," Pete answered. "Lincoln writ everything down. Ten men, two days, at three dollars a head. Five boys, two

days at two dollars. Five dollars payment for a rail-splitting contest —I guess you know about that?"

"Yes."

"And two broken axes, three dollars and fifty cents each. Ninety-two dollars. Lincoln even added a note. If we thought paying for the axes waren't fair, we didn't have to. It was all the same to him. Well, I give Herndon a hundred dollars, even."

"They deserved more."

"It's all Herndon would take." He looked at his old lever watch. "Well. Grub, say, in fifteen minutes? Thankful was around asking for you. She was scared you'd catch cold, lose your specs, cut yourself—" He shook his head. "I used to think she was a right sensible girl but she was in a reg'lar, jasperin' tizzy about you. Yet, she jumped inside her stateroom the minute that wagon brought you to the wharf. Prob'ly, she's fixin' herself special for supper tonight. By thunder, we have *beat* that bend, haven't we? I guess I'll just trim my whiskers before grub. You look spruce enough . . . See here," he said, offhandedly. "You got a few extra minutes. Why don't you borry Sandy's razor? Go on. Take it. Just don't nick his razor too much though with them thick whiskers you grew back in that timber."

I let that last remark pass even if Pete thought it comical enough to repeat twice. I climbed the aft ladder, feeling my legs twitch a little. If it wasn't for knowing Thankful was readying herself special for supper tonight I might have cut grub altogether to stretch on the bunk. But I didn't want her to think I couldn't hold up as well as any of those frontiersmen who were celebrating tonight at the tavern, after building the weir.

For a second or so my mind harked upon Wash Hicks while I plastered a strip of ledger paper over a trifling gash in my jaw. Sandy had certainly honed his razor to a sharp edge. I told myself if I saw Wash tonight I'd keep my boiler level down and take anything he offered. The *Talisman* still came first. After we'd passed over the dam and were around Salt Fork and heading toward the Illinois River it would be time enough to let Wash know which one between us was big buck of these licks.

I started shaving, again, wondering why such a simple thing was so difficult. I could understand now why Pete preferred whiskers. Somebody knocked. "It's me, Pete. Open up." I laid aside the razor, hastily plastered a second piece of paper over a trifling gash from

my left ear, and opened the door. Pete seemed filled with something important—but he stopped short to ask, "Ain't that blood?"

I ripped off more paper, said, "Not much. What's wanted?" and plastered a smaller trifle under my chin.

"Bogue—" Now he'd decided I wasn't bleeding to death, rage took hold of him. His voice sounded thick. "Bogue's here again."

I swung around. "What's he want? Why didn't you throw him off?"

The veins throbbed in his forehead. I thought for a second Pete was going to have a stroke. Even more thickly he answered, "I locked him in the parlor till I could see you. He told me he was ready to offer six thousand dollars for our steamer. I would have thrown him into the river—but what he next told me stopped me. He says we better have a look ourselves at that New Salem dam. We'd better see just how much of a head of water's flowing before we decide to turn down his offer a second time."

I was startled. I remembered speaking to Dave about that dam. His father was half owner along with that Mr. Cameron who was so dead set against steamboats on this river.

"Pete, I know we've enough of a head to carry the *Talisman* over the dam. The steamer only draws two feet. Dave Rutledge told me only an hour ago a thirty-inch head was piling up above the dam."

"I don't know who told you or how right he is. All I know—here's Bogue again. This time that goosy voice sounded more pleased and certain than I've ever heard it. He's got something up his sleeve. You come with me, listen, and be a witness if he tries for trouble. I've already told Mrs. Hicks they'd have to have supper without us."

That second meeting with Bogue was short and it was unpleasant. He was offering six thousand dollars for the steamer, lock, stock and barrel, providing we turned the steamer back first thing tomorrow while there was still time and ran to his landing at Springfield. As proof of his good faith, he'd give me one thousand dollars down with a certified and signed statement that he would pay over the other five thousand to me as soon as my father wrote him back, accepting the offer.

When he was finished, I said I knew the *Talisman* could pass over Cameron's dam tomorrow. A thirty-inch head was running. We only drew twenty-four inches. Bogue smiled sadly at me as if somehow he was sorry for my ignorance.

"That dam has more than a thirty-inch head."

"More?" That was even better.

"I was up there measurin' the thing only three hours ago. You got nearly thirty-two inches. By tomorrow, at full rise, that head ought to swell maybe to thirty-five inches. You see? I'm being honest with you. But just think a minute." He looked at Pete. "Now, sir. What *is* that head? It's milk-water, ain't it? Not solid water at all. That head is half air, Wilmot. You know that. Goin' upstream, yes; *that* was different. The prow always lifts up *against* the current. Traveling

with the current, you'll surge down through that milk-water head. The *Talisman*'ll hit the dam and probably carry away Cameron's two mills, as well. Don't Cameron know that? This time, about, last year, didn't Linkern hang a raft—a small raft—on that same dam? That raft nearly took one mill off the log-pen holding it. The *Talisman* will carry everything. It's what I was telling Mr. Cameron, too, before I rode back to show you how to do this thing right."

All down soft in a rumble, Pete asked, "You've been doing some mighty big talkin' to this fellow Cameron, haven't you?"

"Ain't this a free country? Since when can't a man have a few words with a good friend?"

I said, desperately, "Mr. Cameron ought to know we're willing to pay full damages—"

"Pay? With *my* money—that twenty-five hundred dollars you got off me? Say, you'd need twice that to restore a dam and two mills. Besides, how does Cameron know you got much left? Maybe most has been spent. Wasted on them Clary Grove fellows Linkern jollied into building that weir."

I started to speak.

"No, sir. I don't want to hear no more from you . . ." Bogue faced Pete. "Here's what I say. Help me take this steamer tomorrow back to my wharf. I pay you a hundred dollars. How's that? 'Be fair unto others,' is my motto, 'and they'll be fair unto you.' I got cash in my pocket. Just stick out your hand—"

That was a thundering mistake he made, trying to bribe Pete.

Afterwards from Smoky I heard how Pete had marched Bogue over the gangplank to the wharf where he lost hold of him by having his peg leg get stuck in a knot hole. But when Pete roared and grabbed at Bogue and hustled him out of the parlor, slamming the door, the shakes hit me. All my sand ran out on me. It was Thankful who first found me. She must have heard the commotion Bogue was making and have run up to the hurricane deck.

Pete returned. I was trying to sit up. Mrs. Hicks poured elm bark tea into me which did nothing in general but scald my insides. Everyone cleared out, finally, except Pete. I had a chance to ask if Bogue had been telling the truth. Would that head of water over the dam fail to float us over? He said, "A head of water has got all sorts of air in it. But we'll manage. You'll see. I'll talk to Lincoln and Herndon. Now you get to sleep. I been kicking myself for not seeing sooner how played out you was. And tomorrow you're going to rest."

Tomorrow was Thursday, the fifth. It poured most of that morn-

ing. I had grub in bed. The two women, Mrs. Hicks and Aunty Phoebee, forced me to swallow all their hot gruel. They exclaimed over how I'd cut my face in the timber yesterday. I never could bring myself to admitting I hadn't done it in the timber but with Sandy's razor. Pete came in later. Herndon and he had talked everything over. Herndon believed Cameron would agree to let us run the dam, provided we put up cash, say a thousand dollars, in what was called "escrow" to pay for all damages.

I asked, "How soon are we leaving?" Pete answered that Herndon was waiting to see if Lincoln agreed with us.

"Isn't Lincoln here?"

"He went off somewhere last night with some of them Sucker friends of hisn," Pete said. "But he'll get here quick enough. It's only three hours downstream to the dam, anyhow."

Afterwards, I must have slept some more.

It didn't appear to be raining so hard when I awakened. My legs weren't as queer feeling as they had felt last night. I was stiff, though. I felt like I'd been put through a mill wheel and was just beginning to get back to myself again. I dressed, wondering why we hadn't started off by now.

When I opened the door and stepped out, on the river side, not the wharf side, I heard voices coming up to me from the passenger deck below. It was Thankful's and Wash Hicks's. They were down there below me looking at the river and at the trees, dead skunks, a chicken coop, an old hat, I didn't know what else, everything the flash rise was carrying along on the yellow current. And they seemed to be having a gay time of it.

Wash was bragging about all the relatives he had waiting for him in St. Louis and how important they were. I heard him say his uncle was a constable. A constable! Thankful laughed, light and airy. She said she expected she and Wash would see each other often in St. Louis, wouldn't they?

I didn't want to hear any more of it. I scrooged forward to the wheelhouse. Pete and Herndon were in there together. Pete was saying, "Herndon, you know I like you. But as sure as I'm standing here, I'm going to get dropsy and wither from old age if—you—can't—get them words out quicker. What's Lincoln gone off to Pappville for when he knows we want him here?"

"He's—trying—to—locate—Rutledge.   That's—where—Rutledge—went—to—buy—seed."

They both saw me at the same time.

Pete said didn't I know I belonged in bed? I said I was going to rot away if I had to stay any longer in my bunk and drink any more of that elm bark tea. What were we waiting here for? Where was Lincoln?

Well, Lincoln had ridden to a town called Pappville, twenty-some miles away. Last night somebody at the tavern had told him Mr. Rutledge had gone to Pappville. Before we had even started worrying or thinking much about it, Lincoln had seen we'd have to get hold of Mr. Rutledge. It was necessary to bring him on our side and have him agree we could try to run the dam before we ever could hope to make any headway with the other partner, Cameron.

We waited until after dinner. Not a word from Lincoln. The rain had petered to a drizzle; the sun was trying to shine. If the rain stopped, that meant we'd lose any benefit from the flash rise after another thirty to forty hours. For all we knew, Lincoln's horse might have bogged down in the mud roads anywhere between here and Pappville and he was trying to get back to us on foot.

It was Herndon who decided we wouldn't wait. We'd steam west to the dam. He'd try to convince Cameron to grant us permission to try the dam this afternoon, providing we put up escrow money. So Smoky's men started firing the boiler. Herndon got hold of Jack Armstrong. I'd almost forgotten Armstrong, with everything else. But he'd showed up this morning at dawn. Pete said he'd been in the engine room all morning with Sandy. Sandy had been trying to explain to him how a steam engine worked. We weren't very far above Clary Grove, where Armstrong lived. He told us he knew this stretch of river all right. So he took the yawl, to go ahead and sound the channel for us. I wanted to go with him but Pete got fierce again. I was supposed to loaf today.

We upped gangplank about one o'clock. Everyone living at Sangamontown had gathered, watching us; and Smoky threw in some pitch, a shovel or so, to let them see we were leaving in style. The sun came out in a great warm bursting of light. A rainbow flung over the sky. Thankful said, "That's a good omen. I know it is!"

Wash Hicks said, "Whut's an omen?"

So Thankful had to explain to him, not laughing at his ignorance either. I don't even believe they noticed when I climbed back up to the hurricane deck. I wasn't jealous. I don't want you to think that either. If anything, I felt sorry for Wash Hicks, seeing how he'd combed his hair and had gotten himself into clothes that were clean enough, for once, but as raggy as ever. I expect this was the first

time in his life, too, he'd worn shoes on a day that wasn't Sunday.

Pretty soon that big bluff where New Salem was began lifting up higher and higher over the dark-green line of forestland. We were steaming in a northwesterly direction, if you didn't count the turns. The bluff was almost due ahead of us for nearly an hour. We had to us the grasshopper poles twice. We knocked into another mudbank just above the place Mrs. Hicks said was Bales' Slough. It was a gloomy stretch of river here with thick stands of sycamore on the west shore. The bottom land on the other side was filled with bull grass and wild plum. You could see the road running through the trees. It disappeared where it made a half circle around the bog and came out on the other side below us. Armstrong yawled up to our steamer. In his mild quiet way he said, "Wash, I need some help. Jump in. You know I knew yore paw. I'll take good keer of you. Don't be feared."

Wash hesitated, seemed to grow white—but he climbed down into the yawl. Whether you liked him or not you had to admit that Wash had good quality sand in him. He helped Armstrong tie our hawser to one of the sycamores. We steam-winched the *Talisman* free. Less than half a mile further we passed by Green Branch Landing. Now, the river veered to the right to swing around the prow of that big green bluff lifting in front of us. All at once, there ahead of us, not many minutes off, were the two mill shacks marking where the dam was.

I gripped that wooden railing so hard my fingers must have worn grooves in the wood. It had stopped raining. Armstrong and Wash rowed the yawl ashore near the dam. People were pouring down the road from New Salem to see what happened when we struck the dam. The gristmill and sawmill, off on the west side of the dam, loomed up bigger. You could see windows and the water wheel with a spray of water smoking up white. The river sunk down. You could feel the *Talisman* drop. Pete reversed the paddle to hold us steady.

A gray-haired lanky man ran from the west shore along a wooden trestle built out a dozen yards or so above the dam and river to his two mills. He leveled a musket at us. We were still about fifty rods east of the milky roll of water above the line of dam. Over the chuffing of our own engine you could hear the high whine and grating from the mills' wheel. The man standing on the trestle shouted, his voice sounding thin and angry:

"Don't come closer. I'll shoot. I hev my rights. The law's on my

215

side. Git back from whar you come or take the consequences. Herndon! You hear! Git back!"

"Cameron will shoot," Mrs. Hicks said at my side. "He's wuss than a mule when he gits the fit on him. Thankful Blair! Whar air you doin' up here? Git down! *Git down!*"

So we had to back until we had clearance, turn, the *Talisman* rolling hard on her beam, turn around and steam two miles to Green Branch Landing. Here we had to tie her in close to the river-bank, stem and stern, to prevent the current from fouling our wheel with drift. Some big sycamore branches scraped our roof. One knocked a hole in one of our windows.

Pete and Herndon departed as soon as we were tied, going to New Salem on top of the bluff to have a meeting with Mr. Cameron. Armstrong and Wash had stayed at New Salem instead of returning with us. I wanted to go with Pete. I might even have lost my temper, too. But Pete was firm.

"You might not believe it," he said, "but I've got some sort of re-sponsibility for you. There's nothing you can do at the meeting. There's probably not much I can do either. Herndon'll have to do the persuading unless Lincoln manages to get back.

"I just don't know what answer there is, Jim. I just plain don't know. But Herndon's a sticker, even if he talks slow. We'll stay there all night and next day *and* next day," he said grimly, "until either Lincoln gets back with the other partner or we wear that old buz-zard out. We got money to pay for any damages to that cussed dam. There's no sense in him trying to stop us. It's Bogue's talk of us pulling down the two mills along with the dam what's done it! I'd like to wring Bogue's fat neck."

There wasn't any cheer for any of us at mealtime. Later Thankful escaped long enough from Aunty Phoebee to come up alone with me to the hurricane deck for a minute or so. It had turned into one of those soft April evenings after the rain. We were close enough to the trees growing up from the riverbank to reach out and break off some of the twigs. A big branch stuck clear out, over our heads, closing off sight of the stars, and thumped the cabin roof now and then when the current gave a harder push against the *Talisman*.

It made a dark place up here. I thought if I could have Thankful step in with me where she couldn't see my face I could explain I'd like to have her be my girl, if she'd like to be. But I never got that far. I happened to mention I didn't much care having her waste her

time on Wash Hicks. She blazed up; and we ended with sharp words said on both sides . . .

I tried to sleep, couldn't, and tried to read in that book, remembering I'd promised to give it to Lincoln when I found it—and couldn't. I waited and waited. Pete and Herndon never returned. I heard Denny singing that "Ballad of the Blue-Tailed Fly" while he was standing watch. I got back into my clothes, went down to the boiler deck, ate a sandwich, stayed on for a while with Smoky while he stood his turn at watch; and Pete still didn't return. I climbed back to my office, blew out the lantern and lay down in my clothes, to rest, determined to stay awake until Pete got back and told me the news.

I don't know whether I fell asleep or not. Probably I did, but not clear deep into sleep because I started up in the darkness at a noise. I listened. It was only that sycamore branch scraping and thumping on the roof over me. The current, I thought, must be getting livelier. I lay back. The door squeaked. It shut, again. "Pete," I said. One of those little horn lanterns glimmered in my eyes. Automatically I reached in my pocket for the pewter case where I'd stuck my spectacles. "Pete?" I repeated, hearing my voice slide off, all wrong. I knew it wasn't Pete.

I knew it before Pollock whispered to me. "I want that money in your safe. If you don't get it for me I'll blow a hole in your head."

I'd no doubt at all. He would have. It was like that time when he'd grabbed me by the neck after I'd stumbled by accident against Mrs. Tanner. I hadn't meant anything to him. He'd been all set to snap my neck, for a second or so, until he'd recalled himself to where he was: a river pilot with people watching him. Tonight nobody was watching either of us. In that glow from his horn lantern, I could see one side only of his face. It was all long, pale, shiny, with the visible half of his mouth grinning horribly.

"Not a sound out of you," he whispered.

I got up, unlocking the safe. When I reached in for the tin box of money I felt Pete's loaded pistol behind the box. I was kneeling. Pollock was standing behind me. He'd see me pulling the pistol from the safe before ever I could swing around and point it up at him.

I withdrew the tin box, kicked the iron door of the safe shut. I was afraid he'd look inside the safe to see if I'd left more money there and then see the pistol. He didn't. It took only a second for him to unsnap the lid to the box.

He saw the sheafs of bank notes. His breath whistled. The tin box

was half again as long as that old pewter case which Lincoln had found for me in his barrel of rubbish. Pollock snapped the lid tight, thrust the box into a leather pouch he carried slung from his left shoulder, and whispered, "I've ten Clary Grove men hidden on the banks. If you give an alarm before another fifteen minutes they'll kill everyone on this boat."

He was gone.

I again heard the thump of sycamore branch on the roof as he leaped up in the darkness, outside, swinging himself on it.

I knew now how he'd gotten to my office without giving hue and cry to our night watchman. I even imagined I heard a whinny from a horse tied and waiting for him, invisible in the darkness, at the base of that big sycamore growing up between the road and the riverbank. I felt my fingers digging into the flesh of my palms and took a step through the blackness to the iron safe. He'd given himself away in one thing—saying he had a gang of Clary Grove men with him.

I'd worked with those Clary Grove men. Even if they'd obtained a scandalous reputation by too much skylarking, I knew they weren't thieves of the night or cutthroats. No, Pollock had managed alone. If I yelled before he scamped with all the steamer's funds he'd start shooting.

Below me and a little forward was the stateroom where Thankful and Aunty Phoebee were sleeping. A single shot could splinter through the thin shutters of the window and go worming into Thankful's head where she lay so peacefully on the bottom bunk. I couldn't give the alarm and risk Thankful or anyone aboard who had done so much for my father and for me to help get our steamer this far, risking one or more of them to a murderous fire. I was caught. I could not cry out for help. How much longer would it take Pollock to snake himself to the tree, down to a waiting horse and away with all our money? A minute? With our money gone, how could we offer surety of paying for damages done to the dam? Cameron would laugh in our faces.

I found myself stooping in the darkness, not using precious seconds to light the lantern. I felt for Pete's loaded pistol, stuck it in my belt, slipped out on deck, lost perhaps three precious seconds by hastily having to rid my eyes of my spectacles and place the spectacles in that case; and then, not blind, I wasn't blind in darkness without spectacles, because my fingers became my eyes—and, then, I reached up for the branch which could carry me to the tree.

I dropped to the road, hearing a drumming of hoofs. By the time I'd hooked on my spectacles I saw only a great streaking of something black in that eerie morning light. Next it was gone. I remembered the lane through the pawpaw trees at Hamacher's farm. I'd thought I had sparked up a deer. It must have been Pollock that night spying on our boat.

I began running south on the road, leaving our steamer and the clearing behind. The drumming of hoofs faded away but I still ran, harder than ever. I'd remembered something that had given me a glimmering of hope.

Bales' Slough wasn't very far from here. The river road looped around it, probably crossing by a bridge the crick that had to flow into the slough. The road swung north toward the river on the other side of the slough and again south to parallel the course of the river. There was just a chance, not much perhaps, but enough to try. I could wade or swim directly across the slough to the other side and get to the south side in time to surprise Pollock before his horse came galloping the long way around.

It must have been at least half an hour before sunrise. What light there was had the effect of washing shadows blacker and deeper. I kicked off my boots, wading in to my knees. Bull grass was high. Frogs croaked. A crane startled me.

Halfway across, the slough became deeper. I think the bottom probably sloped in a southerly direction toward the other shore where you could see nothing but a black wall of huge trees. I was holding the pistol above my head to keep it dry and it was harder going and my lungs were trying to tear themselves out from my body and I was afraid I was too late. By now Pollock would have circled the loop to go on south.

Of a sudden I went in deep—and by instinct gave a frog kick with my legs. It was enough just for that second to keep my pistol arm abovewater. I felt mud. I shoved forward. Next something slithered around my left leg. I thought it was a snake. It was only one of the sycamore roots which had been washed loose from the south shore.

I climbed through bull grass and stinking sourgrass, the ground still so soft I was sinking ankle deep at each step. I got through some trees, stretching up and up like pillars of a great church with that queerish morning light filtering down.

And everything was dead silent. I came to the road, just where it swung right to go south again. It was no use. I should have known I couldn't beat a fast horse—

Now I began to hear it from far away, like rapid beats of a muffled drum. I dodged back behind a big gnarly tree. Two drums? I listened. Two horses were racing toward me. Somebody besides me had caught sight of Pollock stealing off the boat and was chasing after him. I had scarcely time to collect my wits, get ready, grasp Pete's pistol, when that great black horse sprung into view. Pollock crouching low. Not ten yards behind him a second man and horse charged after.

I jumped up, hollered, "Stop!" and if I hadn't been on Pollock's left side I would have fallen the next instant with a bullet through my head.

He had to bring his right arm and hand around to aim at me. At the same time his horse shied violently. He fired. The concussion so startled my nerves I must have fired instantly back without consciously knowing my finger had pulled the trigger. The horse reared. Pollock flung up his hands, reeled, and his sugar-loaf sailed off his head.

Instead of going to my help the man chasing after Pollock pulled up his horse and shouted, "Whitey, fur God's sake keep agoin'! Hits only thet half-blind whelp. I'll take keer of him!"

The black horse pulled itself together, leaped forward, and began dwindling smaller and smaller in the half-light, Pollock reeling back

and forth in the saddle like something of straw. I whirled to face the second man, who dismounted.

It was Clem Diggon!

The warts on his face were like specks of black mud. The two men had been in it together from the very beginning! Why hadn't I ever guessed? He lifted his pistol, taking his time, knowing I'd shot my charge at Pollock.

I fell back over a root, grabbing at my spectacles. I heard a sudden drumming of more hoofs. I lifted, seeing Diggon's horse tearing away after the black horse. Diggon ran to the road. I had perhaps twenty or thirty seconds to retreat to the edge of the slough before his voice yelled at me, "Now, you hev done it! You hev stranded me 'ithout my hoss. Well, you whelp. Yore goin' to pay . . ." He was coming at me.

Sometimes your hands do things for you automatically because you've previously trained them. All the time I was backing in, deeper and deeper, my hands had whipped off my spectacles, stuck them into that pewter case, into my wet coat pocket; and I didn't know it, then. I wasn't thinking of them. I was getting breath into my lungs before pulling my head under that scum covering the stagnant water.

I heard a dead branch crack. Something loomed before me. I ducked down under before Diggon could shoot. This was where it was over my head. I held myself down, grasping at the water grass growing from the bottom.

It wasn't entirely without light down here. Some shade through the green scum rippling over me. Everything was all a huge green, moving and twisting around me; and I began to need air. A frog or a catfish rasped my arm, plopped up—and my ears felt a concussion through the water of Diggon's shot. He'd thought it was me surfacing.

I let the current float me along until I was washed against the shelving mud bank. I couldn't stay under any longer. I lifted my head through the grass, blowing out the used air and filling my lungs. I couldn't see very much where I was. I guessed I was a dozen yards down the slough, toward the river. I listened. I didn't hear Diggon. Maybe he'd decided he'd killed me. I let myself rest a dozen seconds longer, exhaling and breathing in. I tried to think. I could float to the river and swim north, toward Green Branch for help while Diggon either ran for it or still was hunting me on this

side. I was filling my lungs to the full before submerging when Diggon took me by complete surprise.

He must have sighted me, and had come wriggling inch by inch closer to the bank. His hand shot out, grabbing me by the hair. All I saw was a shape rearing up with something else, thinner and higher, above his head, and a dull flashing of steel. It was his other arm, raised to plunge his knife into me. His voice said, "This time, you whelp—" I gave a convulsive kick against the mud, feeling his fingers tear at my hair. He gave a cry. His knife hummed and splashed beyond us into the scum. He toppled in with me and bore me down. The green scum closed thickly over us.

If Diggon thought at all in his rage and fury and chagrin, I suppose his intention was to keep my head underwater until I drowned. For my part, I don't suppose I did any conscious thinking, either. You don't at a time like that. But the water had always been my element. I was back to being Turtle Owens. I knew if my lungs could outlast his I was safer down in here than anywhere else.

I don't believe Diggon ever counted on me wrapping my legs around his and my arms around the arms he'd used to shove his hands around my throat. For those few first seconds while we threshed and rolled and got tangled in the slough grass, mud stirred up and darkened the water, blotting all the greenish liquid light away—I don't believe it came to him I was conserving my wind and letting him use up his. It was when he began trying to get his head to the surface to breathe that the real fight came. It was like being in a dark liquid world of no air, in the midst of a snake pit, with long snakes entangling our legs and holding us under the scum.

He'd ceased trying to choke me. He was trying to push at me, to get free, and my wind was nearly used up, too. Then we didn't care about each other any more. We must have drifted off into separate worlds of liquid darkness.

I was trying to get to the surface and couldn't. Snakes were holding me down. I had a vague awareness we must have floated under a bank, partly eaten out by the rains; and we'd drifted into a net of sycamore roots. My lungs were bursting. I had the sensation somehow of my mind being a valve. In another second my mind would let go, open itself; and all of me, lungs, every part in me crying for air, would open for water to go rushing all through me.

It was like being caught under an old sunken barrel, with no air space inside between the barrel head and water. Down! Down! Get under the bottom of the barrel. I had just enough remaining sense to

force myself *deeper*, until I felt cold ooze. I wriggled and kicked and shot up, gasping, green scum splattering. Air!

I dragged myself to the bank. I couldn't get enough air. Diggon? I didn't hear him. I wriggled higher, hiding in old winter leaves and new grass—and there was that same old dreadful business of having to hook my spectacles on even if it cost me precious seconds.

Now, the world jarred against my eyes. Everything shot back in normal shape again. A rosy morning glow seeped through the branches. I didn't see Diggon. Either he'd waded across to the west shore to hunt for me there or had returned to this side, further up, to strike the road. I crawled. I got to the road, listening. A yellow-hammer slung by in a flutter of wings. I jumped.

The road was empty. What to do? If Diggon was hiding on the other side of the loop I still couldn't get back to the boat. After that, the forest was so silent I could hear my heart's blood softly roaring in my ears. My lungs were still blowing out and sucking in air like bellows. From down the road, south, to my left, a voice was singing, at first faint and far away:

> "Ol' massa's dead; oh, let him rest!
> Dey say all things am for de best;
> But I can't forget until I die
> Ol' massa an' de blue-tailed fly . . ."

There was Jack Kelso, walking toward me, his old fishing creel on his shoulder, his fiddle on his back, a tattered hat tipped on his Injun-black hair, his hands in his pockets.

"Why, Owens—" he said, and stopped.

I told him everything. In that filtering of early April morning light he listened to me like the great gentleman he was for all of the opinion Mrs. Hicks'd had of him as the worst scamp in the county and the most disreputable friend Lincoln owned.

When I finished and he spoke, you could still tell that he'd had an education somewhere, although where I never knew or tried to ask. He opened his creel of woven willow splits, handing me from it a small pistol of bluish steel no bigger than the palm of my hand. I knew what it was at first glance. It was one of the pieces Mr. Deringer, in Philadelphia, had been selling of late in considerable quantities to gentlemen and others, I must admit, who weren't but wished a pocket piece and had the price to pay.

"Stay here," said he. "You've had about enough this morning. I'll

do some reconnoitering around the slough. If Diggon's hidin' I'll find him because I've had some experience before in that line."

Kelso was so much lighter and slimmer than Diggon, I didn't like to think of the two meeting. But Kelso laughed silently, opened his ragged coat wider, and pointed to a knife stuck there in his belt. In a second he was gone. He had vanished like the wind into the dark forest.

I sat there for a time, beginning to recover some of my wits as well as my physical being. I took myself up and got back several paces from the road, hiding behind a tree. I saw now that instead of being below, or south, of where originally I'd crossed the slough as I'd thought, actually I was something west on the road of where I'd been fired at by Pollock and had fired back at him. It came to me that Diggon might have outsmarted me a second time, had hidden at the sound of Kelso's song of "The Ballad of the Blue-Tailed Fly." I could imagine his warty face, all stained now with swamp scum, as mine also must be, somewhere on the other side of the road, waiting, waiting until Kelso had put enough distance between us.

Nervously I grasped at the steel handle of the little derringer. I don't know how many minutes I waited in the sycamore forest, perhaps ten, perhaps more. It was an age. All at once came a crashing. A sapling fluttered. Out into the road stepped something all humped and black and shaggy, looking like a mountain, its tiny red eyes searching at me. It swung its huge head. I didn't move, didn't breathe; and the buffalo turned and pushed back into the timber and was gone. Ever since leaving Cincinnati I'd been on the watch for buffalo, hoping to get close enough to one to have a shot. Well, I'd had my chance. That buffalo, after Diggon, was enough to give me the purest undiluted spasms.

What with the buffalo lumbering heavily into the timber, I never did hear or see Jack Kelso's coming. He was before me, again, only the trembling of new green leaves behind him to mark that he had arrived from the edge of the slough and not by the road around.

"Diggon—"

"No sign. He's scamped."

"You're certain?"

"I've an insight in such things. Come. I'll walk with you a ways toward your steamboat."

He took my arm when I tottered. That struggle with Diggon under the green scum had badly unhinged my legs. I asked Kelso what he was doing on the road at this time of morning.

By no good fortune at all, he answered. Wednesday night he'd fiddled for the dance at the Sangamontown tavern. While listening, I had to think out when Wednesday night had been. This was Friday morning. Yesterday, Thursday, after trying to run the dam and being halted by Cameron, we had tied up at Green Branch. When Lincoln had needed a road companion for a journey, Kelso was saying, he had ridden with Lincoln to Pappville. They had located Mr. Rutledge, returning yesterday through the rain, arriving at New Salem about midnight.

We had come to the most lonesome stretch, yet, of the road. Kelso halted, watching me you would think like a hawk sighting down through the air at some awkward, muddy, unresisting species of prey. I felt oddly uneasy from the unwinking stare of those gypsy eyes, although I knew it was my great good luck to happen upon him and have him with me on my way toward the steamer. I was not yet as convinced as he was that Diggon had run off. At Rutledge's tavern, said Kelso, they were arguing at midnight with Cameron. The whole crowd of them had bunked at the tavern. For all Kelso knew by now they had arisen, eaten, and were at it as furiously as ever. What eventually they decided was none of his concern. The river would flow more sweetly if both dam and steamer were blown to dust. Before dawn he had taken himself down the river around in the fresh new blackness before all the cocks began crowing. Two horsemen had ridden by him, nearly trampling him down. Not very long after he'd heard pistol shots. It was not the first nor would it be the last time a solitary man heard pistol shots before cockcrow. Going around the slough he saw nothing. He had continued. He had heard a faint cry come from behind him. He had turned back, his curiosity aroused. When he arrived, he said, I was waiting by the road, looking as bedraggled and dazed a young fellow as ever he'd laid eyes on.

He stopped and pointed the way for me. "Now I shall be leaving you. If it's of interest to you, Rutledge had agreed you steamboaters can run the dam providing you show in advance you can pay for necessary repairs. Between Rutledge and Lincoln, the two of them should persuade the other partner, Cameron—"

"But Pollock has all our money," I cried. "I fired at him and failed to stop him. How can we pay?"

"Here's an easy answer. Send for more money."

"To St. Louis? Will the rise of river wait for us that long?"

"To tell you the truth that is a point I had not considered. No," he

said after a pause, "I had not. Well, you winged your man with your pistol even if you failed to stop him. His leather pouch fell to the road along which I came walking this morning singing a song for my pleasure. Alackaday, I had thought the Kelso luck was with me for sure when I saw all that great fortune . . ." From his creel, Kelso withdrew a familiar-looking black-japanned tin. It was our money box!

I looked at the money box and at him. He put it in my hands.

"One favor for another, Owens," he said. "Because I prefer to keep more of Lincoln's esteem than I deserve, I'm asking you to forget my failure this morning at a bit of secondhand knavery."

Sometimes it's better not to speak. I nodded.

"Now, my derringer?"

I'd forgotten I'd stuck it in my pants. I took our money box in the crook of my left arm, and handed him back his little derringer. I wondered where he had stolen it.

He popped it in his creel and I suppose you could wonder what else he kept secreted in that creel. I began to doubt very much if it ever had held many fish. "You won't need a pistol," said he, "to take you back safe to your steamer. Have no fear. You shan't see Diggon again."

"I wish I could believe it."

"Believe me, I have a strong insight in such affairs. My insight also tells me that you and I shan't ever see each other again, which will be little loss to you. Welladay!" He laughed and it seemed to be at himself. I could not help smiling a little at him myself for very plainly he was put out for having forced himself to return our steamer's money after finding it there by the road in Pollock's pouch. "Although you and I have little in common, I recall we both share a liking for the writings of Mr. Burns. D'you know these lines?" He quoted:

> "The wan moon is setting beyond the white wave,
> And time is setting wi' me, O."

That was all.

But for me they were the two most—most seizing—most poignant lines Mr. Burns or anyone whom I'd read had ever written. However, if there's no particular feeling in those two lines for you, it's all the same. In those days people, I don't know why, liked poetry better than people of these days.

I saw Jack Kelso had turned and was walking away. "Good-by," I called.

He never looked back.

"Good-by," I called a second time.

He went walking away, out of my life, with that old willow creel at his side and his fiddle over his shoulder. Never once did he look back.

The cocks were beginning to crow from that bluff high above me when I rounded the west side of the slough, going mighty slow. It still hurt to breathe. But it was as Jack Kelso had said. No one rose up from the grass to stop me. I passed by safely. I still wonder, sometimes, how Kelso could have been so certain. In my mind I still seem to see him, as dark as any gypsy, wading into the slough and pulling up a hand and arm and finally a face, covered with black warts and green slime. My mind stops there . . .

I came to the boat and Smoky exclaimed at seeing me. What was I doing here like this? He had thought I was in my office, the door closed, sleeping. I hushed him down until we got aft, to the engine room. It was after seven in the morning, I learned. Accompanied by Sandy, Thankful, Mrs. Hicks, and Aunty Phoebee, Pete had had a quick breakfast, and had walked on up the bluff where a meeting was being held to decide whether or not our steamer would be allowed to pass over the dam. Thankful had wanted to have me awakened. Mrs. Hicks had said to let the boy sleep. Those men would be arguing for hours today. She knew Cameron. I'd have time to go up the hill later, if I wished.

Well, I told Smoky some of what had happened—not all. I said I'd winged Pollock. He'd let his pouch slip. I'd picked up our money box. That was all that was necessary to say. I changed to clean clothes after he had poured cold water over me and helped me scrub the slime off my skin. He was as difficult to get pried free from as Aunty Phoebee and Mrs. Hicks when they'd been dosing me with their scalding elm bark tea.

He said, "No, suh, Mist' Owens. You hev time. Missis Hicks says so. You eat dat food before you moves agin off this hyar boat."

It helped some, too, to get food inside my stomach. Because I was beginning to have a private notion of my own, I rummaged in our boat chest for one of our own leather mail pouches and slipped the money box inside. I slung the pouch over my shoulder and started off, again, on the road that ran north a ways under the bluff, parallel

to the river, and turned to go winding up and up toward the town of New Salem. I met Dave Rutledge halfway up the road. He stopped when he saw me, his face shining with excitement.

"Wal, you woke up, did you, at last? Linkern took a minute to whisper for me ter run like blazes an' wake you up and hev you git up here quick ef you didn't want to miss the ruckus. Hurry. Justice Green is thar. Old man Cameron's dead set as ever, wuss even now he's seen my pap swing ter you steamboaters' side. Bogue is thar, goin' at a great rate. Everyone who kin crowd inter our tavern is thar. Some hez brung muskets. Thet feller of yourn, Sandy Jenks, he got inter a fight with Cameron's nephew. Justice Green hez said the law is on Cameron's side. Jes' becuz Pap's one partner, one partner kain't agree to hev the dam wrecked 'ithout the other. Whut kept you so long? Don't you care ef yore steamboat gits stuck here on this side of the dam an' stays til she rots?"

He stopped, waiting for me to catch up with him. "Say, whut's wrong with you, anyhow? Hurry! You act like you hev bin up half the night 'stead of sleepin' like a log an hour past grubtime. *Hurry*, kain't you?" He pointed to the mail pouch hanging from my shoulder. "Whut's thet? Ef you've brung letters, yore too late. The mudwagon left for Springfield forty-five minutes ago. Oh, hurry! I don't want ter miss all the fun!"

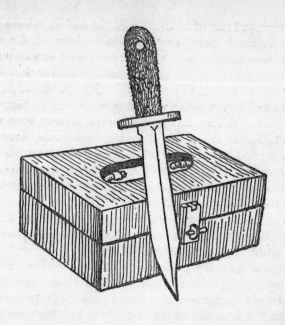

The road taking us to the top of the bluff ran back on itself, south, above the river; and, nearly at the top, just before it curved to the right, Dave pointed to a small log cabin at our left, the door closed, and said that was Offut's store where Lincoln clerked. The dandelions spread their yellow sheen on the meadow and Dave kicked off four or five dogs that ran toward us. "Thar's Pap's tavern. Look at the crowd."

It was a story-and-a-half tavern with the loft big enough, I imagined, under the big shake roof to accommodate a dozen travelers for the night. It was built of squared logs, carefully chinked, not "dog-logs"—as I'd heard logs called with the bark left on, the reason obvious enough, I would say.

It had a narrow door at the end nearest us, probably opening into the kitchen or the Rutledges' private quarters; a single window on beyond; and a larger door, almost hidden by the crowd. Because windows were generally considered a nuisance, the oiled paper or scraped leather leaking water, letting in cold air, with glass too dear to buy, and easily broken, most cabins and half the taverns you saw didn't much trouble with the things. It showed the Rutledge tavern was a cut above the ordinary with a luxury like that window with real glass in it.

We would have never pushed through the people packed around

the second door if Dave hadn't hollered, "Make way. This is a steamboat feller." About forty men and women had packed themselves into the common room to hear the argument, with half that many kids underfoot, wedging themselves into any leftover spaces.

It was no use trying to shove. But Dave knew his own house—or inn. He edged back to me with a box; we got up on that, sighting over the heads of the people in front of us. I recognized the huge man sitting at the table at the far end. He was Justice Green. Off to his left was Lincoln, a good half a head taller than anyone else. Behind Lincoln was Herndon and Pete. I thought I saw Thankful somewhere. All the faces began blurring. Justice Green hit the table with the palm of his hand.

When all the rustling and murmuring and whispering died away, he said, "We've been here now two hours this morning an' we were at it last night I don't know how long after I fell asleep . . ." Somebody laughed. He waited. "We haven't made progress. I'm sorry for the steamboat people. If two partners *can't* agree, why, the law *is* on the side of the partner who wants to keep his business as is. That dam stays. The law says you can't break up another man's property 'ithout that man's permission. I'm sorry." There was a kind of silence. He said again, "I'm sorry," looking toward Lincoln and Pete.

A thin man in neat clothes with a moony-looking, pleasant face, not very old perhaps forty, began standing. I hadn't seen him before because Lincoln hid him from where I was craning my neck and trying to keep my perch on Dave Rutledge's box.

Dave stuck his elbow into my ribs and whispered, "Thet's Pap, now. He's goin' to hev his say agin old Cameron."

Mr. Rutledge had a thin worried voice. While he was speaking I noticed what seemed to me to be an uncommon number, suddenly, of girls cramming their heads through the door of the partition separating the common room from the family's quarters. I decided probably they were a good share of Dave's sisters, wanting to hear their father. I wondered which one of them there was Ann Rutledge, that girl back in the timber whose hands and voice had been so light and gentle.

Mr. Rutledge finished, "Now, Cameron. Ef they are willin' to put up one thousand dollars in escrow, against all possible damages, an' ef Justice Green holds thet money till the steamboat—"

"Rutledge," said a harsh voice to the right of Justice Green's desk, "yore a fool. I jes' won't be bulled." The man speaking was too far to the left. I couldn't see him. Dave whispered it was old Cameron.

The harsh voice ground on and on. "You know steamer traffic will be the ruination of this here river for milldams, Rutledge. We are doing a good business, hain't we? Let one steamer break up our dam —we'll have hundreds wantin' the same— An' you, Linkern. I thought you was a good friend of mine?"

"I am," said Lincoln.

"Here you are, set agin me. Whar do you live in this town? At my place. I give you room and board. I hev welcomed you as one of my family. Why are you agin me? Linkern, I *know my rights*. Tell them steamer fellows they'll hev to wait till next winter when the river rises agin."

Pete spoke from his side of the room. "Mr. Cameron, we'll be willing to put up *two thousand* of our money in escrow to show you our good intentions. I know we won't damage that dam at the most over five hundred—"

"Cameron, don't listen to him!" Bogue pushed through the crowd, sawing his elbows, standing up there now in front of the desk, his brass buttons shining. "First and foremost, I'm a millowner like Cameron. I was responsible for bringin' that steamer up to my mill, yes. I won't say maybe I was tricked. No, I don't go that far. If that steamer draws more water than I was told, it was my fault. I ought to have looked. Yes, I'm ready and willing to admit I made a mistake. But I know steamboaters. They're a shiftless lot for the most part, I'm sorry to say. Two thousand dollars? Where would they find that money? You—all of you listenin' here, now where would *you* get two thousand dollars all of a sudden? I tell you it's buncombe, Mr. Cameron. If Peter Wilmot, here, has two thousand dollars to give into escrow, why don't he show the color of it? Why? *He ain't got it*. That's why. He—" He sighted to see who'd shouted at him.

It was my voice.

Sometimes you can get so fighting mad you forget a whole crowd is listening. I'd yelled that was a lie. We did have the money. Right then I was glad I'd had that notion—feeling—to bring along our money. So they opened a way for me. I walked to the table and took out our money box and said, "There, sir."

Justice Green lifted the lid. He looked at the sheafs of notes, smiled, closed the lid, and laid his hand on the box. Lincoln stepped forward and said one word:

"Cameron?"

"Linkern, I *got my rights*. No."

There it was . . .

Old Cameron *was* like a mule, I expect. He was "sot." The more you argued the more sot he became. I think everyone of us in that common room saw it. I heard a kind of sigh lifting from the air. A couple of men and one woman edged out of the door. They knew the show was over.

But Lincoln didn't appear to know that yet. *He* started speaking. When he turned his back to me to address Justice Green I saw his hands clasped hard behind his back. And he was inclining forward again. Seeing him from the rear you saw how large his ears were. They ran out almost at right angles from his head. Perhaps it came from him pulling that old straw hat he wore out of doors clear down hard on his ears.

And he was laboring to express himself. He was being careful and picking his words and speaking in that same elevated style he'd tried on the storekeeper in Springfield. His voice pitched up high, too high; and you could hear little nervous titters from the people packed in there, watching and listening and wondering just what Lincoln had in mind. At first all Lincoln did was to remind them he was planning to run for election next fall, providing he didn't get chased too far out of the map by old Black Hawk to find his way back. Usually Lincoln's jokes could bring a laugh; but this one fell flat. I felt pure misery. *What was he doing?* Now we'd lost our steamboat had he decided to take advantage of the crowd to canvass for more votes?

He went on. He seemed to get easier with it, not so nervous. He reminded them he had promised, if elected, to advocate for the improvement of the Sangamon River. He felt somewhat at home, he told us, in discussing water transportation. Hadn't he floated flatboats and their cargoes some four thousand miles in the past four years?

I could begin to see now that this wasn't a political speech. He was starting to head toward something that had to do with our steamboat. What it was I didn't yet see. I felt a quivering of excitement. You could sense it from the others, too. Nobody was whispering or murmuring or scratching himself for a stray flea or acting restless any more. It was all a dead silence except for Lincoln's voice. He was smiling a little. He was acting as if he *was* here among friends and not too nervous any more at giving them a speech. He spoke to Cameron, like only the two of them were here.

He said he was his friend. In Cameron's house he had found a kindness which he had been deprived of for too long by time and

distance separating him from his own family. He agreed Cameron had rights. Why, I heard him state Cameron's case against our steamboat better than Cameron had done. When he finished he turned, facing us.

He said steamboat people also had certain rights. He said he had not happened to think of those rights until a few minutes ago when Mr. Cameron had mentioned *his* own property rights to the dam. He was sorry, he told us, not to have thought any sooner. But he had come across those rights a couple of months ago when he was getting material from lawyer John Stuart, in Springfield, while preparing a political campaign.

He paused. Then he said, "Under the Federal Constitution an' its laws no one has the right to dam up or in any way obstruct a navigable stream. Thet dam of Cameron's and Rutledge's—" He paused. *"That dam obstructs thet stream, don't it?"*

He stopped. He didn't need to say anything else.

We won, right then.

There was so much noise you couldn't hear yourself think. The fact is I didn't know why I didn't think of what Lincoln had told us sooner. My father had said almost the identical thing back in Cincinnati, when he'd heard of the project to throw a pontoon bridge across the Ohio from Rock Point. It was true. It was such common knowledge that it was against national laws to obstruct a navigable stream that I expect everyone or almost everyone there also remembered as soon as Lincoln had mentioned it.

The point is—*I didn't think of a dam as being an obstruction.* You don't. An obstruction is a mud shoal or a snag or a toll bridge crossing. That a dam also came under the head of obstructions had never crossed my mind. But Lincoln had thought it out.

My back was sore from where Dave had been pounding it. Justice Green hammered on the table for silence. He rose up, big as two barrels; and he said there was no doubt. Lincoln was right. He didn't know why he hadn't thought of it himself. I expect everyone here was asking himself or herself that identical question.

"Consequently," he said, "neither Cameron or Rutledge can stop the steamer. Furthermore, I must say, they can't ask for any damages done—"

"No, sir. No, *sir!*" That was Bogue. He'd jumped up again. "I say this—the Sang'maw River ain't navigable! That steamer hasn't floated on this here river. You all know that. She's fitted with devices

to walk her way, like she was a wagon. That's what she's done. She's walked and crawfished and—"

"Bogue," Lincoln said, not very shrill at all, "that won't do, will it? The *Talisman* ran all the way from the Illinois up the San Gammaw to your landin'. If you don't call that *demonstrable* proof this river is navigable, I don't know what 'demonstrate' means!"

I watched Bogue start flapping his elbows. His face grew purple. He was so sore and angry and disappointed and chagrined he'd even reversed himself, saying the Sangamon wasn't navigable, after having proven it was. He tried to speak. His throat just closed up on him. He ran out of fuel. I thought he was going to strangle. He gave a sudden hop, put down his head, jammed through that crowd and got away. I heard a horse galloping off. It was that sudden.

Pete was trying to say something. But by this time both Cameron and Rutledge were just beginning to realize how far they were in the wrong. Instead of being able to collect any damages from us, we could blow their dam and their two mills to Kingdom Come. A couple of fellows started scowling. You could feel a new sudden tenseness. But Lincoln he looked around him and rocked back, sort of, on his heels and began laughing as if something had struck him as being comical. Well, when somebody starts laughing you look around, wanting to know the joke.

"Bogue," he said in his commonest country style," is all right. But I sorter think sometimes when he gits ter oratin', like jes' now, his oratory suspends all action of his mind. I don't know anything ter compare with friend Bogue in this partic'lar 'cept thet steamer down thar below, waitin' in the river. It's sich a triflin' little affair when you come ter think of it, bustlin' an' puffin' and wheezin' on our river an' it only hez a five-foot boiler an' with thet big seven-foot whistle, why, you know, every time it whistles the boat allas hez to stop."

That wasn't true. We'd only had to stop once because of low steam pressure; and that had been when we'd been using winch, grasshopper legs, and our stern wheel. But I didn't mind. It struck everyone in here as appropriate and when you thought of Bogue finally running out of his steam and having to stop—well, I laughed as much as anyone. Pete finally got his lick in. He said our offer still stood. We'd pay for all damages done to the dam. I was proud of him, having him say that.

All the town, people, dogs, hogs, every creature in it, trailed along to watch Sandy and Pete and Lincoln measure the dam's head. It was nearly noon.

I don't quite know how it happened but Thankful and Dave Rutledge and I stuck together, going down the road. She wanted to stop a moment when Dave showed her the log store where Lincoln worked.

She asked, "Where's that barrel of rubbish? I'd like to see it."

Dave asked what barrel?

She said, "The one Lincoln found Jim's spectacle case in."

But we didn't have time. Anyway, Dave said, Offut wasn't here to open up the store. He didn't know where Offut had gone to, he told us. Business wasn't very good—too much competition. Instead of keeping the store open while Lincoln was busy with us, Offut had closed it.

When we came to the bank above the river Mrs. Hicks saw Thankful and snatched at her, saying, "See here, young lady. This hain't no proper place for you—"

"Please!"

"They mou't be some cussin', young lady, when thet steamer strikes the dam. You come with me."

Thankful gave us a woeful look and marched off with Mrs. Hicks. I was sorry she had to miss the rest of it. Dave and I waited while the men measured the water. By now, most of the women and girls had cleared off, going up along the road or high up on the bluff to sight down at us. I remembered sighting inside the tavern at four or five pretty faces and wondered which one of them was Ann Rutledge. I asked.

"Ann? She hain't here terday. She's helpin' out at Jim Short's farm. But say—won't she be put out, though, when she l'arns what she missed? Kin you keep a secret?"

"Mostly."

"She's sorter sweet on Linkern."

"Is she?"

"Sorter. She's promised ter marry another feller, McNeil—he was here before Linkern came. Maw says when a girl promises ter marry a feller she has ter keep the promise. But McNeil hain't a happy feller. He's kinder strange. Mebbe, she won't marry McNeil arter all. Say—look thar. Ain't they nearly through?"

I pushed closer. I saw Pete. He was grinning.

"Here," said he. "You forgot that money you brought. You ain't much of a mud-clerk, are you? But don't worry. Sandy's got it, safe. Ain't this a happy day?"

"Can we make it?"

"We'll sure try. Get on back to the steamer. Oh—" He turned, seeing Lincoln and Herndon. "Where's Armstrong? He'd best stay in the yawl . . ."

Well, I was less than a yard from the trestle leading over the water to the dam and the gristmill. It was too much of a temptation. I walked out on it, hearing the big water wheel grinding away, the noise out here so loud you couldn't hear much of the shouting along the banks.

I edged around the first mill, to the trestle connecting it with the second—wanting to get clear on, if possible, to sight at the dam itself. But I saw Wash Hicks was over there, opposite me. He stared at me and I stared back, the millrace frothing and foaming underneath.

All I had to do was give him a shove. That demon seemed to start speaking in my ear and I saw how all Wash's face was bleached almost a soapy white. I could guess what he had done. If I had been terribly scared of something to help cure myself I might have tried to face it—if I had the courage. Probably he'd walked out here on this trestle to tell himself he could go back and forth above that foaming water and have no real reason to be afraid.

I think he saw what I meant to do, too.

He stayed there, not stepping back. He was scared but he had that courage that made him stick there, not retreating, even if he knew I had the advantage of weight and size over him. All at once, though, I knew I wasn't going to push him into the millrace. It seemed to me I'd had all I wanted of trying to settle any accounts. I seemed again to see Jack Kelso's face before me, all gypsy-like and dark. I let loose of the handrail, stepped out as far as I could without falling and shouted, "Go on by me."

He edged closer and closer, staying on the inside. He passed me. There was one second when I thought he was going to give me a push. He didn't. We both got back to the shore and he looked at me maybe two seconds and said, "I shore was thinkin' of pushin' you, Jim, when you give me thet chance."

"I was shore thinkin' of pushin' you, too, Wash."

"I don't yet know why we didn't. But hain't we on the same side, both steamboaters?" He stuck out his hand. "No hard feelin's, no more?"

"No hard feelin's," I said.

And we shook hands.

And the *Talisman* went over the dam . . .

I heard Rowan Herndon describe how we did it. He described it

better than anyone else ever did. We had tied up at an oak about fifty rods below the dam, only long enough for Cameron and Rutledge to estimate the damage we had done, for Pete to pay. It was two o'clock, Friday afternoon. With the lengthening of the days, Lincoln wanted to use all the remaining daylight to steam north toward Salt Fork as many miles as possible before night.

All of us were there on the boiler deck, waiting for old Mr. Cameron to complete his "ciphering." By now two or three hundred people must have swarmed along the bank. I don't know how the other steamboaters felt but I had the feeling you have after, say, the most wonderful Fourth of July you ever lived through and you're dragged out—you can't move—you can't scarcely breathe—but you wouldn't miss the rest of it for anything.

An elderly sort of man with cottony white hair, dressed in good clothes, got across our gangplank. He came to us. He looked familiar. I couldn't place quite who he was. I'd seen so many people since arriving on the Sangamon that often I couldn't connect their faces to their names.

"What's happened? What's happened?" he cried. "I drove up from Springfield to see the boat run the dam. I was comin' yesterday only somebody told me she'd put back and stayed all night at Green Branch. Jes' what happened?"

"What happened?" said Herndon. I couldn't quite believe my ears. He was still so steamed up from what he had done, piloting the *Talisman* over the dam, that for once in his life he was speaking at almost another man's normal gait. "What happened? When we struck the dam she hung. We then backed off an' threw the anchor over. We tore away part of the dam an' raisin' steam ran the *Talisman* over on the fust trial. *Thet's* what happened!"

"Why, friend Merryman—" Lincoln came around our little five-foot boiler which he had joshed at up there on top of the hill. "What are you doin' here? Now we hev crossed the dam, we need a last verse to thet po'm you wrote, two weeks ago, welcomin' the *Talisman* when she arrived at Bogue's mill."

I remembered him. He'd sung his song to us that Saturday we landed.

I heard Mr. Merryman say, "Friend Linkern, I hev written *two* verses to be prepared. I wrote one if you did not cross the dam and I wrote one if you did."

"Wal, friend Merryman, you can t'ar up yore 'did not' and do yore 'did.'"

Dr. Merryman said, "Here it is, then—" but reached into the wrong pocket. "No, this pocket." He took out a sheet of paper, cleared his throat, looked around him, the April breeze blowing his cottony white hair, saw Lincoln, saw Herndon, saw Wash, saw Thankful down there where she didn't belong, saw all of us were waiting and listening. He recited the lines he'd written if we *did* cross the dam:

> "*And when we came to Salem dam,*
> *Up we went against it jam;*
> *We tried to cross with all our might,*
> *But we found we couldn't and staid all night.*"

Well, he'd had to write it in advance. At least he'd gotten in that we had had to stay all night. Personally, I liked those lines Jack Kelso had quoted better than Dr. Merryman's poem; but I didn't say anything. Everybody else cheered him.

Then we cast off, our seven-foot whistle shattered the air, and instead of having to stop for more steam, the *Talisman* began moving away from New Salem. I wished my father had been here to see his steamboat go over that dam. I wished my father and my mother, both of them, had been here. How could I ever tell them all that had happened? I felt like something important to me had ended; but I didn't know quite what it was. Hadn't I wanted more than anything to see our steamer start back for St. Louis?

We made good time. We were traveling with the flow of water. That helped. The April days gave us more running hours of light than we had had last March. We got stuck, yes; by now all of us were old hands at that sort of business. Either we walked the *Talisman* over or hawsered her over, and only, say, a dozen times did we have to rig our grasshopper poles.

Sunday, the eighth of April, we came around the bend at Salt Fork and steamed toward the junction of the Sangamon with the Illinois River above Beardstown. While it was still going to be too close for comfort, it looked more and more like we were going to be in St. Louis a day, perhaps, before the fifteenth of the month.

I never saw much of the Sangamon River after we steamed up and put New Salem behind us. We dropped Jack Armstrong off that night, paying him, and wanting to pay him ten dollars as a bonus. He refused. He said he was satisfied with us, as is, and we "'peared" satisfied with him; and why have to pay out more good money when none was required? He was the first to go.

Pete was already thinking ahead to the day when we'd be going

down the Illinois, with neither Lincoln nor Herndon along to steer or sound for us. He came to me and said, "You an' Wash don't seem to be havin' much trouble any longer."

"No," I said.

"I hear you're aiming to teach him to swim when we get to St. Louis?"

"Who told you?"

"Never mind. He's got sharp eyes, ain't he?"

"Sharp enough."

"Sharp enough? Why, they're like hawk eyes. I thought I might keep him up in the wheelhouse with me and Herndon."

"Go ahead."

"When we get to the Illinois, I've got to stay in the wheelhouse. Sandy's got to handle that engine."

"It'll be a long shift for you two."

"I was thinking. Wash just might be able to spell me a little—not much, once he gets the hang of swinging that wheel. We'd stand in mid-channel, on the Illinois. We won't try running no chutes."

"That's a good idea, Pete."

"Course, that don't mean you won't be in the wheelhouse too. Sure, you will. Don't I know how any young feller nat'rally itches to swing that wheel? I used to have it myself before I saw engines was my proper line. You'll be up there with us. We'll all be up there, enjoyin' ourselves. Now, is that all right? About Wash, I mean?"

What he meant was, I could take the wheel providing he, Pete, or Wash was also in the wheelhouse, just in case my eyes failed to sight a small trifle, say, like a snag lifting up, or a sheen of water showing under the sunlight where shoals were beginning to build.

I said, "Pete, Sandy's going to have a mighty long shift by himself in the engine room. If it's all the same to you and you don't need me too much in the wheelhouse, I sort of thought I might act as Sandy's striker."

"Well," he said. "Well—" he said again. The only way you could tell when he grinned was by his whiskers seeming to bush up, redder than ever.

He saw it was all right for him to begin working Wash in to help at the wheel. Pete knew when to let go of a subject. He did this time. He asked me about something else. "Smoky told me about that— morning when you went after Pollock, Jim. I never rightly got the whole of it. I been waiting. You want to tell me now or wait?"

"Pete—" I said.

I never was very good, I expect, at keeping a stiff face. I don't know what Pete saw in my face but he said, hastily, "There, now, Jim. It's not important," and began stumping along forward on the deck.

So I stayed mostly in the engine room, trying to learn much as I could in a short time from Sandy. You never can tell what will happen on a steamer. We'd be fearfully shorthanded once Lincoln and Herndon left us. A time might come on the Illinois when a strong-bodied man with good eyes, like Sandy, would be needed elsewhere, quick in an emergency. If such an emergency ever did arise I wanted to know enough about our engine to be able to handle her according to the signals sent down from the hurricane deck.

At nights we tied up. Everyone was off duty. Lincoln played his mouth organ. Sometimes he tried to join in our singing, if we would let him. He had the worst singing voice I think of any man alive. He knew it, too, but wouldn't give up. "The Ballad of the Blue-Tailed Fly" was our favorite song of them all. Thankful learned the words. She pitched in even if Mrs. Hicks was doubtful about one or two of the lines in that song.

In the engine room of a steamer, I learned, you had more time for thinking than anywhere else. I could see why most enginemen had a reputation for being a little different breed of cat than all the other steamboaters. It was because enginemen did more pure thinking while sitting there in their shack, listening to the engine, the stern wheel, the flow of the river, all the little sounds and noises—and jumping up in a hurry if the *least* single sound seemed somehow wrong. That meant trouble.

I was beginning to think of how it would be when I saw my folks again. If my father had been my age, and aboard this steamer, even at my age he'd have had the experience from working on the river and with steamer- and rivermen not to have been so casual and careless as I had been, nearly letting Pollock get off with our money. I grew cold just thinking of how close it had been. I'd got my back up; I'd made a big brag at Father when he'd been in bed with a broken leg.

It wasn't going to be so very easy to face him once more and admit I wasn't much of an Owens. There was Wash, too, aboard. Even if we were friends it was going to have to come out to Father how I'd

turned tail and run that time from Wash and his crowd. More and more shameful little details began shoving into my head, of where I hadn't measured up.

Too, I was beginning to think I might not perhaps be cut out to be a lawyer as once I'd thought. But how would Father take that if I backed water and allowed I'd like to remain with the other two members of the Owens family?

Why, he'd even told Mr. Blair, Thankful's father, I was returning to Philadelphia. Thankful had told me. It looked like it was all settled and nailed down in my father's mind to shuck me off next fall. But here I was finding I liked this sort of life! I don't mean I particularly liked being in an engine room. No, I mean I liked the whole thing in general—going somewhere on a steamboat—seeing Thankful—watching accounts—keeping the log—balancing our ledgers—knowing whether or not we'd paid a profit to ourselves—and even being so fiercely plagued by Thankful. It was all something crowded together and good, too good to lose.

I even spoke to Lincoln about a notion I had of staying in this part of the world and trying to make something of myself. He just let me talk on, for once listening. I said I thought I might stay on a year or so more in St. Louis. Maybe I'd get the hang of how a fur-trading concern operated at a home office. Afterwards I might go into the northwest frontier for enough years to get the hang of that side of the business before trying a venture of my own. Lincoln didn't say anything at all, either way. I was slightly let down. I tried not to show it. He'd been lively enough before I had begun speaking to him about my idea of going into the fur-trading business.

I could get excited, thinking of that sort of life. When the steamboat tied up at a trading post for a few days, you would get on a horse and maybe find yourself buffaloes to shoot. I don't know why, but the idea of hunting buffaloes had always taken my fancy as long as I could remember. Even if that one buffalo, probably one of the last remaining on the eastern side of the Mississippi, had nearly scared the living daylights out of me—I still hoped someday to go on a buffalo hunt.

It was no use, though, trying to interest Lincoln in my hopes and plans for a future, not that night or any other. He'd get that look on his face as if all the light inside him had burnt out. It must have been something I said each time that graveled him. I never knew what it was. Perhaps he thought I was being too brash to imagine someday I might own as big a fur-trading concern as old Mr. Pratte owned in

St. Louis. But what was to stop me? Mr. Pratte had started in small, acting as a clerk for a Mr. Astor in New York, hadn't he?

After we had tied up, sometimes only to a tree, and had grub, and joined in together for an hour or so before all turning in, I think what Lincoln enjoyed more than anything else—or almost as much as he enjoyed plaguing us by his attempts to sing—was listening to Thankful sing some of the old old songs in her fresh clear voice. She looked so pretty in the lamplight, her hair growing curly, almost in that light as red in color as some of those redheaded sisters of Dave Rutledge's whom I'd watched peeking through the door to listen to their father and Lincoln. She knew how to tease him, too.

She'd start asking him about that old barrel of rubbish waiting for him in his store. What else did he expect to find deep down in it, anything more valuable than that flint case he'd found for my spectacles? He'd use his broadest style, when joking back with her—but sometimes it seemed to me he was taking himself halfway seriously when he'd say, "Wal, I jes' mou't find something down in thet thar bar'l. Now, who knows? Who kin say?"

I'd look sometimes across at Herndon, sitting there in one of our chairs watching Lincoln. You'd see that kind, patient, horsy face of his wrinkle a trifle in a smile. But he never spoke much. And except that once, when he was steamed up and ready to blow his boiler over the triumph of crossing the New Salem dam, did he ever say one word without making you wait half an hour for the next.

Tuesday evening, the tenth of April, we tied for the night on the east shore of the Illinois River. That was about two miles below its junction with the Sangamon. You would have thought we would have cheered and whooped and have made it a gala occasion when at last we reached the Illinois. We didn't. Perhaps we all were too played out.

We only had five more days. Going with the current it now looked as if we would reach St. Louis possibly as early as Friday night, providing we had no particular bad luck. But Pete was taking no chances. He gave orders we'd leave at dawn. Lincoln and Herndon slept aboard that night. We didn't have anything like the singing and joshing around we'd had together on previous nights. Without saying very much at all, everyone more or less drifted out and got into their own cabins.

In the dull gray light of early Wednesday morning, all of us gathered on the gangplank and foredeck when it was time for Lincoln

and Herndon to leave. They were planning to walk across country to New Salem. A tramp of that many miles seemed nothing to them, I suppose.

Thankful's eyes were all shiny. She looked like she was going to break out and rain any minute. Our roustabouts were there, too. Lincoln was going around to all of them, shaking a man's hand, saying the man's name; but not making any more of his going than that. I don't know when he learned all the names of our hands. He had, though. Herndon was waiting, looking like he would have liked to say something to us, knew he'd wear out our patience if he tried, and being one of the most sensible men who lived, didn't try.

While waiting my turn it came over me all of a sudden that I'd forgotten to fetch the book of Robert Burns's poems, which I'd planned to give Lincoln as a farewell gift, not particularly from me, but from all of us. I'd remembered that night when he'd said, "My best friend is the feller who'll git me a book I hain't read." I turned, running up to the hurricane deck as fast as I could go.

It was the same thing all over again. I couldn't find it. I pulled up the cornhusk mattress. I looked inside the desk, under the desk. The safe! I opened the safe. There it was. I took it in one hand, shut the safe door, out of habit, and saw Lincoln out there on the hurricane deck, bending down his head to peer in at me.

"I looked for you below, Owens," he said. "I come up here to say good-by to you."

"I forgot this—here."

Those big hands of his turned the green leather book over once or twice.

"It got a little burnt," I said. "You can read all the pages, though."

"You found it?" he said. "I thought you had lost it."

"I was saving it to give you as a surprise."

"Wal—" he said. He stuck the green leather book in his pocket. We had a moment or so, neither one of us saying anything. A crane flopped up into the gray light, its wings drawing it higher and higher. Lincoln always had been shy of receiving favors. "I kin pay you," he said. "Pete Wilmot jes' give me my wages. Forty dollars. I never had so much in my life at one time. Thet Pete is a good feller. He'll git you safe to St. Louis. Sure. How much is a book like this wuth—" He stopped. I was shaking my head.

I went by him, almost blindly, clumped against the railing. His hand caught my arm. He waited while I wiped off my spectacles and hooked them back over my nose, his big thumb and fingers still

circling my right arm, not tightly, but just being there. I could see the white scar on his thumb. I remembered him telling me how once he'd nearly cut off that thumb with an ax.

"I'll keep this book of yours t' remember you by," his voice said. "I'll tell you something, Owens. Maybe sometimes you go a *leetle* too hard yet at people. You haven't quite larned a drop of honey catches more flies than a gallon of gall. But I hev never heard you whine or complain. One thing I like about you is when you make up your mind t' do somethin' you don't let nothin' hinder you from tryin'. Ef ever I git to feelin' sorry for the poor sort of feller I hev turned inter, I'm goin' to say to myself, 'I never seed Jim Owens actin' sorry for hisself, did I?' "

I turned around, to look up at him as the sun began lifting over the prairieland to the east. "I *haven't* anything to hinder me from going to the northwest and learning the fur-trade business. Why, a friend of mine in St. Louis owns the biggest—" I stopped, embarrassed. "*My* trouble is—I always get to feeling *too* pleased with myself, and carry on bragging like just now."

"Jim—"

He started bending down and down to bring his face in front of mine. The light fell over my shoulder, shining in the glass of my spectacles. So I saw his face for the last time not too distinctly, one reflection of it appearing wrinkled and grave, the other strangely lit up and young, with both reflections somehow melting one over another. It's hard to describe very exactly, unless you've also sometimes had your eyes try to play tricks on you.

"Jim," he said, "I take thet back. I was wrong. No, I see you hain't got nothin' you'll ever let hinder you much no matter what comes. Yore all right. Yore a good feller. Good-by."

I never saw him again, either.

That morning we steamed south toward Beardstown. Pete was in the wheelhouse. Wash, I suppose, was in there with him. I know Thankful was standing lookout duty on the fore hurricane deck because of what happened an hour or so later. I was in the engine room with Sandy, where I belonged.

Sandy and I sat around and listened to the engine going slick-slick-slick back and forth, to the big stroking thunkity-thunk of the hickory and iron arm, and to the sloshing of the stern wheel as it turned twenty-two revolutions each minute. Everything was steady, regular as a clock—and monotonous and dull. Finally, Sandy said, "For a

fellow that didn't have no more of a singin' voice than a hoot owl he sure did have a way of singin' that song 'bout the blue-tailed fly, didn't he?"

I knew who he was talking about, all right. I said, "Remember how Thankful and he would get going together on some of those old ballads?"

"Jim, we all nearly killed ourselves getting this steamer out of that miser'ble Sangamon River. I thought nothin' ever would please me more than once more steamin' back down the Illinois to St. Louis. Maybe what you and me need is some sulphur and molasses. Maybe that's why I don't feel so sprightly."

We fell silent, each thinking our own thoughts. The stern wheel sloshed perhaps a hundred more times around to shove us that much closer to St. Louis. Sandy raised his head. "Do you think he made up all them jokes?"

"No. I asked him once."

"What did he say?"

"He claimed people told him most of them."

"That don't seem possible. I never laffed so much as I done when listenin' to him. He could make a cat laff if he wanted."

"I wonder how far he and Herndon've got by now?"

"Oh, two fellows like them won't let much dust settle on them. They'll be fifteen, sixteen miles along by this time of mornin'."

"I liked Herndon, too. Didn't you?"

"Say, I liked *all* them Sangamon people. Someday I'd like to get back to New Salem and persuade one of those redheaded girls to sign articles with me."

"Which one?"

Sandy rubbed his jaw. "Now, to tell you the truth I wouldn't be too partic'lar. I'd settle for the first one that would— Say!" He jumped from the engineer's rocking chair. That was Pete's chair; but when Pete had moved up to the wheelhouse Sandy had taken it and when I wasn't minding the engine according to his directions with the wiping rag or tallow stick or can of whale oil I had the cub's stool. "What's Pete blowin' our whistle for?"

I'd jumped up with him. Our whistle was sounding one shattering blast after another. In between ours I heard another steamer whistle blowing off to our larboard. That made no sense at all. We had the only steamboat on the river. Our steam engine was located on the larboard side of the engine shed for the big connecting arm to thresh back and forth through the aft slot to the stern wheel. We

worked the engine from the starboard side; there wasn't much space to get around it to sight through one of the three chicken-head windows on the larboard cabin side to see what was on the river.

So Sandy and I piled out of the engine room, with our whistle forward letting off another blast. Then Thankful came skinning down the aft ladder from where she'd been, high forward on the hurricane, to shout, "Sandy! Jim! We've sighted another steamer. It's dead ahead, quarter mile, coming upstream, labbord!"

Forward, the roustabouts were hollering. Behind us in the empty engine room all our bells began jangling. Pete was signaling down to us to slack off to quarter speed. But Sandy and I stuck out our heads over the larboard railing and sure enough we could see another stern-wheeler pushing upstream toward us, whistling to us, and beginning to curve in to close with us.

Sandy said, "Jim, I don't like the looks of that. Do them fellows think just because they're *second* to steam up this river they're goin' to drive off any competition steamers? You stay here and mind that engine." He reached inside the engine-room door, grabbed a crowbar, said, "Thankful, you hike up to the passenger deck and stay there with Mrs. Hicks till we see what this is, hear me?" and started running forward.

The bells were jangling more violently. I jumped back inside the engine room to reduce speed. Thankful poked her head in and said, "Will they board us?"

"Get up to your cabin," I shouted. "Stay there! Lock yourself in with Mrs. Hicks and Aunty!"

For once she did as I asked, too. I guess my face had drained white and she saw this was dead serious. Sometimes when a new river was first opened up a steamer would try to claim it for the first year or so to grab off the first rush of new business and freight at high prices; or river pirates would take over a small stern-wheeler and hide up a new river to sweep down on the broadhorners and flatboats until enough other steamers were going up and down to make that sort of jump and hit and run business a trifle too risky.

Well, I slacked off to quarter speed. Then I got another jangle to shove to full speed. Next, Pete wanted the engine to back and hold against the current. I thought he and Wash must have gone crazy up there in the wheelhouse. I shouted through the speaking tube, "What steamer is it, Pete? What do they want?" But Pete didn't answer. Wash didn't answer. Nobody at all answered from the wheelhouse.

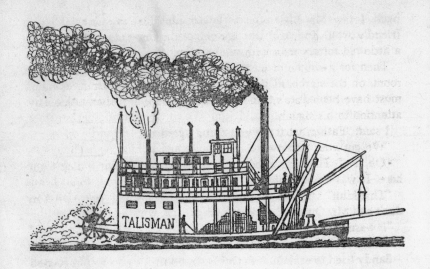

I got another jangle of engine bells. The wheelhouse was asking for just enough forward speed to give hard water to the rudders. I heard more shouts.

Thankful came running into the engine room. She hollered, "Oh, Jim! It's Pa!"

"What!"

"It's Pa and yours, too. They're on the other steamer. They're yawling across to us. Mr. Pratte's with them."

"Who?"

"Mr. Pratte. Oh, Jim!"

She slung her arms around my neck, hugged me, and darted away again.

It was the most convulsing thing in the world! I was stuck there. My father was aboard that other steamer? I couldn't believe it. Thankful's father? Mr. Pratte? I could feel our steamer going cantywise against the current. I got more jangles; Back! Ahead! Slack off! A steamer's whistle was blasting away a couple of hawser lengths away from us. Evidently Pete was trying to hold the *Talisman* steady against the flow of current while a yawl was rowed across.

All at once from the fore boiler deck came *such* a whooping and cheering out of our roustabouts I nearly died having to stay by that sickening engine. Then about a minute later my father walked in— and he said, "Well, there you are!" I didn't care about the engine. He was whacking me on the back. I was whacking him on the

back. I saw Mr. Blair outside in the sunshine, grinning in like a friendly wolf. Thankful was hanging on *his* arm. Behind him was a little old tottery man with wispy white hair, smiling and smiling.

Then for a couple of minutes everyone crowded into the engine room, on the starboard side; and up in the wheelhouse I expect it must have been Pete's turn to have nearly died. Nobody paid any attention to his signals.

I said, "Father, what are you doing here?"

"We got your letters—"

"Oh, Pa," Thankful cried. "We got stuck. We nearly didn't get here. It was wonderful. Jim, you tell—"

"Thankful," said Mr. Blair, "aren't you forgetting yourself? You don't call Mr. Owens Jim yet, do you?"

"I wasn't calling Mr. Owens Jim, Pa. I was calling Jim, Jim—" Then she looked confused.

Sandy tried to explain to Father. "Mr. Owens, we've sort of started calling Jim, here, Jim—"

And that was more confusing, I guess.

Somehow I'd forgotten Jim was my father's name and Horace was my front name until between Thankful and Sandy that Horace thing more or less had been done away with. I told Father, "I'm sorry. I didn't mean to steal your name."

Sandy was saying, "Mr. Owens, Horace ain't no name to call somebody like Jim, here. Why, he done as much as any of us to get your steamer out of that Sangamon River, more even, maybe."

Then Father laid his hand on my shoulder and said, "Why, Jim. You never stole any name from me. Don't you know nearly eighteen years ago I *gave* you that name? My grandfather was Jim Owens. I'm Jim Owens. Your other grandfather was Horace Tate like you know, so we called you Horace James Tate. But I guess from now if both of us happen to be around together I'm Old Jim and you're Young Jim—"

"Mr. Owens!" protested Thankful. "Nobody'd ever call you Old Jim. You're *much* too young looking."

I liked hearing her say that, too. It eased off the tightness taking hold of us all from the delight and joy of having my father and hers —and Mr. Pratte—aboard. Well, the bells were jangling even more violently. Pete was asking for steering speed. So we began to sort ourselves out a little; and Sandy said reluctantly, he guessed he'd have to take over. And he did.

In about a quarter of an hour we got underway again, all of us

excepting Sandy collecting together in the wheelhouse. The steamer *Souvenir,* Parkington master, had given us a final salute from her whistle to commence steaming upriver again toward Pekin. Father said if it was all right with Pete, he'd take the wheel; and Pete said, "Mr. Owens, if it's all right with you I *never* want to stand behind one of them wheels again." So Father took the wheel, and listened to us. After getting the captain's rocking chair from the captain's parlor for old Mr. Pratte, Mrs. Hicks, Aunty, and Thankful sat on the bench and the rest of us stood around and all of us tried to talk at once until Father said, "Now, hold on. Wait a minute."

Father had received Pete's and my letters. Mr. Blair had received Thankful's, all of them swarming into St. Louis on the same mud-wagon at the same time. Father had wanted to go across country. If he did he was afraid we just might have managed to yank ourselves through the lower Sangamon and be on our way to the Illinois. Mr. Blair had learned the steamer *Souvenir* was leaving Saturday—that would have been last Saturday, the seventh—on her maiden voyage up the Illinois to Pekin. So they'd bought cabin space. At the last minute old Mr. Pratte had surprised them by deciding to come along.

Well, we kept telling and retelling, one and the other, what had happened to us all through noon and on into the afternoon. We didn't put in at Beardstown. We kept steaming down the river. Smoky and the steward brought up food to us and Aunty helped serve it and she stayed on to listen; and so did Smoky, with both of them exclaiming and adding on bits here and there to help Father and Mr. Blair and old Mr. Pratte understand how the steamer had been saved.

Father kept looking back at us and saying, "Who's Linkern? Who's Herndon?" or asking for particulars on some other name. Mr. Pratte rocked back and forth and looked like he was enjoying all the commotion. I expect all that time Sandy must have been perishing in the engine room. I wished Mother was here; it would have made everything perfect. Father said he wished he had brought her along, too. But Mr. Blair and he hadn't known what they might run into when they started up the Illinois to see what could be done to save the *Talisman.*

"Save the *Talisman!*" said Pete. "Why, I tell you, Mr. Owens. Them Sangamon people pitched in. The whole Illini country, nearly, pitched in after that scoundrelly pilot of Bogue's ran off with Mrs. Tanner. And Jim here—what didn't *he* do? Let me tell you . . ." And all at once Pete was telling it, clear from the beginning. Now nobody

was saying a word but him. He stretched it, too, when it came to my share. I tried to interrupt.

But Thankful said, "Jim, you keep quiet!"

Then everyone looked at her and at me; and even Father turned around again from the wheel. But Pete wasn't to be stopped. He continued heaping it on. He came to that part where I'd gone after our money. He paused an instant—like Lincoln used to pause when telling a story and wait for you to lean forward. There was such a dead silence. Kind of quiet, Pete said, "I don't yet know all the details, Mr. Owens. You'll have to drag 'em from Jim. But he took after them two rascals by himself and *he saved the money.* Both Lincoln and Herndon told me they don't b'lieve we'll ever be troubled or even ever see hide or hair of either Pollock or Clem Diggon again."

Wash Hicks spoke up. "Say, Mr. Owens, he whupped me, too. He's a reg'lar bobcat!"

Now, that was a lie. They were all heaping it on too much in my favor. I saw too late their scheme. When I hadn't ever known it Pete must have passed the word around about that brag I'd made so long ago to my father. It was the only explanation. Perhaps he'd only told Thankful. I didn't know. But I knew Thankful. She'd stand up behind you and rally everyone else, even if it was to have your own father think you had outmatched him when you never had.

I said, "Father, it's not true. Wash licked me. When I tried to find Pollock I failed—"

"Oh," Wash hollered, "that ain't so!"

"Jim Owens—" said Thankful in a white temper.

"Mr. Owens," said Pete, "I'm goin' to say something if I can make myself heard. Maybe in some ways you'd have matched over Jim, if you'd been his age. Sure. I never knowed you at Jim's age. But I've knowed you eight years. There's one thing I'm saying—if you'd been aboard with us, back there, Mr. Owens, there's one thing you'd never matched him. I heard enough of it to know. Jim went after Pollock and Diggon by crossing that slough. I don't know how he did it. Let him tell you. But you'd never have done it. You ain't no better in water than me. Jim got through that slough—that tangle of stuff in that slough—when nobody else *I* know of could—and he got our money. Him and what Lincoln and Herndon did, all three, *they* got this steamer through. I say, he's matched you up. You have lost your bet."

I jumped up. "There wasn't any bet. Father—"

"Wait a minute," Father said.

251

Mr. Pratte got up from his rocking chair and said, "Mr. Owens, let me have that wheel. I can handle a steamer. I'd like to have the feel of this one, as long as I'm buying it." And he took the wheel from Father, too.

Pete said more strongly, "I never have gone against you before, Mr. Owens. But I'm saying young Jim here—"

"As *I* was saying," Father said—and there was the longest second when he looked at me. "If Jim matched up on this steamer, *I* didn't lose. He never meant to make any brag to me that day I was in bed with a busted leg. I did everything I could to get him to get his back up to me that day. Why, I almost gave up hope when he was taking all the graveling I was giving him and never spoke back. But he *did* have a limit, even with me. Why, Pete—I'd have lost if Jim had lost his brag. Don't you see? Jim's won. But so have I."

Pete looked puzzled. At first I was, too. I felt something almost unbearable carrying at me, though.

Then Father said, "It's one of the great days of my life for rejoicing," and shook my hand like he was shaking another man's hand and not somebody's who all of a sudden was starting to founder and break apart.

That evening we tied up for the night at the Callytown landing, on the west side of the river. There was still so much to say as soon as one stopped for breath another took over. Father asked if I'd seen any buffalo; and I told him about that one buffalo, and about meeting Jack Kelso and I found I could tell him about fighting underwater with Diggon without having my throat clog up and stop my voice.

By and by Mr. Pratte said this had been a long day for an old man. He guessed he would turn in if there was a spare cabin for him. So we got him and Thankful's father and my father established in the spare cabins on the starboard side; and by and by I went up to the hurricane deck, to turn in myself. I wished Mother was along. It was all that was needed—or nearly. A moon was shining down on the river and after all the years I still can remember a fragrance of new grass and new leaves and spring flowers from the shore and how soft and dreamy the evening had become.

By and by somebody slipped to me through the shadows and whispered, "I couldn't sleep, either. I got dressed again and came up here. I was afraid you'd have gone to bed."

Thankful looked at me by the light of the moon and while maybe I couldn't see her too clearly, not as clearly as her eyes saw me, I

252

didn't need to. She whispered, "You can put your arm around me a minute, if you like."

I said, "It's what I've been wanting to—" and I did.

"I've been wanting you to, too. But you're such a poky about such things."

"I tried to, once, but you whacked me because I was so brash."

"I never—"

"It was that time I tried to kiss you and stepped on your hat. I even tried to buy you a new hat—"

"When?"

I told her.

"Why didn't you ever tell me sooner?"

"I didn't get the hat. He wouldn't sell it to me."

"But you should have told me you tried, Jim."

"I did try but I failed."

"I wouldn't have cared. It was having you remember and trying. And I didn't slap you because you tried to kiss me and stepped on my hat. I *wanted* you to kiss me that day. Then I just boiled up when you told me you'd kissed that Laura Melrose woman. It was awful. We'd even heard of her when I lived in Memphis. She's been married two or three times. I hated her. I wanted to—kill her. Oh, Jim! I wanted you to be the first man to kiss me a real kiss and be the first woman to kiss you a real kiss. Then you told me—"

I felt my arm draw her closer. All at once experience in such things wasn't very necessary. I wanted to tell Thankful I had only given that woman aboard the *Star of Ohio* a good-by peck; it wasn't a kiss. For the first time in my life and probably the only time I had a moment of insight about women in general. It might not be too wrong of me to let Thankful persuade herself she had just possibly come along in the nick of time to—save me from any continued interest in some fascinating young woman from New Orleans.

I remembered back to what my father once had told me about Mother and himself. It had been when he and I had been walking on Dock Street in Cincinnati town that long-ago December morning. He had been in love with Mother from the time he first saw her. She had been in love with him. There had never been anyone else for him but her. He had been eighteen when he had married her. She had been sixteen. People were used to getting married young on the Ohio River. People married young along the Sangamon. It looked to me like young people fell in love and got married young every-

where in the nation except in Philadelphia, where it was fashionable for the man, at least, to wait until he was twenty or twenty-one.

I whispered, "Thankful—" and felt her raise up her head. "I can't say this very well but I'm going to try. There has never been anyone for me but you. When we were kids I threw stones at you to keep you from tagging along. But I never hit you. When you got tired of tagging after me, where did I go? Back to your house. The minute you came aboard the *Talisman* at St. Louis I fell all over in love with you again. There's never been anyone else; there never will be. You're all I need if you'll have me."

"But you're going away to Philadelphia!"

"I've been doing some considerable thinking. If I do, it won't be for very many months. I believe Mr. Pratte'll give me a job in his trading concern. Next January, I'll be eighteen. Pa married when *he* was eighteen. At least I ought to be able to match him up there, shouldn't I?"

Then we stayed there and talked in whispers for all hours, maybe most nearly to midnight. Once, I remember, she asked me where I thought Lincoln and Herndon would be tonight. I supposed they would have built a small fire, Indian style, had their grub under the trees, and be stretched out under the stars to sleep. They had at least three more days of steady walking to get themselves back to New Salem.

Thankful whispered, "I wonder if he'll ever find anything at the bottom of that barrel of rubbish he used to talk so much about? The one he paid half a dollar for to oblige a settler going west?"

"Probably not."

"He found your spectacle case in it, didn't he?"

"I don't expect he'll find much else."

"I wonder?"

"What would a settler's family pack in an old barrel?" I asked. "Old shoes? Played-out clothing? Perhaps one or two useless old books?"

"I wonder? I wish I knew," she said, "don't you?"

Ask her a question . . .

About three o'clock, Saturday afternoon, the fourteenth of April, the *Talisman* docked at St. Louis. Mr. Pratte bought her and sent her on one voyage into the upper Missouri, which she completed successfully.

The night after her return the steamer tied next to her blew a

boiler, blazed up, the flames spread to the *Talisman* and she burnt to the water and foundered. Pete and Sandy went with her. They had been fighting the fire and failed to escape. Wash Hicks was saved. When he recovered, Thankful's father and my father took him in as an apprentice in the steamboat works they had established.

At the time I was in Philadelphia, visiting Aunt Iz and Uncle John. Because of the slowness of the mails and their irregularity, it was Thankful's letter bearing the tragic news that arrived before my mother's and father's. Shortly after that I returned to St. Louis, accepted Mr. Pratte's offer of a job; and I never traveled east of the Mississippi afterwards. The shock of losing Pete, Sandy, and the *Talisman*, I believe, must have finished off any trace remaining in me of being a boy. I had grown to full size when I returned to St. Louis. I found I was thinking as a man, thinking of Thankful as a woman, and acting as a man deeply in love with the only woman for him—and there was no longer anything of boy left in me.

I never saw Lincoln or any of the people of the Sangamon again. Of course, as years went by I began hearing his name mentioned more and more. All at once it seemed his name was carried all over the nation. Now it was "Old Abe" or "Father Abraham" or simply "Abraham Lincoln." Sometimes a longing would come over me to leave the new town of San Francisco, where our trading firm of Pratte & Owens was beginning to be more interested in other commodities than furs, and go back to where the people along the Sangamon would still call him "Linkern." But it was too far away. I was needed where I was.

Now and then Thankful would still recall that old barrel of rubbish in his store. The fancy had never left her that perhaps Lincoln had found something of value to him down at the bottom. But that was always her way. If she took a notion to something she clung to it, whether it was a notion about an old barrel of rubbish or someone who stumbled and was awkward on land and saw less and less with his eyes as the years drifted away.

Once she said, "Jim, why don't you write him and ask?"

"Write the President of the United States, when the last issue of the *Alta California* reported Fort Sumter had been fired on? The President may have a whole civil war on his hands. He'd be too busy to bother with such a letter. Besides, don't you think by now he's forgotten he ever once paid half a dollar for a barrel of rubbish?"

"I wonder?" she asked, and sighed. "I wonder?"

It seems only yesterday evening that an April moon was shining down upon a river flowing toward the Mississippi. Thankful was there beside me, in the shadows, smiling, resting her arms on the railing of a trifling little steamboat with a five-foot boiler and a seven-foot whistle, now gone and forgotten.

Again I see all the faces of those people along the San Gammaw. Their names will stay with me as long as I live: Abraham Linkern, Rowan Herndon, Jack Armstrong, young Duff, Hannah Armstrong, "Slicky Bill" Green, Bowling Green, Denton Offut, Jack Kelso, Simeon Francis, John McNeil, Vincent Bogue, Josiah Pugh, Abner Jefferson, William Alvey, Billy Fleurville, Peter Cartwright, Dr. Merryman, John Cameron, David Rutledge, his father and the sister of his whose hands I felt and voice I heard but never saw clearly.

In my mind once more I hear Pete's wooden leg as he stumps aft on the hurricane deck to a mud-clerk's office. Again Sandy booms out the verses of "The Ballad of the Blue-Tailed Fly," one of the songs that Lincoln liked so well. Now I hear Thankful's soprano, so fresh, so sweet, so haunting, as she sung when we were there together, young, our lives before us.

How long ago it all was!

The wan moon is setting beyond the white wave,
And time is setting wi' me, O.